What people are saying about

Katzenjammer

"This is possibly the best book ever written. It's funny, witty, well crafted, full of symbolism, anagrams, and hidden meanings. An overall knock-out! Now, if I can just get it back . . ."
Max Perkins—author of *Mrs. Squigglemire's Bustle*

"Disgusting! Filled with references to sex, bodily functions, and prostitution, it is a moral majority person's nightmare."
Kaplan Fartus—President of Barely Broadway Productions

"Why are you asking me for a quote? I don't even know who this person is. I was raped, you know."
Clarice Butel—head reader at Bandomday Books

"I actually wrote this book, not that McCrae person. He owes me big time. I want credit."
Reeda Rot—movie director (this week)

"You really should buy this book. I'll get a lot of money if you do and then I can quit my job at the mental hospital. Jackson, give me a call—we can work something out, big guy."
Spank Wexmiller—orderly and male prostitute

"Who's writing this crap about me?"
Spong Flagelatte—inmate at Rikers Island Prison

Katzenjammer

Soon to be a major motion picture

Katzenjammer

Soon to be a major motion picture

Jackson Tippett McCrae

The Enolam Group, Inc.

ISBN: 09715536-3-7

LCCN: 2005922684

First Edition

Printed in the United States of America on acid-free paper

Published by
The Enolam Group, Inc.
P.O. Box 2008
Norwalk, CT 06852

Book and cover design © by The Enolam Group, Inc.

For T

Kat-zen-jam-mer (kat´sən-jăm´er); *German* (kät´sĕn-yãm´ĕr) *n.* 1. The book you are reading. 2. What happens to Max in this novel. 3. A code word. 4. Don't ask. 5. A long complicated word that's hard to pronounce. 6. Total and complete confusion. 7. Everything gone wrong.

I wrote to a very famous publisher of a certain dictionary, requesting permission to use the "real" definition of the word *Katzenjammer*. Promptness, it seems, is not one of their strong points, and by the time the book went to press they still had not responded, ergo, my own definition of the word. Life isn't easy—you do what you can.

—Jackson Tippett McCrae

The antonym of synonym is antonym.

— no idea

Prologue

The statistics on sanity are that one out of every four Americans is suffering from some form of mental illness. Think of your three best friends. If they're okay, then it's you.

—Rita Mae Brown

It's her voice that's so disturbing—the equivalent of fingernails on the chalkboard of life—just like the nurse from the movie *One Flew Over the Cuckoo's Nest* if she ever let go emotionally. All that's missing in this place is a game of basketball with Jack Nicholson and the lobotomy.

"He's doing it again," she screams across the room to the nurses' station. Now the orderlies are coming. I can see them running, pushing open the heavy double glass doors. The embedded chicken wire doesn't obscure anything; it just keeps the glass from flying when some of the patients become too violent. They're on a rampage, these goons in white, furious with me for getting out of yet another regime—the taking of my meds. I hate them and the pills they give. They take me away from who I am, where I've been, my efforts to deal with the past.

And now the restraints; the hard hands of the orderlies pressing down on me, their shiny wristwatches Navy-ship-reflecting the sun that streams in through the barred windows of the hospital.

Then, out it comes—something of interest for everyone: "Whosoever sayeth this is snafagoo-goo . . . can eat a willibeeeeeetheeeeeeth!" screams one of the newest pieces of meat to an overly large Deco light fixture that hangs, slightly askew, from the ceiling. (Well *that* made sense.) The screamer is male and totally naked except for a pair of gray satin bikini briefs, the front of which forms the trunk of an elephant. Two crossed plastic eyes hover above the genitals. The lunatic's penis is now becoming erect and Babar is raising his proboscidian appendage triumphantly. It's not a large trunk, but even so the tip of it droops over about two thirds of the way. Someone should have bought a smaller elephant.

As the orderlies lean down, tying my hands to the chair, their stiff uniforms stand out from their bodies momentarily. There's a whiff of aftershave, underarm deodorant, or the lack thereof. White rubber shoes mock-scuff the floor. Theirs are overly muscular forearms, one with a tattoo, another with a large mole that looks suspiciously like the British Isles. God Save the Queen. There's also the smell of urine wafting about—permanent in this place. I think they mop the floors with it. Another of the patients is shuffling by in his bathrobe, saying something about God being dead, about the end of the world, about a sale Bloomingdale's has on ladies' bras that he's interested in, even though he doesn't need one himself. And why does it always seem that people in mental institutions are obsessed with bodily functions? If not theirs, then yours? It's "Piss this," and "Fuck that," and "Shit this," and every other obscene word; so much so that all the soap in the world couldn't clean out these potty-mouthed loonies.

"You know that if you don't take your meds we're going to have to go back to the injections," another nurse says, trying to be firm. She's one of the more amusing ones. Everything's relative.

"Have you ever seen *The Snake Pit* with Olivia de Havilland?" I'm about to ask, but I catch sight of our Lady of Perpetual Insanity, the resident top-loon; the one who's got us all beat. She's behind a glass partition. Again, the chicken wire motive continues. She's standing on her bed, mouthing something at me. I suspect her cloistered area is a result of the Tourette's Syndrome she suffers from—that lovely obscenity-laced problem that involves an individual spewing forth any and every form of verbiage, most of it nonsensical. I try to follow what she's saying, having become an expert on lip reading since being committed here. When she gets really out of hand they lock her away, behind this wall of wire and glass, like some overly large exotic pet at a turned-upside-down Woolworth's, wedged in between the dried-out pothos vines and the aquariums of goldfish. Mint-green smocks, laminated ID badges, piped-in Muzak—it's all that's missing.

Our Lady is bouncing slightly now, her two bandaged trophy-wrists held up for all to see, her greasy hair streaming downward like rivulets of dirty water. Who said there's no counterpoint in this place? She yells at the top of her lungs, yet what squeaks through the inch-thick glass is only a faint reverberation, like some disheveled siren's song from a far-off land with no water, no hope. I can't make out what she's saying. Her lips twist about so that reading them is next to impossible.

"We can pick him up in the chair," I hear one of the orderlies say. They've got me tied to the arms and legs of the thing with nylon rope. I feel like the hostage that I am.

"I'm innocent!" I scream at them, hoping that the three-hundredth repetition of the phrase will finally sink in.

"That's not what they tell me," counters one of the more surly health workers. Just as I'm about to spit in his face, the tape comes out. It's hard, torn, and tasting of petroleum. I've had it before, I know. It gets slapped across my mouth and now I am, for all practical purposes, a complete vegetable—at the whim of those less intelligent than myself. I'm nothing more than a plaything for incompetents and they know it, trying everything they can to erase, scramble, or rearrange my mind. But why should life in this place be any different from the outside?

As I'm carried through the double doors I strain my neck, intent on seeing Our Lady of Perpetual Insanity as she bawls in my direction. It appears to be a warning of some sort, a revelation; a talisman that I am to take with me as they haul me out. I squint. She mouths a word dramatically, trying to will it through, but it's no use—the thing is lost. Heavy doors slam behind and I'm lifted up— a Gandhi high atop his elephant, riding through throngs of the cheering mentally ill, their bathrobes carelessly tied, their hair unkempt. Bedroom-shoe-clad feet shuffle after me.

"Doesn't anyone dress up for a coronation anymore?" I try to shout through the tape, but the attempt is futile, muted, and damp—I'm gagged, out of earshot, and heading down the hall.

Part I

I always wanted to be somebody, but
I realize now I should have been
more specific.

–Lily Tomlin

- 1 -

When you've had sex with over five thousand people it gets to be a job like anything else. At least that's what my friend Robert says. Robert Hickenlooper. That's his name. I asked if he was any relation to Olga Samaroff, the famous pianist, but he had no idea who I was talking about. He really should have heard of her. After all, he was cut from the same cloth when he wasn't turning tricks in New York. I had to explain to him that Olga's real name was Lucy Hickenlooper and that she was originally from Texas, just like Robert. Seems to me that they would have had some kind of run-in, both being accomplished pianists, but when you consider how large the state is I suppose you have to make allowances. And Lucy was a bit before Robert's time.

I pointed out that Robert might consider changing his name just as Lucy had done. Besides, Hickenlooper didn't sound like a name for a male prostitute. Evidently no one thought it sounded much like a pianist either—that was why Olga had changed her moniker to something a tad more Slavic. At that time—the early 1900s—Russian pianists were all the rage, and Olga had decided to ride that particular tsunami onto shore. It was an excellent marketing ploy on her part if you ask me. The unfortunate thing about my suggestion to Robert—about him changing his name— was that he actually took my proposal at one point in our relationship, and things haven't been the same since. Now I'm weaving baskets and soiling my sheets, and he's brightening the bank's lobby several times a week. But we'll get to that.

Robert wasn't always a male prostitute. Before that line of work he was quite the accomplished musician. Trouble was, his lack of exposure; his lack of recognition. He could play anything you put in front of him, tearing through some of the most difficult Rachmaninoff and Scriabin known, but try as he might, he couldn't get a job, win a competition, or put his signature on a contract for a major record label.

He entered one piano competition in particular, year after year, garnering no results. Each time he would practice for hours, honing his skills, technique, interpretation, and musical shadings of the repertoire. Brahms, Beethoven, and Debussy pealed from his fingers. The veritable cornucopia of aural delights never ceased to astound. Hearing Robert perform a delicate Scarlatti sonata or a carefully chiseled Schumann miniature was akin to eating a succulent peach for the first time—redolent of all things fecund, vernal, healthful, and magic.

Each year he prepared his audition tape with the utmost care, always cognizant of what he thought the judges were looking for. But fame was not to be, for it never failed that Robert received a negative response: "Thank you for your interest . . ." followed by occlusions of some unseen person's guilt and a prevarication of excuses. It was always the same.

After three years of reaping the same reward for his efforts, Robert decided to try something different. Depression, apathy, disgust, and a host of other offending emotions will take their toll on a person, and Robert was, well, only mortal. He devised a plan whereby he would search out not-so-well-known recordings of Horowitz, de Larrocha, and Bolet, and after a careful re-recording in a friend's studio to take out tell-tale glitches and a few quirky personal attributes that would have given the true performer's identity away, he created a tape worthy of a great artist—again.

Horowitz offered up an exquisite Bach/Busoni transcription, de Larrocha gave her best Schumann, and Bolet pledged his most mature Chopin. To all of them Robert was most grateful.

But the elation he felt at dropping the audition package in the mail was dispelled several weeks later when a form letter arrived from the chairman of the competition's preliminary judging panel. This is what it said:

> Thank you for your interest in the Twelfth Annual Pan-American Piano Competition, however we do not feel your abilities are up to our musical and technical standards. It is

therefore the judges' decision not to allow you to enter into the remaining levels of this competition.

The letter went on to state that the five finalists who had been selected were all graduate students at top schools and showed great promise. In the end, the winner went on to perform a whopping three concerts and then disappeared from sight for good. Horowitz, de Larrocha, and Bolet languished in momentary obscurity, their contributions no doubt relegated to the circular file, and Robert treated himself to a drinking binge that lasted three days.

This was, in effect, Robert's wake-up call—the slender stalk of threshed grain that rendered useless the dromedary's vertebrate region—a foghorn in the ear if you will, for it set in motion not only his move to New York City one year before mine, but a career change that would affect us both in ways never imagined.

But perhaps I should tell you how I know Robert and at the same time introduce myself. After all, I've been going on about him for a good while now and you're probably asking yourself the question that so many readers raise when they take a book on: the big Why Are You Telling Me This? So here it is, starting with yours truly, for it will take me a while to make my point.

My name is Max Perkins and I've heard all the jokes, references, and whatnot that accompany having a name such as this—a name famous at least in literary circles. How my parents— who never read a book in their lives—came up with this label is beyond my wildest imagination. To make matters even more serendipitous, I'm a writer who, at the beginning of our tale, has finished a novel and is trying desperately to get it published.

No, not this one.

Yes, I know Max Perkins was the famous editor for the works of Thomas Wolfe, Ernest Hemingway, F. Scott Fitzgerald, and a host of others, helping them to shape their books into literary classics and sometime bestsellers. The irony is not lost on me. And I can't help but think that the original Max Perkins and I are somehow tied collectively, if in no other way than by a tale that circulated for years about the original Mr. Perkins.

Here goes.

Another favorite Perkins story concerned his confrontation with his ultraconservative publisher, Charles Scribner, over the four-letter words in Hemingway's second novel, *A Farewell to Arms*. Perkins was said to have jotted the troublesome words he wanted to discuss—*shit, fuck, and piss*—on his desk calendar, without regard to the calendar's heading: "Things to Do Today." Old Scribner purportedly noticed the list and remarked to Perkins that he was in great trouble if he needed to remind himself to do those things.

The story would be a portent of things to come for me—this tale of the long-gone Mr. Perkins—for at some point my life would be made up of these rudimentary functions and not much else. It was almost as if it were a curse, this having a name that once belonged to one of the world's great editors. And about the only other connection I have to this famous man is the fact that we both had/have a penchant for idiosyncratic punctuation. The original Mr. P favored periods, commas, and semi-colons followed by a large dash. Talk about confusing. Me? I never met a semi-colon I didn't like and will stick one in at the drop of a hat. So perhaps there is something to be said for having the same name.

I can't tell you how many times I've considered changing the label on my packaging, becoming someone else, and even giving up writing for something more lucrative, say, like prostitution, but when I speak to Robert about it he says that they're really the same thing. And I guess he's right. I mean, you end up selling yourself to people one way or another, compromising your ethics, baring your soul. So what's the difference? The only one I can see is that prostitutes make more money and get more respect. Writing is not a profession for the faint of heart.

But all this is fodder for another chapter, and in the telling, hopefully something will be accomplished for Robert's career and mine. After all, we're really in the same business.

2

What you should know about me: I was born Maxwell Perkins, June 28, 1966, to a family of wolves in Harrisburg, Pennsylvania. That makes me a Cancer—the fact I was born at the end of June, not the Harrisburg or wolf thing. Okay, so they weren't real wolves, and neither did they have sheep's clothing (with the exception of a sweater or two thrown in for good measure), but my blood relations weren't what you'd call the most likable people. Animals that eat their own young have better parenting skills.

Witness for the prosecution--Mrs. Aldermeyer, our next-door neighbor in Harrisburg when I was young. Here she is: "I remember the family, yes, yes, I surely do. Seemed to me they lived here in the nineteen seventies. Husband was a mechanic of sorts. Wife--just an ordinary homemaker. Well, not exactly ordinary, but she appeared that way if you didn't know what *really* went on in that house. And the husband drank. I don't mean one of those weekenders either. I mean *drank*. Now I don't recollect him ever beating her, the wife, that is, but Lord knows she could've used it from time to time, what with that carryin' on she used to do. Why, she'd get all gussied up in a sports-bra kinda contraption and some culottes, and be out there in the backyard a-yellin' at that kid they had, the whole time with a Tom Collins in her hand. Guess both parents liked to drink. Now I ain't sayin' nothin' bad 'bout them you understand (looks around for spittoon, sees none, spits anyway) but if you ask me they always thought they was better'n they was. The boy, the boy . . . oh yes! I do remember him now. Mike. Mark? What's that? Maxwell? Max Perkins, you say? I thought his name was Mike. Mike P--yes,

your honor, I'll continue. Anyhoo, Mike, I
mean Max, played that trick on me where he
pooped into a paper bag and then set it on
fire. Was hoping I would come stomp it out.
Never will forget how disappointed he was when
I dumped a big ole cooking pot of water on the
thing. Cried for a week. Told him 'What goes
around, comes around' but he wouldn't listen."

I know what you're saying. I can hear you. I can hear most
people. It's like a curse, this being inside other people's heads. "He
can't write a proper exposition. Is this his idea of a joke?" I know
what you're thinking. Well, let me set you straight. Then I'm doing
exactly as I please and you'll see The Big Why if you decide to
venture further. There are a few people I'd like to forget, but not
before I give them a good thrashing about the backside in the old
black-and-white. You want description? Here's what you're
looking for:

> The sun-scorched earth-weighted town of Harrisburg-
> midsummer-Pennsylvania is not the most pleasant of places to
> be born. There's a heaviness that pervades not only the
> suburban areas, but also the sad arts-and-crafts-style homes
> begrudgingly curled up to what used to be the only place to
> shop—downtown. When Maxwell E. Perkins was born, on that
> hot June day in 1966, at least there was a semblance of life about
> this part of the town.
>
> Both parents being hard drinkers, Max was used to the
> slights and turned-away glances of neighbors in Harrisburg,
> witnessing his mother as she screeched warnings of child
> molesters, all the time clad in only the barest of undergarments
> not fit for the eyes of a young child. Between rotations of sun
> and moon the parents would take turns with their intoxicated
> bouts—one could only imagine what horrors were visited on the
> child. An unfortunate incident involving defecation and
> cookware resulted in a nervous breakdown for the precocious
> Perkins boy at an early age.

I could go on.
But back to the situation at hand—the reason we're here.
You need to know all the angles in this little play—*the dramatis
personae*, if you will. To get right to it: I grew up, won a writing

contest, graduated from high school, rarely dated, and finally entered college at Penn State where I met Dory—the third member of our cast. She was the one who introduced me to Robert and I suppose should be blamed for, or congratulated on—depending on which side of over-processed wheat you put your coagulated dairy product on—the way things turned out. I didn't know much about her at the time. I would learn more than I cared to later on.

Dory had grown up somewhere in New York and had made the mistake of giving a mafia family member a bad case of gonorrhea during the summer between high school and college. It hastened her exit out of the Big Apple and she found herself matriculating at Penn State. Her one real claim to fame was that her mother had been in the party scene of the 1969 movie, *Midnight Cowboy*. She insisted on telling everyone this. "Dory," we would say to her, "whose mother *wasn't?*"

Dory eventually graduated from college with a degree in art. At the time I knew her she had a boyfriend named Gray, and the two delighted in telling everyone they were "Dory and Gray." They were inseparable, that is, until Gray fell in love with meditation and became a Trappist monk. He was never heard from again. Well, not for a long time anyway. The result was that Dory never felt complete, and this caused myriad problems for her down the road, making her susceptible to those who prey on individuals with low self-esteem. And no last name, this Dory. Just the one word. It was as if she were some clothes designer or pop star. "Gowns by . . . *Dory* . . . Ladies and gentlemen . . . *Dory.*"

Dory wasn't immune to the slings and arrows that Robert suffered and I would later partake of—those sharp events that make one question one's sanity. She had learned how the real world works in college, just as Robert had learned with his piano competition embarrassment.

Having been a communications major—with a minor in German before changing to a degree in art—Dory had slaved over her first-year final exam. The only instruction the undergraduates had been given was that they were to complete an assignment about communications and bring it to class. All imagination was left up to the student, and a prize was to be awarded for best project.

Ms. D had come up with a process of finding skiers, climbers, and other alpine enthusiasts lost in the snow by means of tiny radio transmitters. Her father had been heavily into electronics as a young man, and although he didn't help her, some symbiosis had occurred during childhood, for Dory was incredibly adept at all things intricate. In fact, electronics had been her passion as a child.

When the results of the competition were posted outside the classroom, Dory was crushed. She had lost to an overweight transfer student from Lithuania who, as far as Dory could remember, had never opened her mouth in class. Questioning several other students that week, Dory learned that the prize-winning project had been composed of raw potatoes cut in half, with a letter of the alphabet carved into each one. The obtuse devices could then be pressed on an inkpad and applied to paper to spell words. It was all very first grade.

"But what did she print with the potatoes?" Dory had asked one of her classmates, completely dejected, hoping that there was some logical reason for her own project being overlooked. "Was it some witty comment? Some long-winded thesis?" she asked.

"H-E-L-P," was the answer.

So Dory had seen where the communications experience was going (especially after discovering that the prize awarded was a potato peeler), and like Robert, opted out for something more practical. A degree in art, if you will. If you're going to be abused, considered useless by society, and neglected, why not go all the way?

She eventually combined her electronic talents with those of paint and canvas—this, when she wasn't cursing up a blue streak—and created huge swaths of New-Age sculpture that blinked, transmitted, and burbled whenever someone came near. I saw one such installation in the Fine Arts building. It was a giant Mr. Potato Head with blinking eyes and a movable jaw. Whenever anyone approached, an electronic device started a recording. "Lithuania is the hell-hole of the universe," the giant vegetable would exclaim, followed by, "I slept with all my teachers in college—me love you *long* time!" Then the starchy head's eyeballs would fall out momentarily on springs and quickly jerk back into place, while jets of steam shot from the ears.

You couldn't help but like Dory.

While my knowledge of Ms. D was slight, my relationship with Robert was even more tangential. Robert was a Texas transplant intent on finishing his degree in music—this (for Robert) after a rather unfortunate semester at Juilliard involving a well-known piano teacher and a flock of Canadian geese. After his expulsion, another attempt at education via the great state of Pennsylvania had been made. It seems that neither of his piano teachers at those two institutions were familiar with Olga Samaroff, née Lucy Hickenlooper, and therefore unable fully to appreciate Robert's talents via the familiar nomenclature he shared with that artist. Olga, where are you when we need you?

I can remember speaking to him several times in the student union building, and once nodding an acknowledgment to him at an orgy (I was there strictly as an observer during the ubiquitous saturnalia that persisted well into the 1980s) as he assaulted from behind the same transfer student from Lithuania that the potato homage had been constructed to, but that was about the extent of our fraternizing.

His exhibition at the co-ed sex marathon was enough to bring me to the realization that Robert, with his athletic good looks and charismatic smile, was at least bisexual. That was fine. I held no judgment on the subject but liked playing for my own team whose uniform I had worn from birth, the exception being some minor experimentation at Boy Scout camp—Mr. Smarmy, wherever you are, you could have been a little more temperate. (To this day, the experience of being thrifty causes me to break out in hives.)

The next time I saw Boy Wonder was in 1989 in New York, at a performance of modern dance that I shall get to in a minute. He still wrapped the afterglow of that college orgy around him like a second skin and his looks had improved to the point of distraction.

Robert was from Bertha, Texas (I looked on the map—I can't find it anywhere), and evidently came from a family that possessed money. He was six feet three inches of well-padded muscle with unusually large forearms and calves; the kind that stand out when you wear short-sleeved shirts and shorts. And while he had some mix of rubicund Irish, English, and German background, he was perpetually tanned, setting off his square jaw, flattop haircut, subtle freckles, and intense blue eyes. Most women, and more than a few men, melted at the sight of him. He looked good in anything he wore and reeked of sexuality. Not in a sleazy way, but in that "I could work for a major corporation, circus freak show, or even landscaping business and still be sexy" kind of way. He was big-man-on-the-campus of Good Times University, both figuratively and anatomically.

With muscular hands—big mitts of flesh with fingers like small exotic bananas—and feet a good size thirteen, he was by definition, a strapping youth. While his hair was auburn, it didn't stop with the flattop on his head. There was a fine dusting all over, especially his chest, which looked like a cinnamon version of the Black Forest. At the base of his throat the pectoral curls were continually attempting to escape from the V-neck of the sports shirts Robert wore, oozing out the top near his prominent Adam's apple like waves of rust-colored testosterone. A small, tasteful gold chain always nestled in the man-foliage as counterpoint. In short, Robert was a stud.

I was twenty-three at the time I ran into him again. It was after college and I was unemployed and living with a family of Mormons in Upper Manhattan, having ventured to the capital of the world in order to seek a publisher for my book—*Mrs. Squigglemire's Bustle*. What else is there to do, really, when one is without a career and a place to live—and touting a novel with a name like *Mrs. Squigglemire's Bustle*?

The Mormon family had taken me in after mistaking a general stupor—caused by lack of food—for interest in the Church of Latter Day Saints. They found me staring at my reflection in that institution's glass façade on Broadway, across from Lincoln Center. I was trying to determine just how bad I looked. They mistook my intensity and sunken cheeks as interest in religion and seized the opportunity to convert. Who was I to argue—they had groceries. I had been in New York only a day, and considering general world conditions at the time—the late '80s—religion didn't seem such a bad placebo.

Nineteen eighty-nine was an odd year to move to the city. Bush (the first one) was President, the San Francisco Forty-Niners won the Super Bowl that year, Ted Bundy was executed, the Exxon Valdez spilled 240,000 barrels of oil into the Pacific, and Oliver North was found guilty in the Iran-contra scandal. As if this wasn't enough, things only got worse after the first few months I entered New York. The month I arrived—September—hurricane Hugo devastated Florida. Then a California earthquake caused an estimated seven billion in damages, and in November the Berlin Wall fell. It was, as times are now, a period of great upheaval, both good and bad. I couldn't help but feel at least partially responsible.

I moved to the city amidst the turmoil, so it was at least somewhat comforting to be found on that fall day by the Mormons—a group of people that, for all of their perceived or actual shortcomings, did rescue me from my withering and hungry reflection.

Thinking that I needed salvation, they took me into their home with the caveat that I at least attempt to attend church each Sunday. It seemed at the time a small price to pay for food and shelter. Looking back on it, it was an extremely expensive proposition, for the attempted conversion felt forced and my eventual ambivalence about religion would prove to be the foot in the door others needed to set my life's direction down a path of anarchy and turmoil.

The Mormon is a strange animal. They're among the most devoted of all followers and at times their enthusiasm is a bit overwhelming. It seems that my upbringing, or lack thereof, left me unprepared for the rigors of life with a church-oriented family. Fortunately at this point, the Mormon unit consisted of only the husband and wife, but many children were expected—nay, demanded—if the young couple's way to heaven was to be guaranteed. So I played, for the time, the role of over-aged prodigal son, unaware of what was right and wrong in a household such as this.

My first mistake had to do with wardrobe. It seems that blue jeans were not allowed and I owned four pairs of them. In fact, that was about all I owned. After much discussion I was given something rather ill-fitting to take the place of the Satan-inspired casual wear—a pair of elephant-leg, floral-print, women's pants. For some reason denim was a no-no, while borderline transvestitism was acceptable. The wonders of organized religion will never cease to amaze me.

My second folly involved not only the buying of a box of chocolate doughnuts, but the even worse sin of escorting them into the apartment. One could only wonder what other lucre I had attempted to take into my seamy bosom, and what additional immoral culinary profits my visits to the local bodegas had produced. And so it was this very suspicion amongst the local brethren that caused the search through my belongings; a search that would propel me into the world of classified ads and roommate services in an attempt to flee this environment. I shall therefore relate it exactly as it happened since it is integral to the story of Robert and me.

> Scene: Manhattan. Apartment building. Circa 1900 tiled hallways with cooking fumes and a permanent echo. Big rooms. Exotic elements coming together haphazardly. Smells. Foods from many lands. A neighbor's argument heard all too clearly through the plaster walls in some non-discernable foreign language. Too many fire escapes and garbage chutes. One bedroom. Shared bath. Camera moves from rooftops down into airshaft, enters large window where Max Perkins is just waking up, having spent a restless night on a futon in a living room. He is roused by sound of the married couple in next room making love. The Mormons, it seems, are trying for bonus points as far as heaven is concerned.

One week into my stay with the Holy Couple, I was asked to assist in a production involving dance and music—an experimentation in the arts that was to take place in some little-known loft in SoHo. All this as a direct result of living in the same

16

space as Mr. and Mrs. Mormon—the preferred career of the former was "costume designer." While I had come to the city to get my novel published and not to hobnob with musicians and dancers, the thought of experiencing New York artists first hand made me feel that I had arrived. Besides, the book was going nowhere, either of my accord or anyone else's, so any experiences I could have—future fodder for pen and ink—would only add to my already fecund and burgeoning talents.

The evening of the production, I found myself standing at the foot of a steep stairway on a dark street. Rain had movie-set-glistened everything and shadows seemed to walk about of their own accord. Thunder rumbled in the distance and somewhere over the Hudson River a crisp charge of lightening flashed. The steep gray-green stairway led up to a landing, fluorescent and narrow. This in turn poured into the performance area. My first tip-off as to how the evening would progress should have been the scarcity of persons normally known as "audience."

"What exactly am I supposed to do?" I asked, as I arrived at the loft, my floral-print elephant-leg pants swinging freely—the direct result of a breeze of hurricane proportions that emanated from a large fan occupying one corner of the studio. Though it was fall in New York, the temperature refused to be coaxed downward. The loft was sweltering.

"You're to operate the light board," Mr. Mormon instructed, while putting the finishing touches on a harem-like outfit that a young woman was draped in. There were small chains hung around the concubine's neck and waist, and she was sporting ankle bracelets and a rhinestone in her navel.

"But I don't know anything about a light board," I said.

"Don't worry, the guy doing the sound will show you. We just need another warm body," he went on, folding some pleats that weren't cooperating. "The board is over there behind the curtain."

Witness for the defense, Mr. and Mrs. Mormon: "We liked Max--found him in a daze in front of the Mormon Center on Broadway on a bright September day in 1989. He was listless; taciturn. We knew it was our duty to turn him

toward God. We like helping people. We don't
expect anything back. It just feels good."
Production note: They are huddled together,
tightly wrapped in their coats. It is the dead
of winter, obviously some time later. They
jiggle up and down slightly and beat their
mittens together. Separately: "Praise God."
Husband and wife at the same time: "Praise
God."

I made my way to the sectioned-off corner of the loft where
the sound and light controls had been banished, careful not to walk
into the plethora of props and costumes that huddled about. Out of
the corner of my eye I watched a young woman (with a rubber
chicken atop her head) recite Shakespeare in pig Latin, the entire
time performing bird-like movements in the open space. Goateed
forty-year-olds and too-thin women stood around and watched,
hands on chins, nodding occasionally. The word "genius" was heard
more than once.

"Otay ebay orway otnay otay ebay, atthay isway ethay
estionquay," the dancer recited while dressed only in a purple
leotard and chicken hat, one foot slapping the floor in front of her
like a fish on land. So fascinated by this outburst of artistic freedom
was I, that I reached the fabric-clad corner and ran directly into
someone on the other side.

"Dammit, watch where you're going, you fu—" a voice
screamed at me. The curtain parted, and I came face to face with
someone who I probably shouldn't have recognized—at least with
clothing on. In the distance the rubber chicken wobbled to a halt via
my peripheral vision, momentarily silenced by the outburst of the
previously unseen person.

"Robert Hickenlooper!" I said before I realized he hadn't
yet recognized me.

It took him a minute to adjust. His eyes focused, and then
he let it out: "Max Perkins, you son-of-a-bitch!" (The Mormons
frowned.) He grabbed my hand with his meaty paw and almost
wrenched it from my arm.

18

"Otay ebay . . ." the woman with the chicken on her head intoned, hoping to draw attention back to herself, and Robert and I continued to shake for a good minute.

3

"You've got to help me," I said to Robert. We were hunched over the light board and sound equipment in the back of the loft, well into the performance of the evening. His return to New York, what territory there was between college, and my recent installation into the family of Latter-Day Saints, had been covered in the spare moments we had. During this enlightening period Robert showed me how to run the lights, what to do for each piece presented, and how to determine what was happening. This was modern dance in New York and the performers and choreographers felt the need to push the envelope pretty much to the point where it now resembled a motley and pockmarked Federal Express box.

"Where are you staying?" he asked as we both watched a woman fling herself across the loft to a tape-recorded auctioneer's voice. "One-leven-leven, two-leven-leven, three-leven-leven, hooooo, do I have a four-leven-leven, five-leven-leven, whaddaya, whaddaya, whaddaya, bingo! Sold!" a twangy-accented man threw out. A flat plywood pig cowered in the corner and occasionally a strobe light went off on the other side of the space—not my doing.

"With a family of Mormons," I said. "What about you?"

"Here and there. Right now I'm between places."

"Shhhhhhh!" someone hissed at us from the back row. We watched the performing area now as some of the dancers pitched themselves out of sight and another group came on. The new piece consisted of seven people sitting in chairs with their backs to us. For the most part they didn't move, and every now and then someone in the group would say a word or two.

"Precious," one exclaimed while everyone sat still. "Recalcitrant," another echoed a few minutes later. "Idiom," loudly mouthed one sultry female, *à la* Greta Garbo. The words were punctuated by group stares, straight ahead, away from the audience and toward the back wall. Then, a minute later one of them burst out with a horribly fake stage laugh. All at once the group began to talk rapidly, still looking straight ahead. "BEELZEBUB OF THE BUNGHOLE," one of the performers was heard to say above the din. Robert and I figured this was our chance to catch up—besides, no one would notice.

"Look, do you think we could find a place together?" I asked, desperate to get out of a situation that contained no chocolate or blue jeans. Robert looked uneasy, and hesitated.

"I don't know," he said. "I've got some complicated things going on right now with my living circumstances and with jobs."

"Jobs?" I said. "How many do you have?"

"MOTHER OF GOD," one of the performers intoned, cutting the space with her voluminous voice. "TAKE ME WITH YOU," another answered, attempting to match volume.

"A couple," Robert answered and looked sheepish. "Look, here's my number, or at least a number you can reach me at. If you really get into a bind, give me a call." He handed me a scrap of paper with a badly scrawled phone number. "And I've got a little something for you after the show," he added with a wink.

We watched the performance for a while longer. Then Robert spoke again—a commentary on the fiasco before us. "All art is quite useless."

"Huh?"

"Oscar Wilde. The quote. 'All art is quite useless.'"

"Evidently," I said.

By now the second group had dispersed and I had managed my meager light cues. There wasn't that much to it really—just a bump up and bump down between pieces with some slides occasionally shown on the back wall. Not having been to the dress rehearsal I had no idea what was coming artistic-wise and was caught totally off guard when the next piece began.

"Please tell me that's not what I think it is," I said, looking straight ahead as the woman wearing the harem outfit and chains waddled onto the stage carrying an enormous papier-mâché macaroon with large plastic eyes and a lolling tongue. The eyes were crossed and a badly styled stringy brown wig sat atop the cookie. "Mother of God," I said to no one in particular.

"Take me with you," Robert answered, still looking ahead, as transfixed as I was. "One of Dory's creations," he added. "Some freelance work while she waits for the rest of the world to discover she's talented." Then he started the tape that was to accompany the piece and I kicked off the slide projector with a click and whirr.

The next thirty minutes were a conglomeration of celluloid, voice-overs, and mime, all dealing with the art of decapitation. There were butchers wielding large meat hatchets, casually cutting off the heads of chickens and other animals. There were people miming the decapitation of stuffed animals. At one point, the film increased to speed-of-light-proportions. The woman in the toga chained herself to the macaroon and began to strain, as if she were experiencing the most exquisite bowel movement, all to the recorded sounds of a slaughterhouse.

Slides of unpleasant animal parts flickered across the screen; there was a "caught in motion" shot of someone writing their name in a snow bank with an appendage reserved mainly for reproduction (what this had to do with anything, *none* of us could figure out); a close-up of a cow's head, and a dog squatting on the sidewalk with an embarrassed look, its head turned almost completely around, staring at the camera. Under its picture was a caption from the movie *The Exorcist*: "You're gonna die up there." The performer was oblivious to the correlation between the quote and what was now happening.

The climax of the piece involved two accomplices who wheeled out a box of foot-deep macaroons, each with small plastic eyes. The "dancer" then gingerly stepped into the box, squishing about for several minutes until my cue to start the tape. Over the speakers came "Dance of the Seven Veils" from Richard Strauss's *Salome*. The toga-clad woman knelt in front of the giant macaroon—with several of the smaller versions now stuck between her toes—and lifted the papier-mâché object slightly, kissing it on the painted mouth when she wasn't lip-synching the words of the opera.

At one point she spread her legs and brought the large cookie between them, making it appear that the John the Baptist pastry was performing oral sex. As the last notes of the opera crashed around her, I brought the lights down. Turpitude reigned supreme.

Robert and I sat dumfounded, not able to look at one another after the tumultuous applause died down. "Gives a whole new meaning to Beelzebub of the bunghole, doesn't it?" whispered Robert.

"Eelzebubbay ofway ethay ungholebay," I said in my most sultry stage whisper.

The problem with most organized religions, Christianity in particular, is that they have no backup plan. If things go incredibly wrong, say, with the discovery of life on other planets or some subject not covered in the Bible, the pontificators of God's word are in a bind. After all, they've taken everything literally—at face value. With zealots, even the smallest mention of rituals and do-not gets attention; that is, unless it falls under that most dreaded heading—Inconvenient. Burnt offerings, women staying at home during menstruation, and dietary restrictions suddenly go by the wayside when modern society beckons. And an even more mangled view of things takes place when one enters the land of Mormon, albeit one that does at least have something to fall back on. Maybe too much to fall back on.

As if things aren't confusing enough to modern Christians with one Bible, the Mormons have *The Book of Mormon* translated from the Nephi plates. If one accepts this new addition to the religious canon, then it shouldn't be much of a stretch to imagine that in the event that some heaven-shattering incident takes place, someone can always try and locate the reason under a tree stump in upper New York State. "Aliens? Life on twenty million other planets? Honest politicians? Oh. Yeah, forgot to tell you about those. Seems we found these 'plates' located under a four-week-old bagel and they describe life on other planets and people who actually want to better the world. Sorry about the confusion."

And so began my instructive journey through Rule-Land in the Mormon household, the main part of which was supposed to take place at church. I attended, thinking, "How bad could it be?"

Each Sunday the Reverend Balding-Pate, sole proprietor of God and Company, would fire off a list of sins which, if laid end-to-end, would circle the world were it not for the fact that we know (thanks to religion) that the planet is flat. And it's this warped logic that brought about my most anxious moment since moving to the city. That story here:

The day after what I will lovingly term "my night in the theatre" with the macaroons and pig Latin, I slept in late, then decided to go to see a film. I knew I had to look for a job but thought I would see some of the city first. There was no pressure yet from Mr. and Mrs. Mormon to contribute to the rent, so the occasional helping out with dance productions in lofts and attending church seemed to be enough for now, short time though it was. Besides, I loved movies of any and every kind—especially old movies—and to my delight there was a theatre in Greenwich Village that specialized in exactly that.

I was turning the corner of Sixth Avenue and West Fourth after seeing that salacious and sometimes overly descriptive film from 1969, *Midnight Cowboy*, when I ran into Robert again. New York was quickly becoming a very small town.

"So, how'd you like it?" he asked. I thought he was referring to the movie.

"Intense," I said, shielding my eyes from the midday sun.

"Not the show, dufus, the pot. How'd you like the pot?"

"What *pot?*"

"The pot. The joint I stuck in your knapsack last night during that abortion they call art, dance, whatever."

"You stuck a joint in my bag? What are you, crazy? I live with Mormons! They don't even like doughnuts. Are you trying to get me killed?" I looked around; caught; desperate. This was not good news. "Oh, man," I said, "I've got to go."

There was no time. I had to get back to the apartment and search the knapsack before someone found the stash. I shouted a good-bye to Robert with the promise that I would call, and launched myself down the subway steps, barely catching the A train in time before the doors closed. My last image of him that day was of his jaw dropping in total amazement. The trip uptown was one of the longest of my life.

When I arrived at the apartment, I found the door slightly ajar. I eased it open, letting myself into the small entranceway. All was quiet. It was not until I rounded the corner that I realized I was

25

in trouble. There, perched on every sofa, chair, ottoman, and milk crate, were twelve rather ominous-looking Mormons, all with arms crossed and sporting scowls on their faces.

"Hey, what's going on?" I asked, trying to act casual, trying to catch my breath.

It was Mr. Mormon who spoke first. "We found it," he said, and the words hung suspended in midair—a Damoclean sword ready to drop and sever me from food and shelter.

"Found what?" I asked, feigning ignorance, immediately asking the Almighty's forgiveness for the earlier scorning of religious literature.

"The pagan herbs," said one of the other members of the church.

"Crapola," I thought. "I'm sunk now. No place to live and no money to do it with."

But something seemed strange. I looked toward my knapsack. It hadn't been moved. It was exactly where I had left it, slightly under a pile of books (read: symbolism for those of you on a mission).

"What pagan herbs?" I asked, turning my profile to the side and squinting, hoping for a miracle; hoping for hope.

It was then that I saw it. At first I couldn't make out the object since it was halfway across the room, but the declamatory word "This," spoken by the member holding the item that I feared would bring about my downfall, ushered everything into focus. There, suspended in the center of the room, twirling lazily in the afternoon light, was a Lipton's tea bag.

"It seems they don't approve of caffeine," I said to Robert as he accompanied me down the sidewalk in midtown. I was on my way to interview at several employment agencies with the hope of procuring a job—agencies that Robert had recommended. Crowds jostled past us, their murmur of everydayness punctuated by the intermittent car horn and howling homeless person. Occasionally someone would eye me strangely, as if I were talking to myself, the way I'd seen so many dispossessed people do.

"That was the problem with the chocolate doughnuts," I said. "Caffeine in the chocolate."

At that moment the scream of an ambulance, insisting on life, slogged its way through a bevy of yellow cabs and delivery trucks. Our conversation was momentarily halted. Then the noise died down.

"Bummer. So what are you going to do now?" Robert asked.

"They've given me two weeks to find a place, which, I suppose when you consider that I've broken some of the most coveted of all commandments—thou shalt not have caffeine or heavy cotton fabrics—is really generous."

"Any ideas?"

"Well, first thing after these interviews, I'll be looking for a place to live."

"Try the *Village Voice*. They've got a lot of listings for roommates," Robert said, as he maneuvered around a blind person standing perfectly still in the middle of the sidewalk. The sightless man was rhythmically shaking a cup of change. Then the building where my interview was to take place came into view and I signaled to Rob that this was my cue to leave.

"Interesting," he said. We began to part company: he for some secret appointment and me for an interview with the first employment agency.

"What's that?" I asked, seeing him walk slowly backwards away from me. He artfully dodged every passerby as if he had eyes in the back of his head. It was very '70s made-for-TV-movie.

"Just thinking about the Mormons. Religion. All the aspects of the thing. Someone who doesn't mind designing costumes for a piece about a giant macaroon performing cunnilingus on Salome, but who flips out about a tea bag."

"Takes all kinds," I said, turned, and headed north.

If buildings could be compared to people, the one where my interview was to take place was standing defiantly in front of me, hands on hips, head held high as if to say, "What do *you* want?" This was my first introduction to agencies that placed people like myself—people who had no real marketable skills in a city that concerned itself with making money. I pressed my way into the slick marble lobby through the whoosh of revolving doors. Stoic men in uniforms sat sullenly at a reception desk—a behemoth of stone with a lighted board containing the names of all the businesses in the structure. No one offered any help. After a few minutes I found the floor number of the office and tried to sort out the elevator configuration located in a separate vestibule. Floors one to eight in one elevator bank. Floors ten to fourteen in another. Then floors fifteen to penthouse in the final one. I looked again. The agency I sought was on the ninth floor. No elevator *went* to the ninth floor. I retreated to the main lobby.

"Excuse me," I started to say to one of the grim uniforms at the front desk, "I need—"

"Take the elevator up to ten. Go into the stairwell. Walk down one flight," a guard said in a flat emotionless baritone, without ever looking up. Obviously I wasn't the first to notice this structural oddity in the building. So I did as commanded.

The stairwell deposited me on purple-colored carpet and I found the room (suite 901) after a good fifteen minutes. It seems that the numbering system, like most things in life up until that point, made no sense.

The second I opened the door to the agency, an avalanche of noise poured into the hallway and covered me. Typewriters, high-decibel office machines, agency badinage, and ringing phones all piled out together—teenagers spilling from an overstuffed Volkswagen or phone booth. I waded up to the reception desk.

The girl sitting at the small table was wearing green eye shadow, green fingernail polish, and green lipstick. In addition to this, the tips of her hair (which was standing straight up) were frosted green. She was grinding one of her nails between two teeth in an effort to dislodge some food particle as she talked on the phone. She sported multiple piercings.

"Well, just tell him that toys are out. You don't do anything you don't want to. And no leather. Who the hell does he think he is?" she was saying in a thick obnoxious (redundancy alert here) Long Island accent. "You just remember that you're a lady. A *classy* lady. And if he doesn't include the cost of the motel the next time in his fee, you tell him you're through. Okay. Okay. Okay. Uh-huh. Okay. Look, sweetie, I've got to go. Uh-huh."

I waited patiently. I cleared my throat slightly. As there was precious little else to do, I counted her piercings. Six, no, seven on the left ear.

"Huh? No way. No way. No way," she continued. "Listen. Listen to me . . . LISTEN. LISTEN TO ME, JOSIE. You tell that no good bum that he can KISS YOUR ASS and mine too. You just remember that your mother didn't raise a lady for nuttin', okay?"

One, two, three, no . . . five in one nostril . . .

The human pincushion continued. "OKAAAAAAY? Look, I've got to . . . uh-huh . . . well I don't care what she said. I was THERE. I KNOW. Okay, sweetie. Yes. I'll see you tonight at nine-thirty. Okay. Okay."

One on each eyebrow and the glint of silver on the tongue makes . . .

She was showing no sign of tiring. "Noooooo. When did that happen? Okay. We'll talk about it tonight. Yes, I'm going next

Tuesday. You don't think I would miss that, do you? Okay. See ya. Ciao."

I finished: A total of thirty-two piercings, but that was just what I could see from her chest to the top of her head. I shuddered to think what the lower extremities looked like. Finally she wrapped things up. The festival of metal and paint had yet to look in my direction so I wasn't entirely sure that she knew I was there. Deftly fingering a rather anemic-looking pothos vine sitting on the upper ledge of the reception desk, I waited. After a few seconds she addressed me—still without looking up.

"Yes? Can I help you? Are you going to stand there all day or are you going to fill out one of the forms?" she asked crossly, and with that she slapped a clipboard onto the edge of the desk with one hand while she flipped through an amalgamation of index cards with the other. "And if you don't have a pen," she continued, "you shouldn't be here." With that she abandoned the cards and immersed herself back into a scruffy dime-store novel she had been reading before her erudite conversation with the "classy" debutante. An overly long lime-green nail underlined sentences while her lips moved. She was only on page six but the paperback looked as though it had survived two world wars.

I took the application over to one of the chairs and sat down, trying not to notice the décor. It wasn't easy. Bright green walls with large floral pictures competed for attention with the purple chairs and carpet. On several small tables were two-year-old copies of *Sports Illustrated* and *Cosmopolitan*. Ten other job seekers in the waiting area were busy transferring information from their résumés to the application forms, their heads bent in studied intensity.

After filling out the form and attaching a copy of my *vita*, I set them on the desk and returned to my seat. Without a word the receptionist got up and took them through a doorway, then returned. About three hours later, a rather thin, crooked-mouthed woman with badly bleached blond hair came through the same opening and called my name.

"Vita? Is Vita here? she exclaimed.

30

"How strange," I thought, "that someone would be called Vita."

"Vita?" She looked around, then added, "Vita Perkins?"

"I'm *Max* Perkins," I said, slightly confused.

She looked down. "It says here Vita. Do you go by Vita or Max? Which one is your name?"

"*Vita* is at the top of my résumé," I said. "It means, well, résumé, you know, what I've done."

She paused, looking confused, as if I were playing some sort of joke on her. "Are you ashamed of having a girl's name?" she asked.

"I don't have a girl's name. *Vita* means—" but I let it go. "Max. I go by Max. Call me Max. Max Perkins."

"Perkins, then," she said without emotion, motioning me to follow her. She had all the panache and eagerness of someone about to give a rectal exam. I followed and sat down on the chair across from her desk. She reacted as if I had just dropped a forty-pound weight on her foot.

"Not there! THEEEEEERE!" she seethed, indicating another chair holding several binders. "Just move the binders," she added. I sat down and looked around after clearing a place. It was one large room with about seven desks. Everyone was on the phone or bent over, and the group looked about as happy as a faction of Holocaust survivors at a Weight Watchers meeting on the first day of their release. Then Brunhilde looked up.

"You're going to starve, mister. Do you know that? You have *zero* skills. Do you even *own* a suit?"

"But, I thought—"

"Don't think. What can you do for *me*? What can you offer *us*, any prospective employer?"

While never one to force my intellectual plumage on someone else, I tried as demurely as I could to state my skills. "Well, I have pretty good writing skills. I have a degree from Penn State— highest average in my class. I studied in Europe one summer. I speak five languages. I've written a book. I type about—"

"I'll be the judge of what you can type," she snapped, cutting me off. "No one cares about your average, and as for the languages, they're useless. And just because I went to the Cayman Islands last year doesn't make me better than anyone. Got it?" Then she stared at my résumé for what seemed like a good hour, which I thought unusual since she had just informed me that I had no skills—what was there to look at?

"How are you at multi-tasking?" she asked, never looking up but scribbling something down.

"All right, I guess. Isn't that a nice way of saying someone has Attention Deficit Disorder?"

She said nothing but shot me an angry look and sighed. Without a word she got up to consult with two other women in the office. I could hear words and phrases such as "speaks English" and "white" bantered about. She came back a few minutes later.

"I've got something for you downtown. Art gallery. Permanent. Pays in the middle twenties. Receptionist. You'll be—" But then she stopped, scrutinizing my application card, flipping it over to look at the back.

"How long have you been in New York? It says here that you lived in—"

"I've only been in the city a short while. I'm just getting—" but before I could finish she was up—back again with her coven, consulting about my latest gaffe. She returned with a plastic smile, extending her hand—a clammy fish, long dead and smelling of hypocrisy.

"I'm sorry, Vita," she said, tilting her head to one side. "But thank you for coming in. We don't have anything right now."

I don't know what took hold of my body, but I found myself walking out the door without saying a word, amazed at her transparency, yet at the same time somehow in denial. I found myself out on the street once more, swimming uptown on Fifth Avenue, trying to shake off the rudeness and the name Vita. I made my way to the next appointment.

At the second agency, the "clipboard-fill-out-the-card-rude-receptionist-bad-decoration-incompetent-interviewer" routine was repeated with only a few minor deviations. The receptionist's phone conversation this time centered on wheat germ and poodle dandruff, and the woman who interviewed me was even more boorish than the wicked witch at the last locale.

"Name?" she intoned to the blotter in front of her when I was finally summoned in.

"My name is on the card . . . and the résumé," I said, gently pointing toward both of them. I had drawn a line through the word *Vita*.

"I asked you your *name*. I'd like to hear you *speak*," she snapped and then began writing while mouthing each word loud enough for me to hear: "Does . . . not . . . follow . . . directionsssssssss . . . weeeeeeelll," she inscribed on the back of my card.

"Max Perkins," I said, even-toned, more than slightly irritated.

"Thaaaaat's better!" she chimed in, now a completely different person. Jekyll and Hyde had nothing on this one. "I've got a temp job—downtown."

"That's nice," I said, trying not to initiate another mood swing, "but I was hoping for something a little more—"

"DO YOU WANT TO WORK? DO YOU WANT A JOB!" she screamed, jumping to her feet.

"I . . . I . . . I . . . I." I was stunned. The outburst had come from nowhere.

"I, I, I, I. Is that all you can say? Is that all you can say? Is that all you can say to me? Isthatallyoucansaytomerightnow? I've got a hundred people sitting out there in the waiting room and you want to argue? Don't waste my time if you don't want to work."

Taking a second to think about her penultimate statement, I realized she didn't know what she was talking about—I had been the only one in the reception area of this particular agency. Then her medication must have kicked in, for she promptly sat down as if nothing had happened. The most disturbing aspect surrounding her behavior wasn't her manic mood swings, but rather the fact that the others in the large room—same attitudes and remorsefulness as those in the first place—didn't seem to notice anything was wrong.

"I'm going to send you to Beaucoup Books." She was once again writing something while talking. I imagined it being along the lines of, "Nooooo ... loooooongeerrr ... pissssssseeed ... ooooooofffffff," but didn't want to waste too much energy in speculation.

"You say you're a writer? At least that's what it says on your résumé. Well, this is a book dealer."

"That's great! Finally, someone who understands," I said with enthusiasm, and immediately realized my mistake. In a city know for its sullenness and cynicism, I had shown eagerness—a death knell if ever there was one. From now on I would have to watch myself.

There was a beat, and then the process of inscription began again. "Tooooooo ... eeeeageeeeerrrrrrrr ..." she wrote, and her mouth molded the words at the same time.

Scene. Exterior shot: Depressing low brick building on Manhattan's West Side--the highway saddling up. Sounds of trucks. No restaurants. No shops. No-man's-land. More like New Jersey on a bad day after a bulldozer has had its way with the place. Our character finds himself standing before a building, looking up at a sign: "Beaucoup Books-- shipping and receiving departments." A long sigh exits his lips. Then he reaches for the door and the building swallows him.

"Hi," I found myself saying to a group of men I happened upon after making my way through an empty reception area and tiled hallway. I had followed the noise of forklifts and yelling toward a break room where several slovenly-looking individuals napped and watched television. One of the men looked up at me, his eyes expressionless. A large piece of onion hung from his mouth. He chewed silently, the mastication of his jaw working the food he had just retrieved from a discolored Tupperware container. Salsa music could be heard coming from a diminutive 1960s transistor radio. "Can you tell me where I'd find Benny?" I asked.

"Who?" a man shouted in back of me. He had stuck his head in through the doorway to the break room.

"Benny?" I asked again, looking at the piece of paper the agency had given me, to make sure I had the name right.

"Let me see that," he said, grabbing the paper from me. Then a smirk came across his lips. "It's ben-aaaay," he said with a condescending tone, attempting a French pronunciation. One meaty finger pointed down yet another hallway and he offered up a curt, "That way," then disappeared.

I followed the direction he indicated. About halfway down the hall I stopped. Something caught my attention. There, to the left, was the "office," a rather worn-looking space with seven or so employees sitting at metal desks. Bare fluorescent bulbs dangled precariously from a water-stained asbestos tile ceiling, and puce-and-green enamel-painted cinder block walls offset the entire (ahem) decorating scheme—each block an alternating color. There was not a window in the place.

"I'm here to see Bee-naaay-kwaah," I said, pronouncing the name as a French person might, but with an overly elongated and nasal sound. I tried to bring up a wad of spit from the depths of my throat, adding it to the last syllable of the name even though none was needed.

"I'm Benny. Whadda you want?" a voice resembling that of a longshoreman said in back of me, and I turned to see a short, pudgy, acne-scarred woman of about forty as she jerked her head upwards. Her hands were on her hips. In addition to her adolescent scars, she possessed a long keloid down the right side of her face, making her instantaneously memorable if ever seen outside the office. A lesbionic haircut completed the scheme.

"I'm the temp. I'm supposed to—"

"You're supposed to be working that's what you're supposed to be doing," she shot back.

"Let me ask you something," I said, widening my eyes and sticking my neck out, "does anyone in New York allow the other person to finish a sentence when they're—"

"Derrick! Get over here and show the temp where to sit," she bawled at another of the workers who sat glumly in one corner.

Before she had finished, Derrick was at my side, herding me over to a metal desk by the door, complete with 1950s ugly oblong lamp and a squeaky vinyl-covered chair. "Sit," was all he said, and left.

"Friendly," I thought.

I soon discovered that the mechanism for stopping the back of the chair from tilting too far was broken. While no one came to my rescue as I lay on the floor, no one laughed either. By the time I had collected myself, Benny had crawled from under her rock and was once more slithering in my direction.

"These bills get filed, sharpen these pencils, take out the trash, and type up these requisitions."

"I'm sorry, but I thought I was being hired as a writer," I managed, and then seeing her reaction added, "but if you want me to do some additional things I'll be glad to help out."

Somewhere in the building someone dropped a pin—and we all heard it.

The pregnant pause continued for what seemed like hours until Benny turned to the rest of the room and jeered, "He thinks he's been sent here to write!"

It took a good half-hour for the laughter to die down.

"Listen, Bub," said a man of about thirty-five, "we're all writers. You don't think we actually get paid for it, do you?" Then he jockeyed back to his metal desk, jerking his head and pulling at his crotch.

Benny chimed in again, a sneer on her face and her arms crossed while one foot beat impatiently on the cold tile floor like a beginner of tap. "You're the receptionist and you do light typing. Understand?"

"I saw a reception area outside—" I started to say, but it was too late. Benny was gone and I was left with a desk full of invoices. I looked down at the coffee-stained blotter on the desk, spreading out like a flat sea of pea soup. One giant discolored area had evidently inspired the last temp who sat here, miraculously forming what the person thought to be a likeness of Jesus. Around the bottom of it the temp had drawn pictures of obsequious sheep, their eyes gazing upwards toward the savior coffee stain. Accompanying this found art was the caption, "He lives."

About three days later, at the end of the work period (five o'clock exactly—no slackers here) Benny presented me with a small yellow note containing tally marks. There were a total of seventeen tallies on this bit of paper. Having no clue as to its meaning I simply put the note under the six-hundred-pound, puke-green 1950s tape dispenser to await further instruction. Each day, I received another bit of paper with a different number of marks on it. This continued for some time.

Toward the end of the second week of my captivity at Beaucoup Books, I asked Benny what the yellow pieces of paper and tally marks meant. I was holding one in my hand at the time, hoping she could illuminate the situation as she walked by.

Seeing the paper and hearing my question, she stopped. She waited for dramatic pause. When she was sure the entire room was focused uncomfortably on me she began: "Those are how many words you say a day."

"But there's only five marks on this one note," I responded, pulling out the least tallied piece of paper.

"Well," she continued, "that's five too many," and turning on her heel, left the room.

"But I'm the receptionist!" I yelled after her.

That afternoon I called the agency to ask that they find me another job. I explained exactly what had happened with the tally marks, Benny's abuse, the general stress of the situation.

"Do you *WANT* to work?" the voice screamed at me through the receiver.

I thought about it, and not for that long a time before I answered.

"I guess not," I said, and hung up.

The act of forgiveness, if done correctly, is a very self-serving thing indeed. I had been given a momentary reprieve from having to vacate the house of Mormon, garnering praise by signing up to be a vitamin salesman in my spare time ("I promise to sell these vitamins to the best of my ability for the remainder of my life") and swearing off denim, coffee, and Satan. The first two items on the list I had no real problem with any longer, but the third one was still in negotiation. After all, neither my book—*Mrs. Squigglemire's Bustle*—nor I were getting any younger. I also had time to clean, do the laundry, and cook caffeine-free meals—all a part of my day of reckoning with Lipton and Co. Besides, the Mormons were hardly at home so I had time to myself—time to spend valuable energy on what I was really here to do—get my book published.

I had done some research and knew that if I wanted to get anywhere I needed an agent. And knowing that the search might take months, I determined that it was best to cover as much territory as possible by typing up a generic letter describing my book and sending it to every known human being in the world who had anything *remotely* to do with the written word. So I did. Thanksgiving was coming soon and something about the crisp New York air invigorated me. I felt optimistic as I deposited innumerable stacks of envelopes into a neighborhood mailbox while bright autumn foliage scampered by.

The response to my letters a week later was underwhelming in content, but overwhelming in quantity. I received virtually the same reply from each agent. Most were quite prompt in their retort, and nearly all of them went something like this:

Dear Author,

> Thank you for your letter; however, we do not feel at this time that we are able to represent your work. Because of the sheer amount of requests we have, we must decline this opportunity. We wish you luck with your future endeavors.

So standardized were these form letters, so close in content and wording, that I suspected they had been concocted at some enormous convention in Los Angeles or New York where agents gathered to agree on the proper rejoinder. "If we can just nail down the right phrases—you know, nothing too harsh, but something firm—then we can all use it. A sort of standardized rejection letter, yes?"

It caused me to start thinking: Had anyone actually read my letters, and if so, what kind of people were they? Did some assistant get my query and, while finishing off a Hostess cupcake, nonchalantly hand over my request to an even more subordinate creature? "Here. Here's another one that gets the form letter," I imagined them saying, wiping their mouth on my expensive stationery as their co-worker's letter opener sliced through another unsuspecting envelope.

It was time to consult the self-help section of my local Beaucoup Books (I got a twenty percent discount after I lied and told them I still worked there), so off I went to look for literature on publishing and agents. What I found was a plethora of tomes on subjects from self-publishing to marketing. There were books describing how to get on *The New York Times* bestseller list, ones touting the latest formulas for success in publishing, and even one explaining how to write a screenplay in three days.

I opened the largest one I could find—a veritable infomercial including everything from names and addresses of book publishers to the latest techniques in editor stalking. "If you must, follow editors, publishers, and others who are influential around the city. Join the same gym they go to, eat at the same restaurants, send them gifts on a regular basis. This will assure that you eventually rub elbows with the right people!"

Fine suggestions for someone living in New York, but what are people in the Midwest going to do? Finally I found the section on agents: "Try doing something unusual to get an agent to notice you," the paragraph began. "For instance, you might send a small tree with your query letter, a bouquet of flowers, or a gift certificate to a fancy restaurant—anything to make yourself stand out!"

At this point, I figured it had to be worth a shot. But where was I going to find a small tree in Manhattan? The gift certificate and flowers sounded too obvious. I needed help, and fast. I consulted the phone book (one of the few things Mormons are actually allowed to have in their homes) and found a garden center in the city that happened to specialize in small trees for penthouse terraces. I called and scheduled delivery, offering to pay C.O.D.

The tree (it was a blue spruce—nothing too fancy, about two feet tall) arrived the following day. Why I didn't have it delivered directly to its final destination is beyond me. Possibly I thought that personally transporting the specimen would garner extra points.

The tree was just small enough for me to carry, and just large enough to be inconvenient. Having spent most of my remaining money from Beaucoup Books *on* Beaucoup Books, I decided that a cab ride to midtown was out of the question and headed over to the subway after determining which agent might be the most receptive to burlap-encased flora.

> Scene. Interior: Subway. Upper Manhattan. Crowded and jostling car comes to a stop. Writer gets on with small tree and backpack, sits down. Across from him a woman with pink hair and headphones casually munches on a hot dog, the condiments spilling out onto her lap. She occasionally sings along with the music. Her mouth is full of food. A bag person sleeps on seats nearest the end of the train. Smells of urine and filth. A young woman begins to recite poetry to no one in particular.

The good news about carrying a small tree on the subway in New York while wearing floral print elephant-leg pants is that no one notices. The bad news is that ... well ... no one notices. I made it to Rockefeller Plaza with Mr. Arbor and myself intact and proceeded to the largest skyscraper I could find—the one housing my coveted agent-to-be.

My spirits were high until I reached the elevator bank located in the middle of the building. A uniformed guard informed me, "tenth floor ... nice pants," his gloved hand holding the door back so that I could drag the burgeoning evergreen into the car. I was going to question how he knew where I was headed, but the door closed and I was hoisted up toward the office I sought.

The reason for his knowledge became quite clear, when, after exiting the elevator and rounding the corner, I was instructed by a building maintenance man that all tree deliveries to that particular agent should be taken to the mail room. It seems that sales, at least in the area of books on how to get an agent, were doing quite well, and the retailing of trees in Manhattan was even better.

8

My job efforts failed and my agent-procuring abilities seriously called into question, I decided to try my hand at finding a suitable apartment. After all, before the hawking of my writing wares could continue, stability was needed. *Mrs. Squigglemire's Bustle* would have to take a backseat to eating and sleeping. And how hard could it be? I mean, this was New York City. The stock market crash of 1987 had opened up more than a few entries in the area of apartment hunting. I figured that I would go out and knock on several doors, meet some people, and in a day or so have something equivalent to the type of place that the Woodhouses had in the movie *Rosemary's Baby*—you know, that multi-roomed, parquet-floored, high-ceilinged space in that little-known apartment building, the Dakota? I assumed that if Guy Woodhouse could afford it on an actor's salary (and not even a good actor's salary), then I would have no trouble with what I would eventually be making whenever I found another job. But then Rosemary and her husband had the help of the devil in the movie—I was still on my own.

After scanning the ads in *The Times* for places to live, my Dakota fantasy was cut short. That and the fact that I asked what Mr. and Mrs. Mormon were paying for the child's shoebox we were all living in, and they told me. The rent was only slightly less than the national debt. This situation would definitely require more cash, being less particular, the real help of the devil, or possibly all three.

I perused the *Village Voice*—a Robert Hickenlooper suggestion. The listings were more liberal and so were the prices. There was even a section for sublets and "roommates wanted." Since the idea of subletting appealed to me more than having to share, I called the first number I saw. Here is how the ad appeared:

Sublet avail. 03/01/88. Bklyn. 1 bdrm, shrd bth, furnished, w/d. Rent: $250.00 per month. Non-smoker and pet lover only. Lovely flat in safe part of Bklyn. English-speaking applicants preferred.

Looking back on things, there were signs. For one thing, it was now October of 1989 and the ad said "available 03/01/88." Then there was the rent. Two hundred fifty dollars a month is cheap in any age, but in '89 it was obscene. Still, my brain had been addled by employment agencies, Mormon regulations, and too many agonizing minutes spent in a garden center. I simply wasn't thinking clearly. Besides, when I called, the woman said I could come right over and she sounded nice enough. So I went.

The subway stop at which I got off in Brooklyn was not the friendliest. Evidently it had a reputation unbeknownst to me, for as soon as the doors opened, all the women sitting inside the train clutched their pocketbooks tightly with one hand and gripped the edge of the seat with the other. I couldn't understand what all the fuss was about since the outer platform was completely empty except for a group of four teenage black males wearing overly baggy pants, backward baseball caps, and a multitude of gold chains. So many chains in fact, that they resembled Cortez's men after his run-in with the Incas. I exited the train.

"Yo, homey, whassss up?" one of the youths called out, complete with splayed and semi-spastic hand gesture and absurd tilt of the head as the train's doors closed behind me.

"Yo, yo, yo, my main man, check it ouuut. Das de vic," another crooned.

"Chill muddahfuckah. I'm down wid dat shit, yo, say, Bradley, hit me wid my toooool," youth number three intoned, looking straight ahead at me. The fourth youngster was evidently along for the ride, having said nothing at this point.

It was then that I realized they had been addressing me, sauntering in my direction, and yielding a rather ominous sharpened screwdriver. It twirled between one of the youth's fingers like a miniature baton in the hands of a majorette. I made a quick retreat up the oily steps and into the sunlight, hoping they wouldn't follow.

"Jer, jer, jer, yo man, look out, de vic be givn' de slip."

"Chill my man, it's cool," and with that they began gaining on me.

After a few minutes of running, I looked up at a street sign for just a second. Myrtle Avenue. "Murder Avenue," I thought. I had memorized the address before taking the train and I was lucky enough to be near the right street. Quickly I scanned a row of turn-of-the-century townhouses, drab and decaying, like forgotten immigrants huddled together—waiting for a return passage from Ellis Island after being rejected. I saw the house number I was looking for and realized the four youths were within a few feet of my back. I was at the bottom of the steps to the house when I felt them suddenly slip away. My heart was still in my throat, my mind racing, trying to figure out how I was going to extricate myself from a miniature race riot.

"Fuck, man whas up wid dat shit?"

"Muddahfuckah I ain't messin' wi-dat."

"Yo, man, step down, step down . . . chiiiilllllll."

They scattered.

I didn't know what the problem was, nor did I care; all I knew was that I would live at least a few more minutes in Brooklyn. For some reason the four angry youths had dispersed, hightailing it when they realized I had set foot on the steps of one of the falling-down brownstones.

I looked up at the house, searching for some visible reason for their hasty retreat. An ancient wisteria vine looped its way up to the top story of the structure. Giant pieces of stucco had fallen away from the façade, and half of the shutters were missing. All the trim was painted a gloss black and the windowpanes looked as though they hadn't been washed since the place was built, which, judging from the architectural details, was about 1880. I ascended the steps and rang the bell marked "Patchin."

A good thirty minutes later someone answered.

" 'Eah!" a voice shrieked out of the dirty aluminum intercom.

"Hi, it's Max. Max Perkins, I—"

"Bzzzzzzzzzzzzzz. Bzzzzzzzzzz. Bzzzzzzzzzzzzzzzzz," the square metal box announced—my cue to push ahead and start

45

moving through the front door. The heavy oak and beveled glass portal snapped shut behind me, echoing in the empty entrance hall. Most of the plaster was gone from the interior walls and the lathe and wiring could be clearly seen. The place looked as though it was ready for the wrecking ball. I was getting ready to turn around and leave when two enormous parlor doors opened and a woman of about fifty years of age appeared. She was using crutches like those of a polio victim, and her legs were in braces. White-haired and in a floral-print housedress, she rivaled my pants for attention. A cigarette dangled from her lips.

"Name's Grace. Grace Patchin," she said in a thick cockney accent—something straight out of Dickens—as she ka-thumped her way toward me, her withered legs dragging slightly behind. An inch-long cone of ash from her cancer stick fell to the floor as a silver amulet bounced between her two huge sagging breasts, most of which were visible as her housedress was barely buttoned. Each time she spoke, the cigarette lurched up and down like some manic baton of an orchestra conductor whose imaginary music was reaching its most orgasmic climax—vintage Berlioz or Franz von Suppe on amphetamines.

" 'Ome on in," she said, turning toward the back hall. I followed slowly—an unsure traveler. "Yuh mus be the fellow what's called about the flat."

"Yes, I saw the ad and—"

"Weeeeell, just don't chu worry 'bout ah thing. We'll get you all fixed up 'ere in a jiffy, see?" she went on, leading me into what appeared to be a kitchen area toward the back of the house. The room was filthy, looking as though it hadn't been cleaned in decades. A cast iron stove huddled in one corner—the type that burned wood or coal—and there was not a refrigerator in sight. But the most anomalous feature of the room was the left wall, for stacked against it, one on top of the other, were six washing machines. Their circular cyclop-eyes were going full steam, rolling about what appeared to be acres of dirty laundry amid a sea of soapsuds, all of it slightly pink.

" 'Ave a seat, dearie. Make ye'self 'omfortable," she said, indicating a rickety-looking chair. Then she yelled toward a dilapidated set of steps at the end of the kitchen. "Laura-Louise, we've got a guest. Get your arse down 'ere an make us some coffee!" She took a long drag from her cigarette and exhaled, addressing me once again. "Laura-Louise is me companion, what since me divorce and all. Me ex-husband is a bit-o-a nut case, if you know what I mean. Always tryin' to, how d'ya say, psychoanalyze me and such. Was an American, that one. Like yourself. A regular tinkerer." Then she stubbed out her cigarette and looked at me squarely, matter-of-factly.

" 'Et's get to the point. I don't 'ave time de waste, wha-ee-ees, so I'll be layin' it on the line. I've 'ad me share of young ones that wanted no part of it."

She waited, I suppose to see my reaction, to see if I had figured out what the reason was for the apartment not being rented. When a few moments had passed she let it out.

"Yuh don't mind Devil worship, now do-yuh?" she asked, looking at me sideways. Then she lit another cigarette.

"Excuse me?"

"*Deh-vul* worship. Yuh know, Satan? Animal sacrifices—blood-drinking—at sor-uh-thing."

I didn't know what to say. I thought she was joking, but things were starting to add up. The ad had been running a long time, the rent was cheap, and something had done a number on four street toughs from this not-so-great neighborhood in Brooklyn as they were about to shish-kebob me with a sharpened screwdriver. It's amazing how quickly the mind can piece together a scenario in moments such as this. Or not.

"Are you serious?" I asked.

"As serious as if I was speakin' to 'er majesty 'erself," she replied and took another drag.

Now, I don't know why, but for some reason I didn't run screaming from the room. Perhaps it was my desire to see the thing played out; to see if she was joking; to see if she was just trying to scare me away. For whatever reason, I sat there, reasoning that an explanation was hiding someplace in this pigpen. It wasn't.

"Owe, you wouldn't 'ave to participate none, not unless you wanted to." Then addressing the ceiling, "LAURA-LOUISE! GET YOUR BLEEDIN' ARSE DOWN 'ERE AND FIX THE GOD-DAMNED COFFEE!"

"I'M COMING YOU STUPID BITCH!" a voice responded from above. It was Laura-Louise, making her way down the back stair, speaking with an almost equally thick accent—this one Brooklynese. "Pain-in-the-ass old woman," she muttered, "making me *do* shit."

"Sheesh," I thought to myself as I listened to the badinage, "the only things missing are Oliver Twist and a bowl of gruel." I wondered which might offend the Mormon clan more if they were here—the Satan worship or the suggestion of caffeine.

Laura-Louise, by this time at the kitchen sink, was clearly visible. She looked about forty with jet-black hair, black fingernail polish, black lipstick, black jeans, black shirt, black shoes, and, well . . . you get the picture.

Mrs. Patchin turned her attention to me as I looked around. "Now dearie, as I was sayin' . . . oh, I sees you're wonderin' 'bout me washin' machines, yes? I caught you now, didn't I? Well now, we 'ave lots-a dirty laundry 'round 'ere, what with the sacri—" But she stopped. "You know, you look like a nice young man. Wha' is it exactly you do?"

"I'm a writer," I said. The words seemed to stick in my throat. It always sounds pretentious to me, even if that's what you do.

"Yeah, sure you are," said Laura-Louise under her breath to a bag of Bustello as she slapped three serving spoons full of coffee into a beat-up samovar. "And I'm the Queen Mum."

"A rawe-tuh! 'Ell, 'ow nice! Oh, I loves me them artistic peoples. Now you take my girl—she's gone, living away from New York right now. 'At's why the sublet, me flat upstairs, is available. It's her room, really. Now you come on, dearie, and I'll show you," she said. "We 'ave to wait for that coffee anyways."

As she got up from the table and positioned her crutches I wondered how she was going to manage the stairs. She spoke as we moved back into the foyer.

"Like I was sayin', me girl is away. An artist, much like yourself. Real bright, 'at one. I told her she should stay at 'ome to save money, but you know how kids is. Now look dearie," she said, standing at the bottom step, " 'ears what's got to 'appen. You an' Laura-Louise is goin' to 'ave to each get on one side-ah me an *hoist* me up them stairs."

"Look, Mrs. Patchin—"

"Grace," she said, and then bellowed toward the kitchen, "LAURA-LOUISE!"

"Look, Grace, I really don't think—" but before I could finish, a blood-curdling scream emanated from the back of the house, followed by a chanting of some sort.

"Now don't you go worrin' your head none 'bout that. Just a little annie-mule sacrifice, it is. Like I was sayin', you an' Laura-Louise would 'ave to carry me up the stairs, every day, 'cause I'm not likely to grow me new legs anytime soon. Oh, an' dearie, me urine bag gets full from time-to-time, so's I'll be needin' you to empty that . . . if you would . . . be . . . so . . . kind."

I began moving toward the door, hoping I could get out before Laura-Louise came and turned me into someone's cat.

"You're not leavin' so soon, is you?" a bewildered Mrs. Patchin questioned as I turned the knob, my adrenaline pumping full volume. I was halfway down the front steps when I heard her last remark. She had managed to clump over to the door and was standing in plain view of the neighborhood: "You 'aven't even seen me flat yet, what with the new curtains I made an everythin'?"

9

After Mrs. Patchin and her little shop of horrors, I was considerably more careful with my next choice of advertisements. I had decided to try the roommate situation, thinking that, while it sounded less logical, having experienced what I had so far of New York, it probably made sense—in a backwards kind of way.

It didn't.

The first ad sounded innocuous enough. It was someone looking for a roommate in Queens. The person who had placed the announcement asked that you be normal, neat, clean, and quiet. Above all, no drugs, sex, or alcohol were allowed in the apartment. While it failed to say "No devil worship," I *assumed* (a word I would rarely use after my visits to apartments advertised in newspapers) that the person offering the share was relatively straitlaced and an upstanding citizen.

When I arrived at the apartment in Queens, I was shown in by a pleasant-looking young man of about thirty years of age, dressed casually, with no urine bag, cigarette, washing machine, or crutches. Things were looking up.

I was shown my prospective room—a twelve-by-fifteen-foot space with four distinct but not unpleasant types of wallpaper and a large bay window. It was affable enough, if Spartan and a bit in need of redecoration. Everything seemed to be going well until I asked if we would share a bathroom.

The interview came to an end when I was informed that I would have to relieve all bodily functions no fewer than fifty miles away since he was from a galaxy where this sort of thing wasn't tolerated in the home. He ended our meeting, seething with anger, showing me a gesture of upheld splayed fingers and a "knook-knock-screech" sound, evidently alien for "Get the hell out."

"Well, that went well," I thought to myself when I was finally able to regain my composure. I was sitting inside a subway train, traveling back to Manhattan from Queens. Although dejected, I knew I couldn't give up. First stability, then the book. I was doing this for art's sake. I have to admit, after my first two attempts at a new place to live, the Mormons weren't looking so bad. Perhaps I could give up caffeine and denim indefinitely—it seemed a small price to pay to live in the city. I secretly hoped for a new set of scriptures, discovered under some over-sized flowerpot or abandoned car; anything that would explain or put right the five boroughs of New York.

The next ad I chose in my quest for a place to sleep and bathe advertised a "share" in the Radio City Apartments, located right in the heart of midtown. The name certainly had cachet enough—Radio City. I envisioned peering out my window at limousines and celebrities, free tickets to performances; even having to call downstairs and request that the Rockettes keep it down. But my fantasy was short-lived; the apartments weren't actually *in* Radio City. As a matter of fact, they were several blocks away.

After finding my way past the front desk, I arrived at unit twenty-four. A nice-enough-looking man about my age answered the door. At first I thought I was looking at the janitor's closet, so small was the space. The room was at best twelve feet by eight feet and part of that was taken up by what some New Yorkers euphemistically call a kitchen—a one-foot by three-foot space with a sink the size of a postage stamp and a hot plate that would barely hold a can of beans.

"Dude, come on in," the guy gripping the doorknob said. "Here, have a seat," he went on, pulling up a milk crate.

"You advertised for a roommate," I began, looking around at the space. The "room" was barely big enough for one person, much less two. There was only a twin bed, several milk crates like the one I was sitting on, and a poster of Raquel Welch. Yellowed Scotch tape held the beauty to the cracked and even more yellow walls.

"Yeah, here's the deal," he said, "I work nights. Only here in the day. You said over the phone that you worked days, right?"

"Well, actually I don't—"

"So here's my plan. We have to—both of us—sleep in the same bed, but since I work nights and you days, it won't matter. The way I figure it, I'm not here at night, so I might as well make some extra cash by letting you sleep here. Why leave a bed empty when someone could be using it?"

"Well, there may be a problem with that plan," I said, getting up to leave. "See, I just quit my job and I don't have another one, so I actually might be working nights—it's just that I'm not sure yet." I was trying to think of something else, anything in order to buy time and get near the door. And I didn't need that much time—the door wasn't far away.

He promptly began to have a small seizure, reacting pretty much the same way as the last interviewer in Queens had, only this time it took even less effort for his ire to build. I wrote this off as the difference between the outer boroughs and Manhattan—everything was quicker right *in* the city.

"What! You don't have a job and you're interviewing to be someone's roommate?" He had now surpassed the last interviewer in weirdness. "Dude! I need someone responsible. I can't have just *anybody*, just any fly-by-night-bum sharing my space. I've got *valuables* to consider."

I looked around at the room: dripping faucet, whining toilet, filthy gold shag carpeting. A bong the size of one of NASA's rockets leaned against one corner of the twin bed's torn and ratty mattress.

"Fly-by-night—" I started to say, but he had me by the arm and was pushing me out the door.

"Just get out, man, I've got twenty other people to see today. I'm sure they all have jobs," and with that he threw me from the apartment and into the hallway.

"So much for the Rockettes," I thought.

I called about the next ad—it was another place in Brooklyn. I decided I would do a little interviewing over the phone before I made the arduous train journey back to the land of devil worship and street gangs. The conversation started off well enough, but after discussing where I would go to the bathroom, any religious preferences that might get in the way, bed schedules, and "exactly how I felt about Satan," I was told, quite out of the blue, "My apartment is Art Deco, you know." The interviewer's voice was overly pompous—a regular Mr. Mooney from "The Lucy Show."

When I asked what this had to do with anything, I was informed, "Well, I have all my statues, my ashtrays, my chrome furniture—everything. You won't be allowed to move anything, even in your bedroom. I have pieces of tape under objects and if anything gets moved I'll know it. You can sleep in the bed, but you're not allowed to move a lamp or anything else—my apartment is a showplace. I'm very visually oriented, you know. Anything that's the least bit ugly or out of place irritates me. Everything has to be just *so*."

I asked at that point, why this was important, and I was told, "Well, after all, I'm related to Danny Kaye."

"That's it," I thought, "something that in the past would not have made sense, now, for some reason after all I had been through, did." It was probably my decision to hold this interview over the phone that caused my first tinge of retribution toward these people that lorded their power over me—these ad placers, these holders of the keys to where I might live—but for whatever reason, I felt something starting to rise in me. Then I spoke:

"Oh, we totally understand," I said with my best wide-eyed optimistic voice, full of Shirley Temple sweetness. "You could trust us not to touch anything. We'd be just the best little roommates you ever had! But there is one thing . . . well . . . and this is hard to say . . . so I hope it's not a problem . . ."

"Wait a minute," the voice on the other end said, panic rising, his vocal chords tensing up, "you said 'we.' I'm only looking for *one* roommate."

"Well, yes, *we* understand that," I continued in my makeshift sweet voice, thinking only of avenging myself on this person for all the wrongs done to me by want ads, "but you see, I'm a Siamese twin and joined at the head with my sister. You'd really be getting two for the price of one. She's a very nice person, that is when her colostomy bag isn't full, but then that's only a problem for *her*—we merely share *some* of the same organs. And I don't know if you like boys or girls, but you'd have one of each if we move in. Perhaps you're bisexual? That would be perfect. She's really a very sweet person," and then I changed my voice slightly while turning my head away from the receiver"—*"Not as sweet as you, pumpkin"*—"but she's prone to outbursts of hives and projectile vomiting"—*"Don't tell him that"*—"so I hope this won't be a—"

But it was too late. Before the audible click there was a palpable feeling of disgust being transmitted via Alexander Graham Bell's invention; a vision of some anal collector of the Deco arts in Brooklyn, writhing among his coveted slim-hipped ceramic women, sleek-lined furniture, and pastel color schemes, all before the line went dead.

10

Charlie Chaplin once entered a contest for Charlie Chaplin look-alikes . . . and lost. It seems that somewhere in the long line of Hitler mustaches, bowler hats, and swinging canes, the judges got confused and awarded the prize to someone who was not only completely void of acting ability, but who didn't even have "Charlie" as a first name. Go figure. And Mr. Chaplin, whose illustrious career had started the contest in the first place, was left out, shunned for not being enough like, well . . . himself. A strange story, but one that nevertheless makes a point about the people running things such as contests, publishing companies, corporations, and countries.

"But I can't," I said to Robert. We had met for lunch at one of those outdoor cafés so unsuitable for Manhattan dining. Something about squealing tourists, diesel fumes, honking taxi horns, and the occasional bag person begging for money always mars the experience for me. Call me crazy. Paris it's not.

"You have to. You need a job. That's all there is to it," he said, trying to look over the gigantic bill of fare (it was a good three feet tall but only two inches wide—some New York menu designer's idea of contemporary).

"Yes, but to go and actually work for an agency, just like the ones I went to when I first came here, seems, well, like joining the enemy."

"What do you think about the shrimp scampi? It's either that or the sole. I can't decide."

"Besides," I continued, "how do you know that your friend of the friend of the cousin you never met is going to be sure I get the job? And why would you do this for me anyway?"

"I think the sole. Less garlic. Have to be careful, you know. Let's just say that some people owe me favors, and that I'm doing this for an old friend. Besides, you have to work. You've got no money. You've got no permanent place to live. You need to get settled." There was a moment of silence between us. "And the pear-and-Gorgonzola salad. That sounds nice. What are you having?"

But before I could answer, we were interrupted by a high-pitched female voice being volleyed over the low canvas partition that separated us from the peripatetic public of New York.

"Robert! Darling! How nice it is to see you!" the woman squealed as she careened over an underdeveloped boxwood in an attempt to meet Robert's cheek. He had only half stood, causing the poor woman to do most of the work. Her handbag slammed into my head as she reached out to meet him.

"Katherine. Good to see you," Robert offered. I could tell he remembered the name but not much more. His wheels were turning, trying to place her.

When they had regained their own space, she turned to me and absent-mindedly fingered the corner of her purse as if to soothe any damage I might have done to the bright red patent leather. "And who is this?" she asked, one corner of her upper lip twitching, "another client?"

"I'm Max. An old friend of Robert's," I said, getting up and extending my hand. She extended hers but the effort was only half-hearted.

"And are you in the business also?" she asked, mildly interested. Then she took out a silver cigarette case, removed one cylinder of tobacco, and aggressively tapped it before putting it between her lips and lighting it.

Fortunately, Robert jumped in at that moment. "Well, no. Max is an author. We've known each other since college."

"Hmmmm," she said and exhaled a long column of smoke. "You two could be twins," she said looking me up and down. Then she squinted, as if I were some long-lost taxidermied specimen in the British Museum. "About the only thing different is a few pounds and the haircut," she said to Robert. Then she turned back to me. "You might consider the 1950s flattop—it's done wonders for Robert." Then to Robert again, "Well, darling, I've got to be going, but I'll give you a call soon and I hope we can get together. See you, Rob, and nice to meet you, Mike."

"Max. My name is Max," I said, but it was too late—she had already become a part of the teaming masses, yearning to find the latest pasta shop and dress boutique in SoHo.

After we settled back down and placed our order, Robert leaned onto the table, one forearm resting on top of the other, a tuft of chest hair sticking out of his sports shirt. "So, Katherine thought you might be in the business. You interested?"

I knew Robert had been secretive about things: his living situation; where he worked; the people he hung out with. We had seen each other from time to time in the city since that evening we worked together at the dance performance and I had enjoyed his company. But there was always a shroud of mystery about him and the reason for this was becoming clear.

"You don't perform anymore—the piano, I mean?" I asked, hoping for more than just a yes-or-no answer. I was stalling. This was the first time I found out what Robert really did for a living.

"Hey, guy, come on. You know what's going on. Don't pretend to be so naive." Then he leaned back, crossing his arms. Blue veins stuck out from his bulging forearms and one rough meaty hand folded over a muscular bicep. Robert was an attractive guy. I just wasn't sure I was ready to admit that other people thought so *and* paid for the privilege of being near it.

"We suffer for what the gods give us," I said, to no one in particular, shaking my head.

"You're not the only one who can quote Oscar Wilde," Robert responded. "What the gods give they quickly take away."

"What's that from?"

"Some old movie."

"Look, I'm not judging what you do," I said, still not verbally admitting that I knew how he made his living. "But whatever it is, in a city like this you've got to be careful."

Who was I to give advice? I had almost moved in with a Satan worshiper and had been abused by every ad placer and employment agency in the city, and now I was going without brushed cotton and iced tea.

"What is it exactly that you think I do?" Robert asked.

I didn't say anything, but looked sheepishly away at a woman walking a miniature poodle. The dog sported a pink plastic raincoat and matching booties even though the sun was shining.

"Come on," he repeated, "what is it that you think I do? I do all kinds of things. I work the theatre circuit doing odd jobs, I sometimes get gigs in piano bars—I do a lot in different areas. Thing is, it never quite pays the rent. You know me, Max. I tried. I really tried. The whole piano competition thing, the teaching, the applying for jobs. It's fixed. It's all fixed. It's who or *whom* you know, depending on whom the who is and what your level of correct English usage tends to be. Has nothing to do with talent or persistence or training. It's all a game. I saw a long time ago that I wasn't going to be let into the inner circle. That whole fiasco with the piano competition where I sent in the tape of Horowitz playing and they came back with a 'no.' Fixed. Everything is." He paused and looked around. "You need a steady job. I need a steady job. So I do something that some people call immoral, unethical, even dangerous. I look at it this way: I'm doing something I'm probably going to do anyway—hormonally speaking—so I might as well get paid for it." He waited again. "And it's no more unethical than what agents and publishers and competitions and judges do to people like us." He paused. "Take for example, your book. How's that going?"

He waited. I didn't answer.

"Thought so," he said.

We sat there for a moment, watching the waiter deliver our entrées. Neither of us touched our food. Then Robert spoke again. "I know you probably don't approve, but at least if you ever wanted to break into the business, you'd have a chance. I mean, you're not a bad-looking guy and Katherine thought you might be involved in things, if you know what I mean. So . . . you interested?" Again a pause. "You said you didn't want to go work for an employment agency. Maybe you should get involved with something else—you know, give something back to the community."

"You mean like syphilis?" I asked.

There it was: the polemic of the day, served up on a two-inch-wide menu. I was insulted he brought it up.

"Interested in being at the beck and call of neurotic women and even some men for their twisted, sick pleasure? Interested in being abused, told what to do, taken advantage of? Interested in selling myself? I don't think so, Rob. Aren't you afraid of AIDS, the other things you can catch? It's not for me." I shuddered at the very mention of AIDS—that pernicious pyramidical virus scheme in which no one came out the winner. I continued: "What, wait until my T-cell count is so low that I have to name each one? I don't think so."

"Hey, I'm getting you into this agency, if you want—that's a real job. But you said you didn't want that. What *do* you want? I'm not pushing, I'm just trying to be your friend," he said, showing no offense at my latest tirade toward his line of work. "As far as AIDS goes, I'm very careful and the majority of my clients want things that are so kinky that the typical sex act doesn't even come into play."

Then he added, a smirk coming across his lips as he turned his head to nod hello to someone across the street before turning back to me, "Besides, you're a writer, and if you're interested in ever being commercially successful, the way I see it, there's not a lot of difference in what we do. Think about it," and with that he turned to nod to yet another person, showing his strong jaw and muscular neck. Then, never moving his head, he cut his eyes back to me, and smiled.

11

When I was fourteen, I attempted suicide. The repercussions were that my parents sent me to therapy, I skipped a semester of school, and I learned what self-esteem was at a day camp for depressed teenagers ("Now let's use our construction paper and paste to make some pretty flowers! Does everyone have his *dull* scissors? Thaaaaaat's nice.") Looking back on my experience with Babley Associates—the employment agency for janitors that Robert got me into—I would have been better off to have finished the job I started at fourteen rather than take the one he recommended nine years later.

I started at the employment agency—Babley's—the day after my discussion with Robert involving his "profession." The interview was short and to the point, and a meager salary was agreed on. What else could I do? I needed the job and the head of the agency knew it. And at least, in my mind, this was better than what Robert did.

First days on a new job should be relatively uneventful if one is to settle in properly. This was not the case at Babley. I was shown to my office, (a tiny dimly-lit cubicle with filthy baby-blue burlap walls and no air), and told to immediately start filing a stack of résumés on janitorial technicians. Babley "excelled in the procurement and placement of the nation's finest janitorial personnel and services," or so the large blue-and-white sign bolted to the reception wall said.

Now I should have known there was something unusual about the place when I first went for the interview. As you entered the front door, you were greeted by badly stained gray industrial carpeting, a few wooden cubes used as tables, and a torn Naugahyde sofa, the color of which resembled the excrement of a cat whose diet contained nothing too healthy. Greenish-yellow comes to mind. There was also a single copy of some magazine, most of its pages torn beyond recognition. Then the natural effluvia that come with territories of this sort: fumes from paper, shirt starch, the ozone effect of fluorescent lights on industrial carpeting; the smells brought in by subway, bus, and taxi. God forbid it rains—then the whole thing reeks like a corporate wet dog.

But the most disturbing aspect of the place was a three-inch-thick bulletproof glass that separated the waiting area from the portion of the office where I and two other people sat.

My cubicle was positioned so that I could view the scratched partition, and in the event that someone actually came in to apply for a job, I would get up from my seat, saunter over to the glass, and speak through a circular pattern of holes.

"Can I help you?" I would say to some slovenly-dressed young man with bloodshot eyes and a runny nose.

"Be wantin' a job, muddahfucker. Got to be gettin' me sumptin' to EAT!" was a typical response.

So when I wasn't categorizing résumés of the janitorial astute, I handed out clipboards through a vent under the glass and learned to use an emotionless tone and be slightly condescending. At the time I didn't allow myself to remember when I had been searching for a job, albeit one that didn't require bullet-proof glass between me and the receptionist, and so by the third day I had the routine down pretty pat. Still, it wasn't totally lost on me that I had become what I hated.

"Just fill out the front of the card and attach your résumé . . . if you *have* one," I would say, grinding the last four words with my teeth. The clipboard would "ka-thump" down a metal chute and into their eager little hands. When they were done they "ka-thumped" it back into another chute. Even though the pen had been attached to the board with a heavy metal chain, acres of tape, and a piece of well-chewed gum, it seldom came back. Rarely could I read any of the handwriting, and frequently the signature was a mere X. But all of this was the upside of the job, for as bad as the applicants were, what passed for employees on my side of the glass was even worse.

What can I say about Anastasia? While her name conjures up images of the Czar and ball gowns ornamented with pearls, sequins, and jewels, the more immediate thought for me concerning this co-worker termagant was the firing squad during the 1917 revolution. At least that's what I hoped for her in an updated version of the story.

Anastasia was allegedly from a wealthy family in Boston and made sure everyone knew it. I found her name ironic, if not impossible, until she explained that she had bestowed it upon herself after dumping the one she had initially been given.

She prided herself on her manner of dress, which would have been acceptable—the clothing part was normal enough—were it not for the enormous jewelry she sported each day. Earrings the size of pie plates, necklaces with baseball-like beads, and rings containing fake stones whose circumference was only slightly less than the equator ornamented her three-hundred-pound frame.

The jewelry took on a life of its own. Even a simple task, such as walking to the break room became a feast for the senses. The beads would sway, the hubcaps hanging from her ears would flash signals to far-off life forms in the universe, and the floor would shake as she waddled toward the latest stash of Hostess cupcakes and Twinkies stored in the faux-wood cabinets. All of this would have made her a sad and pathetic figure were it not for the fact that she was the ultimate nasty female dog on wheels. I imagined her as a child, asking for a rhesus monkey torture kit for Christmas, along with other sundry devices she could use on the neighborhood children when they failed to comply with her draconian regimes.

My other office mate was male and on equal footing: greasy black hair, pocket protectors, synthetic clothing, Hush Puppies, no skin pigmentation to speak of, and a badly repaired cleft palate—the scar size of which was only slightly smaller than the San Andreas fault. He was painfully thin with an oversized head and a neck no thicker than a pencil. The overall effect was that of a Tootsie Pop that had been badly damaged during shipping. And the fact that he spoke only sentences from Bette Davis movies in order to communicate and had been convicted as a child molester several years before didn't help his overall demeanor.

Malcolm had served his jail term and was grateful Mr. Babley had hired him, swearing off children as a source of enjoyment, but the usage of movie lines from *All About Eve, Now,*

Voyager, and *Jezebel* had only intensified during his prison stay—a useful ploy in confusing even the most hardened inmates, especially when being assaulted ("The gentle atmosphere is very Macbethish. What *has* or is about to happen?"), and he employed them without restraint in our current office environment.

One day, while wearing a pair of cymbals as earrings and what appeared to be the fender of a Mercedes Benz as a brooch, Anastasia rolled over to my cubicle from hers, placing an envelope of some sort on my desk. Then she proceeded to do the same for Malcolm.

"It seems that Leslie wrote a letter to Hammond asking him to come to the bungalow on the night he was killed," Malcolm said, quoting a scene from *The Letter*. He used a pretentious 1940s Hollywood actor's accent without looking up as Anastasia placed the envelope on his desk.

"It's an invitation to my wedding, moron. Both you and Mac are invited."

"Max. My name's Max, not Mac."

"Who cares?" she shot back. "You'd better come. It will probably be the best meal you've ever eaten. Judging from the way you dress, you couldn't have very much money. Besides, you can see what real people act like—real people with money. And class. My relatives have lots of class, just like me."

"Yeah, you and the receptionist at the first place I interviewed," I said, then added, "Geez, Anastasia, pull your fangs back in." I should have known better.

This was Malcolm's cue. "What about her teeth? What about her fangs?" he voiced over the partition; his best Bette Davis imitation when she's arguing with Gary Merrill in *All About Eve*.

"Can you even *speak* English, cleft palate?" Anastasia threw back. "I think they must have done something to your head in prison. Sheeeez." And then: "Oh, great, here comes another low-life," she said, seeing an applicant at the window. "You get up and get this one Mac—I'm tired of dealing with the riff-raff today."

"Max. My name is Max, not Mac, and don't refer to these people that way, it really gets me mad sometimes. I know they may not be—"

"Mad! Darling, there are certain characteristics for which you are famous, on screen and off. I love you for some of them in spite of others. They're part of your equipment for getting along in what is laughingly called our environment," sang Malcolm in a haughty theatrical tone to no one in particular, a continuation of the *Eve* script.

"Would you shut up," countered Anastasia. And get the window . . . whatever your name is."

I didn't feel like arguing today. Besides, this was at least a stable job and I figured that if Mr. Babley could keep two vainglorious and distorted loons like Anastasia and Malcolm, then he would probably make me president of the company within a week. That and the fact that while he was out of the office today he had put the American Princess in charge and I wanted a good report to come back on my character. An unfortunate choice in my opinion—this installing Anastasia as commandant—but nothing I could do about it. I got up to see what our latest applicant wanted.

"Just fill out the top card and attach your résumé if you have one," I said to the holes in the glass.

"No-uuhhh, no-speaka . . . me . . . you . . . half . . . somebody speak-a-de Spanich?"

"Giuseppi, turn the car *around*," offered Malcolm *(Now, Voyager)* from inside his cubicle. He could hear English-deficient Pedro through the small holes in the glass from where he was sitting.

"Look," I said, "just fill out the front of the card, sí?" I nodded a few times, just in case "sí" was misunderstood.

"Qué?" I got a blank look back, but after ka-thumping the clipboard down the chute, the applicant took the offering and made an attempt at filling out the information requested.

"You two idiots need to respond to that invitation by next Friday so we can tell the caterer who's going to be there," said Anastasia while filing her fingernails. "If you're not coming I can get someone else. And don't try and skimp on the gifts—I'm from a classy family, so I'll know if you bring something cheap."

I just shook my head and slouched back to my cubicle. Both Anastasia and Malcolm had pulled reams of applicant résumés out of the files in an attempt to place them in situations, and I was left to clean up the mess. I began sorting through the stack, thinking about how I still needed to find a new place to live—away from the Mormon household.

"And you can bet I'm going to be one blushing bride on my happy day, what with all the money my parents are spending," added Anastasia, still working the wedding routine to death.

It was then that Malcolm offered up his latest line, continuing his *Now, Voyager* imitation: "I'm not surprised you blush. I was in the room when William took the books from the shelves. And let me say that what we found hidden there was a very great *shock* to me. I can only hope that this shameful episode in your life is completely past."

Anastasia waited a full minute, finished filing one obstinate nail on her left hand, and then said with as much dryness as she could muster, "Malcolm? Would you shut the hell up?"

12

"And Manhattan is getting a new look this week," the oily-voiced anchorman announced to the camera, "as hundreds of small trees are planted along its avenues and in Central Park. The Park Conservancy said that so far six hundred and thirty-seven trees have been donated by publishing houses, literary agents, and bookstores in the last six months. Officials in the New York area can't say exactly why these people in the book business have such a sudden access to this outpouring of flora, but they're happy nevertheless."

I turned off the television, deciding that I'd better get some work done. I had feigned sickness and the Mormon coalition had gone out for the day, to Sunday morning services. I was left alone with my guilt about not having yet procured an agent or done anything that might get my book published. After all, wasn't that why people put up with New York—in order to get what they had come after?

Six hours later and a multitude of letters and writing samples from my novel ready to send out to a new set of agents, I sat back, staring at the ceiling. It seemed that my life was nothing more than a combination of searches: jobs; places to live; agents; networking; jobs; places to live. I needed stability. I needed structure. I needed money. I needed . . . a break.

Two weeks later they started coming in—the rejections from that Sunday's efforts. I had hoped I would get numb to the sensation of seeing the self-addressed stamped envelope with my own handwriting being returned to me, all too flat and insignificant to contain any good news. Bad news was always like that—short, flat—one page. The only time it wasn't was when someone was trying to sell you something. The exception to this mountain of mail was a small brown package addressed to me with no return address. Opening it up I found a book that everyone needs: *Jokes for the John*. I put it aside, not giving it much thought, and began the long and boring job of opening the rejections that had accompanied it. Needing a break in the process some time later, I called Robert.

"They're relentless," I said. "They keep coming in by the hundreds."

"Well, how many did you send out?" he asked.

"Hundreds."

"Therein lies the problem."

"But what am I supposed to do—sit around and wait for someone to discover me? Work at a job I hate for the rest of my life?"

"Max, you're pushing too hard. It's all there for you, for the taking—life; the pursuit of happiness," Robert persisted.

"I was watching a rerun of that Roman Polanski movie, *Rosemary's Baby*, on television the other night. You know, the one where Rosemary's husband agrees to allow the devil to impregnate his wife in exchange for success as an actor? I only got to see the last bit of it—been years since I've seen the whole thing. The year One; Hail Satan—that whole scene?"

"Don't remember that one," Robert's voice came back. He sounded as if he were cleaning under his fingernails with a kitchen knife or picking lint from his bathrobe. His voice had a calculated yet distant quality.

"The point is," I went on, "at this time in my life, with the way things are going, if I tried to sell my soul to the devil I'd probably get a note back saying, "Thank you for your interest in hell, however . . .""

"Don't be too sure," Robert said, but there was a strange quality to his response, again, as if he were doing some menial task and only his subconscious was responding.

I decided to change the subject since he sounded bored. "So, when are you going to invite me over? I've been in the city now all this time and you haven't once extended an—"

"Look, guy, I've got to shove off. Got some business to attend to, but it was real good talking to you, you know?"

"Sure," I said, feeling as though I had just received one more letter from a literary agent, and with that I hung up.

Days later the rejections were still coming in. At one point I even tried embedding antagonistic messages into some of the new query letters and writing samples that I sent out, putting the offending bits somewhere in the middle, just to see if anyone was actually reading my correspondence. "I plan to come to your home, dismember you and your entire family with a butter knife, then cook and eat everyone," I stated, somewhere in between "The market for the book is the baby-boomer generation," and "I look forward to speaking with you soon about my book."

Nothing. Even the police didn't show up.

I was about to abandon all hope when one of my envelopes boomeranged back (one without the cannibalistic threat), bearing my handwriting and signature nature stamp. Then I noticed something: It looked a good one-thirty-thousandth of an inch thicker. I tore into it. Behold: It contained a rejection notice, but, like manna from heaven, also a fuchsia Post-it note which curled up slightly and was inscribed in a dark blue ink. It was as though someone had given me a vital organ that I needed, for it was hand-written and personally addressed to "author" in a not-too-hurried script. I was overjoyed. I leapt emotionally into the air. Finally, someone had noticed me; someone had taken the time to write back; someone had shown some interest in my writing. Here is what it said, complete with a black line through the word "author."

Dear ~~author~~:

I don't know who you think you are, sending me letters and a sample of "writing" (your words—not mine) but we are NOT interested. Go find yourself a story editor who can help you make something out of this mess.

Good _day_.

The word "day" was underlined and the person responsible for the added personal touch had obviously been bearing down with quite a bit of pressure, for it appeared that the writing implement had broken apart at that point, sending a skewering of ink off the paper. I pressed the form letter and the small note to my nose, breathing in the scent of a real agent's office where it had originated. The fuchsia paper smelled slightly of perfume. Half a ring from a coffee cup graced the back of it. Someone had doodled a three-dimensional box in one corner. For the rest of the day I sat enveloped in ecstasy; filled with an indescribable joy over the fact that an important person had taken the time to personally contact me . . . and my hopes rose from the lowest despair.

13

"Mr. Babley would like to see you right away." It was Anastasia speaking, and in none too pleasant a tone. "And by the way," she added, turning around and sneering, the very act of which set off a cacophony reminiscent of a bad freeway accident, "you're not coming to my wedding, so just tear up the invitation."

It had been less than a month since I started at Babley's. The weather—like Anastasia—had turned cold. Each day I made my way from upper Manhattan into the gray and brown canyons of midtown, jostling through throngs of tourists, office workers, and street people. My days were filled with filing résumés, ka-thumping clipboards, abuse from Anastasia, and myriad lines from every Bette Davis movie ever made. But during this time Mr. Babley had never once spoken to me after the initial interview. And in this short amount of time Anastasia had somehow managed to push all of her work off in my direction. It seems that filing one's fingernails and talking on the phone about what color to dye the bridesmaids' shoes took more time than expected. She would often toss a folder from her desk to mine while she screamed mercilessly at some poor reception hall attendant who had ordered the wrong chairs or committed some other egregious gaffe. "Can't you people do anything right? My parents have money, we can paaaaaaaay! I want some service here!"

"Do you have any idea what Mr. Babley wants?" I asked Anastasia, who was now bent over, picking at a run in her hose, trying to calm herself from a recent telephone conversation involving marzipan icing. Two large hubcaps dangled from her ears, and in this bent-over position she looked as though the weight of her sidewalk-bought accessories was too much for her. She had more than a modicum of trouble straightening up.

"No idea. But I'm sure it's something negative. Always is with Babley. The guy is sick in the head if you want my prognosis. Maybe he has a brain tumor or something."

Malcolm felt this his cue. "I think I'll have a large order of 'prognosis negative'. You know, oeufs sur le plat, *prognosis negative!* Do you know what 'prognosis negative' means, Doctor? Explain it to her, or have you? It means a few months of pretending you're well, then blindness, then . . ."

Anastasia straightened up. She stood frozen, confused; looking at Malcolm. Then she turned to me, her face one big question mark.

"Dark Victory," I said. "Nineteen thirty-nine. Best original score by Max Steiner."

Anastasia pulled a blank expression, pursed her lips, and sat down. I got up and headed toward Mr. Babley's door. It was a massive oak thing—two inches thick with huge gold letters, "Horace Babley, President and CEO."

I knocked.

Nothing.

I knocked again. This time there was a grunt from the other side so I manufactured courage and walked in.

"You wanted to see me, Mr. Babley?" I asked as I made my way across an acre of flat-weave carpeting. Golf balls littered the make-believe green and a nine-iron rested on a comfortable overstuffed chair.

"Sit down, Perkins," he said, looking up at me over bifocals. Then he dug through some papers on his desk, occasionally scratching his balding forehead. Large pieces of dry skin flaked off, kamikazing onto the blotter in front of him. After what seemed like twenty minutes he addressed me, all the while continuing to dig through files and scratch.

"We've got a problem here, Perkins," (flip, flip, flip, scratch, scratch) he began, still not looking up. "Seems that your work is not (flip, flip) up to par." Then he paused and looked up to see my reaction.

"What problem?" I began. "I thought I was doing pretty—"

"Well, you're not (scratch, scratch, flake). You're not doing well at all. At this company we take pride in our work and yours needs addressing." He finally found the file he had been looking for and opened it. Then he presented it to me. "Here, take a look at this and tell me what you see wrong."

I took the file and began to look at reports I had prepared for him on invoicing, credit applications, and write-offs. All the numbers seemed to be in order. I couldn't make out what was missing. "I'm sorry, Mr. Babley, but I don't see anything wrong with these numbers. Could you tell me what it is you want?"

"What I want! What I *want!* You want me to tell you what I want?" He took off his glasses and wiped his eyes. Then he laughed to himself softly in a condescending way. He finished with an even more patronizing shaking of the head, then a look that said, "You just don't get it, do you?" Finally, he spoke.

"Seven." (scratch)

"Sir?"

"Seven."

"Seven?"

"Seven."

"I'm sorry, but I don't understand."

"The number seven. What's to understand? Look at it," and he pointed across his massive desk to the file I was holding. "You put a line through your sevens."

I waited for a moment, still not sure where this was going. "And?" I said with an upward inflection, tilting my head in his direction, my eyes bigger than normal, my face open and eager.

"And I don't *like* lines through my sevens. You're to stop doing it immediately, do you understand?"

At first I thought he was joking, but then I noticed a lack of anything human about him—a dearth of fuzziness. Evidently the surgical removal of senses of humor had been perfected long ago and Mr. Babley had been one of the first recipients of the procedure.

"Mr. Babley," I began, as cautiously as I could, "I've been putting a line through my sevens for as long as I can remember. It's a European thing, really. I *could* possibly stop doing it, but the time and energy it would take for me to concentrate on that would—"

"Do you *want* to work here?" he demanded, angrily picking at his flaking head. Evidently this was a popular phrase in New York, not only with employment agencies, but with despotic bosses as well. He waited a moment for dramatic pause, then added, not allowing me to answer. "No, I don't think you do. You want to argue. That's fine. You're entitled." He was now rummaging through the top of his desk. "And I'm entitled to do what I need to," he continued, "after all, the agreement was to hire you and I've done that. The agreement was never to *keep* you." Then he brought out a checkbook and began scribbling. "Tell you what, Perkins. I'm not a mean man, but I don't like being taken advantage of. Here's two weeks salary. More than generous, if you ask me." He ripped the check from the book and handed it to me across a sea of folders. I found myself taking it, mouth open, in too much shock to comprehend what had just happened. I wanted to ask what agreement he had been babbling about, but couldn't muster the strength. Part of me wanted to stay and argue but another part wanted to jump into the air, click my heels together, and say, "There's no place like home." I settled for leaving quietly.

"Now go. Get out of here. I don't want to see you ever again," he finished, waving his hand and resuming his pillage through the land of manila and dead skin, even before I was out the door.

"I know now why you went to his office that day," Malcolm sang after me—yet another Bette Davis quote—as I headed out the door, not even bothering to tell Anastasia what I thought of her. "To beg him to marry me out of pity. You're kind, Dr. Steele. You're both so kind. So long, my friends."

And with that I was gone.

Part II

The very purpose of existence is to reconcile the glowing opinion we hold of ourselves with the appalling things that other people think about us.

– Quentin Crisp

14

The release from janitorial placement hell was a blessing. While I needed a job in order to eat, I didn't need one that resembled a day care center for emotional cripples. I called the only real friend I had in New York: Robert.

"What's with you and the job and the apartment thing, guy?" he began.

"I know, I know. I'm really trying. Look, I need some moral support. Could I come over just for a little while?" I asked.

"Not a good time, buddy. I've got things to take care of. And I'm tired. Got in late last night—Metropolitan Opera performance of *Don Giovanni*. Man, does that one take a lot out of a person. Listen, here's what I'll do: I'll give you a number of someone who can get you into this arts organization. You like Broadway, right? You'd be perfect for this company, and besides, I sort of know the guy that runs the place—through a friend of a friend of a client of my brother's friend's next-door neighbor."

"Sounds promising," I said sarcastically. "I don't know. No offense, Rob, but you hang with some really strange people."

There was about a minute of silence. I could tell Robert was irritated. Finally, he spoke: "Do you *want* to work?" he asked, and we both let an uncomfortable silence hang in the air—a stalled propeller plane just before it begins its long plummet toward earth. Then he hung up.

I called Robert back a few days later after daytime television and lack of food had taken their toll. By the end of the week I had a new job, but it, like everything else in New York, came with conditions attached.

Before I started my new position, I decided to explore the Upper East Side one day—a sort of clearing of the head if you will, before plunging into yet another Robert-recommended occupation. Deciding that I would stop at one of the more moderately priced restaurants on Lexington Avenue to have lunch, I entered the first one I saw, settled into a booth, and began to peruse the menu. What happened next shouldn't have come as a shock, but it did nonetheless, for just as I was deciding on the crab cakes, in walked Robert. It seemed to me at the time that he lived in the cafés and restaurants of New York, and I was forever seeing him pop up. The thought flashed in my mind that he was following me, but that idea was quickly shot down when I saw the look on his face.

Accompanying Mr. Chiseled Jaw was someone I hadn't seen in years—Dory, of the famous Dory and Gray combination in college. Robert's eyes scanned the bistro, looking for a hasty exit, but Dory and I had seen each other and I waved her over.

"Fancy meeting you here," Robert said uncomfortably, and the two of them sat down. After scrutinizing the menu for a moment, he summoned a bored actor to take our order. Dory looked up, then around the table, then back at the waiter. There was tension between Dory and Robert—something I couldn't put my finger on.

"Vodka blushes all around," she said, taking the situation in hand. I noticed a palpable uneasiness in Robert. He squirmed in his seat. The waiter left. Dory continued: "Ich möchte geschleccht mit ihrem llama haben."

Blank stares were the order of the day—Dory could be strange, this much I remembered from college—but she seemed to be teasing Robert.

"I would like to have sex with your llama," she said, translating.

"Who wouldn't," I said, trying to break the tension.

"So," continued Dory, looking directly at me, turning a slender breadstick between her fingers before biting off the tip, "heard any good jokes lately?" And with that remark, Robert shot her a *most* unfriendly look.

15

Everyone has thought of committing murder at one time or another, and that fantasy, more times than not, is reserved for one's boss. If suicide had been an option over employment at Babley's, then murder was definitely the route to take at my next place of service. Barely Broadway—the name pretty much says it all. Why no one seemed to notice this slighted title was beyond me. And the most clueless person in the whole affair was the owner himself: Kaplan Fartus.

Kaplan Fartus was unlike any other life form on the planet. This poor excuse for a human being was challenged in every way. He was overweight, under height, nearsighted, rude, incoherent, tone-deaf, illiterate, dim-witted, badly dressed, and president of the halitosis club. But worst of all, he held power over my life. The realization that I needed to keep a job for a period longer than one month was beginning to sink in. But what made the situation with Fartus and his play business truly unbearable was the fact that I was the only person in his office. It was just him and me. No one else to cut the tension. No one else to take things out on. And because of the close proximity and lack of warm bodies, he noticed my every move and made my life a living hell. I was in New York for one thing—to get my book published—so I took a deep breath and held on, telling myself that I would someday reap rewards I had yet to imagine.

> Scene. Interior shot: Fartus speaks to Max. "I'm going to place a call now to my best friend at Johnson Associates, Max. They gave us quite a bit of funding for Barely Broadway last year and have been a contributor since . . . oh, well, it doesn't matter. Watch and learn, my friend. It pays to know the right people. You'll be thanking me in a few years for all I've taught you."

We see Fartus at his desk, waiting for someone to answer. "Yes, um, this is Kaplan Fartus, and I'm calling to speak with Mr. Johnson at your firm. Yes, yes, thank you." Fartus waits to be transferred. In Fartus's office we see some binders containing material from Broadway musicals, a dead rubber tree, and sickly-blue fluorescent lights. Fartus's buttocks squeak in his fake leather chair. "Yes, hello Bill, it's Kaplan. Listen I just wanted to ask how much you were planning to give . . ." (uncomfortable silence) . . . "Kaplan . . . Fartus. Yes, that's right. And I was just wondering . . . Barely Broadway. Yes, and what . . . we're a musical organization of show-stoppers with over . . . Fartus . . . Kaplan . . . I got your number from . . ." and then we hear the phone go dead.

K.F. was a bit of a loser to say the least, but he did have some good qualities. One of his more endearing ones was his uncanny ability to communicate. Here's an example:

"Max, where is that thing I gave you earlier?"

"What thing?" I asked.

"You know, the *thing*."

I held up a fund-raising letter I had been working on. "This?"

"No. The *thing*."

"This?" I said, holding up a ledger with that day's ticket sales on it—all three of them.

"No, the *thing*, the *thing!*" he began, becoming wildly agitated. "Give me the thing, the thing!"

"What thing? Could you be a little more—"

"THE THING! THE THING! GIVE ME THE THING! I WANT THE THING!" he began to shout hysterically. I noticed people in the building next to ours looking out their windows, perfectly able to hear Kaplan's screams even though both buildings were hermetically sealed and a bounty of street noise wafted up between.

"Do you mean the memo you—"

78

"THE THING, THE THING, THE THING, THE THING, THETHINGTHINGTHINGTHING!" he shouted, and I thought his head would explode. Finally, he gave up in disgust and I was never privileged enough to know exactly what "the thing" was. As he was walking away I held up the copy of *Jokes for the John* that I had brought to work, but I didn't really believe that was what he was looking for.

So that was Kaplan. When he wasn't screaming at me, he pretended to conduct off-off-off Broadway musicals, sans sets, actors, or musicians. Oh, he had people to go through the motions, but they weren't professionals. Most were rejects from some junior college music education program or newly released twelve-step group. And the performances were truly off-off-off Broadway—like, New Jersey. Still, he thought of himself as a gifted theatre person; an impresario who couldn't be bothered with minor details like paying royalties or remembering his one employee's pay check every week.

Without fail, every Friday, which was payday, he would conveniently forget to compensate me. That is, until I had complained, cajoled, and threatened, and until the banks were safely closed for the day. Then he would begrudgingly hand over the check, always managing to let his fingers linger just a fraction of a second too long at the edge so that a tiny piece of the sky-blue paper was torn off. Nothing extraordinary, just a piece about the size of a pencil's eraser.

One day when he was out, I was snooping around his office (in order to discover why he used a complete roll of paper towels each day while his door was shut for an hour during lunch) and pulled open the bottom drawer to his desk. It was filled with what looked like several thousand small pieces of sky-blue paper, all about the size of an eraser. Fartus had been in business, it seems, for years.

Now, working for K.F. was bad enough, but the fact that his penuriousness extended to office machines didn't make things any better. This was the end of the '80s and most businesses had computers or at least word processors. So the fact that the only mode of typing in the office was a Brother Selectric II (at least you could correct on it) did not enhance my Broadway experience. And there wasn't a copying machine to be found for miles.

Each day, Mr. F would give me no fewer than two hundred fund-raising letters to type. It seems that the three tickets sold for each concert somehow failed to pay for musicians, singers, actors, and waiters, so the poor man was reduced to begging for money from his imaginary friends. At any rate, there I would sit, typing each of the letters. Even though I knew his aversion to anything that might make my job easier, I tried suggesting that he could save money if he photocopied the letters and I typed the names and addresses on each one—they were all the same with the exception of the person and company they were going to.

He would have none of it, insisting that people would be able to tell a photocopy from an original. I wanted to tell him, "Yo, Fartus, wake up. Ain't nobody reading these things anyway," but didn't. I tried explaining that I'd have more time to do the other chores he had for me (wincing at the word "chores" as if we were surrounded by bleating sheep and clucking chickens) such as polishing the wastebasket (an obsession of his) and dusting the lint from the seat of his chair (he claimed he could feel it through his pant material—who was I to argue?), but he wouldn't budge.

And to make matters worse, each of the letters was a good six pages long. So there I would sit, typing the same six-page letter over and over, the only change being the company and person to whom the correspondence was addressed. If you even *mentioned* the words "computer" or "word processor," the man would break out in a rash.

But this wasn't the worst of it, for if ever a mistake was made in typing *any* page of *any* six-page letter, and I ventured to correct it with the "self-correcting" typewriter, Fartus would become hysterical. He would hold the pages up to the light, scrutinizing each letter, each comma, each exclamation point, until he had found what he so coveted.

"Perkins! Get in here," he would yell in my direction. "Look at the 'E' in line six hundred and forty six. You corrected it. I can see it plain as day. Here's what I want you to do: You will go back and type this entire letter over from beginning to end and this time with no mistakes!"

"But Mr. Fartus, if you're that upset about the 'E' then all I really have to do is retype that *page*," I said, hoping to appeal to some shred of sanity the man might have found or stolen.

"No, it's more than that. You've got to *learn*. And I want the entire letter moved up one-sixteenth of an inch on the page."

"You're joking, right?" I said. Then I thought about the fact that he had asked me to call housekeeping earlier because the baseboard behind his credenza had a smudge on it and he wanted them to repaint it pronto. I kept quiet. I had to keep this job. I couldn't get a roommate or apartment without showing some stability so I bit my tongue. Besides, I kept telling myself that it built character. Whose character I wasn't sure. And so I did what he wanted—I went back and retyped the entire letter.

16

"**T**alking to the guy is like trying to herd cats," I said to Robert over the phone. "What did you get me into? How do you know this bozo anyway?"

"I don't know him. I know someone who knows him. Long story."

"He's a pervert," I said. "He makes me put on rubber gloves to take the lettuce off his sandwich every day. Claims that he's allergic and that the deli downstairs adds it just to get even with him for licking the sneeze guard on the salad bar. He's loony-toons. The only thing missing is the straitjacket."

"Max, you've got to stay there for a while. People aren't going to take you seriously unless you show them you're stable. Besides, January is no time to be looking for a new place to live."

"Show them *I'm* stable? What about these other . . . people, for lack of a better word? And Fartus had me work on Christmas Eve, all because he claimed the doorstops needed a fresh coat of lacquer."

Exasperation was setting in. Hell, it wasn't just setting in, it was signing the lease, moving in furniture, redecorating—the works. I couldn't hold a steady job or stay in one place, but boy, Exasperation sure could ("And now, if you'll just step this way, I want to show you the lovely dining room . . . oh, and there are four bedrooms—you *do* have children, don't you, Mr. Exasperation?")

"I'm just about done, Rob," I said. "We've known each other since college and you've helped me out, but something's got to give. I can't go on this way. There are just too many unanswered questions: your secretiveness about where you live; the way you always meet me at some out-of-the-way place; the way you're careful not to be seen in certain parts of the city. I just don't know. I get the feeling you're leading me down a path I'd rather not take."

"Would you like me to bow out? Stop helping you find places to live and jobs? Is that what you want?" he asked.

I had to think a moment. I hadn't done well left to my own devices, and if the response I was garnering from life with Robert's help was this bad I could only imagine what it would be like without it.

"No. Sorry. I'm just getting tired of beating my head against a wall and having nothing to show for it," I said.

"Just hang in there for a while longer. I'll see what I can do. And if it's really that important for you to see where I live, well, I guess I can do that at some point. Give me a while. Then maybe you'll understand a few things."

I hung up after a few more minutes of speaking with Robert, feeling better that he had opened up. But for the present time I still had Kaplan Fartus to deal with.

About two weeks later, while I was combing the carpet in the office with a small dog brush (Mr. F aspired to the fluffy look even though it was an industrial indoor/outdoor weave), the phone rang.

"Who is this?" a voice hissed over the line in a thick Indian accent.

"To whom did you wish to speak?" I asked in my best English accent, hoping to intimidate the individual with a reminiscence of Imperialism—think pith helmets and tea parties.

"Listen. There is not much time. You must pay attention to me," the other party continued. "You *have* to help me, help us . . . the foundation."

"Who is this?" I asked, not at all intrigued, thinking that it was just another actor recently escaped from the latest Broadway flop.

"My name is Poopa Goopta. I work for ASCAP, the American Society of Composers, Authors, and Publishers. Can I trust you? To whom am I speaking?" The rhythm of her voice was clipped and bouncy.

"Poopa Goopta is a name?" I said. In the background, Mr. Fartus hummed to himself. It was something from *The Student Prince*.

"Listen, there is not much time. Where is he sitting?" the voice asked, curry-thick and redolent.

"Who?"

"Mr. Fartus!" the voice responded with determination and overemphasis.

"I don't know, he's in his office, I guess, he's—"

"I tried to get this information from the last person who worked there but he fired her before she could finish. We've got to hurry before he catches on to—"

"Oh, Max? Maaaaaaxxxxxx?" Fartus called, interrupting my foray into the land of elephants and monsoons.

"Just a minute, Mr. F," I said, "I'll be right with you." Just then, another call came in.

"Fartus," the new caller's voice said, clipped and short on the other line. It was more of a command than a request. I could hear a parrot screech in the background and the woman sounded as though she was at a party.

"Just a minute," I said, and put the call through. Then I returned to my first caller—Poopa.

"Look, he's asking for me now. I just put another call through to him, but I know what's coming—he's going to start cracking the whip. You'll have to call back, okay?" and I hung up just in time to turn around and see K.F. in back of me.

"Who was that?" he inquired seductively, having finished the earlier call I had put through to him. A sick grin was forming at his lips.

"No one. Just a friend," I said.

He waited a moment, looked around the office, and then offered a little smirk.

"Getting a little, eh, Perkins?" And then he reached down and goosed me in the ribs. Evidently Fartus, while a married man with three children, played the field. I had long suspected he fooled around on the side by the sleazy glint in his eye, but one look at his out-of-shape body, oozing milk-white flesh, and bad posture confirmed that if he did, he had to pay for it.

"Yeah," I said, thinking that I hadn't had sex or even a date since I'd moved to New York, "a little on the side," and with that he seemed satisfied and bounced back into his office.

One week went by. One hellish week involving a copying machine, three "concerts" and what I like to term the beginning of the end at Barely Broadway.

It started like this: Mr. F decided that he wanted photocopies made of all the music for his stage fiascos, so as not to muss the originals (which were bad copies themselves). He decided that I was to take all thirty-five million pieces of music that he possessed down to the nearest copying center and have reproductions made. I did this in between typing the six-page fund-raising letters, and by three o'clock Wednesday returned to the office with the equivalent of a wheelbarrow full of paper.

Mr. F immediately took the top copy from the stack and began to peruse it. A few minutes went by and then he sauntered over to the filing cabinet where I had replaced the originals. Then he made his way back into his office and I waited, knowing that something was coming, but thinking, "What could it be—I've already polished the door hinges three times today—what could he complain about?"

But he found something, for just as I launched into the last page of one of the many fund-raising letters, typing in "Broadfay" instead of "Broadway" (I would have to start at page one again as he counted the sheets of paper he gave me to type with), I heard my name being mellifluously called. Melpomene in person, this one.

"Yes, Mr. Fartus," I said, disgust rising in my voice. His antics were endless, like a mentally ill fox terrier with a thyroid condition.

"Come here. Look at this," he said, and called me over to his desk. He had the original piece and the one that had been copied positioned over one another. Then he held them to the light. "See that? The copied one is smaller. I knew it." Then he set them down. "Here's what you do," he said, his voice calm and controlled. "Go back to where you had these done and tell them this is unacceptable. I will not tolerate a one percent shrinkage in my copies."

"But Kaplan, a copying machine automatically shrinks things one percent. It's such a small amount that no one notices."

"*I NOTICE*," he bellowed at me, rising from his desk, fury shooting forth suddenly. "And it's 'Mr. Fartus' to you!"

"Okay, okay, okay. I'll go. Just don't get upset," and with that I trudged back to the copy place with the duplicates and the originals.

Evidently they saw me coming, for by the time I made it up to the counter, the entire staff was waiting with arms crossed and feet tapping.

"He's not getting away with this anymore," one of the employees started saying. "He's infamous all over town. We're the only shop that will even do his work, so you just go back and tell him 'No.'"

"I see you've been down this road," I said.

"One percent? Yeah, we've been down it. And just so you know, here's what he's going to want: He'll want us to blow up the size of the originals, and then reduce them however many times it takes for them to come down to the same size as the primary copy. The last girl who worked for him had a nervous breakdown. Take my advice—get out while you can."

So back I went to the office, not looking forward to what was about to take place. Me? I had a book to peddle, agents to stalk, small shrubs to buy. I couldn't be wasting my valuable time on a man like Fartus and his complicated games with score reproduction. I'd keep the job, but there were limits to what I would put up with.

"Well, you just tell them to blow up the originals and then reduce them enough times so that there's no one-percent reduction," he said, his tone indignant and hostile.

"That's what they thought you'd say."

"And they refused? They *refused?*"

"Hmm."

"I'll take care of this," he said and proceeded to dial the phone after scouring his Rolodex for the number. Just then the other line rang and I went to answer it, retreating to my desk. I had to pick up by the third ring. If I didn't, I was forced to vacuum Fartus's entire toupee collection. In addition, Mr. F. had been very specific as to the wording he now wanted used in the phone greeting and I was told not to stray from the script.

"Good morning, Barely Broadway productions, Kaplan Fartus founder and director since 1963, this is Max Perkins speaking, how may I be of help to you on this lovely day?" I said into the receiver. It occurred to me that if any poor soul had randomly dialed, hoping to get someone to call an ambulance in order to take them to the hospital because of a heart attack, they would be dead, embalmed, memorialized, and on their way to their next reincarnation by the time I finished the particular bouquet of words that were required of me.

"It's me," said a voice. Ordinarily I would have found this statement more than a little self-serving and egotistical, but because of the thick Indian accent I said nothing.

"Can we pick up where we left off? You've got to help me," the voice continued, in desperation. "It is of utmost importance."

"Poopa, right?" I asked.

"Yes, this is correct."

"Good," I said, "just wanted to be sure. So many people call me with Indian accents that I've got to cover all my bases." Then I looked around the doorframe to make sure Mr. F was busy on the other line, still trying to cajole less than a one-percent reduction out of Copy Cat Copy Services.

"Okay, now," I said, turning my attention to Poopa, "how can I be of help?"

17

Having a steady job allowed me to look for a permanent place to live. Life with Mr. and Mrs. Mormon had been for the most part quiet, but I needed money for new clothes since my blue jeans had been burned in an exorcism ceremony, and trying to keep up my energy level without caffeine was taking its toll. Granted, I didn't make much money while working for Barely Broadway, so looking for a place to live in Manhattan was out of the question. I perused the *Village Voice* again and found ads hawking more reasonably priced roommate situations in the outer boroughs. I tried to put the previous experiences out of my mind. Momentary denial can be a wonderful thing. It was February now and a deep chill had settled over the city.

The first ad I called in this new theatre of cruelty was for a roommate situation in Queens. Having endured the Art Deco experience with one of Danny Kaye's relatives some time back, I was cautious, feeling the person out on the phone before giving away too much information about myself, and it was a good thing I did.

After about three minutes of conversation I was informed that I would be expected to join the Queens Militia—evidently an organization dedicated to the abolition of minorities in all five boroughs of New York—so I pretended I had a Chinese food delivery at the door and went on to the next number.

I suppose that I had to get lucky at some point, and it seemed as if some desirable type of Fortuna had come my way, for the second person I spoke with about his ad actually sounded somewhat normal. The situation was this: a share in Brooklyn, on what was then the D train line, someplace near Newkirk Avenue.

Sounded nice enough, but when I finally arrived everything seemed off-kilter, and in more ways than one. I made my way up five flights of stairs after being buzzed in. The first room of the apartment I entered was incredibly tiny, maybe five feet by eight feet, and appeared to be a bathroom—a fact that was apparent since there was an enormous and ancient claw-foot tub against one wall. It was then explained that this room was the bathroom room *and* the kitchen. And everything else.

As if this wasn't bad enough, I began to notice a sickening feeling in my stomach which, strangely enough, had nothing to do with the enormous chunks of plaster that were missing from the ceiling or the offensive colors of the beanbag chairs stuffed in one corner. The enormous green-and-pink vinyl sacks were patched with gray duct tape and covered with dust. Against another wall was a stereo—faux wood grain with an out-of-date turntable, and monolithic "Woodstock" speakers that seemed to suck what little air there was out of the room. The only space left in the place was a pathway about one foot wide. I felt as if I were going to fall over and put my hand out to steady myself by touching the wall.

"You get used to it," the guy who answered the door offered. "Name's Spong," he said, and stuck out his hand. "Vertigo," he continued. "Happened to me the first time."

"Spong Vertigo?" I asked. "That's an unusual name."

"No, just Spong. You know, like Cher or Madonna. Vertigo is what you're experiencing." I would find out later that Spong's last name was Flagelatte. No wonder he only went by the first part.

Spong looked no more than eighteen years old. With black hair, a perpetual five-o'clock shadow on his baby face, skin the color of dirty underwear, thirty pounds underweight, and bad teeth, he was a walking poster child for ugly. He also had a limp that appeared to be the result of being hit by a car. I would later discover that outside the apartment the limp was quite pronounced. Inside, however, it was barely noticeable as the floor was in about as bad shape as he was and the two cancelled each other out. I stood looking him over, then decided to turn my attention to matters only slightly less angst-provoking—the room.

It was then that I put together what was wrong with the apartment. One of the walls was leaning at about a forty-five-degree angle. I took stock of the floor—it slanted downward toward an ancient and now defunct radiator in front of a window that was covered with a burglar gate. A large masking tape "X" plastered itself over the filthy glass of the window. Another wall leaned in a direction opposite the first one, and to make matters worse, the door and window frames weren't parallel with any of the angles of the floor and walls. Thankfully, the ceiling was almost gone, saving it from the angular fate of the fun-house walls and floor. The only things missing were mirrors that made you look fat or thin and an evil piped-in laugh.

"It's a really old building. Used to be a slum," Spong offered, seeing my interest in the problematical geometry of the place.

"Used to be?"

"The place got a face-lift several years ago when some squatters moved in and made some repairs. Then the landlord decided it was in good enough condition to charge rent and threw the drug addicts out."

My first reaction was to run screaming from the (and I use this term loosely) "room," but after a moment of reflection on what I had gone through so far trying to find a place to live, I held back. I wanted something to pan out in my life and so I stayed, at least to ask questions, my morbid curiosity getting the better of me.

"So, where are the bedrooms?" I asked. I should have known then to leave, but again, the draw of living and working (loose terms) in the greatest city in the world held me fast. This may have been Brooklyn but it was still New York.

"Bedrooms?" Spong asked, as if I had just requested breakfast served to me in my own personal harem. "Dude, there's only one bedroom." Again, this wasn't such cause for alarm. I was getting used to just about anything after my New York experiences, so I took the bait after an awkward pause, thinking that having to share a bedroom wouldn't be so bad.

"Do I get to see this bedroom?" I asked, realizing that Spong wasn't moving.

"Well, you can, but it's my room," he said, as he lurched toward one of the walls. When he had managed to swing open a door and expose a closet, I thought there had been some mistake. Granted, it was a big closet, it just wasn't another room.

"I don't get it."

"I've been told I'm really cheap," he said, rolling his eyes.

I walked over, as best I could, to the place where Spong was standing and peered into the small dark space. There was a sleeping bag bunched up on the floor along with yet another beanbag chair (How many do you need?) and a few books. An empty beer bottle completed the plan. The entire space was the size of a refrigerator.

"How—"

"I don't mind. I sleep either sitting up or in a fetal position."

I was really afraid to ask my next question but thought I'd better get it out in the open since things weren't looking so good. The only real room of the apartment was barely big enough for us both to stand in. I dove in, head first. "If you sleep in the closet, then where would I be sleeping?" I was beginning to realize that the entire apartment, with the exception of the closet, was this one small area with a bathtub along one wall. I feared the worst since we had discussed over the phone the fact that both of us worked during the day. At least with the Radio City apartment fiasco I would have had the bed to myself *some* of the time. Now I had visions of sharing a closet.

"You get a really good deal," Spong began, and gestured toward the tub. "The bathtub is really roomy. You could fit two in there comfortably if you ever have company. See, the only thing is, you have to be out of it by seven each morning or else wait until eight."

"I'm not following," I said, completely confused. "The bathtub?"

"That's where you sleep, man, in the tub. It's really big."

If you look in the dictionary under "uncomfortable silences" you will find a picture of me standing in front of a claw foot tub, somewhere in the recesses of Brooklyn.

I couldn't move.

Some sick inner thing glued me to the spot. And the worst aspect of the experience was this: It somehow made sense. After everything I had experienced, I wasn't totally mortified. It was as if my few months in the city had somehow warped all logic and now, being given a different set of rules, a different set of criteria for happiness, for success, for everything, I had acquiesced to what was

91

being handed over. I was the consummate abused individual who suddenly turns the term "victim" into "survivor."

And to prove this miraculous transformation, when Spong suggested that I get into the enormous porcelain receptacle, I consented and found myself supine, staring at what little was left of the ceiling. I felt as if I were trying out a coffin; as if I'd made some deal with a gangster and was not only relinquishing my right to live, but actually forging ahead and picking out my own resting place so as not to bother anyone later with the details.

"It *is* roomy," I said, thinking that no amount of money would convince me to move in with this nut case, hoping to quell any anger he might have that was waiting to burst forth at my refusal to accept his invitation. I just wanted to appear amiable so he didn't attempt to kill me before I could make it out the door. My reclining act was just that: a performance to try to appease the gods of wacko-land and buy some time before they smashed me like an insect. "But it's awfully hard," I said, wrinkling my nose, which I hoped he interpreted as the ultimate sort of, "Yes, I'd dearly love to sleep in your bathtub, but I've got to move to Helsinki next week and discover the cure for cancer," gesture.

"I've got some blankets you can put down, that is, after you wash it out," Spong offered.

"Wash the blankets out, but—"

"Not the blankets, the tub. You'll have to wash it out each night before you get in. At least that's what I'd do."

"What do you mean, 'each night,' " I asked, still not firmly grasping the situation.

"Man, we have to use it to get ready for work each morning. Sometimes anyway. Most mornings I go to my gym and shower before heading to work so there's no problem. At any rate, you still have to be out by seven or wait until eight."

The question hung in the air for me—the one I had yet to ask. I should have known better, but after all I had been through I still hadn't learned when to stop.

"Why out by seven or wait until eight?" I asked, thinking that there couldn't possibly be a reasonable answer. I was right.

"Man, I have breakfast between seven and eight," Spong responded. I didn't say anything, but a good portion of my forehead went up and my eyes got bigger. He read the signs.

"I put a big board over the tub and use it as a table each morning. That's where I have my breakfast," he said, motioning to a three-foot by seven-foot piece of water-stained plywood that was stuck between the tub and the wall. One edge of it peeked out sheepishly from behind the monstrosity—a seemingly unwilling participant in this folly called living.

Spong continued: "I'm on a strict schedule. I've been late so many times now that the head of accounting has threatened to fire me. Big television is like that. NBC is the same way. I can't be late again, so I have my breakfast at seven exactly. If you sleep late then you get covered up until eight. If there's one thing I insist on it's punctuality, so if you decide to sleep in, you'll have to stay in there until I'm finished. There's also a toilet down the hall that we share with the other tenants on this floor," he added, probably thinking this would smooth things over.

"Thank God for the little things," I said.

"It's best to keep a flashlight in there with you just in case," Spong added, turning back to the subject of the tub and his breakfast schedule, pointing to the porcelain Grand Canyon that occupied most of the room, "that way you can at least read if you get sealed in."

And while this should have been clue enough for me to jump directly from the window and impale myself on one of the spikes that topped the turn-of-the-century cast-iron fence in front of the building, I again stayed, veering into that no-man's-land called insanity and asked the question, "It takes you an hour to eat breakfast?"

18

A nd so here we are once again at Barely Broadway. When last we left, our cast of characters included Kaplan Fartus, that unctuous and turgid bit of bile, and Poopa Goopta—a mystery woman in need of something. Now let me say that things were starting to look suspicious. First of all I found myself engaged in employment and conversation with two people whose names resembled functions one most often chooses to ignore. This would be a foreshadowing of things to come, for the reference to odious elimination of waste material and the gasses accompanying such actions would raise their ugly heads (imagine it how you will) later, and prove to be an even more tangible and reluctant manifestation of the dirty deed. Poopa and Fartus. I'd like to tell you that I pulled these from the depths of my psyche, but alas, truth is stranger than fiction and the workplace in New York City reigns supreme when it comes to the bizarre.

> Witness for the prosecution, Kaplan Fartus: "Max came to work for me in the winter of 1989. I thought there was something strange about him but hired him anyway. As you know, I run Barely Broadway and we give a series of concerts each year that . . . what? . . . oh, yes . . . well, as I was saying, I always thought there was something a little off with Max. I mean, he couldn't even handle simple tasks like typing or photocopying. I felt rather sorry for him if you want the truth."

Add to this the way life was handing me people and names that went together. There was the list of places that I had worked: Beaucoup Books; Babley's; Barely Broadway. You may have noticed the *B* connection without my mentioning it.

I somehow imagined that the universe, in its sordid way (is there any other?), had turned against me, grading me less than first-rate. Whenever anyone inquired as to where I had worked, I would rattle off the list of names, sounding like a babbling idiot or worse, Bing Crosby doing an orange juice commercial. While I was still employed at Barely Broadway, I was looking for a new place to live, a new job, and trying desperately to get published. And the rejections kept piling in.

I decided to take the advice of the last agent who had so kindly recommended that I seek the help of a story editor, and called her personally. What happened uncomfortably resembled Mr. F's attempt at fund-raising.

"Hi, my name is Max Perkins and you were kind enough to send me a note back that—"

"Click."

Well, that was that. I would have to search elsewhere for a story editor, and where should I turn but to my old friend, Robert. I called late one Saturday and asked for his advice. "You might as well come over," he said, resignation finally overtaking him, and gave me the address.

Now as I said before, Robert is a good-looking guy: six feet four inches, flattop, works out—you know the type, not a gym bunny but takes care of himself; has a natural proclivity toward the beefy side. He has to, being in his current profession—a profession which wasn't looking so bad after the few jobs I had endured.

So I fully expected him to keep company with birds who possessed plumage much like himself; good-looking and well-muscled types who mainly spoke in monosyllables and drank too much beer. Let's just say that I wasn't prepared when Marcel, his roommate, answered the door.

"Hi, you must be Max. Come on in," a bodiless voice said when I finally made it to Rob's apartment. My eyes, seeing an empty space where a person normally would be, dropped down to the level of a small ottoman. There stood Marcel—all two and a half feet of him.

"Heeeey!" I said, bending over and using my best "I'm not surprised, I see this all the time, most of my best friends are vertically challenged, I'm just so glad to finally meet someone I didn't even know existed" voice that reeked of phony cheeriness.

"Yeeeessss indeedie!" I continued, suddenly realizing that I was treating him like an overgrown lap dog. I cleared my throat, pretended to cough, and then scratched—anything to cover up my astonishment. Robert appeared behind Marcel and motioned me in. He was on the phone and indicated that Marcel and I should begin getting to know one another while he took care of business. "No discomfort here," I thought.

"Robert tells me you're a writer," Marcel said, oblivious to the strained surroundings. I looked around nervously. A recording of Liszt's "Mephisto Waltz" played in the background—*sotto voce*—and there was an open bottle of wine out on a table.

"Well, I don't write much right now," I said. "I'm trying to get settled, land a steady job, you know—that sort of thing. I haven't had time to write lately. That and I'm busy trying to find an agent and publisher." I waited. Marcel was attempting to crack a walnut with his teeth. "And yourself? What do you do?" I asked.

I could hear Robert in the background: "Two hundred is not too much. I have to buy the outfit and shave my legs. And that won't go over too well with some of my clients."

"Me? I'm—" (craaaack! and a piece of walnut flew into the air and landed on a chair). There wasn't that far it could have gone—the apartment was only a small studio. No wonder Robert hadn't offered to take me in. I imagined a changing of the guard as far as bed duty—like the one proposed by an earlier prospective roommate—or a closet where the Brooklynite slept. Then I saw the opened bottom drawer of an ornate antique dresser, its contents a pillow and comforter. I did some first-grade math and came up with where Marcel snoozed. At least it wasn't a bathtub.

"I run a cleaning agency. Work for myself, if you know what I mean," Marcel finally responded.

"How interesting," I said, thinking that I could rival his banter with the extensive knowledge I had gleaned from Babley's; grateful for a least a common thread. How often does one get to meet a dwarf who owns his own cleaning service? (I understand the term midget is politically incorrect.)

"What kind of cleaning services do you offer? I mean, is it for people's houses or is it commercial?" I went on, hoping to keep the conversation going until Robert had successfully negotiated his tryst—the price was going up by the minute now that false eyelashes and a riding crop were involved.

"Suicide clean up, murders, that sort of thing," Marcel responded, and then began to dig at a piece of walnut lodged between two molars. "When I'm not doing that I'm Robert's pimp. Well, sometimes anyway." By now he had secured the coveted nutmeat of the walnut and was chewing away. He went on, seeing my confusion at Robert's attempt to negotiate price and conditions of the sale. "I'm letting Rob handle this one. It's my day off," and with that he bit into another nut. With his size and talent for cracking things with his teeth, I couldn't help but visualize him being carried off the stage by a group of rabid sugar plum fairies at Lincoln Center during a performance of *The Nutcracker*.

"You guys getting along?" asked Robert, after tying up the loose ends of his negotiation and joining us.

"Yeah, I guess," I said. "Going to have to shave your legs?"

"Not if I can help it. There were two clients this guy wanted me to handle. The first one I just said no to. The second one I've done before—many times. A real odd unit. Forty-something-year-old. Never married. Into some kinky stuff, man, let me tell you. I have to dress up in these S&M outfits, but it doesn't much matter since she blindfolds herself before I ever get in the door. I'm not allowed to speak during the session, and before I leave I have to take a picture of her with a camera she has set up. And some of the physical abuse she likes borders on the psychotic. But enough about my profession. You're here to get some advice on getting that book published and I promised you a story editor."

"Anything, Robert. I've got to get out of that hellhole I work in too. I don't even want to know how you're connected to Fartus."

We spoke as he rummaged through the uppermost portion of an enormous roll-top desk. It took up most of the room, just as the tub had done in the Brooklyn apartment I had seen. My eyes scanned the room as I waited.

"How's Dory?" I asked, seeing a picture of her. It sat on an end table to my left. I remembered the run-in at the Upper East Side restaurant and was attempting to make conversation and get in a dig at the same time. I recalled how uncomfortable Robert had been with all three of us in the same room and I wanted to see if he remembered the incident. But before I could continue, something out of place caught my eye. It was a strange envelope next to Dory's picture. I noticed it because it wasn't addressed to either Robert or Marcel. There was no way that three people lived in this tiny studio apartment.

"Who's Ray-Bob Ramssey?" I asked.

"Boy, you're just full of questions today," Robert responded. He looked irritated for a moment, then went back to his search for the editor's name and address.

"Okay, I guess. We're not as close as we used to be," he said.

"Not close to Ray-Bob or Dory?"

"Dory."

"So who's this Ray-Bob person?" I persisted, picking up the letter. Marcel shot me an icy stare and Robert lifted the envelope out of my hand, replacing it with a slip of paper, ignoring my last question.

"Reeda Rot. That's her name. The editor," Robert said. "The person I'm sending you to. Ray-Bob is a nobody. Must have been the person who lived here before me."

"Let me get this straight," I said, "Reeda Rot is a person's name?"

"So I'm told."

"It's very Astro from *The Jetsons*."

"I've heard she's the best in the business, at least with regard to helping writers polish up their work and get it ready to be published. I don't know her personally, but that's what they tell me. A friend of a friend. Six degrees of separation, that sort of thing," and he flashed a large grin showing perfect teeth and two enormous dimples. "You're supposed to mail a copy of the manuscript to her first, then call."

"Doesn't she live in New York?" I asked.

"Lower East Side," Robert responded. "Trust me, do it this way. It's what she wants. And from what I hear, she knows all the right people—agents, publishers—the works. If you play your cards right she might just be your ticket to success."

I looked at Marcel. He raised his wineglass and smiled. Then I glanced at Robert. We all looked at each other and there was a moment of silence.

"At least it's worth a shot," Robert said, and he finished with his address book, placing the letter addressed to Ray-Bob inside it.

"To fame and fortune," Marcel intoned to the room. Robert gave an uncomfortable little laugh, then added, "Rots-a-ruck!"

"Well, at least to one of them," Marcel said, and proceeded to drain what was left of his wine.

19

"I can see you at three, no ... four o'clock on Tuesday the eighth," the voice on the other end of the line said. I could hear a pen scratching over the phone, along with what sounded like a Tarzan movie playing in the background. Since it was February in New York I figured Reeda was watching Johnny Weissmuller and Cheetah in an effort to keep warm.

"But I have to work then. What about some time after five?" I didn't want to be difficult, but life at Barely Broadway was not easy and I didn't want to cause any more problems than necessary. Fartus and I had been warring against each other as of late.

"Listen, I'm very busy. You're lucky I'm taking you at all. I have a waiting list of people who want to study with me. I'm only accepting you because you're so talented. That and because Robert is a friend of someone I know. He recommended you, did he not? I've read your script—"

"Manuscript," I interrupted. "It's a book, not a movie."

". . . and I really think we can work together, but you have to do things my way. Four o'clock, Tuesday. I'll see you then." Her tone attempted hyper-professionalism. Her sentences were cold, clipped; short. There was a defensiveness about her. And the sound of her voice—a screech of sorts. Like metal on metal. Irritating beyond belief.

"All right," I said. And then not wanting to end the conversation with her antagonistic tone hanging in the air I added, "I really like those old Tarzan movies too. Which one is this?"

"I don't have the slightest idea what you're talking about," she snapped. "See you at four," and with that she hung up, leaving me staring into the receiver as if the object in my hand had just committed the solecism itself.

I didn't know what I would tell Kaplan but I knew I'd think of something. Besides, if what Reeda said was true, I was lucky to get her as a story editor; someone to help me get my manuscript in shape so that I could win over an agent or publisher. And hadn't she said I was talented? Well, that felt good. She was making a place for me even though her schedule was jam-packed. Besides, we both liked Tarzan movies.

The next day I approached Kaplan and asked to leave early on Tuesday. His head blew off completely, his limbs thrashed about like an octopus on methamphetamines, and I think he may have even wet himself, but by the end of it I had procured the extra time to visit the story editor who would shape my book into a bestseller.

That Tuesday I made my way to the Lower East Side of Manhattan, careful to sidestep passed-out junkies, pools of freshly regurgitated vomit, and several angry-looking pit bulls with their rib cages on display. I found the building—a squalid yellow brick thing with enormous streaks of rust careening down the side. The proverbial assortment of beaten-up garbage cans stoically stood guard out front, and I noticed that the freshly applied graffiti on the sidewalk still seemed wet.

Approaching the front door, I pressed the cracked and greasy black buzzer and waited.

And waited.

Three ominous Puerto Rican youths slouched by sharing a paper bag with a bottle inside. A two hundred-year-old homeless woman snail-paced her way in front of the building. At one point, a diaper—freshly used—came plummeting from an upper window and landed with a plop only a few feet away. The sounds of bastardized Spanish could be heard following its nose-dive to the sidewalk. Beekman Place it wasn't.

"Yes?" Finally. The voice came out of the aluminum grid.

"It's Max. We spoke on the phone—" and then the long buzz to enter the building. Timing was of the utmost importance here. As with most non-doorman buildings in New York, it is necessary to go through two doors: first the outer one, and then one leading directly into the lobby. A badly-timed peripatetic journey could leave one stranded in the tiny inner vestibule between glass, the end result being that the visitor would have to go back outside, ring the bell again, explain what had happened, hope to be believed—that this was not some elaborate plan to slit every person's throat who lived in the building—and try for better timing next go-around. Fortunately I made it in through both doors. I felt myself to be the consummate New Yorker.

Like most walk-ups in the city, the hallways smelled of cat pee. And not just any cat pee. These things had obviously been fed a steady diet of asparagus. I walked past doorways emitting either bad food smells or arguments, or both, until I found my destination. "Why," I wondered at the time, "was I forced to wait a good five minutes before I was let in? Perhaps she couldn't hear me because the Tarzan movie was playing so loudly?" The reason became obvious shortly.

"Don't let the iguana out," a voice said as a crack appeared between Reeda's door and the frame. Then an arm pulled me through a three-inch opening. I felt as though someone had broken a window in a plane at thirty thousand feet and I had been sucked out—into a strange and foreboding atmosphere. Fortunately it was quite dark in the apartment, otherwise the initial sight might have been too much for me. The din was certainly enormous. Deafening. And the place smelled only slightly better than a garbage dump.

"Take your shoes off. I have to keep my carpet clean," Reeda snapped. And then to the room, "Quiet! Everyone quiet! Shush, Daisy-May. Cletus, get down from there! Pongo, I'm not going to tell you again to stop chasing Miss Marple."

I did as I was instructed in the small foyer, careful not to set my shoes down on the iguana. My eyes adjusted to the dimness. The tiny studio was filled with what looked like no fewer than twelve birds of every description (one a completely featherless African Gray), six cats, one dog with no fur, which was hooked up to some contraption involving wheels, assorted rodents, the iguana that had answered the door, and a badly moth-eaten-looking cougar, its fangs adequately displayed. The cougar wobbled slightly as an oversized macaw landed on its back. The large cat had not been subjected to the best of taxidermy jobs. It was the only one of the tribe to be stuffed—so far.

I turned my attention to the dog—the one missing most of its fur. Its back legs were withered and someone had made it a set of wheels like those used on bicycles for beginners. They were attached with a harness enabling the poor pooch to pull himself about with his front legs while the back ones hovered just inches above the ground. I immediately thought of Grace Patchin—that devil-worshiping landlady with her useless legs—and imagined her with the same contraption. Then I looked up to find the woman I had come to see extending her hand.

"Percy."

"Excuse me?" I asked. "I thought your name was Reeda."

"Percy. The iguana is Percy. I could tell you were wondering," she said and waved a rather violent "be quiet" to the room. "I'm Reeda—the one you spoke with on the phone," she said, and extended her hand again.

"Right," I said grasping it.

"What are you doing?" she asked, a puzzled look on her face. She drew back slightly.

I looked around, confused. "Shaking your hand?" I said, hoping this was the right answer. I had played hopscotch with vomiting winos to get to her neighborhood, almost been decapitated by a dirty diaper while waiting to be let in, and an iguana had answered the door—I wasn't too sure of anything.

"Oh, that!" She laughed uneasily. "I wasn't shaking hands. People make that mistake all the time. I thought you were going to give me the cash you brought—you know, for payment of the session."

"But we haven't had the session yet. Wouldn't it be more normal for me to pay you afterwards?"

"Don't be silly. Everyone pays me before. Come over here to the sofa and we can talk," and she motioned me over to the center of the small room.

I followed her as best I could, sidestepping a sleeping cat, three piles of *something*, an overturned chair, and two boxes of kitty litter. No wonder it had taken her so long to buzz me in. On my journey to the sofa a parrot swooped down too near my head and a chinchilla ran across my foot. In the process I managed to get a look at Reeda: six feet tall, bleached blond hair (punk-rock short), thin as a broomstick, and two enormous black outlines around her eyes. But she had evidently been fat at one time for enormous wattles of flesh hung from her upper arms—the only areas that had not been affected by her weight loss. One immediately thought of some fifth-grade teacher at the blackboard, writing furiously with a nub of chalk while her sagging and aged triceps flailed in the wind—"And now class, the capital of Bolivia is . . . (flap, flap, flap) . . . La Paz."

"So, Reeda, you like animals, huh?" I asked, hoping to break the ice.

"You're not here to talk about my animals. You're here to talk about your book."

"Warm," I thought. But then perhaps she was just really good at her job and could afford to forgo the niceness.

While I thought we would settle in to work on *Mrs. Squigglemire's Bustle*, most of the next hour was spent with her telling me the cost of the consultations. "Now, let's see, I can probably get this book into shape in three, no, five, six . . . perhaps ten, twelve sessions. And trust is important; you must have complete trust in me and never question anything I do. I'm only taking you because you're so talented. I have students lined up who want to study with me."

Being told once that you're talented is a compliment. Anything after that becomes sycophantic. I squirmed in my seat.

I was informed Reeda charged one hundred and fifty dollars an hour. I did the math in my head. It wasn't pretty. The rest of the session (five minutes) consisted of her telling me everything wrong I had done in my writings, always accompanied by, "But don't worry—that's what I'm here for." Somehow I wasn't comforted.

"Now, I don't want to begin working on this book just yet. We've got to get your writing skills better honed," she said, offering a peanut to a sullen cockatoo sitting to her right. "So what I want you to do is write an essay on something like, say . . . boogers, for next week. We'll take it from there."

"On what?" I asked, thinking I had misunderstood.

"Boogers. I want an essay on boogers. Capeesh? Listen, I'm a novelist—that's what I do, write novels. That's why I can help you. You want to write a novel—"

"Uh, I've already written a novel, Reeda, I ju—"

"Don't interrupt me. I'm here to help you—you *did* bring cash and not a check today? At least this first time I want cash. So do you understand that you have to put yourself in my hands?"

"I think so," I said. "Could I write on something a little more . . . accessible? And yes, I brought cash, but you know I'm not sure I can afford to—"

"So you don't think boogers are accessible? What did I say about complete trust? Do you *want* to get better? Do you *want* me to help you?" she asked, and then began making notes in a rather nasty spiral-bound book while she spoke out loud to herself. I imagined her a relative of the employment agency person, taking down my every fault for future reference—"Doooooeees . . . noooooot . . . liiiiiikkkee . . . boooooooooggggerrrrs."

She continued: "I'm connected. I know everyone. Agents—publishers—media—print—you name it. If you follow my lead I can get you in; get you an agent. We're talking big-time here. But you have to do things exactly as I want—what I say, when I say it—no questions."

I sat there trying to make sense of everything I had experienced in New York. The living situations, what you could call jobs, the things that passed for art. I was here to get a book out. I kept telling myself to focus, to trust people. After all, they had been doing *something* right to live in this city. Finally I spoke.

"Mucous is fine," I said, and left it at that. But somehow Reeda's list of contacts, my possible literary success, and the subject material for my essay . . . well . . . they just didn't seem to go together.

20

D eciding that spending eight hours a night in a bathtub (with or without water) was too much for me, I continued my journey through the land of escaped mental patients, determining that of all the places I had seen, the one in Brooklyn with someone named "Spong" was the worst. That is, until my second week's look through the newspaper ads.

One such advertisement I called involved a sublet on Avenue B, on the Lower East Side of Manhattan—Reeda's territory. Alphabet City, as it was known then, was not exactly a prestigious address. Even some of the homeless people and drug dealers avoided it, so bad was its reputation. Still, I wanted at least the crumbs of the American—and more specific, New York dream— and felt my tenacious self ascend to the occasion.

While everything checked out on the phone, the minute I showed up at the apartment I knew something was wrong. I was met at the door by a Korean man and the odor of kimchee, so overpowering (the Korean man, not the kimchee), that I had to keep my hand to my nose the entire time. He explained to me that while, yes, this was a sublet, his wife would be staying there as well and that I was expected to sleep with her each night as the couple wanted a baby so that they could sell it on the black market and buy a one- way ticket to Antarctica. (I didn't ask.) I looked behind him to see an almost completely toothless woman with crow's feet as deep as the Grand Canyon, gingerly fluttering her fingers at me—a meager attempt in any culture to say "Hi."

I moved on.

The next ad I called involved a single male with an extra bedroom and free reign of the bathroom facilities. And the price was reasonable. I should have known that something was wrong, as that particular animal—an affordable share in a two-bedroom apartment in Manhattan—doesn't exist without some serious compromises. And I had learned one lesson: Just speaking on the phone, making a judgment about the person via their voice, didn't always allow them to fall on the right side of the fence when it came to normal behavior. So I made the pilgrimage to the West Village, to a lovely old building with marble floors and high ceilings in the foyer, trying to keep my optimism at a minimum. And it was a good thing, for the moment the renter opened his door things started to go downhill.

He invited me in. The apartment was pitch dark even though it was the middle of the day, and the greeter was wearing sunglasses. Expansive black cloth shades hung over the windows and not a light was on. I followed his silhouette as best I could, into what I was told was the living room—a place that would be communal. Slivers of sunlight squeaked through the edges of the black shades and the occasional digital clock or light on some appliance punctuated the space. I sat.

My questions about what he liked to do in his spare time, the quality of the neighborhood, and what he expected in a roommate, were met with monosyllabic answers. "Nothing," and "Okay," were for him the equivalent of an overblown paragraph in an encyclopedia. An open book he was not.

Just as my eyes were adjusting to the lack of light—my pupils now the size of a black hole in the outermost reaches of the universe—he began to come alive verbally. This would prove to be . . . not a good thing, for his statements gave new meaning to *non sequitur* and at best he was caustic.

"You know, I could have anyone I want, anytime, anywhere. The most gorgeous man came by the other day. He was a model and worth millions. We both adore Fra Filippo Lippi. Do you even know who Lippi is?" His voice suddenly contained enough anger to power a small town. I did know about Lippi the artist, but thought it best to keep my mouth shut. At least I would have my own bedroom in this place.

"We sucked and fucked for hours on this floor," he continued, pointing to a swath of sheepskin rug beneath my feet. I unconsciously fidgeted, imaging two writhing bodies where my soles now rested, thinking that his last comment was just a *wee* bit more information than I needed.

"He told me he loved me and that he wanted me to marry him," he went on.

My eyes were beginning to adjust even more to the lack of light and I could now see that he looked in one direction the entire time. Then it hit me—the shades, no light—the guy was blind. A red-tipped cane leaning to one side confirmed my suspicions. I couldn't resist.

"How did you know he was gorgeous?" I asked, really more out of curiosity than chiding.

He exploded: "I *felt* him, you moron!" Evidently tempers are at a premium in the Big Apple, especially when it comes to asking questions of potential roommates.

He continued. "Do you think you could love me as much as he did? Do you think you could be my slave; service me on a daily basis; cater to my every whim?" He was foaming slightly at the corners of his mouth, the whiteness visible even in the cave-like atmosphere.

I thought a moment of all the people I had interviewed with for a place to live. "I could give it a shot," I said, thinking I'd have a door to shut and an actual toilet. It was then that things heated up, for he must have thought I was being sarcastic. I wasn't.

"You have to leave! The interview is over! I could never love anyone as stupid as you!" he spewed. His entire body was shaking. An epileptic seizure came to mind—if he wasn't having one now I certainly wished one on him.

"I don't want to love anybody," I said, "I just want a place to sleep and go to the bathroom." Evidently this is something difficult in the city of New York. Who knew? Had these people all been spawned from the same creature? Why was it so hard to find a place to live?

"Get out, you moron!" he screamed and jumped to his feet. This was getting tiring, this being at the mercy of every nut case on an island that had been bought for twenty-four dollars worth of beads from Indians who didn't even live there. Perhaps this was the supreme joke, the supreme retribution for the massacres, the alcoholism, the smallpox blankets. I began to make my way to the door as best I could in the darkness.

"Fool! Ingrate!" he hurled at my back as I fumbled nervously for the doorknob. I finally managed it and now that I was safely on the other side I couldn't help but ask a question that had been nagging me—the one other than, "Does anyone these days actually use the words *fool* and *ingrate?*"

"If you're blind," I asked, "then . . . how can Fra Lippi be your favorite painter?"

"I can *feel* him, you cretin," he seethed and slammed the door in my face.

After that it was on to a penthouse apartment on East Seventy-Second Street in Manhattan where I was told by a three-hundred-pound eunuch that I would be required to paint the living room once a month—a different color each time—as part of my rental agreement. I was also informed, "You know, I could cut you up in my bathtub right now and no one would ever know." Bathtubs in Manhattan, it seemed, had myriad uses, the majority of which included anything but bathing. At least I wouldn't have to sleep there.

Some part of me was attempting to calculate my painting skills and how best to hide the knives. "Let me think about it," I said, and slipped back into the elevator. At this point my brain felt like a number two pencil being used at an SAT exam and anything was possible. Think teeth marks.

Directly from my interview with Sweeney Todd I went to see an apartment in the Gramercy Park area, and when I asked if I could come in to discuss the living situation, I was hit with, "Oh, you want to *talk*. Well, I don't *talk*. You either take it sight unseen or go find someplace else." So I did. I found some other place to go. Plus, the guy wanted four times what I could afford.

It was only a day. That's all it took of looking at ads and interviewing for a place to live; all the time it took before I found myself heading back to Brooklyn and the *Cabinet of Dr. Caligari* with Spong and the claw foot sarcophagus where I would sleep each night. Secretly I prayed the tub had not been rented to anyone else. On my subway trip back to the land of slant, I got out my notebook and began writing. My journey through rental-land had not been a good experience, so I made up a list of what people actually mean when they put an ad in the paper—just to remind myself if ever again I started looking; if Spong and the tub didn't work out. Here's what I came up with:

> If the ad says "quaint" the actual living space will be so filthy that you will need a spatula to scrape the dirt from the walls and floor. Don't even think about using the toilet until a new one has been installed, and even then you may want to keep a brick on top of the lid to hold it down during the night—rats *can* swim up through the pipes, you know. All of this is, of course, dependent on whether the place you move into actually has a toilet. Be sure to ask.
>
> If the ad says, "cozy" you will not be able to open the refrigerator and the front door at the same time. You may also have to sleep standing up. Note: Cozy and quaint often go together.
>
> If the ad says "convenient to transportation" the wall on which you will put the headboard of your bed (*if* you have one) will be underground and within three feet of several major subway lines. Still, you will need to walk forty or fifty blocks once outside as there will be no direct route to actually enter the subway station in your immediate neighborhood.
>
> If the ad says "reasonably priced," someone was murdered in the apartment, no one bothered to clean up the crime yet, an outer wall is missing, and the landlord has now decided to charge you five hundred dollars a month *more* than the previous (deceased) tenant.

Hold on. There's more. This is, after all, Manhattan—that urban sprawl of whatnot. Greatest city in the world? Yes, but . . .

> If the ad says, "pets okay," this means that the rat and cockroach populations in the hallways are so extensive that Fluffy won't be noticed. Plus, the landlord's pit bull needs something substantial to practice on before his next fight, so feel free to let your Pekinese wander the halls unattended. It could also mean that the Vietnamese restaurant next door has a deal with the super of the building. Better keep Fido on a leash.
>
> If the ad says "no pets" this means that the current landlord has not been able to rid the apartment of the smell of cat pee and hopes that by having you live there you will find a way to abate the stench, thereby making the unit more valuable

after he has evicted you *and* raised the rent by twelve hundred percent.

If the ad says "a must see," the landlord is hoping that you're from out of town, don't have time to visit the apartment, and will take it without first viewing the space.

If the ad says, "won't last!" this means that it has been on the market since before the birth of Jesus and that the few people who have been foolish enough to make the trip to the South Bronx to see this crack house are now suing for mental damages that the trip has caused.

If the ad says "different" this is the wild card that screams, "prepare yourself for the worst" and might allude to the fact that the walls, floor, and ceiling form angles that even the most advanced geometry can't explain, or that there aren't any stairs or elevator leading up to the unit, even though it is located on the twenty-third floor. It also can mean that the drain from the Ethiopian restaurant next door backs up three times a day into your kitchen sink.

"You're back!" a cheerful voice said—Spong—greeting me over the intercom after I rang the buzzer.

"Yes," I said, thinking that at least I could remain in one piece and relieve myself inside, albeit down the hallway with immigrant people who had probably never even *seen* an indoor toilet. "I've always wanted to experience the best that New York has to offer," I said, and so began my journey into the land of stable housing.

I paid the deposit that day as requested—up front; two months rent—and was on my way back to the Land-O-Mormon to collect my meager belongings with visions of chocolate doughnuts dancing in my head.

On the subway I thought about the character I had just agreed to live with. Something—more than the strange angles of the walls and the fact that I would be sleeping in a bathtub—bothered me. Spong was odd, but then, if I avoided everyone who seemed strange, I would have to move *very* far away. Still, something about Spong wasn't right. Spong: purveyor of gold chains, fine clothing, and someone with a decent job. Yet he lived in a hole. He worked for a credit union as an accountant at one of the large television networks in Manhattan, and liked to dine out and dress well. I sensed he was overzealous in his longing for the cash stash, but since I didn't have any myself, I wasn't too worried—he wouldn't be taking mine. Plus, denial is a wonderful thing, and tiring of wearing only floral prints and clogs—my waterproof "duck" shoes had been deemed footwear of the devil by the Mormons—and weary from a lack of caffeine, I plunged ahead, intent on making a new go of it in Brooklyn.

Witness for the prosecution: "I don't know why my parents named me Spong. Yeah, it's my real name. So I like nice clothes--comes from having nothing as a kid. The folks were cheap. Their idea of Christmas was underwear and socks and not even the good stuff. You'd think I'd get rid of my acne at my age, but I'd rather spend the money on what I wear. What? Oh, yeah . . . I'll try to stick to the case at hand. Cushy job mine, at the credit union. Work in accounting. Number crunching. Bunch of saps. Heads up their asses. Wasn't thrilled about the new guy moving in--he slept in the bathtub, which was fine. And he didn't have the last roommate's problems--ate all the food in the place. Ate everything. Only way I could keep that guy from my stash was to buy Gerber. The baby food. Tastes like puke but he left it alone. And yeah, I'm conceited. What of it? My idea of a good time is young pussy and no extra gifts that come with it. Can't stand that shit; yeast infections, VD, all the trimmings. Trouble is, I have to go to their place. Man, it's hard to fuck standing up in a closet. Oh . . . sorry your honor. Yes, I'll try and clean it up. No . . . no, I want to cooperate. What did I think of Max? In one word: Stupid. But then, most people are who come from any place but here. I always acted nice around him. Hell, why not. He had no idea I hated him. I just wanted someone to pay all the rent. I told him he was paying half, but

in reality it was the whole shebang. What
an idiot."

Okay, so Spong was not the most charming individual. As a
matter of fact, he was reprehensible, a word I rarely use, my life not
being the most pristine thing on display. But I will say this for him:
he was industrious beyond belief. He claimed he didn't make that
much money but I saw him with rolls of it. Big wads of hundreds.
And his clothes? Only the best. Like I said, when he wasn't eating
baby food he was dining out at expensive restaurants, going on ski
trips, buying stocks. The guy was a money hound. Everything he
touched seemed to turn to gold. That is, with the exception of the
fleapit we both lived in.

21

"You're late again." It was Fartus, chastising me.

"I'm really sorry," I said, putting down my backpack and settling in at my desk. "Problems with my roommate this morning. Nothing I can't straighten out. It won't happen again."

Spong had warned me that seven to eight was breakfast time and I had been awakened by the sound of him placing the makeshift tabletop over the tub ("Sorry, guy. I've got to have my Wheaties and banana.") No amount of pleading would convince him to remove the wooden top and every time I tried to push up on it he screamed like a girl.

Fartus didn't say anything. He just stood there, glumly concentrating on another photocopy that had yet again been reduced by one percent. He held it up to the fluorescent lights, squinting at the misalignment of notes on the sheets of music.

"You know," he continued, all the while scrutinizing the page, "if this lateness happens again I'm going to have to let you go."

"But I've only been late twice since I started, and we're talking about a total of ten minutes. That plus I stay till seven or eight o'clock several nights a week because you like to work—"

"That doesn't matter," he cut in, his eyes glowing, "you're tardy and I don't want it happening anymore. Do we have an understanding?"

"I guess so," I said, as I started to dig through the piles of mail on my desk. "Who uses the word *tardy*," I thought. What was he, an elementary school teacher? As Kaplan made his way into his office he shouted in my direction: "And someone called for you this morning. A Guppie someone. Wants you to call her."

As soon as he stopped haranguing me, I turned my attention to his fund-raising letters and other useless items. In all the morning commotion I hadn't noticed a small gardenia plant on the credenza across from my work area. About the time I saw it, Fartus called out again, pointing out the flora in case I'd missed it.

"That came for you this morning, that plant. I have to wonder if the reason you're late is because of your amorous escapades before work," he said, still in his foul mood. I walked over to the plant and picked it up. No card, but the blossoms were out in full force, and *loud*.

Then Fartus vaulted another irritated condemnation my way: "And take that thing home. God knows the smell is going to kill us all."

I tried to concentrate on work, paying a few company bills and listing all the horrible ways Fartus could die. Then I called Poopa. There was the uncomfortable silence after introductions and she started in—Indian accent thick as ever. I was all ears.

"First, just let me ask you how well you know this Kaplan Fartus, your boss?" she said, her voice tentative.

"Well, I've worked here for a while . . ."

"Does he treat you well?"

I waited, not sure where this was going. "Look, just get to the point. What is it I can help you with? And did you send me this gardenia?"

"No, I do not know of this . . . gardenia you speak of. I am sorry, but I did not have the botanical specimen sent to your person."

"All right, all right," I said, eager for her to get to what she needed.

"I wanted to be sure of something first, but I'm going to take a chance and figure that you dislike the man as much as your predecessors. And he got rid of them before they could help me."

"Well you wouldn't be too far off on that point," I said, looking around the doorframe to see Fartus shuffling through some papers. He softly hummed "The Girl from Ipanema" to himself,

"I'm not crazy about him," I said. "Shoot."

"Here is the situation. We spoke about the number of concerts he gives—you were kind enough to give me those statistics last time we conversed, along with the names of the composers he uses. I've done some computing, and now I am ready for the second part of the operation. Here is the problem: he has never once paid a cent for royalties."

I let it sink in. Fartus was now assaulting "Somewhere My Love." The humming was so loud that a faux brass lamp on his desk vibrated on certain pitches. I turned my attention back to the problem at hand. It was starting to add up: his penuriousness with regards to every atom in the universe including my paycheck; his obsession with photocopying—all of it.

"So the only problem is that he hasn't paid royalties for using the music?" I asked.

"As far as I know, sir."

"What about copying the music? Is that something that would cost him also?" I asked, trying not to show that I knew the consequences of copyright infringement.

"Oh, definitely. That would be a most heinous thing to do," Poopa cooed into the receiver. We could bring him up on these charges and also force him to pay the royalties, if only . . . well, we need your help."

"What can I do? I just work here as his personal slave," I said. I was now being subjected to "One Touch of Venus," complete with Kaplan's inserted mock-sexual groans at the end of certain phrases.

"We need to have copies of every single program he's performed—ever. And if you could get the receipts from the copying, that would be helpful to us also."

"But don't you need the actual copied pieces of music?" I asked, thinking that it was risky garnering this information for someone I had never met. I wasn't sure I entirely trusted her, and the collecting of the goods could take weeks.

"I'm not sure the actual copies would do that much good," continued Poopa. "You see, unless they've been reduced one percent to show they were copied, we're not always able to use them as evidence."

"Gotcha. Just give me a little time," I said, and took down her address. I wasn't sure whether I would let Fartus have it just yet. It was one thing to dislike someone because of his eccentricities, but another to land him in jail or bankruptcy court. This one would take some soul searching.

Before I hung up, I asked, "About how much money do you figure he owes—I mean, with royalties, fines, copyright infringement, the works?"

Poopa paused and thought. I could hear her doing some additional calculations in the background. "I'd say . . . from the records I have estimating his wrongdoings . . . about two hundred thousand dollars, provided that most of the composers and publishing companies prosecute him."

I started to respond, but at that moment Fartus called me into his office. "I have to go now. I'll get back to you," I said to Poopa, and hung up.

"Have a seat, Max," Fartus said as he indicated a second-hand office chair probably made around 1940. I eased onto the cold dark green cracked vinyl, hoping he hadn't heard any of my conversation with Poopa. I waited nervously for a sign but none came.

Then Mr. F began to bellow pompously, as if giving a speech at some political rally. "Dear Mr. Brachaeus . . . Barely Broadway, New York's foremost performing group, would like to invite you and the Kensington Spastic Society to sponsor the latest in a series of—"

I looked around. Fartus was speaking into space, his arms crossed; he was leaning back in his chair. His voice was ostentatious and authoritative.

"Excuse me?" I managed, cutting him off. He came out of his reverie, leaning slightly forward.

"Take a letter, take a letter! I want you to take a letter, Max. Why are you just sitting there?" His eyes were beginning to glow again. I chalked his bad mood up to the gardenia and tried to hold my temper.

"But . . . why didn't you say that to start with? And you know I don't take dictation—we discussed that in the interview. You can't just start spouting off—"

"TAKE A LETTER! WHAT ARE YOU DOING? WHERE'S THE STENO PAD? TAKE A LETTER! YOU'RE WASTING PRECIOUS TIME!

117

JESUS CHRIST!" he exploded, his eyes bulging. He flung his hands in the air and proceeded to rant wildly, shaking his head so violently that I thought it would come off. I sat back, stunned. Finally, he caught his breath and waited. "Well?" he asked, his eyebrows a good three feet higher than normal.

"Yes, Mr. Fartus," I answered, completely shaken by this latest tirade. It had come from nowhere considering his forays into popular song while I conferred with Poopa. One minute it was "I'm Just a Girl Who Can't Say No" and the next it was his best Tasmanian devil impersonation. This was, even for him, getting to be excessive. I got up and came back with a yellow legal pad and sat down, the whole time thinking that I needed this job so that I could get another apartment and be free of roommates who ate baby food; roommates whose parents had named them Spong. Already I was planning to move. The tub was doing a number on my lumbar region.

As soon as I sat down again I noticed that Fartus had his head in his hands. He spoke through his fingers, addressing the blotter in front of him, teeth clenched, anger seething from every pore. "Not a yellow legal pad, you *fool!* I . . . want . . . a . . . steno pad! STENO PAD! STENO PAD! STENO PAD!" and with these last words he leapt into the air and began beating on the top of his desk.

I didn't know what to say or do. I jumped up as fast as I could and ran to find the coveted steno pad. Then we proceeded to move ahead with his letter dictation. But given the fact that I didn't know shorthand, and that the steno pad was minuscule, a letter that would have normally taken two pages now took me twenty.

"The festival of Broadway will present," he continued dictating, as if nothing had happened, back to a calm and semi-euphoric tone, "a series of concerts throughout the New York area, celebrating the music of—"

"I'm sorry, was that 'series of concerts?' " I cut in, as my writing was slow.

"Keep up, keep up, Max!" he yelled

"Yes, Mr. Fartus," I said sheepishly, thinking of the agonizing hours left in the day. And then the other thought that kept rolling around inside my head, the one that seemed to make everything all right was, "Two hundred thousand dollars. The man owes two hundred thousand dollars."

22

A recent survey concluded that people are more aware of their nasal mucous than previously thought. Even though the planet blankets itself with wars, serial killers, floods, famine, and Republicans, it seems that everyone is still very much focused on their nose goblins. I know this because of a recent poll taken on the subject. Out of a hundred men and women (ages twenty to forty-five, lest the reader think this is some sort of child's play), thirteen actually admitted to picking their nose and wiping the substance on some inanimate object—say, a chair, or under a table.

More disturbing was the fact that four of the individuals in the survey admitted to wiping the procured mucous on a *person*—while said person wasn't looking, of course.

A whopping thirty people admitted to rolling their harvest into a small ball, over and over, until the thing no longer stuck to their fingers. They would then flick it in some direction. Northeasterly was most preferred. No explanation for that compass direction was given.

Twenty-three admitted that they were partial to wiping their nose bounty on a wall rather than on some object, and an amazing fourteen admitted to holding their finger out the window of a moving car after excavating the offending bit of produce, allowing the wind to take the object away.

Nine said they wiped their secretions on their clothing, four said they actually *had* no mucous, and a comforting zero said they didn't own a "fruit of the proboscis" collection and therefore could not claim to donate to that organization on a regular basis. At least those making this last statement didn't check that particular box off so we're assuming they don't reap what their nose sows.

Folks, this leaves only three people—we are still left with these three who did not respond. Given all the bases covered in the poll—the fact that almost no nose was left unpicked—the mind reels at the possibilities. Was it that the remaining three simply forgot to respond? Or were they hiding something—some deep, dark secret that was too monstrous to share with even understanding people such as ourselves—those of us who do not gather our own snout secretions on a regular basis for fun or profit. Or could it be that they actually used something as exotic as a tissue in time of need? Or that they simply weren't cognizant of their own miniature nose-flags and went about their everyday routines with joy and glee? Kids, don't try this at home.

If these one hundred people are a good cross section of the country, I fear that we have larger problems than wars and politics. For the sake of argument, let's say that there are a total of seven people out of a hundred who don't play with their face gifts. Seven. Not a big number, and we're giving three of them the benefit of the doubt. We're actually believing those four who claim they can't give because they're nasally bankrupt. So now, think about it: If you try, you can come up with one hundred people that you know. I don't mean just friends, but people in your everyday lives: the dry cleaning man, your accountant, neighbors, relatives, door-to-door salesmen, the five people you went camping with, school chums—even the guy that sold you your latest mattress. Stay with it—you *can* come up with a hundred.

Now, keep up with me—this is not rocket science. Out of all those people you know, only seven do not admit to contributing to the beak fairy in some way or another. Seven, I repeat, seven. And we're assuming that you are one of these seven. That leaves thirty that say they roll and flick. Look around you the next time you're in a crowded movie theatre. More than thirty people there, if the film's not a complete bomb. And even if they don't pass the recently garnered object right then via airmail, well, a movie is two hours long—you do the math.

Now, think about driving down the highway. Passed a hundred cars yet? Probably. And what number did we come up with for people who hang it out the window? Fourteen, if memory serves. An investment in window-washer fluid and a good set of wipers might not hurt. And you were worried about gravel trucks.

While I won't bore you with all the possibilities and permutations of the poll, how many people you know, etc., let's imagine that the group of people (four, according to our survey) who prefer to wipe their honker baubles directly on *you,* are within arm's reach. Comforting, isn't it?

Just think, you're in a room of one hundred people. Let's say it's a wedding reception, a funeral, a high school reunion—Grand Central at rush hour. Out of those one hundred people, at least four are going to try and attach some former part of themselves onto another person. This is one sweepstakes you *don't* want to win.

Now I know what you're saying: "Why me? Couldn't they just as easily wipe the offending present on someone else? What if I kept moving? What if I watch people's hands?" And all I have to say is, give it up. It's bound to happen sometime, and besides, at least you'll know where their stray bit of body secretion is.

So the next time you start to reach for your schnozzolla, just remember: be creative. Don't become one of those people who garner their first-grade candy and then flicks, wipes, or rolls it into oblivion. Give the thing some thought first; be the exception to the rule; think outside the box; find the new paradigm; and for God's sake . . . use a tissue.

There was silence. Reeda sat with the paper in her hand, scanning the page, one finger to her lips. Her eyes cut back and forth, then she reached down and began playing with one of the cats that had approached.

"That's a nice kitty," she cooed to the animal, using baby talk, "yes-um *is*, yes-um *is*." A pause, and then, "Yes-um *is*, yes-um truly *is* . . . oh, yes-um truly—"

"Excuse me," I said, trying to control my irritation, "I don't mean to be rude, but I *am* paying one hundred and fifty dollars an hour and I'd like to know how I did on the assignment."

"Um *is* a truly nice kitty," she continued, having heard me perfectly but choosing instead to participate in the control game. She looked at the paper again and made some "Hmmms" and "ummmms" before glancing up at me with a big fake smile.

"Not good," she said, clipped and to the point. "I asked for an essay on boogers and you haven't even used the word once in the piece. If we're going to work together then I must have complete control over your writing. You must do exactly as I say." She rose up slightly in the chair and thrust her right hand out, palm toward me as she turned away in mock disgust. "Forget everything you've ever learned. We're starting all over. This may take years," she continued and then began reaching for her ledger and calculator. "Let's see, my estimation is that it will take twenty, no, fifty more sessions than previously expected at" (and at this point she began to calculate—clickty-clickty-click-click-whirrrrrrr-bramp-bramp-bramp—it was an adding machine—in order to determine exactly how much a summer share in the Hamptons would cost), "two hundred dollars a session is . . . with the added . . . and then . . ."

"Two hundred!" I said. "I thought I was paying you one fifty?"

"My rates are going up next month. I have so many students that I need to weed some out and this seems the only way. And what I hear you telling me is that you don't want your writing to get better. I hear you saying that money is more important to you than art."

I looked around the room, attempting to diffuse my rising anger with anything that would take my mind from it. Two large hamsters rolled across a nearby tabletop, attempting to mate. A mourning dove cooed gently underneath a rickety chair in the corner. Occasionally the completely featherless African Gray parrot would screech some obscenity. "Eat me!" it exclaimed, gingerly picking up its feet to walk sideways on his perch while I sat in thought.

"Now back to the business at hand, if you're over your momentary bout of cheapness," Reeda continued. "The story, the essay, is all wrong. What we want are facts. Here, let me show you," and with that she got up and moved to a large writing tablet like the ones used in conferences at large corporations—flimsy metal stand, large flip-over pages, multi-colored markers. She shooed off a motley parakeet and began to scrawl.

"You make a chart, *comme ça,*" she said, drawing numbers down the side. "Then you fill in . . ." and she began to write, all the while speaking out loud. "Line one—people that pick their boogers and roll . . . fifty-five; Line two—people that flick them . . . twenty . . . seven."

"Is it in yet?" the parrot exclaimed, and then let out a perfect replica of a human belch. "You're so big!" it then announced—a completely different voice this time. Reeda was oblivious.

"But that's not an essay, that's a chart," I said. "You asked me to write an essay and I did the best I could without trying to be offensive, if that's even possible with the subject that you gave me. And the numbers are wrong," I continued, fending off the same low-flying parakeet that had been perched on top of the writing tablet. It swooped toward a corn plant and then landed with a thud against the only window in the apartment. The stunned bird slid to the floor, managing a meager "ki-chirp," before flopping around at the base of the plant.

"Stoo-pee-da bitch," the naked parrot muttered with an Italian basso buffo accent, and then with out-of-the-blue gusto, back to the Sweet Polly Purebred imitation, "*Fuck* me big boy!"

"I'm here to help you. Do you want help? Because that's what I do. I write essays for a living," Reeda continued, still completely oblivious to Polly's antics. "I'm an *essayist*. You've got to exaggerate things. Make them stand out. Nobody cares if only, say, ten people roll and five people wipe."

"I guess," I said meekly, thinking that I must need a lot of help, what with all the rejections I had received over the years dealing with my work. About this time the one dog that Reeda owned came wheeling over to the chair I was sitting in and leaned up against it. I noticed that there was only about one square inch of fur left on the creature. The animal appeared to be older than the universe itself.

"That dog belong to Methuselah?" I asked, hoping to bring some levity to what was becoming a bad experience.

"That's *Dog*," Reeda replied, obviously irritated at being taken away from her deep thoughts on how my essay should have been written. "*Dog* is his *name*." The summer share, it seemed, would cost more than expected. The minutes were ticking by.

Then, just at that moment, "*Dog*" let loose one of the most horrendous-smelling pieces of sphincter gas known to the world, for it rose up and engulfed the entire room in a matter of minutes. Lucky me, I was at ground zero anal epicenter when it happened. I waited for the wallpaper to peel itself from the walls while four of the more exotic birds appeared to drop dead and fall from their perches. At the door, two of the cats meowed and pawed, begging to be allowed to escape. A solitary ferret began hacking in its cage, and Percy the iguana (I noticed now that he had only three legs) scampered—unevenly—under a chest of drawers. Even the naked parrot was quiet this time, so horrified was it by the smell.

"Does he do that often?" I asked Reeda, nodding toward the dog.

"Do what?" was her wide-eyed response. Reeda, it seemed, had no sense of smell.

23

When Kaplan Fartus wasn't abusing me verbally, he participated in two rather strange habits: he would either lock himself in his office with a roll of paper towels for over an hour at lunch, or he would journey out for a few minutes and then return with some sleazy-looking blond who was wearing hot pants, knee-length boots, and a short rabbit fur jacket. It was always a different woman but the same outfit. I imagined them changing under the West Side Highway, chattering in thick Long Island accents: "And don't get gum on the fur again, Shelly. Gino says he'll take it out of your be-hind next time. Ah-hhhhhhaaaa."

If Fartus did go out and return with a happy hooker, he and his lady friend would giggle and coo the allotted amount of time in the sanctity of his office, and the paper towels would remain intact. Either way, these escapades took exactly one hour—no more, no less. Fartus was, above all, punctilious.

The fact that he had a wife and kids didn't seem to matter. As with most people in business, ethics was not his strong point. Oh, I was sure he didn't want his family to know, but he made only a meager attempt to hide the truth from me. A very meager attempt.

"Max, this is Trixie," he would announce, coming down the long hallway that led from the front door of the office to my desk. "She's a musician . . . yes, yes, that's right, a *musician*, and she's going to . . . uh . . . audition for me now. You know how we're always needing new musicians, don't you?"

While the same woman never appeared twice, they all somehow resembled each other. More than one offered an over-manicured, too-long-finger-nailed-hand in my direction, as if she thought I would touch my lips to it, while she chimed some platitude direct from a 1930s movie. "Charmed, I'm shoo-uh," was not unusual. After that Kaplan would escort her into his office. There wasn't much for me to do with this information right now, but I filed it away for future use, knowing that Fartus's wife stopped by the office occasionally.

One day, while K.F. was amusing himself with his paper towel collection instead of Miss Cheap Trick 1990, I decided to thwart the boredom that was raising its ugly head. I still had a stack of the fund-raising letters to send out, but before I did, an ingenious plan came to mind. When I told Robert about the eccentric leanings of Fartus, he seemed more than slightly amused. I had also told him about the endless fund-raising letters, the dictation sessions, the pomposity of the man—just about everything. So I thought it would be fun to rewrite one of the company's letters with a new twist and send it to Mr. Stud-You-Like. Just one letter, and sent only to someone who would appreciate it. I began composing the masterpiece and thought it would be amusing if I included an actual name and real address of a high-profile company that existed. You know, such as the National Endowment for the Arts, American Express, or even some high-up individual in politics—that kind of thing, just to make it look more real. And so I did. Here is what it said:

Dear Mr.—

Barely Broadway, New York's most putrid and disgusting company (if you can call it that), would like to invite you and the Male Prostitution Society to sponsor Bad Broadway Reproductions at the newly landscaped Staten Island garbage dump.

The concerts will again present a major series of six hundred and thirty-three thousand utterly worthless shows, celebrating the music of a number of outstanding Serbo-Croatian and Icelandic composers, with solos, ensembles, and a ménage-a-trois from their absolutely worst and most turdish musicals.

Sponsors of last year's shows included . . . let's see . . . I don't think anyone was actually stupid enough to sponsor this piece of yak feces last year, but no matter—that's no reason for you not to.

Based on the absolute "bomb" we had last year (and we're talking hydrogen—kaboom), several of our potential sponsors have already moved and left no forwarding address.

A pity.

The shows will include the following productions:

The Best of Achmed Ashbamvngpznbdnthrzkf and his American-hating taxi company (Arabic musical theatre at its best, containing the new hit, "I'd Like to Buy a Vowel.")

Please Go Fuck a Cactus (Western medley)

Songs My Mother Sang in Her Whorehouse While Screwing the Club-Footed Goat Boy (the torch song series)

The "Go to Hell Review," complete with Satan himself (a devil of a good time)

A Good Old-Fashioned Case of Herpes (a musical look back at friendlier STDs)

Mr. Fartus Himself and the Tiny Pencil-Dick Players

These shows, offered free (You kidding? Who would pay for this stuff?), are sure to be jam-packed with nerdy turgid louts that wear polyester, smell bad, have anal warts, and possess no dental plan at work.

Each concert will run two hours too long, but that's your problem, now isn't it? What we want here is money. I'm talking chips, moulah, green ones. Just to prod you along on this journey, here's a sampling of the reviews that our Mickey Mouse organization has received over the, oh, let's see, past several years.

The *New York Dimes* describes Barely Broadway as . . . "One of the most putrid and unprofessional 'high-school-like' productions ever to appear in this universe or anywhere in the solar system. Halfway through their performance I tried to kill myself by taking an overdose of sleeping pills, but the production was so bad that I threw them up. The *Dimes* is currently suing for mental anguish and loss of valuable prescription drugs. Avoid this joke of a show at all costs."

There are no good reasons why someone like you should care about an organization (if you can call it that) such as ours, but we'd like forty million dollars by next Thursday. Thank you.

Looking forward to having you mount me in a donkey suit in the near future.

Sincerely,

Mr. Kaplan Fartus (Head dingbat for this joke shop called a business)

Just as I finished the letter, Mr. F called me into his office. I slipped the fake letter between two other letters and went to see what he wanted (the contents of the waste paper basket needed counting again). When I returned to my desk I finished preparing the remaining letters, stuffing the envelopes, placing the stamps just so (Kaplan was a stickler for detail), and finally dropping them in the mailbox. I slipped Robert's letter into an envelope, having no time left to look it over for typos, and went home.

Several days later, Robert called to ask why I had sent him a letter on Barely Broadway stationary, asking for money, and why the letter had someone else's name, company, and address on it.

"I thought you'd get a kick out of it," I said, "knowing what I've gone through with the man."

"Why would I get a kick out of something like this?" he asked.

"You know, Achmed and his American-hating taxi company, go fuck a cactus, the bad *Dimes* review."

"What the hell are you talking about?" Robert asked, and then it began to sink in. I felt a knot in my stomach.

"Read me the last line of the letter," I said to him, "the one right before 'Sincerely'. Does it say, 'Looking forward to having you mount me in a donkey suit?' "

"No, it says, 'Looking forward to speaking with you in the near future,' " Robert said, and therein followed an uncomfortable silence on my end.

Somewhere, someone—some legitimate company—had received the letter intended for Robert, and Barley Broadway's name, address, and phone number were right there on the letterhead, just waiting to be contacted.

24

Each day when the phone rang, I held my breath. "Good morning, Barely Broadway productions, Kaplan Fartus founder and director since 1963, this is Max Perkins speaking, how may I be of help to you on this lovely day?" I would say into the receiver, praying to God that no one asked when they could be mounted by Fartus wearing the donkey suit. Out of all the letters sent, I had no idea which envelope it had landed in. All I could hope was that the person receiving it didn't read it. After all, what fund-raisers actually read their mail? Judging by the meager amount of calls that Fartus received, not too many were jumping up and down to give him money. My plan was to hold on just a little longer until Robert could secure what he politely termed "my next place of employment." After a heartfelt outpouring one evening at his and Marcel's apartment, they had both agreed that anything was better than having to endure the many eccentricities of K.F.

Marcel had agreed to allow me to work for his cleaning service until a more permanent place of torture could be found. But not wanting to waste time, I sent my résumé out everywhere I could think of. The few responses that did come back sounded strangely similar to the rejection letters I had received from agents and publishers. "Thank you for considering us, but at this time we have nothing that fits your work experience." Who would?

The plan was this: I would continue working for Fartus, and in my evenings I would show up at Marcel's company and train to become a professional clean-up man.

I tried not to feel dejected my first day of instruction as my fellow cleaners showed me how to get into the special contamination suit. Marcel's company was really nothing more than a garage on the West Side Highway, near the Village and Chelsea. The nearest subway was blocks away and it was necessary to traverse the fat-and blood-soaked streets of the meatpacking district in order to get to the training seminars. After two weeks of intense instruction on how to remove a corpse from an apartment, what not to touch with regards to evidence of a crime, and what chemicals best cleaned up blood and body fluids (evidently it was necessary for one to become certified in these things), I decided to force the situation at Barely Broadway. And it was not a moment too soon.

"Oh, nooooooo. No, no, nooooooooo." It was Fartus uncomfortably convulsing as he opened the mail. "How could this have happened? This is a disaster! I'm ruined. Everything is gone. What am I going to do?" He stewed in his office, tearing at the few strands of white hair on his head. I waited, imagining someone had taken him up on his offer for the quadruped outfit with anatomical addition. Then he came out of his office toward my desk, his face red and bloated. I expected the worst.

"I'm afraid I've got some bad news," he started in.

"Boy," I thought, "you're not kidding if you got the response to that letter that I think you did." But I said nothing.

"Barley Broadway owes several hundred thousand dollars in royalties ... and they say that I'm accused of copyright infringement," he continued, staring at the letter. "I don't know how this could have happened. I don't understand. I was so careful."

"You never paid royalties on the music you used for the shows?" I asked, knowing full well what had happened. I thought about the late nights there; him gone, me getting copies for Poopa and ASCAP; how it had felt to hand deliver them to the Indian princess herself.

He turned suddenly pompous; indignant; self-righteous: "I shouldn't have to pay royalties or worry about copyrights! Who cares if the composers and lyricists get their share—it's hard enough for me to make ends meet as it is."

I thought about this last statement. In addition to all my other duties, I kept the books for the company and Fartus conveniently paid himself over a hundred thousand dollars a year while my pay was somewhere below the poverty line. The people with food stamps in my neighborhood bodega were better fed than I was.

A few days later he called me into his office and announced that he'd have to let me go as there was no more money; that he might have to close up shop for good. It was agreed that I would be given two weeks to find a new job. Fartus was most apologetic and on some level I felt sorry for him, but I hadn't decided to totally forgive him for all the abuse he had heaped on me.

The next day I could tell he was preparing for one of his trips to find a new accompanist to play his . . . (ahem) . . . organ. Probably the stress of having to give up his salary set off some raging hormones in his antiquated body. Sure enough, like clockwork, he left the office at exactly twelve. By some miracle of God he didn't run into his wife who appeared at our workplace no more than two minutes later. They must have taken separate elevators in the lobby so close was the timing. I couldn't believe my good luck.

"I know I'm late, but I thought I'd catch Kaplan before he left and we could go get some lunch," she offered as she walked down the long hallway from the front door to where my desk was. "I guess I should have called first, but I was in the neighborhood and thought I'd just pop in."

"You just missed him," I said, trying to think on my feet. "He's coming back in a minute. Said he hoped you would stop by— must be one of those ESP things—that if you did, you were to wait for him in his office," I continued, gently escorting her past my desk and into K. F.'s cavernous space. "And you'll be nice and comfortable in here," I added. "I've already picked the lint off the chairs and brushed the carpet."

"You know, I have to do the same at home," she said and gave a little shrug and smile.

"I bet you do," I thought. "You just make yourself comfortable and he'll be here in a minute," I said.

I went back to my desk to wait it out. From where I was sitting I had a clear view of the front door to the office. It was a good thirty feet of narrow hallway that emptied into the area I sat in.

133

If I looked the other way, I had a clear view of Kaplan's desk—the very one his wife was sitting at.

About ten minutes later the door opened and there was Mr. F and his new plaything. This one was really done up—enormous fake black wig, fishnet stockings, bright red lipstick that had been applied with a spatula, and to top off the whole thing, an eye patch, no less. I couldn't have asked for anything better.

"Geezy peezy," the hooker ejaculated, pulling her fake fur closer, jerking slightly away from Kaplan, "where's yous takin' me anyways?" and with that the two of them flounced toward my desk. Just as they got to the corner of it, at the point of no return and only a few inches away from being visible to the woman waiting on lint-free office furniture, I chimed in, using my cheeriest voice—loud enough for everyone involved to hear.

"Your wife is waiting for you, Mr. F."

Mrs. Fartus looked up, the hooker looked sideways, and Mr. Fartus looked embarrassed. Time stood still for a brief moment and I basked in all my glory. Then . . . kaboom!

25

"Today we're going to work on rewriting your novel. I've gone over the manuscript again, and by the way, I'm going to have to charge you another three hundred dollars since it was longer than I expected. But don't worry; you can work it off somehow. Now let's begin with—"

"Three hundred dollars!" I said. "What are you, nuts? First you give me one rate and then tell me it's going up, and now you tell me you're going to charge even more because you underestimated the length of my book, when all along you knew—" but I stopped when I saw her expression. It lasted for a good three minutes. Even the animals were quiet, having seen the one raised eyebrow, the frown, the complete stillness. The reek of bad karma was everywhere.

"What did we say about trust?" Reeda finally asked. The sarcasm and condescension meters were going off their scales. She was seething.

"*We* didn't say anything about trust. *You* said something about trust."

"So, are you saying you don't trust me? Is that what you're saying? Because I've got a waiting list for students—students who *want* to work on their writing skills with me. So let's start over, if you please." Then she flipped through the binder containing my book—the one I so desperately hoped she would help me get published.

"As I told you in the beginning, I'm perfectly willing to act as your agent and get you a publisher, but first we're going to have to work on this manuscript. Ordinarily, acting as your agent, it wouldn't be ethical for me to charge you anything until the book is sold. Then, at that point I would get a cut. But before I can even represent you, we have to clean the manuscript, polish it, bring it up to the next level. And for this I need complete control. If I ask for additional money it's only because I'm thinking of you and your needs with regards to getting published. After all, it's *your* book, not mine." She waited. "So can we cut the attitude? Yes, Mister Needs-Help-Getting-Published?"

I glared at her. "Okay," I finally said. "But you never mentioned acting as my agent. You said you would *get* me an agent." She ignored me.

"Now, first of all, I want you to read aloud the beginning of your book. I want you to see how it sounds—what's wrong with it. Now, start."

I felt as if I were in the third grade again, but something kept nagging at me, and it was this: This is New York. Everyone here knows more than me. I need help getting published. No pain, no gain, and myriad other expressions and excuses. That, plus the fact that I wanted to believe her. I wanted to believe anyone and everyone but myself, so why not start with her? I swallowed hard and began to read—the opening of *Mrs. Squigglemire's Bustle*:

It was February 18, 1889, when Mrs. Henrietta Squigglemire sat down on her tufted sofa, causing the music box contained in her bustle to begin playing "God Save the Queen." She immediately stood up, as did everyone else in the salon.

"For Christ's sake, Henry," crowed an older gentleman with an oversized handlebar mustache and brandy snifter, "why can't you wear a normal bustle like every other woman? Why does it have to be that music box contraption?"

"It was a gift from Sir George, Basil, and besides, I want to show my support of the Empire." She sulked toward a melancholy sentry palm, the long train of her velvet skirt trailing after her. The others in the room, Maude Clempirwaggle and her husband, Cedric, along with Basil, kept standing, not sure if Henrietta would alight again and extract from them another show of English nationalism.

"And it seems to me," continued Basil, "that it is most inappropriate for Sir George to be giving a bustle as a gift." By the time Basil had completed the last three words, his pince-nez was pointed down toward the floor and his eyes were looking over the spectacles. Cedric and Maude said nothing, but rather watched the verbal volleys silently, holding drinks in hand.

"Sir George is accustomed to giving bustles as presents, Basil. That's what he *does*," responded Henrietta. Then her sudden outburst from nowhere: "Dagnabbit! Bitch! Hell's bells! . . . Shut up, shut up!" accompanied by a rocking motion and several facial tics. There was a brief pause after her momentary tirade and then she continued as if nothing had happened. "After all, he does own a bustle factory."

Basil spoke: "Still, it seems to me a gesture rather outside the official *mores* of today's society. You will give me that, surely." Cedric and Maude turned now towards Mrs. Squigglemire, awaiting her response. Everyone had conveniently ignored her last outburst of nonsensical drivel. They knew the manifestations of Tourette's Syndrome, having had the illustrious Dr. Georges Gilles de la Tourette over to their home in Paris many times for dinner.

"Oh, Basil," Henrietta said, turning the jardinière that contained the palm around so that the more ample side of the plant was directed toward the center of the room, "must you go on about it so?" Then she touched her nose to one elegant frond—nine consecutive times. Satisfied that the horticultural specimen was now at its best, and her obsessive-compulsive disorder momentarily satisfied, she moved toward a wobbling finial on top of a lamp, intent on assaulting its leaning state. After touching it twenty-seven times (she often multiplied the last number of times she had touched something by three) she proceeded to screw it more firmly into its receptacle.

"Will you be still for one minute!" shouted Basil with such horrible ferocity that everyone including Henrietta hurriedly took a seat on the nearest ottoman and fainting couch. Immediately "God Save the Queen" began to peal from the poor woman's buttocks and the evening's guests popped up— reluctant jack-in-the-box clowns at the mercy of a precocious child.

The palm of Reeda's hand, held high in the air, halted my reading. Then, "Stop, stop, St-ahhhhhhhhhhpppppp! Do you hear it? Do you hear what you just read? Can you see what's wrong with it? Yes? And what's with the Tourette's Syndrome? Who needs that?"

I sat there, not knowing what to say. I wanted to belt out some modern obscenities along the lines of *Mrs. Squigglemire* but held back, managing a shrug.

Reeda offered up her deepest sigh and fake smile. Then she shook her head. "Pity, pity, pity, pity. Poor pity party. Precious poor pity party for Mr. Perkins." Another silence followed and then she began.

"Okay. Look. Here's what we'll do. I will rewrite this first part for you, just so you can see how it's done. That's what I do—I rewrite. I'm a re-writeeeeeer. I'm a novelist and a person who rewrites." She then took the binder out of my hands and began making a series of marks. These were punctuated by "hmmms," and "ummms," and one "not bad." Then she looked up. "Here," she said, handing back the manuscript. "Read now."

"Read what?" I asked, looking at the few scratches on the page.

"There on the left. Start there. That's how it's done."

Here is what she wrote, and what I read:

```
    Scene. Interior: Living room. 1989. Mr.
and Mrs. Smith are engaged in a fight. Things
heat up. An argument ensues. Bob screams at
wife.
```

I looked up after reading, my face one big question mark.

"Yes? Yes? Can you see now how much more clear that is? We've actually got something to work with now. None of this dialogue and description—just the real *meat* of what's happening," and on the word *meat* she made her hand into a claw-like gesture.

I sat still for a moment, not sure if this was some kind of joke. "But what about the bustle?" I asked. "You cut out everything about the bustle?"

"Don't need it. Never did."

"But the entire novel is about the bustle and what happens to it—where it came from, where it ends up, what happens to the lady wearing it. And you changed the date from 1889 to 1989."

"Doesn't matter. The writing is so much better now. Everyone can understand it. Not like what you had before. No one is going to read that thing with all the three-dollar words you've got in there."

"Three-dollar words? Where?" I looked down at the binder. "Can you give me an example of a three-dollar word?" I asked.

She took back the binder, jerked it out of my hand actually, and ran one of her claws over the now scratched-out sentences. "Here. Here's a perfect example," she said. "Melancholy.

138

Melancholy is bad. People can't read words that have more than one syllable. You should avoid any word with more than one syllable."

"You mean like the word syllable?" She didn't respond. I continued: "Melancholy is not a three-dollar word. Perhaps a dollar-fifty-word, but not three dollars. And you took out the names. You changed the lady's name to Smith. What happened to Squigglemire?"

"No one can pronounce it. You would have to put in a pro-nun-see-aaaay-shun chart at the beginning of the book. And then the chart's name would have more than one syllable, so if people tried to pronounce it they would become confused. You have to understand that today's readers are stupid. No multi-syllable words or big names. And a plot is suspect also. The book shouldn't actually be *about* anything. This tends to confuse people. We should also change the title from *Mrs. Squigglemire's Bustle* to *Mrs. Smith's Bottom*. Or better yet, *Smith-Butt*." She waited, a finger to her lips, her eyes squinting; thinking. "We could ... even leave off the last *T . . . Smith-But*."

I tried to ignore her, telling myself that as soon as I got out of her apartment I would take a bath. But while I was there I continued, intent on finding some shred of help.

"And what's with the word *scene*?" I asked. There was an uncomfortable silence.

"Treat the head good," the obscene parrot chortled to a plaster bust of Shakespeare that was sitting in one corner of the room. "Lick under the balls."

"I write scripts. That's what I do. I'm a *script* writer," Reeda replied after taking a sip of tepid coffee that had sat the entire session, untouched. "It's a script technique," she added. "Scene. A house in England. Trees. A young woman—that type of thing. It lets the reader know the information without all that ... those ... *words*. Afterward, when we get the thing in script format, we can take out the word *scene*."

I looked around. "But I'm writing a novel, not a script," I said, trying not to sound defensive. "It would seem to me that part of good writing is creating descriptions, complex sentences, and wording things in such a way as to be interesting—creating poetry."

She smirked. "You're going to have to sell it as a novel *and* a script. Might as well get used to it now."

I didn't know what to say. I wanted to run screaming from the room. I wanted to reach over and strangle her. I wanted to do anything at that point but continue. But I also wanted to be a writer and live in New York, and knowing that I had experienced rejection upon rejection, and knowing that at least there was one person who would sit down with me and discuss what I had done, albeit questionably, I stayed.

"Besides," Reeda continued, reaching down to scratch the ferret that was gnawing on the chair's leg, "you'll have to try and sell it as a script if you want to make any money. You won't get anything for a book, no matter what it's about."

"I thought you said you were a novelist," I offered, looking for an "in" to irritate her, remembering her most recent comment about being a scriptwriter. "What was the name of your novel?" I asked.

"I'm all things to all people. I'm a writer. That's what I do. I write things: scripts, novels, plays, articles. If you want to be successful you'll have to do the same. I haven't actually written my novel down—it's in my head. You don't have to have written a novel to be a novelist."

"You don't?"

"Absolutely not. Look at me. I haven't written one and yet . . . I'm a novelist."

"I guess," I said and sat with my arms folded. "Does that mean I'm a novelist?" I asked.

"Not yet," she said. I tried to follow the logic, but like everything else of any importance in life, it seemed to evade me.

"Suck that cock!" the parrot suddenly intoned, his head turned sideways, his look pointed straight at me while his claws dug into Shakespeare's plaster hair, "Treat the head gooood." Reeda ignored the nude bird and I couldn't help but think that its words had some prophetic meaning.

I planned to attend more sessions with Reeda—I thought I could get something out of it; if nothing else, then fodder for a future book—so I played along. It wasn't so much that I didn't trust her at this point, but rather that I was still feeling things out in New York; trying to get a handle on exactly what she knew and how good she was; see how much she'd read and how in tune she was with the world of publishing and writing—not that the two have anything to do with one another.

Reeda was always drumming into me the rules of writing—as if there actually are any rules—citing examples of what was wrong with the plot and the characters. Publishing houses are notorious for the same thing, always telling authors that the book they've submitted is not the genre they're looking for, when only last month they published three similar books, all of lesser quality than the unpublished one.

So as I sat through this session I decided to try something; an experiment if you will, during my next few meetings. By our next get-together I had what I needed.

In order to test her, I typed out a complete chapter of *Huckleberry Finn*—a chapter from the middle of the book. Then I presented it, along with the statement, "I'm working on something new as you've convinced me that *Mrs. Squigglemire* isn't any good."

"This is a perfect example of what I'm talking about," she started in after skimming Twain's work right in front of me. "You're *telling* the story instead of *showing*. As this stands now, you'd never get it published. Your use of English is deplorable, and the phrase is *African-American*—not *nigger*. And why would anyone want to read about the Mississippi River anyway?"

The next week I tried a chapter from Faulkner's *Light in August*.

"Boy, do *you* need to learn to write!" she said, settling onto the sofa. "You're lucky you came to me. I can really help you with this sort of thing. Do you even know what a sentence is supposed to sound like?"

Truman Capote's *In Cold Blood* was next.

"People don't generally like reading about this sort of thing," she said, her eyebrows up. "You'd be hard-pressed to find a publisher for it but if you agree to work with me for the next year—payment in advance—I should be able to help you whip it into shape. We have to start by taking out all the violence. That never sells." And then she added, "Just how many examples of your bad writing attempts do you have?"

Her response to three complete chapters from Hemingway's *The Old Man and the Sea*, again typed out so as not to look suspicious, garnered the comment, "Didn't you do *anything* interesting at all on your summer vacation?"

In an attempt to see just how far I could push the envelope, I began to send samples of famous books to various publishers, reasoning that they were as inept as Reeda. I attached my name and a different title, just to see how they would react. I knew that the samples would either be ignored, read by some ignorant twenty-year-old whose idea of great literature was the *Peanuts* comic strip, or given the proverbial "shove-off" letter. Strangely enough, I actually got back responses instead of the usual form letters. Perhaps it had something to do with the fact that I lied about having an agent and being wealthy enough to fund my own marketing campaign.

For the first three chapters of Harper Lee's *To Kill a Mockingbird*, which I called *Morning Aubade*, I received the response, "Works like this are generally not publishable and there has never really been a market for this type of thing."

In response to the complete *Nine Short Stories* by Salinger (it took me two weeks to retype them all), I received, "We are not in the habit of printing the work of fifth-graders. May we suggest a writing course at your local junior college?"

And then there was the response to Steinbeck's last three chapters from *The Grapes of Wrath* which I had re-titled *California Dreamin'*. "We suggest you try one of the lesser-known publishing houses for a work of this genre as the market for this type of thing is usually small. Also, you may want to change the ending as the breast-feeding of the hobo is a bit over the top."

One acquisitions editor at a major house even had the intelligence to recognize the name Max Perkins and accuse me of pretending to be someone I wasn't. "I happen to *know* the real Max Perkins," she wrote, "and as soon as I put this letter in the post, I'm calling him up and letting him know that you're using his name." I wanted to wish the acquisitions editor luck as the Max Perkins she was referring to had been dead at that point for forty-three years.

But the best response was given by one of the city's most elite houses, which, after I had sent in the book of Genesis from the Bible—double-spaced and in twelve-point type, just as they had requested—wrote back with the pithy quip, "Dear Mr. Perkins, if you insist on plagiarizing Shakespeare, we suggest you at least give him credit for his 'creation' somewhere along the way."

So it was confirmed: No one in publishing knew anything. I decided to carry my plan even further at that point, intent on covering all who wrote, read, or pretended to.

At one point, in order to test the waters and see just how many burgeoning and desperate writers there were in the world willing to do whatever it took to get their work published, I put a notice in *The Village Voice* and in some other New York papers:

> Help! Editor has lost the only copy of client's manuscript—*Mrs. Squigglemire's Bustle.* Accidentally left on the first bench just inside the Forty-Second Street entrance of Grand Central Terminal yesterday at three o'clock. Printed on yellow paper and has a small drawing of a cross-eyed sheep in the corner of first page. No reward offered, but please return as I will lose my job if work is not found! Have not read it yet!

I included my address and instructed the papers to run the ad in the most microscopic type they possessed. Even with a magnifying glass the text looked like nothing more than a blur when it came out.

I arrived home a few days after placing the ad to find a cavalry of mail trucks delivering over three thousand encyclopedia-sized packages, each containing a different manuscript and professing to be the lost book. Regardless of the content of these literary Trojan horses, all were titled *Mrs. Squigglemire's Bustle* and printed on yellow paper. The drawing of the sheep varied from copy to copy, the most interesting of which sported a plumed hat and abnormally large genitals. It took well over a week to feed every dumpster in Brooklyn these attempts at literature, and the follow-up letters alone could have filled Yankee stadium. In the end it confirmed my worst fear: I was just one of many—an *E Pluribus*

Unum of wannabes with no hope of ever seeing my book through the Fifth Avenue plate glass windows of a major book store.

26

My internship at Marcel's cleanup company was short-lived. The first day on the job was a disaster and I took it as a foreshadowing of things to come. I was now free from Kaplan Fartus, but the phrase "Out of the frying pan and into the fire," doesn't even begin to cover what happened.

Witness for the defense: My name is Marcel Smith, I live on Thirteenth Street in New York City. I own a Bio-cleanup company-- Bye-Bye Bio-hazard. The company is designed to abate, disinfect, deodorize, and do general cleanup of biohazard areas involving, but not limited to, accidents, homicides, suicides, natural deaths, and decomposition. Max Perkins came to work for me after a two-week training period. He seemed bright, energetic; intelligent enough to do the job. It wasn't his fault, really. It wouldn't have been a pleasant situation for anyone--even a seasoned cleanup person. We had been called to the scene of a homicide in Queens. Two-bedroom apartment; overpowering smell. The whole place was done in the Art Deco style with posters of Danny Kaye all over the walls. We could tell this was going to be a nasty one.

But that wasn't too unusual; it wasn't too out of the ordinary for us. And well, Max, wanting to show initiative, walked right into the bathroom where the body was. Most people don't understand how intense this business can be. They don't know what they're getting themselves into until they actually see what we do. By then it's too late. Problem was this: the corpse had been there for days and the gasses had built up inside the body. As soon as Perkins got close to it, the whole thing exploded. Intestines, eyeballs, last month's lunch . . . everywhere; all over. Max just stood there in shock, that is, until a piece of the guy's colon (which had stuck to the overhead Deco light fixture) came plopping down on his head. Timing. I'll tell you. Lucky for him the protective hood was still in place. Guess he just lost it after that. No more questions? Would you like the phone book back now? I don't think the next person is going to need it to sit on.

27

Montgomery Clift and I were spending a great deal of time together in late February of 1990. Our visitations consisted mainly of me complaining (sorry, Monty), and him listening. At least I think he was listening. I couldn't be too sure since he had been dead for several decades. The incident with the light fixture and colon attachment had exacted their toll. I wasn't feeling well and had started spending quite a bit of time in the Quaker Cemetery in Prospect Park, Brooklyn, just up the subway line from where I was living with Mr. Condescension himself— Spong. Roomie had now initiated me into not only his morning breakfast ritual, but had seen fit to add an even earlier one as well. Monty was getting an earful.

It was always the same with Spong: Sometime around three o'clock in the morning—every morning—I would be awakened by the sound of talking. Squinting myself awake I would see him perched on top of three beanbag chairs, staring into the tub while citing a litany of the various ways in which he planned to kill himself. Between ruminations on the merits of death by carbon monoxide asphyxiation or hanging, he would manage to scoop a spoonful of baby food—puréed carrots mostly—and slurp himself into further depression.

"Why don't you just take an overdose of Valium?" I offered one morning as the first rays of light began to peep through the window. It was still well before seven o'clock so I had time to escape before breakfast.

"Have to take too many," he responded in a dreamy voice. "Takes too long."

"Well, if you start hoarding now, I'm sure you'll have enough by this weekend."

Nothing I did would convince him to stop the nocturnal ramblings and baby food fests, and just as I was getting used to his routine, he upped the stakes by climbing into the tub with me one night (with a newly procured jar of creamed asparagus), and proceeded to tell me his life's story. I decided then and there that I would start my apartment search all over again. Spong's moods vacillated between nocturnal depression and midday hate fests, and despite what I knew about the rest of New York I wanted something—anything—but Spong as a roomie. After all, only three hours of sleep a night was taking its toll and I had to save all of my energy to look for a new job. Ah, the never-ending spiral of life.

The Saturday after Spong's latest apricot diatribe I made my way once again to Prospect Park to ask Monty what to do. He rarely had good advice, but listened well, so I gave it a shot. The trees silhouetted themselves against the gray winter sky and there was no snow on the ground, but the air was crisp and stinging.

"He eats baby food," I said to the tombstone, pulling my jacket tighter around my waist. "And he wakes me up every night with stories about his childhood and how he's going to kill himself and who he's in love with and blah, blah, blah. It's too much, really."

Monty didn't respond, but just as I finished, I heard another voice from somewhere behind me.

"He's not going to be that much help, guy, after all, he ran himself into a tree." I turned around to see Robert. "I followed you—been yelling after you ever since you got off the train. You come here a lot? To talk to dead people, I mean?"

"Things are not good lately."

"Are they ever? What now?"

"Roommates again. Look, I know I can't stay with you and Marcel, even for a night or two, but I've got to find a new place to live. And the commute from Brooklyn into Manhattan isn't exactly quality train time either."

"Wouldn't you miss Monty?"

"To tell you the truth, he's not very good company."

"Listen," Robert said, as he put his arm around my shoulder, "I've got a friend who knows someone who runs a roommate service. Maybe he can set you up with something.

"If you had this 'friend' why didn't you tell me about him before?" I asked as we traversed the rocky brambles of the park, out of the cemetery.

"Just met him the other day."

"So, he's a close personal friend, huh? Who *don't* you know?"

Robert didn't say anything for a moment. We stood watching a group of Haitians play rugby in a clearing some yards away, all of them wearing ski parkas and sweat pants. He squinted as he held his hand up over his eyes even though the sun had yet to break through the clouds. "Do you *want* a place to live?" he asked, never turning to look at me.

A week later:

"Dude, you've got to get it together," Robert was saying as we walked down Seventh Avenue. It was eight o'clock at night; a Saturday. "I can help you out with this next hunt for stability, but after that I'm finished with the job situation and apartment search. I've got clients to service, places to go, people to do."

"I know. I really appreciate everything you've done, it's just that, well . . . I didn't know things were going to be this hard. I mean, with a living situation, a job, trying to get published, Reeda, Percy, the naked parrot—everything. I'm losing it. I just need a decent life—I'm not asking for anything too cushy—just a decent place to live. Is that too much?"

"In New York? Yes."

"Seriously."

"Okay. I'll see what I can do."

People jostled us as we wove our way downtown toward the Village. We walked on in silence for a few more moments and then I turned to Robert.

"Was that a woman with a beard walking hand-in-hand with a three-hundred-pound man wearing a tutu?" I asked. Robert smirked and shook his head.

"Yes, it was," he said. "But what's even more disturbing was that we saw them a good twenty minutes ago and you just now noticed. Guess you're a little preoccupied with things," and with that he turned down a side street, waving good-bye.

While I waited for Robert to come through with a new job and apartment I forced myself to think creatively. Nothing was said to Spong about my job loss or a prospective move, and having just paid that month's rent I at least had somewhere to sleep at night. But I was beginning to see how things worked in the city. I had often heard that places like New York were full of corruption, vice, and a lack of morals. What I didn't realize was that it simply wasn't possible to make it in such a place and be an honest, hard-working, upright individual. At least not without some serious connections, a major inheritance, or a penchant for lying.

If things were going to turn around for me I was going to have to change, and in a big way. And what better way to start than by becoming someone else—lying about who I really was? I might still need Robert's help, but in the meantime I was going to help myself. I had been honest up until this point—honest about previous salaries, where I'd worked, what I had expected. Why not make things up? Why not stretch the truth? What's the worst that would happen? I wouldn't get the job? Hell, I wasn't getting the ones I wanted anyway.

That day I picked up the mail as usual. The customary fare was there, crammed into the too-small brass mailbox located in the lobby of the building. There were several magazines for Spong, the phone bill, a plethora of junk mail, and two more rejection letters for me. The privileges of forwarded mail. Then I looked closer. One of the letters was indeed a rejection from a company I had sent my résumé to, but the other belonged to Spong and I had opened it by mistake. And it wasn't a rejection.

Dear Mr. Flagelatte,

Accountants Today magazine would like to request your presence at a focus group. We are asking twelve accountants to attend the function on March 5, 1990, at 7:00 in the evening. Refreshments will be served and you will be invited to participate in a panel discussion regarding what you like and don't like about our publication.

Please R.S.V.P. by February 20th in order to reserve your place. Participation is on a first come, first served basis, and we are offering seventy-five dollars to the first twelve accountants who respond.

The letter was signed and there was a 1-800 number to call. I shuffled it back into the envelope and walked into the apartment, intent on distributing Spong's mail. But something stopped me when I got to his closet. It was probably a combination of things—his rudeness toward me, the fact that I needed the money, my assumption that he wouldn't miss the letter, his general lack of resemblance to a human being—but for whatever reason I didn't put the envelope on his pile of belongings as I normally would have. Instead I kept it. My recent revelation about how I would have to lie to get ahead was feeding off this recent find. It was as if someone had heard my plea and decided to help. Who was I to argue?

"Hello?" I said, as the receptionist on the other end of the line picked up. "I'd like to reply to your offer for the seventy-five . . . I mean, for the accountants who want to be a part of your panel discussion."

I waited.

"Yes, yes, that's correct. Yes. My name?" I said, thinking that I would call Robert later and ask him to cancel the appointment with his friend at the roommate service, "My name is Spong Flagelatte."

Part III

Most people are other people. Their thoughts are someone else's opinions, their lives a mimicry, their passions a quotation.

— Oscar Wilde

28

"You're not getting to the heart of the thing. You're not letting me see your pain, your emotions. The writing is just plain; empty, without drama." I sat listening to the comments, trying to take them in and understand. I had endured several sessions with Reeda and wasn't sure where this whole escapade was going. I was still laboring under the delusion that something could be gained from my hour spent with her each week. After all, she did know agents and publishers. I had pretty much determined that she was illiterate but then, if I threw out everyone who worked in the publishing industry who didn't know Shakespeare from the Bible, I wouldn't have a lot left to work with.

I was running out of money, but the thought of her connections held me fast to her filthy sofa collection. I hadn't mentioned Fartus, Robert, Marcel, or the exploding body to her. I figured it was strictly business and what time she gave me was costly. Besides, the less she knew of my personal life the better.

"But you stripped everything down," I stated. " 'Scene: A room. Two people. A chair. There is a fight.' That's what you wanted." We had gotten through the entire book between my Twain, Capote, and Faulkner writing styles, and Reeda had managed to reduce the original four-hundred-page novel to three double-spaced pages.

"That's what we had to do initially to get to the truth. Now we've got to go back and figure out what the entire book is about."

"But you said this would take a certain number of sessions and now it's running into months. I don't have this kind of money. I'm starving to death and I just want—"

"So what you're telling me is that you don't want your writing to improve." She was cold; a concrete emotionless wall.

"That's not what I'm saying at all. I'm just trying to explain that I don't have a lot of money and that you initially said this would only take a certain amount of time to fix and now it's run into overtime."

"You think I'm trying to cheat you? Is that what you think? Are you always this insulting to people trying to help you?" She was cool; reserved; sitting immobile and ignoble, like some self-glorified psychiatrist who's bent on seeing what makes their patient tick.

"I didn't say you were—"

"You didn't have to. I'm a mind reader. That's what I do. I read minds."

"I thought you were a writer," I said, rather sarcastically.

"So, you *do* think I'm a writer. Then why are you trying to discredit everything I've done?" And with this last statement she began scribbling something down in a notebook on her lap. Proof, I suppose, that she actually could write.

"Can we stop this and get on with the book?" I asked, but just then the phone rang and she proceeded to have a twenty-minute conversation with someone regarding the fact that she could help them with their sagging movie script if they would be willing to lend her their house for the summer. Reeda had more angles than a ninth-grade geometry textbook. When she finished the conversation, which was conducted on my time and money, she sat down once again across from me.

"What I want here from you is the truth. What really happened in the story. What the story is all about. From what I can gather, it's autobiographical."

I blanched. Autobiographical? It was set in England in the 1800s! Where was she getting autobiographical?

"We've set it in present day now, done away with things like Squigglemires, Tourette's Syndrome, and bustles, and now we're getting down to the meat of things. And I have to tell you, Max, I think the humor that's there in the story is just a cover-up for your twisted childhood. Until you can accept what really happened to you—your sick relatives and the bustle you wore as a child—you'll never be a good writer.

"What are you talking about, what happened to me? Nothing happened to me. I didn't wear a bustle. Are you compl—"

"You're not being honest," she said, leaning forward, looking directly at me. "You have to write this story to tell what really happened."

"It's a comedy, for Christ's sake. What's with the gloom and doom?" I was getting exasperated. I looked around the room. Even the animals were bored. The parrot that usually had some new obscenity to offer was calmly cleaning between its toes. Percy the iguana was sound asleep on top of a bookshelf.

"Listen," Reeda began melodramatically, reaching out, grasping my hand and leaning over, "you've got to tell me the worst thing in your life—what your worst experience was. Then I can begin to help you. I can't work with you until you do that." The entire apartment was becoming a made-for-TV movie.

"But I need a story editor, not a shrink," I said, folding my arms and digging in. "I need you to help me write the story the way *I* want to, not the way *you* want it. Besides, no one wants that 'look what happened to me' kind of thing anymore."

"People are still reading it," she said, sitting up straight, holding her arms out in front of her like some semi-paraplegic version of Vishnu. "People *want* the horrible things. They want sex. They want *disturbing*." Then she paused for dramatic effect, sitting back, crossing her arms in answer to mine. "Give it to them. Give them your pain." Now she leaned forward, again taking my hand in hers, her brow furrowed, her bottom lip quivering, a mock tear forming in her eye. The melodrama was going full tilt. "Give them what pain you have, Max, and let *them* decide. Let them see what hurts the most." And at this point she shook my arms slightly and nodded a *yes* several times.

But just as she finished, the moment was shattered by the featherless parrot who finally decided to join the party. "Oh, yeah, big boy!" he crooned, "Use that cat-o-nine tails! *Whip* that butt!"

29

It's not so much that I long for the past, but that I'm not that comfortable with the future pressing down on top of me to the extent that it does. Sure, some part of me still wants to be able to ring for servants, worry about whether or not the *Titanic* will sink, and anticipate the invention of the television, but I'm perspicacious enough to know it's more realistic to settle for a time when women didn't leave the house without hats and gloves and Nixon wasn't yet President. Hell, I'm not that picky, I just want people to buy pants that don't hang off them like sacks and wear a baseball cap in the right direction. My point is this: You know you're getting old when youth starts to scare you, when you no longer recognize current music, and when a trip to the dry cleaners requires a nap for purposes of mental and physical restoration. Hence my desire to write a book—*Mrs. Squigglemire*—set in the past. Hence my lack of verve for having to sit through focus groups, all of which dealt with the "now," the "here," and even worse—the "future."

Imagine my surprise when I arrived at the first focus group, pretending to be Spong Flagelatte, and found that everyone was a good three years younger than myself. I hadn't counted on this. While I thought I knew Spong's age, I had reasoned that the people in charge of the focus group were interested in accountants, not children. I didn't realize they wanted really young accountants. And is anyone ready to be anything, especially an accountant, at around age twenty? I don't want anyone who hasn't had three children, two cars, and at least one mortgage handling my money, much less some post-pubescent party animal with raging hormones, suicidal tendencies, and a proclivity for puréed vegetables.

Now I don't consider myself old, but the group I found myself ensconced in was definitely borderline crib material. You may have forgotten, but when you're in the late teens or early twenties, two extra years is the equivalent of ten in more mature circles.

Since I was deep in rumination over these issues at the hotel suite that *Accountants Today* had provided, I hadn't noticed myself and the others being herded into a paneled room, one side of which was almost entirely covered with mirrors. We shuffled in that direction like cattle to the slaughter. As if I wasn't queasy enough impersonating someone I disliked intensely, I now had to contend with what looked like a giant pair of reflective sunglasses—some rather badly disguised two-way mirrors. It wasn't hard to imagine tiered rows of market researchers taking notes on what we wore, how we spoke, and what we said about the magazine. I glanced nervously at the shiny wall and then told myself I wouldn't look again.

But no sooner had I made this decision than I realized that everyone had scrambled for seats around the table, musical chairs style, and I was left with the one in the center, facing directly into a reflection of seen and unseen faces. My own visage stared back—an uncomfortable proposition.

"We'll begin today by going around the room and introducing ourselves. Tell us your name, what company you work for, and what training you have," the moderator started out.

I hadn't thought about this. Actually, all I *had* thought about was the seventy-five dollars. I'd envisioned a lax environment where one didn't have to speak unless the mood struck, not this show and tell reminiscent of first grade. Thank God I was sitting in the middle and would have time to imitate some examples from the others. I figured that, this being accounting, the moderator would be super orderly and start at the end nearest her.

"Let's start in the middle with you, sir," I heard her say, and chairs on each side of me swiveled in my direction as if I had just been elected president of the lottery club. There was no escaping it; no "Huh, who, me?" that I could pull off. Everyone was staring and I had to think fast.

"My name is Spong Flagelatte and I work at . . . ('Oh, my God, I don't have a frikkin' clue,' one part of my brain screamed silently) . . . I'd rather not say. You see, it's a private company and . . ." but I could see people weren't buying it. "I work for Hickenlooper Associates," I said, giving in, not wanting to be discovered. It was the only thing that came to mind—Robert's last name. "We're a privately owned company with over two hundred employees," I lied. "I attended NYU here in the city and worked at the company I'm at now, Hickenlooper, to get my C.P.A. certification. Oh, and I like to ski and go mountain bike riding," I added, just to pad the thing up. I smiled, congratulating myself on the ability to think fast, and when I was finished, I turned to the person on my right with raised eyebrows as if to say, "And now you? If you will be so kind, please tell us about yourself?" I had no idea where the chutzpah had come from, but nonetheless enjoyed my newfound talent. It was a quick transition. Thank God something was working in my life.

I basked in success during the first half of the meeting, managing to recapitulate what others had said. I was the master tautologist, spewing back to this group of self-serving, over-inflated number crunchers their own insipid comments about computer software and profit-and-loss statements. And I did it all with zest, couching it in condescending terms and with such a sense of cynicism that everyone seemed impressed.

I was so into the role I was playing that I started to fake answers, offering up my opinion even before anyone else could speak, mentally feeling about the room as I went. When asked what I thought about the new layout of the magazine, I quickly jumped in even though I had never actually seen a copy.

"I was a little disappointed in it," I said, raising one side of my upper lip for added effect. "I thought the old format was better. More user-friendly. Easier to follow." Several others in the group agreed, nodding their heads and taking notes down on the yellow legal pads we had been given. I looked down at my own notes: A series of three-dimensional boxes, fake-looking flowers, and a margin full of my attempts to practice my signature—Spong Flagelatte, complete with a flourish underneath—stared back at me. Getting bored with the process, I got even braver, thinking only of how much time was left and salivating for my seventy-five-dollar check.

"Can we talk about the editorial content?" I asked, going out on a limb. "I liked the articles that were appearing a few months ago. I thought they had a more concise, more focused numerical orientation, and I could relate to them better."

"Can you give me some examples?" the moderator asked, momentarily throwing me for a loop. But I was saved by several others in the group who now raised their hands, eager to follow in the footsteps of a zealous participant.

By the time the focus group was over I was exhausted but seventy-five dollars richer. On my way out, a marketing person who had been on the other side of the mirror approached me. He asked if I'd be interested in participating in another group, this one involving a slightly older crowd that was a little more outgoing—all subscribers to *Accountants Today*—who were really interested in having a hand in where the magazine was headed. I stifled the yawn in my head, thinking that I couldn't possibly suffer through another boring meeting with people whose idea of a good time was discussing ledgers as if they were talking about the Academy Awards.

"We're paying twice the going rate for this next group," he said, breaking me out of my reverie.

"I'd love to participate," I said, walking with him over to the registration table. And then added, "Just put me down for as many of these as you'd like."

When an autopsy was performed on actor John Wayne, it was reported in various circles, tabloids, and news groups, that his colon contained thirty-five pounds of fecal matter. After a few days in the news it was possible to find certain accounts that claimed the weight of the famous intestinal material was closer to seventy pounds. Further investigation to date on my part has revealed that some sources claim it was a mere fifteen pounds. And if one truly doesn't have a life and spends countless hours of research at various libraries, one can find just about every amount conceivable. Here lies the problem and the culprit: PR. Public Relations. Press Release. Practical Rubbish. Publicity. Advertising—or the lack thereof. Selling the public something they neither need nor want. Y'all come back now, hear? It's all about what we're told—what they want us to know. And what they don't. Information.

But most of all it's about being known. A household name. You could axe-murder twenty people, be related to Hitler, and claim to be an alien from Planet Killalltheearthlings, but if your name is recognized you'll be a hot property for writing a book. Why? Because the world already *knows* you and most of the work is done. Write a book—any kind of book—and hordes will flock to buy it if you are famous, infamous, have committed a crime, or are related to one of the editors (the amount of advertising they'll spend on a relative is *amazing*). But if you're the greatest writer in the world and you didn't cook and eat thirty people to make the six o'clock news, forget it. The agents and publishers don't want you unless you already have a name. That way they don't really have to do any work.

And lest you think any of the great authors happened to send in their work blindly and suddenly become published and famous, let me clue you in on how three great American authors came into being via the first Mr. Perkins at Scribners. The story in a nutshell:

F. Scott Fitzgerald knew Shane Leslie, a writer of some note who was already well ensconced at Scribners and a recognizable name in bookstores. (Ever heard of Leslie? Me neither.) Leslie was Fitzgerald's *in* to Perkins. Fitzgerald then pushed Hemingway on to Mr. P. And finally, a woman named Madeline Boyd who was the wife of a literary critic (how lucky!) happened to mention a crate of loose papers belonging to a certain Thomas Wolfe. Intrigued, Perkins asked to see the manuscript and, after he got through shuffling that enormous deck of cards, the crate became known as *Look Homeward, Angel.* A small book. Nothing too important. You've probably never even heard of it.

Through all this, Perkins lent money, smoothed ruffled feathers, and hand-held to such an extent that it is a wonder he had any time left at all to actually read. Stories circulate of him begging for manuscripts from not only Hemingway, Wolfe, and Fitzgerald, but almost every other author as well. He had to; Scribners had made these men's names hot commodities, and so they were expected to perform like the trained seals they had become. This is not to say that the aforementioned writers were not talented, but rather that they had help; that someone noticed them; that they were pushed along toward recognition; that they had support and were nurtured until they became household names at which point they were valuable. How many great writers are out there with no Max Perkins to prod them along?

Segue into . . .

Okay—stay with me. So this begs one of several questions on the part of society. First, exactly how much macho poo-poo did the Duke have in him when he died, and second, do we really care? Well, it's too late to know the truth now, so that pretty much takes care of number one. And number two, yes, evidently people do want to know since the information was passed around quite a bit at the time of Mr. Wayne's demise and can still be found in various sources. You see, Mr. Wayne was a commodity—a name, a recognized and salable piece of goods—and, because he was famous, didn't screw up too much, was heterosexual, white, and over six feet tall, we *care* about the contents of his colon.

Now, at this point, you are probably asking yourself where I'm going with this—John Wayne; his colon; advertising. It's quite simple. The whole *tableau vivant* of Mr. True-Grit-and-His-Tummy-Contents seems to me to be the perfect metaphor for what would be my next area of employment—publishing. They churn out a bunch of fertilizer by a one-dimensional artist and then manage to get everyone to buy it. And this phenomenon is due to a particularly nasty animal, known by its professional and cloistered ivory tower names: *promotion, publicity, and marketing.* Its definition is much like that of diplomacy: Telling someone to go to hell and doing it in such a way so that they look forward to the journey. It's all the "higher ups" who decide what will be the next bestseller, what you will wear, and which products are poisonous this week (in the 1950s smoking was actually thought to be good for your health). Don't fool yourself into thinking that because you see a book on the bestseller list, it actually *is* a bestseller.

Now, I've not got anything against Mr. Wayne. He only took what chances were given him and worked hard. But how many other actors deserved a shot at what he had and didn't get it simply because they weren't already known and recognized?

I hear you asking, "Why have I started this chapter in this manner?" That will become clear if you read on, for it has everything (literally, unfortunately) to do with the next job I was to procure; the job to end, well, almost all jobs; the place where I was to make a name for myself.

Publishing appeared to be a logical route at the time. I was, after all, a person putting pen to paper. Babley Associates, Barely Broadway, and the brief stint in Marcel's cleaning company were only marking time. Publishing: It seemed where I was meant to be—that proverbial foot in the door for a writer. I had plans. Plans for my book.

It was Robert who caused the whole thing—this new job. He was always coming into a situation, meeting people, doing things for others so that they owed him a favor. And looking back on it now, I should have seen what was coming. But I didn't.

He called one balmy day in late April to tell me that he had found a job for me as a reader in one of the city's major publishing houses. After I finished screaming and running around the room in circles, I picked the receiver back up; Robert was still on the line. It was at that point that the " . . . and, I've got bad news" part was related to me. It seems that he had told this person he knew, who in turn knew the individual at the publishing house, that I was a former concert pianist, not a writer. Quick thinking on his part since publishing houses want anyone *but* someone who is a writer. Go figure. I suppose they don't want a gaggle of wannabes pushing their goods in the backdoor like backstage groupies at a boy-band concert—which is exactly what I planned to do.

So I was instructed to lie on my application and become someone I wasn't, taking over Robert's past career.

Not a problem for me.

In the last couple of months, because of my zealous entrepreneurship and a proclivity for stealing others' mail from our neighborhood in Brooklyn and even from a few upper-class environs in Manhattan, I had participated in focus groups as a baker, a junior lawyer, a used-car salesman, a butcher, a taxi driver, a speech pathologist, and even a housewife from New Jersey (it was a total misdirection of the mail—not even the correct state, and I will never again wax or wear panty hose). It had all worked out well enough, so I figured becoming a concert pianist, albeit one with carpal tunnel syndrome who would now be employed as a reader, wasn't going to be too much of a stretch for me. More like a walk in the park. After all, I *could* read, which was actually more than some others in the industry could do.

One week later, with Robert's help, I was Max Perkins, former pianist who wanted to do nothing but read bad manuscripts and pass judgment on them. I told personnel in the interview that I had no aspirations to be a writer and in fact didn't even know one. My phony résumé was done, the interview went off without a hitch, and by the end of the next week I found myself standing in the lobby of the personnel department at Bandomday Books, waiting to be escorted to my new office.

While this was to be my new full-time job, I held onto my Spong impersonation just in case something went awry. Things had been so unpredictable up to this point I wasn't sure where my life was headed.

I was excited.

Bandomday was located in one of the glitziest buildings on Sixth Avenue. The skyscraper reached up in competition with its fellow neighbors for front-runner in the "most-steel-and-glass category." So far, my building was winning and I imagined myself on the fortieth floor with a nicely paneled corner workplace. I would pace my luxuriously carpeted office when I wasn't practicing putting with a titanium golf club, aiming for a highball glass. I would feign irritation at my secretary as she buzzed me, wanting to know if I needed lunch reservations ("Yes, Miss Vanderschnoozy! What *IS* it!") I would scowl at one of the sofas in my office, insisting that it be re-covered by the end of the week, and I would toss manuscripts into the garbage can with an ear-shattering thud, deeming them unreadable ("I don't care if it *is* a long-lost Hemingway—the thing is just *bad!*"). After work I would dine at Twenty-One, take the limo home to my penthouse apartment, and crawl into my custom-made bed with designer sheets, next to a gorgeous super-model who would writhe underneath my amorous attentions until we were both ready to—

"Come."

It was simple. One word. A command. It had interrupted my reverie, like some gaseous belch in the middle of a dinner costing five hundred dollars. And a woman doing her best to imitate the wicked witch from *The Wizard of Oz* had delivered it. The only thing missing was a bicycle and the small dog in the basket. If her one-word command wasn't enough to convince me that I was to follow, then her crooked arthritic finger was surely another clue. I followed, imagining her ire at my having gotten the last corner office with mahogany paneling while she was forced to share an airless broom closet with a blinking fluorescent light and moribund geranium.

But something was wrong, for as we entered the elevator she pressed the button marked *B* for basement. As in "The basement in the building."

I fidgeted, pretending to look more closely at the button panel, then turned so that I could get a look at her name and ID tag. "Phyllis Stein," it read, "Personnel Director." I said her name to myself several times, running the first and last together. It seemed to work.

We passed several floors where throngs of anorexic women wearing black got on or off, their knobby knees rubbing together with rhythmic condescension. A few older men, all of them easily in their eighties, hobbled on at different floors. At one point a cafeteria worker pushed her way in, the cart she was attached to reeking of ziti and over-cooked vegetables. Finally the car bumped to a halt with just Ms. Stein and myself in it. Nothing happened. The door didn't open, and after a second Ms. I'll-Get-You-My-Pretty punched the alarm bell with enough force to dislodge an intelligent sentence from a presidential candidate at election time.

"Clarice!" the woman bellowed into the crack between the two doors. "Clarice! The new boy is here!"

"Boy?" I thought to myself. "And as long as we're calling names . . ." But I didn't have time to finish the thought, for within a matter of moments a rather ugly crowbar was wedged between the doors—from the other side—and we fell onto a cold gray concrete floor.

The noise surrounding us was deafening. All around sprawled a collection of massive pipes, gears, and valves.

"YOU'RE LUCKY I WAS WALKING BY," screamed a girl of mongoloid proportions, looking from the personnel woman and then to me, "ELSE YOU'D HAVE BEEN IN THERE FOR HOURS."

Ms. Congeniality from personnel rolled her eyes and jerked her head—evidently a company indication for her to leave and let Clarice take over, as though I was some sort of human wand in the relay race of publishing. I found myself following Clarice automatically, hoping she would have a way out of the noise. I was

165

still confused by the lack of plush offices. By the time our peregrinations were complete and we had arrived a good distance from the clamor of the boiler room, I had taken stock of her attributes.

Clarice was in her mid-twenties, slightly overweight, pale as a ghost, and sporting an enormous blond wig. The hairpiece alone was big enough to claim its own zip code. It was a good three feet tall and had the requisite 1950s blue bow imbedded in the middle, causing her to look like something from a bad *Gidget* movie. Top all this off with her expression, which was a completely blank face with two enormous protruding eyes and an O-mouth that was continually agape, and you pretty much have the picture. She looked as if she had been stuck full force in the buttocks with the most enormous hatpin, and her face had frozen the instant that realization took hold.

"That elevator door sticks several times a day," Clarice explained. "We keep the crowbar handy. You never know."

"Why are we stopping here?" I asked as we made our way through two enormous heavy metal doors and into an ugly room which was nothing more than a concrete cinderblock shell—not even painted—with multiple "Fallout Shelter" signs. Five ratty-looking cubicles—even worse than those at Babley's (still in the proverbial filthy baby-blue) were mashed up against the colorless walls, and a collection of flickering lights punctuated the space, their hum an eerie counterpoint to the flipping of pages.

"This is it," Clarice said, moving toward the worst of the cubicles. "Your space." Then she turned to me and within a second changed into a completely different person from the one who had escorted me down the hall. "Let's get one thing straight," she said, crossing her arms and jerking her head upward defiantly, "you work for *me*," and on the word *me*, her right hand and index finger shot from her body and struck me in the chest. "You *got* that? It's my way or the highway. You treat me with some *respect* and I'll do the same for you. Got it?"

"Okay," I said, and nodded, hoping that one of the exposed steel and fire-retardant-flocked beams in the ceiling would fall on her. Then her mood changed again, back to the first person I had encountered. She was bending over the shelf in my cubicle—there was no desk—and pulling out lists of manuscripts I was to read.

"If you like," she said, her voice resembling that of a human being once again, "just start with these three and then if you have any questions you can come get me. I'm in cubicle number one. And here's a list of questions you need to answer for each book. Just get settled in and I'll come by in a little bit to see if you need anything. Okay?" Then she turned and retreated back to her own cubicle.

Possibly I was too stunned by the lack of paneling, a personal secretary, and a complimentary set of golf clubs to really notice where I was. It took a few minutes for the reality to sink in. I told myself this was the dream sequence in my next novel but I knew better. After all, the whole experience was too surreal to be a dream.

```
        The   cast:   Four   worker   bee   employees
besides    Clarice    occupy    the    room    in    the
basement at Bandomday Books. First, Frasquina:
a   small,   irritable   woman   from   Jamaica   who
speaks  virtually  no  English.  She  is  arrogant
and  has  an  inflated  sense  of  self-worth.  She's
been   with   the   company   now   for   over   fifteen
years.    She    frequently    threatens    to    kill
everyone  and  keeps  a  large  butcher  knife  on
her  desk  in  case  the  opportunity  should  arise.
Second,  Cloud:  A  rather  mousy-looking  woman  of
perhaps  twenty-five  years  of  age.  She's  half
black,  half  white,  and  has  frizzy  red  hair  and
light  skin.  Claims  she  is  American  Indian  and
that   her   full   name   is   Big   Rain   Cloud   Over
Meadow.  Cloud  will  do  for  short.  (Does  anyone
have  a  normal  name  nowadays?)  She's  all  bad
teeth  and  ugly  shoes.  She  tells  the  boss
everything,    hoping    for    Brownie    points    and
usually  gets  them.  Half  of  her  nose  is  missing
from  cocaine  use.  Then,  Perkel:  Puerto  Rican.
He's  perhaps  twenty-two  and  has  nine  children,
not  all  by  the  same  woman.  All  nine  are  living
with  him  and  his  present  wife.  He's  a  know-it-
all   with   a   chip   on   his   shoulder.   Fat,
obnoxious,  racist,  and  rude.  Then,  there's--
```

"You. What are you doing? Don't you have any work to do?" I looked up to see a woman of about fifty years of age, standing over me with proverbial hands on hips. She had greasy gray hair and no makeup.

"I'm sorry, but who are you?"

"Who am *I?*" Then she turned to the room, hands still on hips. "Hey, everybody, listen up. The new guy wants to know who *I* am?" The room roared with laughter. It echoed off the concrete walls. It was very Beaucoup Books.

"I just got here, and I'm—"

"Pokey."

"Well, I'm not really late, I've been—"

"No, *I'm* Pokey. My name. Pokey. I'm the supervisor around here, that's who I am. And don't forget it." Her finger shot out just as Clarice's had, hitting my sternum. I imagined it to be a Bandomday trait—the corporate culture. In my mind I practiced jabbing my finger into everyone's chest I came in contact with but quickly decided I didn't look good with two black eyes.

"But I thought Clarice was the supervisor. She told me that I worked for her," I responded, hoping to clear up the confusion, turning slightly in my chair. Pokey glared at me. Then she bellowed in the direction of Clarice's cubicle without turning away from me. Her eyes bore right through me while she screamed. Evidently all supervisors in Manhattan went to the same school, specializing in condescension and attitude. At least Bandomday thought enough of their employees to include the finger-pointing seminar. I was moving up in the world.

"Clarice! Did you tell the new guy he worked for you?" she yelled at me, despite the question being addressed a good twenty feet in back of her.

Clarice appeared now, standing in the center of the room, out from her cubicle, the same dumb bug-eyed and open-mouthed expression that I had noticed on our first meeting a few minutes earlier.

"Gosh, no. I would never do a thing like that," Clarice responded. "I only have the utmost respect for you, Ms. Pokey. I could never undermine your authority." She was sickly sweet and obsequious. I wanted to hurl.

"So," Pokey threw at me, "a liar to boot! That's all we need," and with this she turned and started back to her office. I noticed she was dressed in an obnoxious striped pants suit that appeared to be made out of burlap, and she looked as if she bought her jewelry from the same place as Anastasia from Babley's. Only most of Pokey's jewelry was plastic—hoops, Rubik's Cube earrings, finger ornaments that looked like scarabs. I looked over at Clarice. She only shrugged and returned to her cubicle.

"Mon, dat iz one fooked-oop chick. Me tink she pee-pee panny fooooot."

"Excuse me?" I said to a small black woman wearing an ensemble that was knitted entirely of chartreuse and fuchsia yarn. It was Frasquina, the Jamaican immigrant. She was speaking in what I would later learn was a cross between Ebonics, patois, Caribbean mumbo-jumbo, and make believe—heavy on the last item.

"Cuyah, she gwan like she nice eee. Choble nuh nice. You ina big choble."

"What—"

"She said, 'Look at that, she acts like she is so nice. Trouble is not nice. You're in big trouble.'"

I turned to see Cloud, the company rodent, another of the "readers" with her frizzed hair and gaunt face. She was holding an armful of manuscripts and sporting a pair of putty-gray orthopedic shoes. "You'll learn it after a while," she said, putting the manuscripts down on the ledge in front of me. Then she continued, seeing my confused expression: "Frasquina doesn't speak English. If you want to communicate with her you have to speak patois." Then she added, "Mi cyan help yuh wit dat problem."

I stared.

"And Pokey used to make doorknobs for a living before she came here," she went on.

"And you're telling me this because . . ." I said.

"Her parents escaped from Nazi Germany so that would explain some of why she's the way she is," Cloud continued.

"I'm sorry," I said, "I had no idea Pokey was Jewish and her parents had been the victims of prejudice."

"Not *Jews!*" Cloud screamed. "They're not Jews, they were Nazi scientists who escaped before the Americans liberated the camps. They tortured people at Auschwitz," she said, and walked off.

I was trying to figure out who was more charming, Cloud, Frasquina, Clarice, or Miss Pokey, when Perkel, the token Puerto Rican, came around the corner and threw three more manuscripts in front of me. "Have these done by tomorrow, Jew-boy," he shouted as he walked away.

"Well," I thought, "at least he speaks English."

I waded through what I could of the book proposals and tried to settle in. About midday the mail arrived and in it was a package for me. "Strange," I thought. "It's my first day. Who knows I'm here?"

Opening it I found a game—Scrabble. Attached to the inside lid of the box was a rather cryptic note: "The name is an anagram." I was puzzling over the thing when Miss Pokey walked by and snorted.

"So, the new guy's got time to play games, does he?" she chortled to the room. I was about to respond when she jerked the box out of my hand, leaving only the note.

"You can pick up your toys when your work's done," she snarled, and I just sat there, stunned, staring at the piece of paper.

"The name is an anagram," I said to myself. "But *what* name?"

32

The focus groups were getting easier and easier, and the money helped to pay for my sessions with Reeda—that paragon of ever-changing careers and benevolent Saint Francis of Assisi clone—a real chameleon. Plus, they took my mind off Bandomday.

Managing to rummage through the mail at home every day, I was able to become Spong Flagelatte, the focus group guru for over twelve nationally distributed magazines. There was a skiing magazine, two or three publications on men's issues, health and sports, one on sailing, another on computers, and even one called *Decorating for Men Today.* This I found ironic considering Spong's living situation. What was he going to do, wallpaper his closet and put in track lighting? And I was other people as well: Mr. Waldermanick on the fifth floor; Mr. Bradeis on two; even the super, Mr. Sanchez, in the basement (I explained to the coordinator that my mother was of English derivation, hence my lack of Latin pigmentation).

Within the period of two months I had dazzled moderators of several illustrious publications with my knowledge about, well, everything. "I find Vail to be far superior to Taos," I would say, taking on a haughty air, crossing my arms in defense. I had been no further west than the state of Ohio but felt I could conjure up forty-five-degree slopes covered with snow in my head with no problem.

"That article on hot tubs in Calgary left out some of the more important elements," I might say. Or, "The layout of *Men's Sports and Sex* is good, but—and I hope I'm speaking for everyone here," I would state, leaning onto the conference table for added effect—"what we all want is an extended swimsuit issue." High fives and a goosing in the ribs followed comments such as these. I was a regular "one of the guys."

I finished that month off with a *National Geographic* group, having actually read one of the issues. "I have to tell you," I said, making my bottom lip quiver slightly, "that the story about the plight of the gorillas, well, it made me weep. And I'm not ashamed of it," I added, straightening up in my chair. "Can we have some more of that?" and several heads nodded in agreement. After the session, three women asked me for a date.

Despite the money being good, I was worn out. Between my magazine focus group impersonations, my job at Bandomday, my living situation, and Reeda's Rube Goldberg method for finding the book within, there was little energy left for socializing or a relationship. There was no time to take in one of the opulent Broadway shows I saw advertised on marquees around Times Square; no time to visit the museums; no time to explore much of the city, and well, no time to really be the person I was supposed to be—whoever that was. I was beginning to lose my identity. At Bandomday I was a failed concert pianist, faking my way through the position of reader. After work I was an arrogant oddity, filling endless conference rooms with Spongisms and slinging around his conceit and over-inflated sense of self worth.

So it came as no great shock to realize that my defenses were down; that I was unfocused; easily caught off-guard. There may have been warning signs—I don't know—and I'm willing to admit that I contributed somewhat to the situation, but now, looking back on it, I can't blame myself too much. Things were so hard, life so difficult, and so many obstacles in the way that I don't see how I could have done things differently. It just never occurred to me that I would be sucked into certain events, like a helpless and fragile leaf in some vast and all-powerful vortex, floating for a moment on the swirling surface before the circular tendrils of the whirlpool pull it to the bottom.

33

I had been going to Reeda Rot now as often as I could afford, scraping up money from the focus groups and my Bandomday job, and saving what I could by eating as little as possible. I also had zero social life—a great way to save *and* be depressed. While I didn't agree with most of what Reeda said in our sessions, I was used to her and the menagerie that inhabited her tiny apartment, and in some small way I looked forward to these visits—if nothing else, for the amusement they produced. They were, sadly, one of the few stable elements in my life. So I was unprepared when I showed up at her building one day, was buzzed in, and then met at the door by her scrunched face. It poked out through the crack she made between the entry and the frame.

"Here," she said, squeaking her hand and five dollars through, "go get me a coffee, light, and get yourself anything you want. I still have a . . . student, yes, yes, that's it . . . a student . . . so come back in ten minutes." From the sound inside the apartment she had several students.

I didn't know what to say. Her actions seemed exceptionally rude and out of character, even for someone as out of touch as she was, but I figured that it must be some big shot she was helping and loped off down the street to look for the nearest deli. Being the punctual person that I was at that point, I made an attempt to look at my watch every minute so as not to be late in returning—or early.

Approaching her building once again I noticed several rather rustic characters emerging, complete with strange-looking cases and an assortment of clothes. One of them had some theatrical lighting equipment and a large boom microphone. As they were leaving, a young man of the group held the door open for me so that I didn't have to be buzzed in and I found myself at the ugly brown enameled door, knocking timidly while trying to balance the now tepid cups of coffee between my arm and chest. I mentally wrote off the coterie of misfits that had oozed from the building as just another artistic group working in film or photography.

"Good! Just in time," Reeda said, opening the door. "I'm sorry about that, but he's a very important client. Has a screenplay that one of the major studios wants pronto and I agreed to help him. They all come to me. The good ones, that is." Then, "Aaaaant!" she admonished. "The shoes! Take off the shoes!"

I don't know how I could have forgotten. This was one of her obsessions—the removal of one's shoes. The apartment was a pigsty with animals coming and going over every square inch. I always had my pants dry cleaned immediately after a visit since the first time I contracted a bad case of lice simply by sitting down— fully clothed—on a vinyl chair. And here she was, insisting that I take my shoes off so that the dirt of New York City's streets wouldn't contaminate her living space. I obeyed and shuddered to think what my socks were picking up.

"Come in, sit down," she commanded, indicating a new filthy sofa as today's place of instruction. She was always doing this—changing the seating so that I never knew where we would be working. One imagined her scouring all of Manhattan for the latest urine-stained recliner or '60s-style coffee table with cigarette burns. I sat, and immediately a bad spring came up to stick me in the buttocks. I moved slightly.

"Fidgety today?" she asked and sat across from me in one of the cold metal folding chairs that were some of the more attractive pieces of furniture in the room. Perhaps she had experienced the lice herself. I noticed the place smelled slightly antiseptic, like a veterinarian's office.

"Now, let's get started where we left off. We had decided that you were emotionally unavailable for your readers and that we needed to get to the real pain of your novel."

"I know. I thought about what you said, but this is supposed to be a funny book, you know, not much characterization. It's supposed to be anecdotes, amusing stories."

"But the basis for comedy is pain."

"Like I don't know this."

Just then the phone rang and she answered it. Why she couldn't have let the answering machine get it was beyond me. I was, after all, a paying customer. But thankfully the conversation was short with an "I see" and one "That's too bad" thrown in. As she hung up she explained to herself as much as to me the content: "Just lost a huge chunk of funding for a movie I'm working on. The guy thought he could swing it but they took him to court for all kinds of things a while back—copyright infringement, not paying some royalties. Now I'm going to have to find it somewhere else." I could see her crunching numbers in her head as she made her way over to me, her brain one big machination on how to squeeze the remaining pennies from my pockets. One part of my subconscious mind picked up on something she had just said, wanting to delve into things, but another part said, "Let it go," and I did.

"Why are we fighting? We just need to find your pain and then we can work it into the novel," she said, picking up where our last conversation left off—the one I was *supposed* to be paying for. "Let's get to it. Let me see what you've written since last time. We spoke about how we had stripped down the novel to scenes and now we're going back and find the pain. Come on, let me see what you have," and with her last statement I handed over the binder I kept my revisions in. She scanned each page, muttering to herself and making annotations in her own notebook. Five minutes passed as she allegedly read forty or so pages. Her anorexic arms cut through the air as she flipped the pieces of paper, one over the other.

"Better. We're getting somewhere now. But you have what appears to be a mystery, a semblance of a plot so to speak—that's not good."

"But I want the book to be about something as well as be entertaining."

"Can't do it. Won't sell. Now, this part here, about Mrs. Smith—I see you took my suggestion and did away with Squigglemire, good, good, good—it's not, well, how shall I say it? You're not letting me into the story." She joined the fingers of both hands together as if to replicate a Chinese finger trap, then attempted to pull them apart, thinking that this illustrated her point.

It didn't.

"I feel left out. I need to know what she's all about, this Mrs. Squigglemire or whoever—what makes her tick," she went on.

Oh, to hell with it. I was getting fed up. We had stripped down my life's work, taken out any words with more than two syllables, written and rewritten scenes in first, second, and even third person, and all through it she had wanted some inner truth, some heinous secret about the characters. This entire experience wasn't going in the direction I wanted it to, so at that point I decided to have some fun. I felt as though she had been playing with me for months now, so I figured I might as well turn the tables on her. Besides, I was beginning to question how many other students she had, if she knew agents and publishers, and what her real story was. I shuddered to think that the definition of success in this business meant shopping for furniture on the street.

I lapsed into an uncomfortable silence, my head bowed, much like an acting student when he tries to get into character.

"I . . . I'm not sure I want to go there," I said, haltingly. "I . . . it's just that . . . well, it's painful. I want this to be a humorous book and . . ." but I stopped, trying to make my bottom lip tremble. Then I jerked my eyes quickly to the left as if looking for some escape route, then back to her. Good. She had bought it.

"I can see you're uncomfortable with this process, but we need to continue. That is, if you can. I want you to just sit and compose yourself. Take a deep breath. Look up at the ceiling. Thaaaaat's right. Now close your eyes and exhale slowly. Thaaaaaat's good. Now I'm going to count from ten, backwards, and I want you to relax with each number as we go lower until I get to the number one. At that point you will be completely relaxed and at peace." Then she began to count backwards in an attempt to hypnotize me or perform some such mind-altering experience. It was all I could do not to burst out laughing, but I kept calm, telling myself that the game would be worth it. And who did she think she was? Did she think she could count backwards and anyone would drop off and start spilling their insides? That, plus the fact that she was illiterate helped quell my smirk. I remained solemn; appearing as if I were really going under, ready to delve into my own personal artifacts—a regular *de profundis* of the psyche.

When she was done counting, she adopted the voice of someone in a bad B-movie dealing with Oujia boards and séances. "You're going back, going baaaaaaack," she said, and it was all I could do to maintain my deadpan expression. "Now start, from the very beginning. Your childhood if you like. I need, I mean, the *reader* needs to know your innermost thoughts."

I played along, pretending an emotional disturbance inside. I made my eyelids flutter and then swallowed hard. She was truly in her element and enjoying this immensely. As soon as this became apparent, I played it for all it was worth.

"Now I want you to begin speaking and just let the words come out. Begin," she commanded, and as if some genie had placed his hand on my shoulder I began a series of moans and groans, as if a spirit were coming up from the depths of my being.

"Paaaain," I said, "feel . . . pain . . . childhood . . . family, father . . . hitting me . . . uncomfortable . . . help, get out, get out!"

"Thaaat's right, just let yourself experience the pain. We need to know the pain for your book. This is *your* book and you need to share with us your pain and experiences that happened to you as a child. So tell us what the pain is, what's happening to you. We need you to blow us out of the water with your pain—tell the world every detail. Don't be afraid to make an explosion with this gift of pain."

"Blow us out of the water?" I thought, while staying in character, "now *there's* a phrase you want to hear while hypnotized. No connotations with *that*." My lips began to curl upwards so I thought about what she charged per hour and the smile quickly faded.

I had to think fast. She was buying my hypnosis act and if I was going to play her for all she was worth and recoup some of my dignity, then I had to suddenly become the consummate actor. I grunted and felt myself slipping into the role of spellbound groupie that I suspected she wanted me to become. And I would have carried it off except for the fact that at the very moment I was ready to speak, to tell the dreaded revelations that she so wanted to hear,

178

to "blow her out of the water," the featherless parrot shook himself, squawked, and let out his loudest and best JJ from "Good Times" imitation.

"Dyn-o-MITE!" the thing exclaimed, and I grimaced horribly.

It was as if Reeda was comfortable in these two worlds— one, her squalid apartment, and the other, that of Dr. Make-Believe-Freud—for immediately and on cue she continued, addressing the featherless bird as much as me, in her same B-movie voice, "Not *that* kind of explosion . . . the *other* kind."

34

New York City is known by several names, one of which is Gotham. G-town was originally an imaginary village in England where the locals were known for their antics and foolishness. It was Washington Irving who bestowed this title upon what was to become one of the world's greatest metropolitan areas after experiencing all that the 14,272 acres had to offer, deciding that it was overrun with "persons pretending to have great knowledge." Not much has changed since Mr. Irving's time. New York—that giant rabbit hole that makes *Alice in Wonderland* look repressed—is a metropolis where you'll find every possible Freudian permutation and then some. A place with a tessitura that stretches from palooka to genius in a matter of seconds. Irving's description rolled through my mind as I made my way to work at the city's latest version of a modern-day concentration camp—Bandomday—land of instability and confusion.

Three torturous weeks had passed since my first meeting with Clarice and the gang. Franquina would yell at me in one of her languages ("De wata is dutty so don't play inna it"), Clarice continued her somnambulistic-like strolls around the squalid area, her exophthalmic brown eyes looking as if they would pop from her skull, and Cloud and Perkel would take turns throwing manuscripts they didn't want in my direction. Whenever they let up for one instant, Miss Pokey was on my case, wanting to know why my work wasn't finished. I tried to stay out of the fray, digging into what I had been given to read, but the task proved arduous.

The first three manuscripts I read were nothing special. All were some "coming of age" type of novel in which most of the words were misspelled and the author had never heard of the term "transition." But the fourth was actually somewhat interesting although far-fetched. It involved a gay advertising salesman who was a vampire and could time-travel into the future. He would get up every day and step into his time machine for the sole purpose of procuring a new account. Because he could determine what products would be selling light years away, he could service his clients (both literally and figuratively) in the most extraordinary ways. Where the writer really lost me was the chapter in which we find out the salesman is actually Jesus and is now the head of a major movie studio that produces documentaries about plant life at the bottom of the ocean. The inclusion of a radioactive pony named Glowstick didn't help the plot any, and I hacked my way through to the end. Still, it was an improvement over most of the drek I was supposed to read.

Now as I said, the reason for taking this job, and more importantly, for sticking with it, was that I eventually wanted to use my position to get my own work read. That is, when I finished revising it and shelling out some serious payback to Ms. Rot. So I bit my tongue about the substandard manuscripts as best I could and waited.

One day, after having finished reading a twenty-thousand-page tome about the color yellow and another (even longer one) titled, *Sparky! The Adventures of a North American Porcupine!*, I was called into Miss Pokey's office.

"Perkins," she began, not looking up at me, "I want you to be supervisor of the department from now on. No pay increase; more work; no back talk. Understand?" The term "out-of-the-blue" would be appropriate here. I had no idea where she was going with this.

"No," I said, "I don't understand. Everyone else has been here longer and, well, aren't they going to resent it? I mean, I've only been here three weeks. Why me?" I tried to focus on her bad dress, her lesbionic short hair—anything to keep on even keel.

"I don't think I have to tell you what a zoo this place is, do I? Have you spoken to Frasquina, or should I say, tried to? Clarice is a piece of work herself, and Perkel and Cloud, well . . . you decide." She had obviously attended the same school as Reeda, enjoying clipped phrases and a rude demeanor. Both had graduated with honors in my opinion.

Miss Pokey was writing something during our conversation, never looking up at me. "Besides, you read faster than anyone else.

Don't think you're getting out of that. You still have to fill your quota, but I need someone to oversee things, and that's you."

It stuck me as ironic that she was telling me how fast I read when only yesterday she had admonished me for not having my work done.

"I'm flattered, but—"

"Don't be. It's nothing special. Just do your job and mind your own business." Then she softened somewhat. She stopped writing and looked up at me. She set her pen down. "You're a good worker," she added, "and I'm glad you came to us. I know I have my moments, but I can be fair and honest also. I hope you won't take advantage of it."

"Okay, Miss Pokey," I said, inching my way out of the office before she could change her mind. I wanted to leave on a good note, so few and far between were they.

The first words I heard upon leaving came from Perkel. "What's happening, Jew-boy?" he asked and grabbed my ass.

"Perkel, for the last time, I'm not Jewish. Stop calling me that. And don't touch me—anywhere—anymore."

"Okay, *fat*-boy."

"And I'm not fat, either," I said. The irony of this wasn't wasted on me. Perkel was at least three hundred pounds, and like most obnoxious people, was completely unaware of his shortcomings. He wore the tightest fitting pants and cheap sweaters he could find and these only served to accentuate the rolls of lard that spilled over his straining belt loops. You wanted to be careful not to frighten him or do anything that would cause him to turn too quickly as the rolls of padding under his chin would take a good minute to catch up to his face when he jerked his head around. The result was none too pleasant.

"Okay, *fag*-boy."

"Perkel. Lay off. I'm not gay either." I didn't want to get into an argument, what with my one-minute-old promotion, but I was tempted to let Perkel know that he had better watch his step. "Can't we just try to act civilized around here?" I asked, not really expecting an answer.

"Okay, *cry*-baby. *Jew*-boy. *Fag*-boy."

I didn't even respond. I just sat down and tried to get into the latest manuscript that had landed on my ledge. It was titled simply *Tongue!* and as the synopsis and cover letter stated, was the story of a model living in Switzerland whose tongue takes on a life of its own. According to the memo from the writer's agent, the tongue develops its own brain and even a complete digestive system. It eventually decides to leave the model's body without her knowing it. It seems that models don't use this part of their body that much, at least not for speaking, and so the event went unnoticed for some time. Bandomday was supposed to publish all genres of books, but I was fond of telling people they specialized in mysteries. That is, how anything as bad as this stuff got published was a real mystery to me.

I had been told by Miss Pokey to give the manuscript my utmost attention as it had come from one of the top agents in New York and the writer had won several major awards. So I slogged my way through chapter upon chapter for the next few days, trying to convince myself that readers would be amused at a part of the human mouth decked out in high heels and clutch purse, shopping at some of the finest boutiques in Paris (air fare, evidently, was only half price for members of the body that seceded without the knowledge of the host).

About half way through the book (not my term), the tongue decides to get itself pierced and somehow gets mixed up with the Croatian mafia who are vacationing in Paris (this is fiction) and ends up with not only a silver stud in its navel (imagine it how you will) but a set of concrete dentures to encapsulate it. This, after a brief affair in a doctor's office during which time the tongue falls for a "tongue depressor" and becomes suicidal, having listened to hours of woeful stories told by the lithe wooden medical instrument. My attention started to wane after the tongue promises to fulfill three wishes of each mafia person if they can each answer a riddle about Diana Vreeland and a blind poodle with glandular problems.

Toward the end of the week I was getting to the part about poor Ms. Vreeland and the poodle, when I was interrupted by Miss Pokey who called me into her office once again.

"Perkins," she said, "I want you to do something about Clarice. She's on the phone constantly and not getting her work done. She has that manuscript about the modern dance company—the one that has only one work in its repertoire—and she hasn't even started it. You need to do something."

"I'll get right on it," I said, bowing and scraping. At least I had learned this much about dealing with Pokey: she loved to have someone's lips touching her posterior. And her announcement to the staff earlier about my promotion had not gone over well so I at least needed *someone* on my side. Perkel was even more antagonistic than usual and Clarice was now refusing to work at all, spending much of her time airing her toes on the top of her desk while she leaned back in her chair, constantly talking on the phone to her fiancé, Beau.

No one could gauge Frasquina's reaction except Cloud, as everything she said was in voodoo-speak. And Cloud was sulking as she thought her stint of service at Bandomday should have pushed her to the top, over me. It still wasn't clear why Pokey had done this—promoted me of all people—but it did have a few advantages, the least of which wasn't my ability to try to avoid being stepped on by my co-workers.

As I walked up behind Clarice, intent on carrying out Miss Pokey's wishes to extricate the receiver from her ear, I could hear her conversation. It brought back unpleasant memories of Anastasia at Babley's.

"Beau, we've already set the date and I've ordered shoes for the bridesmaids." Pause. "I know it is but . . . God damn, Beau! You filthy pig . . . how dare you call me that! And after all I've done for you. Maybe we should call the wedding off . . . YOU GO TO HELL. DON'T TELL ME TO GO TO HELL!"

Pretty much everyone was used to the screaming by now. I was told it had been going on for months before I came. According to the others (sans Frasquina) Clarice was on the phone non-stop, discussing wedding plans, the price of tea in China, what the latest fashions were in Swaziland, and well . . . a little of everything. But the most disturbing aspect of her conversations involved a call each day to Beau at exactly nine-thirty every morning.

After leaving the room for ten minutes, she would hit her speed dial, wait, and then deliver the message. "Two pounds," we would hear her say. Then on another day, "Three pounds." One day she seemed ecstatic. "A seven-pounder!" she exclaimed, loud enough for all of us to hear. We endured this for the longest time until one day Cloud could stand it no more and asked Clarice, in earshot of everyone else, what the weights were all about.

Without missing a beat, Clarice explained that she would call Beau after each of them had a bowel movement and they would compare how much the waste material in question weighed. Repulsion on the part of her co-workers gave way after a few moments to an even bigger problem. It was a question, really, and was put to Clarice by Perkel as Cloud and I were in shock and Frasquina didn't understand English much more than she spoke it. Even before it was asked I shuddered to think what passing a seven-pound bowel movement felt like.

"I hope I'm not being nosey," Perkel started in, his arms crossed, leaning up against the outside wall of her cubicle, "but how do you *know*?" None of us were sure we wanted the answer, but in a moment we had it anyway. Clarice pulled a scale from her enormous purse. Relief set quickly in as we realized it was the kind for weighing an entire person and not some portion thereof.

"I weigh myself in the morning before I come to work, then I weigh myself after making doo-doo. The difference is what my bowel movement is," she said, hoping to have placated our curiosities. She blinked largely and slowly, several times. We just stood there, perplexed yet mesmerized. Finally, Cloud asked the question we were all thinking. She began it with a face—the kind someone might have who's just eaten a bad piece of cheese—followed by gritted teeth and a wrinkled nose.

"Why," Cloud asked, "would you even *care?*"

Again, without missing a beat Clarice explained: "Beau and I are trying to get our bowel movements synchronized. We figure that since we're getting married, that we should try to get our lives as coordinated as possible. Beau says it's a true sign of love—to have bowel movements that weigh the same."

"I'll bet," was all Cloud said, and walked away. The rest of us drifted back to our cubicles, hoping that things would be in sync soon.

And if you thought I couldn't pull John Wayne and the contents of his colon into the publishing industry, just wait—it gets even better. Bandomday was, and is, a never-ending metaphor for what passes as literature in some circles.

35

The New York Philharmonic was tearing through the first piece on the program. Robert had garnered a free pair of tickets from one of his rich Upper East Side clients and we found ourselves sitting in the fifth row of Avery Fisher Hall. Robert sometimes accepted gifts rather than money for his services, just to keep monotony at bay, and he had been particularly keen on attending this concert. After a flourish of brass, the first piece on the program started, moving on to the quipping chirp of woodwinds, the "ka-ching" of cymbals, and then the rousing and turbulent upward rush of strings. The orchestra was full into "Marche Hongroise" from *The Damnation of Faust* by Hector Berlioz. Robert sat enthralled—glued to every note. His musical background was showing.

After a pause, the ensemble continued with an equally raucous number: Richard Strauss's *Don Juan*. An upheaval of strings flung the notes toward us as the musical journey pulsed with aggressive repeated horn motifs and a jovial, virile melody. As with all Strauss, the instrumental offerings seemed to toss themselves from the stage and into the audience with reckless abandon, tethered only by musicians who held the reins. With the exception of a somber oboe passage and the twiddling-down ending instead of the expected heroic muscle flexing that Mr. Strauss is so noted for, the entire piece was stunning and glittering—a veritable rollicking good time of youthful abandon, love, and triumph. At intermission Robert and I made our way out to the lobby to see what libations might be had.

"Which piece did you like better?" I asked, taking two champagne glasses from the bar and handing him one. An overly vocal crowd of svelte concertgoers mingled slowly about us, their voices echoing in the cavernous high-ceilinged vestibule outside the hall. Above us a modern sculpture suspended itself from the ceiling.

"The first one. I liked the first one better."

"The Faust?" I asked, but Robert was busy making eye contact with a forty-year-old Philharmonic matron whose husband had turned his back, jocularly attempting badinage with what appeared to be a fellow country-club-goer.

"The Faust?" I repeated. "You didn't like the Strauss?"

"What? Oh, no, they were both great. I just hate to see Don Juan not come out on top—you know, big finish, lots of hero's trumpets and bass drum at the end." He sipped his champagne, scanning the room.

"Do you ever stop working?" I asked, becoming irritated at his roving eye. "Do you think Lothario could keep it zipped up for five minutes?"

"Can't afford to. Besides, this is one of the best places to get some new clients. You don't think I wore the Armani for my health, do you?"

"No, I guess not," I said. I waited, wanting to change the subject. His profession sometimes depressed me and not just on one level. Part of me wished I could have his life, or at least the life I imagined he had, and part of me wanted to run from the idea, screaming, into the middle of the street.

"See that one?" Robert said, indicating a beautiful woman of about forty with frosted hair and jewels the size of walnuts.

"Hmm."

"I should be paying her as good as she is in bed."

"You've had her?" I asked, incredulous.

"Not only her, but her husband as well," he continued, pointing out a dashing salt-and-pepper-haired gentleman who could have passed for the president of a bank. "Just not at the same time. And neither one knows about the other's goings on. They haven't had sex in years—at least not with each other—but boy oh boy, separately they're something else. My gain."

"At least you don't have to deal with the odd collection of people I have at work," I went on. "That and the strange things that have been happening to me—things sent to me since I've been in New York, the phone calls."

"What kind of things?"

"Nonsensical things. Someone sent me this book—*Jokes for the John*. And then a gardenia. I never figured out who. Now, at Bandomday, I get this package of some greenish-brown stuff. I had no idea what it was, but Frasquina—the voodoo princess—claimed it was tannis root. Something to do with evil spirits. I don't know. Oh, and then I get this Scrabble game sent to me and it's got a note attached that says 'The name is an anagram.' What the hell does that mean? And sent to me right when I started at Bandomday."

I looked at Robert. With the champagne glass turned up he still managed to keep an eye on the crowd and listen to me as well.

"And then there are the calls," I continued. "One time someone called and just kept repeating the word 'castanets' over and over. At least I think that's what they were saying. They just kept repeating it until it all seemed to run together."

"How very *Carmen.*"

"You're telling me."

"Is it a guy or a girl that calls?" Robert asked, more curious now, slightly disturbed.

"Always a girl—same girl. Sounds like she's trying to disguise her voice too," I said.

"And what else does she say?" Robert asked. He seemed irritated, yet engrossed at the same time, as if he knew something about the calls that I didn't. I noticed he gripped his champagne glass unusually tightly. It was as if he wanted to feign indifference but couldn't. Just watching him was a show in itself. I had never seen him this way.

"Different things," I said. "Sometimes it's someone's name—Vidal Sassoon, a Donald somebody—sometimes it's a motorcycle."

"Motorcycle?" He looked confused.

"Yeah. One time she called and just said 'Yamaha.' "

"Sounds like you've got a stalker, man. I'd be careful if I were you. And by the way, Yamaha is also a brand of piano, not just a motorcycle. Just hang up on the bastard if he calls again."

"She," I said. "It's always a 'she'."

"Whatever," Robert said, putting down his glass on a passing waiter's tray. "Ready to go back in for the rest of the concert?" he asked.

"Yeah. What's on for the remainder of the evening?" I asked, clumsily thumbing through the glossy program in an attempt to familiarize myself with the next piece.

"The rest of the program is devoted to Offenbach," Robert said, walking slightly in front of me, trying to edge his way through the crowd. "*Orpheus in the Underworld,*" he continued. "Music and the devil—what a combination," and with that we found our seats and headed into the realm of the outlandish musical adventures of Mr. O.

36

If Clarice's bowel movement accounts weren't enough diversion for our group at Bandomday, she had other methods of entertaining us. I decided that she was an escaped patient from Bellevue, and was dialing them one day for the purpose of having them retrieve her, when she came running up to my desk, more wide-eyed than usual, and in a state of semi-hysterics.

"I'm sorry I'm late this morning, but as I was getting out of the shower, someone rang the buzzer and I thought it was Beau because he said he would be coming by . . . but it wasn't." She was out of breath and keyed. "When I went to open the front door I realized it was my ex-boyfriend and he pushed his way into the apartment before I could do anything." She was picking up steam now, gathering energy.

The strange thing was that I noticed all the others—already at their desks, at work, and within earshot—weren't paying Clarice the least amount of attention. I, on the other hand, was riveted.

She continued. "So my ex rushes in and he starts screaming at me, 'You *bitch!* I'm going to kill you! You *bitch,*' over and over and over."

I was caught up in the story, forgetting all about the weight of her turds, her phone obsession, the fact that she was one of the oddest-looking people I had ever known.

"So then he grabs me and pushes me down on the sofa and he rapes me and rapes me and rapes me. It was horrible. I couldn't say anything; couldn't scream since he had a gun to my head. Finally he left and I called the police. I had to go to the hospital so they could examine me."

"Oh, my God, Clarice!" I said, "Are you all right?" I was concerned—she seemed pretty shaken up.

"I'll be okay. I mean, he was an old boyfriend," she said, wiping her nose and drying her eyes. "The police said that because I let him in, that they couldn't do anything; that since he was an old boyfriend it was his word against mine. I'll be okay if I can just get back to work now and get settled in."

"Listen, you take all the time you need," I said, "and if you want to talk to me about it, I'm here for you, okay?"

"I appreciate that," she said, and sulked off to her cubicle.

"Is the dutty duppy man dweet," said Frasquina to herself in her strongest Jamaican accent, and I could hear her flipping through the pages of a manuscript she had been working on since I had come to Bandomday—*Logarithms and Antilogarithms of the 1950s*. I imagined her with her lack of English and sixth-grade math skills trying to figure out the author's intent.

A while later, after Clarice had calmed down—she was now on the phone with Beau, pleading for him not to be angry with her over the rape—I approached Cloud, who was reviewing a book proposal for the many uses of cooking oil outside of the kitchen.

"Poor Clarice," I said, hoping to start a conversation. "She had a rough morning. I'm thinking of letting her go home early."

Cloud didn't say anything at first, but rolled her eyes and smirked. "I wouldn't get too upset if I were you. These kinds of things happen all the time."

"Cloud, try and show a little compassion. After all, the girl was raped this morning," I managed in a loud whisper, anger rising in me at Cloud's insensitivity.

"Yo, mister man, boss-boy, Perkins. I've got to cut out early. My twins have a fever and I've got to get to the emergency room." It was Perkel—his arm through his backpack, heading out the door.

"Why can't your wife go? She stays at home all day. Doesn't she—" but he was gone, out of earshot before I could finish.

"What is it with you people?" I said to myself as I walked back to my desk.

> Witness for the prosecution: Name's Clarice. Clarice Butel. I live in Queens. I work for Bandomday as a reader. I've been there for six years. Max Perkins was my supervisor. He had it in for me from day one. I never did anything to him, but he hounded me

192

constantly about being on the phone and then accused me of lying. I wasn't lying. My father will tell you I wasn't lying. And if you ever need a ballpoint pen, whatever you do don't buy one. My father has thousands of them. He actually has an entire room in his house as big as Madison Square Garden, and it's filled to the ceiling with nothing but ballpoint pens. They're all the same kind. So don't buy one. He has more ballpoint pens than *anyone*. Can I step down now?

37

Her voice was seductive; slightly dirty, hungry: "She ate the words out of his mouth as he fed them, close up. 'I love you'—breathy and hot, his mouth on hers, his hand at the side of her face, their bodies touching, pressing together. The moment was intense—a bursting flame on which has been thrown more fuel. He writhed on top of her, his thick meaty pole pressing down, both of them not bothering to undress, not taking the time. Skirt up and pants down they found each other and as his breathing intensified, mounting her with fervor, he pushed into her flower-soft folds. They became as one and shuddered together—the original sin made complete by animal instinct and the dizzying drug-like lust for the moment. She had seized on his man-meat with her love box, sucking him into—"

"Clarice!" I screamed in the direction where the soft porn was coming from. "What are you doing?"

She paused from her reading for a moment. "I'm just reading Beau a section of this manuscript in order get his opinion. He's an expert on love, you know."

"All I know is that you live on the phone and you're not getting any work done. So get off right now." I was yelling at her from my cubicle, having perfected the Bandomday technique of talking to someone while not looking at them. I knew it was Beau she was speaking with because he was the only one that she ever called. He never called *her*—she never gave him a chance—and she dialed him no less than twenty times a day to discuss the weight of her excrement, the upcoming wedding, and everything in between. While I felt sorry for the sexual assault she had endured, her time on the phone had increased. And it seemed odd that someone who had just been raped would want to quote a pornographic novel.

I could hear her arguing with Beau now, telling him to calm down. Then things must have heated up for she began to scream, her voice choking with emotion. "I WAS RAPED, DAMMIT! DON'T

YOU CARE? DON'T YOU CARE ABOUT ME?" she spewed into the receiver. I tried not to listen. I tried to concentrate on my work, this latest manuscript by a New York doctor on the merits of toenail fungus, but Clarice was driving me to distraction. I decided to take care of some personal business since I couldn't make any headway on that particular manuscript or the other one I was supposed to be reading—*How to Improve Your Life and Get Rid of Your Husband.* The latter was a pamphlet by a housewife with no professional credentials. The reading was excruciating as the would-be author attempted to relate the virtues of making your own soap and what the end result would be on your husband's mood after he had attempted to bathe with the homemade object—"Don't tell him that it's made up of ninety percent lye, just let him find out on his own! You can save over ten dollars a year by doing this!"

I decided at that point to take care of some personal business and try to find out who was calling me with the puzzling messages—the ones I had told Robert about at the Philharmonic concert. I proceeded to call the phone company about a new service I had heard of, termed Caller ID. The service wasn't yet available in New York in 1990, but I wanted to know when they thought it might be introduced to the general public. I was growing tired and a bit worried about the hang-ups and strange calls I'd been receiving. The last message had contained a name—a Donald Baumgart—and I thought perhaps this was the person annoying me. Somehow the name was familiar, but I couldn't quite place it.

"You're sure it's not available now, anywhere in the area?" I asked the girl on the other end of the line. "See, I've been getting hang-up calls and cryptic messages from—" but it was too late, she too had hung up.

Trying to slog through some bills from home and a mail order catalog occupied the rest of my time. By lunch I had managed to kill most of the morning.

As if the day hadn't been wasted already, Clarice, because of a lover's quarrel with Beau, decided that I would do as someone to talk to. Lucky me. About twelve fifteen I looked up to see her standing next to the opening of my cubicle. I waited, thinking that if

I ignored her she would go away, but she persisted, open-mouthed and wide-eyed, looking for an opportunity to pounce.

"So we had this really intense thing happen yesterday," she began, regardless of my obvious lack of interest. "We've been getting these calls from someone for the last year. Really obscene ones. My father always answers the phone."

"The guy with the pens, right?"

She turned suddenly defensive; paranoid. "How did you know about that? That's government knowledge. You're not supposed to know about the pens."

"Clarice," I said, pursing my lips, "*you* told me."

"Oh . . . yeah . . . right. Anyway. So we've been getting these obscene calls. The person says things like, 'I'm going to come over there and cut your pecker off, you pantywaist,' or, 'I just had sex with your wife and she rode me like a pony.' "

"Clarice, spare me the details. I think you've been reading too many manuscripts."

"Honest! This had been going on now for over a year and my father was furious. So he says to the caller, 'We've got Caller ID and I *know* who you are. I'm calling the police because I can see your name."

"Caller ID?" I said, thinking about my approach to the phone company that very morning regarding the service. "Do you live in New York or New Jersey?" I asked.

"We live in New York. Queens. What does that have to do with anything?" Clarice asked, but not letting me answer, continued with her story. "So my father recognized the name and realized it was our next-door neighbor. He goes over there and confronts the guy and there was this big fight and our neighbor pulls out a gun and shoots my father in the head twice. He's okay. They rushed him to the hospital and they say he'll make it, but it was a really close call."

"Your father was shot in the head twice?"

"Twice," Clarice said, holding up three fingers for emphasis. I found this last visual aid more worrisome than the story itself as Clarice had been an accounting major in college. I wondered if she knew Spong.

196

"Don't you mean that your father found out it was the neighbor some other way—not by Caller ID?" I went on. "He couldn't have seen the caller's name and—"

"No, it was Caller ID. I was standing right there and I saw it too. You could see the guy's name and number—everything."

I waited, partially out of pity, partially out of wonder, partially out of drama. Then I looked her square in the face and let go: "Clarice, New York hasn't gotten Caller ID yet. I just called the phone company this morning to ask about getting it. It's years away and they don't even have prototypes available. Your family doesn't have it. No one does."

Clarice just looked confused for a moment, caught in her own trap. There was no escape. Her eyes widened even more than usual and she fidgeted. Then she spoke.

"Well, we're *going* to be getting it," she said and walked away.

38

I knew that if I wanted to get even with Reeda for the runaround she had given me I would have to wait; bide my time; prepare the set-up. Initially the plan had been to have her find me an agent after I finished paying for her vacation to St. Bart's, then work on finding a publisher. But now with my job at Bandomday I could afford a little leeway in our relationship; I could afford to play with her a bit. Plus, I was working hard on my own, reconstructing my novel separately from the revisions I showed her; getting it in shape to slip in amongst the drivel that came to the readers' department. But I needed to teach her a lesson, not only for myself, but so she would think twice about taking advantage of the next unsuspecting wordsmith.

My plan was to make her think I was crazy—and dangerous—just to scare her. I couldn't just become psychotic, but rather had to ease into things. I had begun the process last time when I purported to be hypnotized. At my next appointment—the one right after my subconscious revelation of "what had happened to me as a child," I decided to play another hand and give my character additional dimensions. After some harmless badinage with the iguana, two hamsters that were stuck together, and the ferret, I started displaying a twitch. Nothing too obvious, just a minor facial tic that occurred every ten seconds or so. I made sure I did this while petting one of the animals.

Timing was everything here. While Reeda hacked out a fee schedule with some unsuspecting student on the phone, I managed to speak a smattering of Russian to the two hamsters, some Greek to the ferret, and a totally made-up language to the iguana. I made sure this happened just as she was winding down her conversation with her latest victim.

"Bleepahapa moneyubu goonadub?" I said to the iguana who seemed to understand perfectly. He showed me the tip of his pink tongue as if to say, "Finally, someone is going to do a number on this bitch—I'm with you all the way." I could hear Reeda in the background with her usual spiel: "I don't really have any time right now for a new student, but since you're so talented, I'm going to make an exception." The cup overflowed with obsequiousness ($3.25).

"Vi takzhye znayetye, shto Natalya Eevanavna iz Navaseebeerska (You also know that Natalya Ivanovna is from Novosibirsk") I said in phonetic Russian to a mourning dove huddled under a chair.

"What language is that?" inquired Reeda, finally hanging up.

"What language is what?" I said and gave her a blank look. Then I continued my facial tic.

"Well, then. Anyway. Let's get started since— "

But she stopped when she saw me. I had doubled over on the floor. I started to shake and cry and then get hold of myself. "I'm sorry. I don't know what came over me. It's just that, well, ever since I've been coming here and you've been talking about getting to the truth in my writings, I've been thinking a lot about things and . . ."

"Go on. You can tell me," she said, hurriedly settling onto the folding chair, pen poised at paper. I waited until I was sure she was ready to write down my latest childhood revelation.

"Certain things—incidents," I said, cutting my eyes to the side, bowing my head, "have been . . . coming up for me. You know, sort of a past life regression type of thing."

"This is normal. Yes, go on." She had suddenly become the model of professionalism, taking on the persona of a psychiatrist. She was on the edge of her seat, eager to see what secrets would spill forth.

"Well, these images have been coming to me, just out of nowhere," I said, "and some of them are really disturbing." I waited. "But you know," I continued, teasing her, "I probably should be telling this to a licensed psychologist since I think my problems could be quite serious."

"You can tell me. I'm a psychologist. That's what I do. I psychoanalyze people. And I'm less expensive. Go on."

I wanted to stop, come out of character, and tell her she *wasn't* less expensive, but instead proceeded to relate some horrific visions I had made up on my way to the session, filling in with a little gore and a lot of angst for good measure. By the time I finished she was enthralled, so much so that she hadn't noticed we had gone over my allotted time by twenty minutes.

"Oh, look," I said, pointing at the clock on the wall, "I've gone *waaaaaay* over."

"Don't worry about it," she snapped, and waved the matter away with her hand. "I'd like to put you under hypnosis now and we can see what hidden things affected you to this great an extent."

"I don't know. I'm a little tired today and the hypnosis thing scares me." I could tell she was frustrated—right where I wanted her. I needed to make her beg for my made-up psychosis, my hidden angst, my abused inner child. "I'm starting to get more than a little uncomfortable with this whole process anyway. Do you think we could go back to the writing?" I said.

"No! Don't you see? This is a major breakthrough for us. You will never be able to write until I have healed you of your pain, your sickness."

"But I don't feel sick," I said naively.

"But you *are*. You're very sick and you need help. And I can do that. That's what I do—I help people."

"Oh," I said, my eyes wide like Clarice's, my mouth agape, "I had no idea."

39

"I'm not touching it."

"Well, you can count me out. Call housekeeping. Call the police. Hell, call anybody but just get it out of here."

I walked up just in time to get the tail end of a conversation between Cloud and Perkel. "What's going on?" I asked, approaching the door to the concrete bunker where we worked. The din from the basement machinery churned around the corner and I had been lucky today with the elevator—no stuck door or crowbar had been in the scenario.

"That," said Cloud, and pointed to a plastic baggie filled with some sort of brown substance.

"What is it?" I asked, bending over slightly. "Oh, God, I hope that's not what I think it is."

"That's what we thought," said Perkel. "Look at it, man."

"It can't be," I said, straightening up. Thank God the person leaving the gift had sealed it. "You guys are nuts. Is this some kind of a joke? You guys are playing me for an idiot. I know you've been upset since I was made supervisor, but this is too much."

"Hey, don't look at me," said Perkel, throwing his hands up. "I use the can like a normal person." Cloud just rolled her eyes and walked away.

"Well what am I supposed to do with it?" I asked loudly, but Perkel and Cloud had gone inside the office. I followed, settling in and getting my desk in order before I called the janitorial staff.

"Yeah, I need one of your guys to come remove something from in front of our door. Yeah, we're in the basement. The readers' room. First door on the left. You'll see it. Trust me, you can't miss it," I said to the person on the other end of the line. By noon it was gone and the excitement of the day was over. But the next morning, it—or a very good facsimile—was back. And this time the plastic bag wasn't sealed.

"Oh, man, get a whiff of that," Perkel said as he whisked by me. "They didn't even seal it up this time." He was coming out of the office, heading to the elevators and it was only 8:30 in the morning.

"Where do you think you're going?" I asked, seeing him carrying his backpack.

"One of the boys is sick. And my wife's got the flu. There's a book proposal for you on my desk," he added as he disappeared down the hallway. About that time Frasquina appeared at the doorway to the office.

"Lawd have mercy pon Miss Percy," she said as she looked down at the brown gift. It sagged inside the baggie and slumped to one side. "Put de sinting inna de bag," and with that she retreated to her cubicle. I was just about to call housekeeping *and* security when Clarice appeared at my desk.

"I'm sorry I'm late," she said, having come in behind me, completely oblivious to the "present" someone had left on our doorstep. "Beau's grandmother died this morning and we had to go to the hospital but it's not a big deal since she had gangrene and the leg had to come off anyway."

I just looked at her for a moment. Then I composed myself. "Okay, Clarice," I said, and then I managed to choke out a "Sorry to hear about Granny."

That seemed to placate her and she slunk off to her cubicle.

When I eventually got in touch with housekeeping they were none too pleased and suggested we post a sign in our office indicating the way to the restroom. Nevertheless they came to clean up the offending article and we made it to lunch before too much else happened. While I was out looking for a deli whose line wasn't too long, I ran into Cloud, chain-smoking and leaning against a shiny granite wall of one of Manhattan's skyscrapers.

"Eaten yet?" I asked her, trying to make conversation.

"I'm still trying to regain my appetite after this morning," she said and stamped out the remaining bit of cigarette with the toe of her shoe. Then she lit another one.

"Know what you mean."

"If you want my opinion, which you probably don't but I'll give it to you anyway, I think it's Miss Bug-Eyes," Cloud said.

"Clarice?"

"Think about it. Who else do you know that weighs their waste material? She's probably got some new method. Besides, I haven't seen the scale lately."

"She's a wack-job, but leaving last night's dinner on the doorstep? I don't know." I thought about the person who had been calling me, sending me things in the mail—the tannis root, the gardenia, the Scrabble game, and lately a bottle of the perfume—*Detchema*—and wondered if they were the same person who was now making nightly deposits. Still, I didn't say anything to Cloud about the mysterious items and phone calls.

"Well, somebody's doing it and it was there when I came in this morning, so I know it's not you and I know it's not me," Cloud continued.

"Perkel?"

"He's never here. Always out with one of his sick kids."

"There's Frasquina. I know she hates me. At least I think she does from what I can understand," I said. "You know, doo-doo that voodoo that you do so well?" We stood watching throngs of office workers search for someplace to eat; the ebb and flow of New York humanity. I wondered how many other places of work were blessed with the problems we had.

"Don't think so. Frasquina is the type who would leave it directly on your desk, not at the front door."

"You do have a point. But why would Clarice do it? What's it going to get her?"

"Look, the girl is pathological. The only thing missing is the pinecone swags and 'made in the Black Forest' inscribed on her back."

"Huh?"

"Cuckoo. She rants constantly on the phone to Beau about the wedding and this and that. No one can get any work done because of her. She doesn't get any calls from anyone else and she only calls him. And she calls him twenty times a day. It's very distracting. *And* she lies about everything under the sun. Who else could it be?"

"But she's the senior reader. She's making decisions that affect hundreds of thousands of dollars for the company. We're talking about a girl who gets to suggest which books get through to be published." I shuddered even as I said it. I wondered how I was going to get my book past not only Clarice, but Perkel, Cloud, Frasquina, and Miss Pokey. Then there were the higher-ups to consider.

"And she shits in a baggie and leaves it outside the door," said Cloud.

"I fail to see the connection."

There was a beat; a pause. Cloud looked at me as if I had two heads. Then she spoke. "Have you seen the bestseller list lately?" was all she said, and that pretty much shut me up for the moment.

40

The problem with having credentials of any kind is twofold: First, if the person is an academic who has secured some position within fifty feet of a building designed for the purpose of learning, they are so entrenched in the philosophy of their cronies and contemporaries that they've brainwashed themselves into actually believing the ideas they preach—an unfortunate side effect for those studying to make a living in the field of writing, art, music, or just about any other form of expression. Our great halls of learning are littered with composers of squeak-bonk music, artists who believe anything that can be seen with the naked eye is ready for a museum, and writing that would make even James Joyce offer up his best "Huh?"

The second problem with having credentials falls in the lap of those working in the real world—you know, that place that actually makes money and keeps track of things? Generally speaking, if someone toils on planet Earth in a corporate environment, they've so fallen in love with their own perceived success and importance that there is never room for anything deviating from the plan that got them there. In short, and in both scenarios, they have their heads so far up their asses that they just keep going around in circles, wearing the grass out so that the enormous playground of life looks like a landing pad for flying saucers.

Enter publishing.

If you don't believe my theory about the professional world, just look at the bestseller list for the past ten years—all the same names because, God forbid anyone would take a chance on some newcomer for more than one week. And the books aren't exactly complicated. "The story of a woman who is determined to find out who murdered her best friend," the one-line description in *The New York Times Book Review* section might read. Now that's original. The writing's probably about as good as the idea. The whole enterprise of publishing is a vainglorious and indefatigable secret handshake that even the most tenacious writers can't figure out.

And this leads us directly to the problem with Reeda; that never-ending fount of concepts and criticisms; that almost-combination of academia and business; that anorexic succubus with pets. This was the encapsulation of her ominous pedigree, for she was caught in even more circumscribed territory—a land that is neither academic nor professional; a place void of not only tattered lists of safe reading for the bovine and closed-minded, but one that is also void of professional experience. In short, Reeda was a con artist.

It had taken me a while to figure it out for several reasons and even then the process wasn't absolute. First, I wanted to believe that she knew what she was doing. I needed to believe it, and more importantly, I had to believe it—I didn't have a lot else. In the second place, I assumed that because she was from New York, had her own apartment, and actually made a living doing something, she was intelligent. And thirdly, well, she just plain out-and-out lied. So I don't really blame myself too much with a combination like that. When you want something desperately enough, the mind is capable of bending into some pretty yoga-like positions. And if the average position for most people was lotus, then I already had two legs behind my head.

It's hard to say when the exact moment was that I fully admitted it to myself—the fact that she was totally inept and a fraud—and I think it was essentially a slow process as my subconscious might have known that I needed time to adjust.

Oh, I had played with her mind already, but there was still that slim thread of hope, that thought in the back of my cranium that said, "Perhaps just this once I'm wrong and she's right." Between having to sleep in a bathtub, impersonate accountants, clean up other people's excrement in a baggie, and generally be mistreated by every living entity in sight, I suppose my inner self wanted some semblance of stability, and in a way Reeda did offer that. I knew that each time I went to her for help, she would bleed me emotionally, financially, and spiritually until I was left completely drained and feeling suicidal. There's something to be said for a routine.

Today would have been no different except for the fact that something was happening to me. I was experiencing some chemical or emotional change where my body was saying a very loud and definite *"No"* to things. And it was saying it to her—this woman of cons and schemes. She had played me like some broken and out-of-tune violin, and so now I would return the favor.

"We're going to spend the first half of your session on the rewrites, and then the second half on more hypnosis," Reeda began, all the while scribbling notes in her binder. "Hey, pumpkin," she said to a hamster, sitting on one half of the binder. "Yes, um did a piddle, didn't um?"

"Should you really be performing hypnosis on someone?" I asked, even though she had failed to actually put me under.

"That's what I do. I'm a hypnotist," she said. "I hypnotize people."

"I thought you were a novelist, screen writer, essayist, short story author, writer of articles, and Grand Poo-Bah of the literary world," I said, wanting to see what she would do.

She ignored me. "Now, let's get back to your novel. When last we spoke you were going to do another rewrite for me where you added in your pain and we fleshed out the characters somewhat."

I handed her the binder with my mock rewrite and sat back while she scanned it. The usual groans and muffled sounds followed.

"What if," she began, finger to her lips, "we introduced something for comic effect. Hmm? What about that?"

I sat with arms crossed. "And where would this item go?" I asked.

"Well, I think it should go at the beginning."

"I thought you said we needed to get to my pain, that we needed to get past the comedy and get to what the real story was."

207

"Well, yes, I did say that, and that's exactly what we're going to do after this, but first we need some object, some *thing* for the story to be about." Then she rolled her eyes upwards before closing them, took a deep breath, and exhaled. The wildlife in the room was unusually silent today—all watched her from perches, under chairs, and on top of bookcases.

"I'd like to introduce the idea of something attached to Mrs. Smith," she began, as if reading some ancient scripture that only she could see in her mind's eye. "Something behind her. Some object, some . . . humorous effect that would pull the story along."

"Perhaps something attached to her rear end?" I asked.

"Yes, yes, that's it! Something attached to her rear end! It could be a metaphor. It would have to be something large that was carried around, like a pillow or something. I know, I've got it! She could always have to sit on a pillow—no—no, there's something else . . ."

"How 'bout a bustle," I said, my tone flat and sarcastic, thinking the comment would irritate her.

"A bustle would be perfect," she responded, as if the idea were totally new. "But we've set the story in the 1980s now, so we'd have to move it back, say . . . to the late 1880s."

I couldn't believe she was doing this. The only thing scarier than having been manipulated into completely changing my novel and then having to put it back exactly the way it had been, was the idea that Reeda might not actually realize what she was doing. I couldn't resist.

"Do you not remember the first draft that I brought in?" I asked, my eyes squinted, my arms still crossed.

"First drafts are sacred. Remember, we spoke about that."

"I remember. Do you? The first draft I brought in was set in the late 1800s and dealt with a woman who wore a bustle," I said.

"I don't remember that. I think you're making that up." Then she began to physically close up, become tight. "Why won't you give me credit for helping you? Are you so afraid that I might get some credit out of this?"

"I'm not afraid of—"

"Do you think I'm going to want a percentage of the sales of your book? Is that it? You think that just because I gave you the idea of a woman wearing a bustle in the late 1800s, that I'm going to come after you for a percentage? You think I'm that low a person? I've got news for you, I do what I do for the love of my students. I want to help them write better and I don't appreciate you twisting things around this way."

I had seen this coming. It was the next logical step in her illogical process. As I said before, the realizations had been gradual, but evident nevertheless. I knew that if I wanted to play with her as she had done with me it would be necessary to keep my temper and not show my true feelings. That plus the fact that however much a nut-job she was, she might actually *have* connections with major publishing houses, agents, and editors. It wouldn't have surprised me to find out she and the people at Bandomday knew each other.

"I wouldn't do something like that," I said. "I'm really grateful that you've agreed to help me. I really meant no offense. It's just that I'd like to wrap this process up so that we can get on with selling the book instead of spending all this time changing things."

"The work is nowhere near ready. You've got a good fifteen or twenty rewrites before I can allow you to put it out there for an editor or agent to read."

"Fifteen or twenty!" I exploded, and then caught myself. "Okay, okay, okay." I made myself take several deep breaths. Even the naked parrot was silent. I glanced over at him and he seemed as confused as I was. Percy, the iguana, managed a yawn.

"Now, what we need to work on is a plot. The book, as you've written it, has no plot, no idea, no premise."

Part of me wanted to reach across the room and pull her voice box from her throat. "You-told-me-several-weeks-ago-that-a-plot-was-suspect—that a book shouldn't have a plot," I managed to say evenly between clenched teeth.

"All books have to have a plot. Without a plot, no one is going to read it."

"This week," I said, sarcastically.

"I beg your pardon?"

"Nothing."

And so things went on this way for a good thirty minutes. By the time she was finished with me, I had decided to be finished with her—agent or no agent.

"We need to begin your hypnosis session," she said, getting up and rummaging through her desk. She produced a tape recorder—at least twenty years old—and set it down on the coffee table.

"What's that for?" I asked.

"So that we can go over what you've said during hypnosis. You won't remember anything once I put you under, so we'll need this. Believe me, it will help with your writing. You've improved a lot already since you've been coming to me."

"I guess," I managed, half-heartedly, thinking about the character I was to play in a moment.

Then she began her usual routine: breathe deeply; count backwards from ten to one; feel your body sinking down into the floor; counting backwards again; look up even though your eyelids are closed. Finally, when she was convinced I was "under," she continued, her voice breathy and seductive.

"Maaaaaax. Maaaaaax Perkinnnnnns. You will hear me and do as I bid. Do you understand? Raise your right index finger if you understand."

I raised my right index finger after a second or two of making it quiver slightly. "Bid?" I thought to myself. "Where did *that* come from?" I wanted to say, "Yes, your majesty," but kept quiet instead.

"Good. Now, we're going to go back to your childhood. You're floating back over the years, becoming younger and younger. You're now fifteen years old. Now you're ten. And now you're going back even further. I want you to go back to your first painful memory and relive it. You are safe. You may go back now. Take your time."

It was hard not to smile, and to make matters worse, just as I was about to speak I felt something warm on my right leg. *Dog*, or rather the excuse for one, was peeing on my ankle.

"I feel all warm and tingly," I said, trying to replicate tired jaw muscles.

210

"Yes, yes, this is good. You're warm all over," Reeda responded.

"No. Just my right leg," I said, and opened my eyelids enough to see her look down and grapple with the animal. As she picked it up and carried it to the other side of the room, wheels and all, an arc of urine shot out and I could hear the droplets fall across the mass of papers on her desk. Then the scamper of Percy's iguana feet as he scrambled to get out of the line of fire.

"That's right, you're warm and floating, floating back to your first painful memory. Can you remember that, Max?"

"Yes," I began. "Horrible . . . painful . . . what's going on . . . can't . . ."

"Tell me what's happening, Max. What do you see?"

Now I know I should have prepared something beforehand, but I hadn't. I felt at that moment like someone who's forgotten his homework assignment and has to make up an excuse. I stalled.

"Hurt . . . father . . . room . . ."

"What's in the room, Max? Tell me what you see." She was back now, sitting down across from me. I could sense her. The dog had either been relegated to its bed or was too tired to hobble back across the room. A pair of wheels squeaked timidly in the distance.

"Jamaican man. Cocaine. There's . . . a room full of pens. My father is a pen salesman," I said, trying to be more lucid now. "Someone is calling us . . . threatening . . . neighbor. A Jamaican accountant with nine children is threatening us. He's got Caller ID, and he's . . . NO, NO!"

"What is it, Max? What do you see?"

"He's doing something inside a plastic bag . . . can't . . . he's . . . oh, God!"

"You can do this. I'm here for you."

"He's going to the bathroom in a plastic bag and . . . leaving it outside our door! Oh, God, and now . . . I'm buzzing in someone to the apartment and now . . . he's forcing me into the bathtub and he's . . . he's . . . OH, IT'S REALLY SO HORRIBLE!"

"I'm here, Max. What do you see? I can help you." She was scribbling everything down.

211

"He's raping me and . . . calling me . . . fag-boy, Jew-boy . . . and now, everyone is . . . oh, no, this is so . . . awful. They're putting a piece of . . . plywood over me—over the tub—and they're all eating baby food! Oh, God! Baby food! Then a man with a cleft palate is quoting something . . . some Bette Davis movie . . . 'Fasten your seatbelts!' Oh, God, help me!"

I waited a moment for dramatic effect. Then I swallowed hard and pretended anxiety to the level that I couldn't speak. I moved my mouth but let no sound escape, just as I had seen actors do on bad made-for-TV-movies.

"Max? Max? I want you to continue. Will you do that for me?"

I nodded and managed a sniffle.

"I want you to stay in this place and tell me what you see. Be brave. You must do this for your writing. You will never be able to write anything until you've dealt with this and accepted what happened to you. Do you understand?"

I nodded again.

"Okay, now. What do you see?"

"There's . . . a . . . group of . . . people," I continued. "The Jamaican accountant, the one . . . that raped me, is now organizing everyone . . . in a circle. They're . . . they're doing some type of chanting. And there's Art Deco fixtures everywhere. The Rockettes are there and . . . Satan. It's some type of Satan . . . no, devil worship. They're all eating baby food and chanting something about magazine subscriptions," I continued. But by now I was growing tired of the game. I waited a moment and then began to wheeze heavily and snore. Then I came to for a second, eyes open and face alert. "All for now," I said, a completely new voice, signing off. Then I let my head drop again.

"I'm going to count to ten, and when I snap my fingers, you will come out of this hypnotic state and remember nothing," Reeda said, and then began her tally. When she reached ten, I opened my eyes and looked right at her, pretending to leave off where we had been previously, discussing the plot of my novel.

"You really think a plot is that important in order to have a successful book?" I asked, suddenly changing my attitude to perky and interested, now completely coherent and void of all angst.

"Oh, absolutely," Reeda said as she scribbled down notes in her binder. "It's a must."

41

"I'm sorry I'm late, but we were driving back early this morning from Atlantic City and one of the persons in the backseat reached forward and slapped me on the back and a huge puss-filled blister broke and Beau had to rush me to the emergency room and the police started chasing us and followed us to the hospital and while they were trying to arrest Beau for speeding we discovered there was no one there to sew me up so Beau slaps the nurse in the emergency room and says, 'I'll sew her up,' and then he gets the policeman's gun and holds everyone at gunpoint with one hand while he sews up the boil on my back with the other and then we managed to escape so now I'm here but I'll work through lunch to make up the time."

Clarice had spewed this out in a single breath—at the speed of light. I needed a nap after just listening to the thing.

"I see," was all I said. I hadn't even looked up from the latest manuscript—*Was Moses Really a Woman? The True Story of Biblical Politics*. This was nothing new—Clarice's stories about any and everything. I had learned, as most had in the department, to ignore her. She was still circumspect as far as the baggie incidents were concerned, but they hadn't happened now for several weeks and we thought the whole affair was over.

Still, she spent most of the day on the phone, screaming at Beau about the choice of flowers for the wedding, the fact that he never called her, and how she was going to kill herself if he didn't sleep with her more often. Toward the end of this particular day, Miss Pokey called me into her office.

"Perkins, you're the supervisor," she started in. "You've got to get a grip on these people. Perkel is out twenty-four seven with those brats of his, Frasquina is still on the logarithms manuscript, Cloud is hooked on nose candy, and Clarice is driving everyone nuts with the phone calls."

I sat down. There were issues I wanted to discuss and I felt that digging my heels in was the only way. Miss Pokey had basically put me in the position of supervisor so that she didn't have to deal with everyone's problems. She didn't want to know anything about anyone; she just wanted things to run smoothly.

"I'm open to suggestions," I said.

"You're supposed to know what to do. It should be instinct. I shouldn't have to tell you anything. I just want the department to shape up, but since you asked, I'll give you my opinion. First of all, let's take Cloud. She's in the bathroom constantly, snorting cocaine. Sure, she gets her work done, but she's strung out. I suggest you take her out to lunch, talk to her. Perkel: Tell him to get his butt here and stay here. I don't give a damn about his kids. Frasquina: It will be up to you to teach her English. I suggest you do this after work hours. She can come to your apartment. She's been here long enough to learn the language and I want her to stop using that hocus-pocus mumbo-jumbo. Finally, Clarice. She lives on the phone. It's going to have to be surgically removed from her ear. You may or may not know that we had a complete new phone system installed last year. It tracks all phone conversations within the company—who called, when they called, what calls went out, what time—everything. No one here can make a move on the phone without it being recorded in the database. It's even ahead of anything the phone company has. Here's the number of the woman in charge. Ask her for records. You'll need to write Clarice up for excessive phone use. I want people here to know that you're the boss. It's time you stepped up to the plate and took charge."

This was the longest conversation I had ever had with Pokey. She usually locked herself in her office and avoided the department as much as possible. Any attempt to bring a problem to her was met with hostility and angst. I figured that this latest interest in the department stemmed from the rumors floating around concerning a possible promotion she might soon receive. I should have known not to push, but I couldn't help it.

"Excuse me, Miss Pokey, but don't you think asking me to teach Frasquina English is a little outside the bounds of my duties at this company?"

At first she didn't respond. Then she snorted. "You!" She left a space for maximum discomfort. "I'm so tired of everyone shirking responsibility. I never want to hear 'It's not my job' again as long as you work here. As far as I'm concerned, *everything* is your job."

"Yes, Miss Pokey," I managed, gritting my teeth, and left her office. I had wanted to mention that someone had been defecating in a baggie and leaving it outside the office door, but given her mood and the fact that she wanted to know as little as possible, I thought this might be too much information for her to handle.

When I called a meeting the next day to discuss the group's behavior, the readers sat silent, taking in everything. No one responded, and in my naiveté I thought this good. It wasn't, and had I known I might not have delved into things as thoroughly as I did. I set up separate appointments with each employee.

The lunch date with Cloud was a disaster. I never came out and accused her of anything but tried as gently as I could to see if she needed help with any problems—emotional, physical, or chemical. She was cold and indifferent, saying that I was accusing her of a drug problem. Well, duh?

Perkel wouldn't even speak to me after hearing that I wanted to discuss his absences. He stormed out of the office and came back five hours later, indicating to me via eye contact alone that I had better lay off.

With my meager knowledge of Jamaican I managed to glean from Frasquina that if I didn't want an effigy made in my likeness with pins stuck in the genitals, I had better seek solace somewhere else. She finished by asking for a lock of hair and any fingernail clippings I might not need.

That left only Clarice, but before I could confront her I had to get some ammunition. I couldn't call the department that was in charge of communications to ask about the phone records—everyone could hear what was said in the office as we all had cubicles except for Miss Pokey—so I found my way upstairs to the appropriate floor and sought out the person in charge. After explaining my predicament, giving the phone extension and department, I was assured that the records I sought would be ready in a week or two. It seems they were backed up with requests as the department also handled other aspects of the company's business.

So, with the underlings' problems addressed—all except Clarice's—the hostility in the room was thick and fetid. And it therefore came as no surprise when, arriving early the next morning, I found a small plastic bag filled to the brim with the usual "gift," forlorn and sagging against the door. The top of the baggie was open and it was positioned precariously so that it had to be handled, sealed, and discarded before I could enter the office. Obviously my meeting the other day regarding the lack of professional conduct had hit a nerve. But what struck me odd was that Clarice had been the only one I had not yet confronted face to face, and it had been she who was the most likely candidate for depositing the putrid cache each night.

When I finally settled down at my desk, after having taken the latest offering into the men's room and gently placing it into a garbage can, I took stock of the situation. It was becoming clear now why Miss Pokey had put me in charge and I was feeling used. Still, I knew that if I wanted to climb out of the pit of readers, I would have to prove myself and somehow find a way to set things straight. And Miss Pokey had made it clear that she didn't want to know anything—she just wanted things to run smoothly and not be bothered with details.

I waited for Clarice's phone results, for Frasquina to finish her voodoo doll, for Perkel's wife to become pregnant again, and for Cloud's supplier to get back from vacation. While I did so, I amused myself with a visit to the security department of Bandomday Books. It was conveniently located on the same floor as the communications department, and after explaining what had been going on with the nightly offerings, they, while intrigued, were somewhat reluctant to implement what I was requesting.

"We'll have to get an okay from your boss, Miss Pokey," I was told when I mentioned that I wanted them to install a hidden security camera and have it focused on the doors to the office.

"Fine with me," I said, "but she's not going to like being bothered. She put me in charge of things." I waited for them to call her.

When the security officer returned shaking his head, I knew I had been correct.

"She wouldn't even wait for me to tell her what it was about. Said she didn't want to be bothered and to go ahead with whatever it was."

"Told you so," I said, and signed off on the necessary paperwork. That weekend, the device was installed and I waited, for the first time eagerly, for the next deposit.

Two days later Miss Pokey called me into her office. She was sneering even before I sat down.

"What's up with you and your attitude?" she asked, not bothering to cloak the question in even a Salvation Army coat of civility.

"What are you talking about?"

"You. Your relationship with the staff. You've managed to alienate every one of them. What are you doing?"

"I'm just doing what you asked. I've addressed most of the problems you told me to look into and everyone is giving me a hard time. As a matter of fact I need your support since they've really been uncooperative."

She waited a moment, chin on hand. Then she looked up without moving from her position. Her attitude seemed to change. "You're right. I only got their side of the story. I shouldn't have jumped to conclusions. Call them all in here now. I want to speak with everyone in the department. I'm going to let them know that *you're* the boss and whatever *you* say goes. It's about time they learned some respect for you, for me, for this company. Call them in."

I doubt that I have ever moved more quickly in my entire life. I was up in a second and within a matter of moments had collected my staff and herded them into Pokey's office. Some sat, some stood, and Perkel, with his arrogance, lifted his slovenly frame onto a low filing cabinet and proceeded to kick the front of it rhythmically with his heel.

"I've called you all into this meeting for a reason," Miss Pokey began, looking around the room at everyone. "Max has been telling me that he's been asking you to do certain things, questioning your alleged over-use of vacation time, and requesting overtime to get certain jobs done. And that he's been addressing your problems individually. Is this correct?"

They all nodded. Everyone had their arms crossed and all glared straight ahead, not looking at either me or Miss Pokey.

"Has Max apologized for his actions?"

"Nooooooo," they all chimed in as if the whole thing had been rehearsed.

I couldn't believe what I was hearing. What was going on? Just a few minutes ago she had said she was going to tell everyone who was the boss. I had gotten not only the rug pulled out from under me, but the entire building as well. I couldn't let this go.

"Wait a minute," I said, holding up my hand, getting ready to explode, "just a few minutes ago—" but I wasn't allowed to finish, for Miss Pokey had stood up and was directing her comments to me now.

"Max, you are to apologize to your staff for your behavior and then I expect a more professional attitude from now on. If you can't handle that, then we'll have to have another discussion and I can promise it won't be pleasant."

I was speechless. I looked around the room and the entire staff was glaring at me, smirking, their arms still folded. I couldn't believe this woman had done this to me. She was insane—a Munchausen by Proxy Syndrome with feet.

"Now everyone get out of my office," Pokey continued, "I've got work to do," and with that we all filed out the door. At some point you know when to retreat in order to prepare for the next round. Plus, I was in shock. Pokey had taken what little wind there was out of my sails and I was dazed, still trying to figure out how it all had happened.

"Guess you'd better watch your step," Perkel sneered at me, turning around to deliver the insult before returning to his desk.

A few days later I received a call from the Personnel Department. They informed me that Miss Pokey had set up an appointment with the company's psychiatrist for the following Thursday and that my attendance was mandatory. I thought for a moment about all the things I had been through since the move to New York and was getting ready to write my resignation letter. Then I remembered why I was here, suffering the slings and arrows of outrageous fortune. I had formulated a plan to get my book through the necessary channels of the publishing world, and I knew that if things were to go as needed I would have to persevere for a while at Bandomday. Besides, Reeda was not panning out as a connection so I needed to keep from making waves—for now.

"I'll be there," I heard myself say to the snooty voice on the other end of the line, "but first I want to come talk to you. Okay, fine, I'll take down his name . . . Dr. Patchin. That's the shrink? At three?" and as I hung up the phone I tried to remember where I had heard that name.

"Patchin, Patchin, Patchin," I said to myself, but couldn't place it.

42

Scene: An intimidating office on a high floor in one of Manhattan's sleek skyscrapers. Midtown. Posh furnishings; thick carpets. Ms. Stein, the bony and obstinate shrew from personnel who first interviewed Max, is seen emerging from a set of thick teak double doors. She says nothing but motions for him to follow. Reluctantly we see him get up and walk toward the back offices.

View from outside her office through a glass partition: We can't hear what's being said, but can see her sitting smugly behind a desk, hands folded in front of her. We see Max rising out of his chair, gesturing wildly. We can tell by his level of animation that he's yelling. He begins to pantomime sniffing cocaine, then starts to make motions as if he's sticking pins in a voodoo doll. Additional gestures follow and he ends with a semi-squatting position, motioning behind and pretending to seal a baggie. He finishes--his eyes bulging--by leaning over the desk. She looks at him impassively and begins to write something down.

"They want me to go to therapy! Me! They want *me* to go to therapy! I've got one employee who's Marie Laveau, another who's never at work because he can't keep it zipped up, and *another* who's so into nose candy that she's strung out all the time. And let's not even talk about Pokey. Oh, and one who's got the phone permanently attached to her ear, weighs her bowel movements, and who leaves the dirty deed outside the door each morning. And they want *me* to go to therapy!"

"Look, just play along with them. You know everyone in publishing is crazy. Just consider yourself lucky that Bandomday has an in-house counseling center." Robert seemed impassive, unconcerned with my latest run of bad luck. He sat opposite me at a diner on upper Broadway, casually looking over the cheeseburger deluxe that had arrived before him.

"I asked for mustard. They didn't give me mustard. I can't believe these people," he said, and then gestured, trying to get the waiter's attention.

"Forget about the mustard! I've got bigger problems. That excuse for a boss went to personnel and complained about me. Since when is what I've done any worse than what anyone else has done in that frickin' company?"

"I asked for mustard," Robert said to the waiter who had now appeared tableside. "And can I get a refill on the Coke?"

"Jesus! Would you listen to me for a minute and forget about the burger? I've got a manuscript that needs publishing and these people are wasting valuable time."

Robert gestured for the waiter again and the swarthy Greek man returned, head tilted, lips pursed. "Can I get some Thousand Island dressing?" Robert asked, putting forth his best charm.

There was a beat of silence.

"Vhat for?" the waiter asked, showing no emotion.

"For the lettuce and tomato," Robert explained, gesturing to the oversized garni that had come with the burger and fries.

"You want the dressing to put on the burger with the lettuce and tomato or you want to put it on the lettuce and tomato *only*—on the side?"

Robert squinted and looked at me. "On the side. I want to make a salad out of it."

"Then I have to charge you extra for a salad," the waiter added after another moment's pause.

"No, I've already got the lettuce and tomato. I don't want a salad. I just want the dressing."

"Look, if you wanted a salad, you should have ordered one. If you want the dressing for the burger, then it's free. If you want it to put on the lettuce, then I charge you. Got it?"

Robert looked over at me again. All I could do was shrug.

"Fine. I want it for the burger. I'm not even going to use the lettuce anymore. Just bring me the Thousand Island."

"I'm not doing that, my friend. You already told me you wanted it for the lettuce and tomato so now you are lying to me. You want dressing—you get charged," and with that the surly waiter stormed off.

"This is just very *Five Easy Pieces*," I said, moving my grilled cheese from one side of the plate to the other, momentarily forgetting about my required therapy session, and Robert nodded.

43

The test looked innocuous enough: a list of questions about age, sex, background. But on closer inspection the interrogation began to veer off into gray areas. "Have you ever held a grudge against anyone?" the survey asked, and later, "Do you ever have trouble taking criticism?" I continued down the list, thinking that the options would improve, but they didn't. "Do you ever exaggerate?" it asked. "Do you ever feel uncomfortable in large crowds of people?" I held back with the pencil, not sure where this was going. Finally I looked up at the receptionist outside Dr. Patchin's office. She caught the question mark my face had turned into.

"You have to finish the test before the doctor can see you," she said coldly.

"I'm going to have to speak with him first," I answered, trying to keep my voice firm but non-defensive.

"Suit yourself," she said, and returned to the book she was reading.

"One of ours?" I asked, trying to get a look at the cover and at the same time break the ice.

"One of our what?"

"Books. Is that one we published? One of Bandomday's?"

She stared for a good thirty seconds, furrowing her brow, setting her head back into her neck and sneering. Finally she spoke.

"Noooooo," she said, twisting the word in enough directions to encompass the entire tonal range of a Wagner opera. I let the subject drop. Two hours and twelve magazines later the doctor emerged and beckoned me into his office.

"Patient before me run into overtime?" I tried to joke, again to break the ice. The doctor sat down. There was a moment of silence and I took this time to take in what the top of his desk held. There was a silver-balled perpetual mobile machine and an assortment of small electronic gadgets. It appeared as if he had taken several transistor radios apart.

"There was no patient before," he said, looking at a folder on his desk, totally devoid of humor.

"I was just trying to make a joke," I countered, smiling.

He paused and then leaned back in his chair, folding his hands in his lap. Then he squinted and turned his head slightly sideways. "Why would you joke about something like that?" he asked, his tone dead serious. I looked around the room, hoping that something would happen to change the way the meeting had started. Then something did. Things got worse.

"You haven't filled out the questionnaire," Dr. Patchin stated, hostility spewing from his eyes. He focused in on me—a boa constrictor that had not eaten in six months staring down a nappy rabbit.

"Yeah, about that," I began, trying to sound casual, "some of the questions really bothered me."

"Such as?"

"Well, they ask things like, 'Have you ever treated anyone unfairly,' or, 'Do you ever feel you deserve praise for a job well-done?'—that sort of thing."

"So . . . what's the problem?"

"Well, as I began looking down the list, they were all like that—'Have you *ever*.' Of course I've done all of them at some time or another. Who hasn't? So I was worried about answering them. I wasn't sure where the test was leading and I didn't know if I should answer 'yes' to the questions just because I may have done something once. Was that the point? Or was I only supposed to answer 'yes' if I did the mentioned items all the time?"

"What did the questionnaire ask?"

"It said, 'Have you *ever*.' "

"Then that's how you answer."

"But everyone's expected praise at some point in their life, or felt uncomfortable in a large group at one time, or lied about something, or—"

"Why do you feel the need to be difficult?" the doctor asked, leaning forward over his desk now, writing something down.

I was shocked. The question was even more absurd than those printed on the test. He was writing furiously. I tried to rationalize that writing down everything someone said was a New York phenomenon—a sort of big city habit.

"I wasn't trying to be difficult," I said, my voice devoid of any hostility, sarcasm, or anger. "I was trying to point out that it wasn't clear how to answer the questions and that they didn't give me a lot of room for gray areas that—"

"You need to answer the questions before I can help you," the doctor continued, cutting me off. "It's a standard psychological profile test that will determine what type of personality you have. If you've ever done any of those things mentioned, then you need to answer 'yes.' Have it completed and bring it back tomorrow," he said, handing me the questionnaire, a clear indication that today's meeting was over. "And see the receptionist about making the appointment," he added coldly.

The company graciously allowed me time away from my reading duties. The next day I returned, hoping that Herr Doktor would be in a better mood. He wasn't. Psychiatrists are the lawyers of the mental health world: They can take anything you say and turn it into a balloon animal that in no way resembles your original meaning ("How's this . . . *squeak, squeak, squeak* . . . a giraffe? And you thought you'd said 'Good morning.' Nurse! Get the electro-shock treatment ready!")

"How are you today?" I asked, entering Dr. Patchin's office once again. I was trying to keep my demeanor even and void of anything that could be construed as hostile. I figured I should make the best attempt possible at being friendly since we had gotten off on the wrong foot the day before.

"What kind of crack is that?" the doctor inquired, his eyes narrowing.

"I'm . . . sorry . . . I don't understand," I stammered, staggering toward the chair across from his desk in order to sit down. "I was just asking you how—"

"You were asking me how I was when you don't even know me. Do you try and manipulate everyone this way?" he went on, but before I could answer he continued. "So, you finally decided to cooperate," he said, addressing the paper in front of him. I had given the test to the receptionist earlier and she had passed it on to the good doctor who was now writing, evaluating, marking up the copy. "Hmms" were followed by pauses, a few grunts, and then an ominous, "I see." He could have been Reeda's first cousin. The doctor leaned back in his chair and I knew from the previous meeting that this was not good. He was silent. I feared the worst.

"I tried to explain last time that I was uncomfortable answering 'yes' to some of the questions since things aren't that black and white, so I'm hoping that . . ." I was stalling, praying I hadn't messed up too badly. Finally I gave up and fell silent.

"The news is not good," he said, still leaning back, a slight smirk forming on his lips, "but I can help you. Tell me, how do you feel about the company mandating that you come to therapy because of your aggressive behavior?"

"I find it unusual that I'm the one they want in therapy when I've got someone on my staff that likes to save last night's digested dinner and show it to everyone," I said, beginning to lose what control I had. His smugness was nauseating.

There was a good minute of silence in which the doctor simply looked at me—emotionless, thank God—and then delivered his line with dramatic expertise. "What you say about other people," he began slowly, "is often a reflection of yourself." He was even, clinical; condescending, as if he'd been waiting years for an opportunity to use the line. I secretly winced.

I waited, searching the room for something to take my mind off his murder; any distraction that would bring me momentarily out of the realm of his reality, or lack thereof. I took a deep breath. "What did the test reveal?" I finally asked innocently, holding back my emotions, gathering calm, figuring that since he had me pegged as a long-term patient I might as well play it for all it was worth.

"That you're a (he looked down at the verdict) multiple personality . . . paranoid schizophrenic . . . and . . . extremely psychotic." He delivered the words as matter-of-factly as if he had been a mechanic relating the need for an oil change, self-congratulatory in his verdict, thinking what the emotional and monetary bill would eventually be for such a pronouncement.

"Don't you think that's an unfair judgment since you've never had more than a five-minute conversation with me?" I asked.

"The test doesn't lie."

"Multiple personality? Paranoid? Psychotic?" I said. "Those are the labels *du jour?*"

"Correct," he quipped.

"But you just said, Doctor," I replied, measuring my words with calm evenness, without emotion, rising from my chair and preparing to leave, "that what you say about others . . . is often a reflection of yourself," and by the time I had finished the sentence and was heading casually for the door his eyes were bulging and I could clearly see a large vein throbbing in his forehead. It pounded with the rhythmic pulse of a late '70s disco tune.

Robert was perfectly still as he stood directly in front of the painting. I noticed how he seemed to be focusing on the magpie in the picture. On closer inspection I noticed that the painter's calling card was held in the bird's beak.

We had agreed to meet at the Metropolitan Museum of Art for an outing before his rendezvous with a client. I needed to vent my most recent frustrations with Spong, Miss Pokey, Bandomday, and the therapist I had been assigned. As usual, we met on neutral territory.

"I've never been a big fan of Goya," I heard myself say, a little louder than I would have liked. My voice echoed in the cavernous room and several others viewing the European paintings that morning turned to scowl in my direction. Robert didn't respond and we walked on in silence. Finally he spoke.

"Don Manuel Osorio Manrique de Zuñiga. Possibly 1790s," he said to no one in particular and a good minute later.

"Huh?"

"The Goya. *The little boy in the red suit.* Three finches in a cage," he continued. "Three cats eyeing them. Caged birds are said to be symbolic of innocence in the Baroque. They represent the soul in Christian art."

"Why the sudden lesson in painting?" I asked as we moved through rooms containing vast and imposing canvases. "Besides, they've got these docents who walk around giving out valuable tidbits of information—you know, like the one over there." I pointed to a svelte black-clad young woman with a group of elementary school children in tow. "Daddy's trust fund is paying for that while she waits for a husband," I added. "Probably went to Yale to get a degree in art and now the parents have figured out there's no money in anything pleasure-related and—"

Robert stopped me cold with a look of disdain.

"Okay, there's no money in *some* things that give pleasure, like painting, music, and writing," I said. "I wasn't thinking about prostitution just at this moment. That's an entirely different discussion."

"Which we might need to have pretty soon," Robert said, looking at a Vermeer.

"Why does the light always come from the left in Vermeers?" I asked. "And why would we need to discuss your current occupation?"

Just then the tour guide came closer, filling the yawning space with her authoritative voice and mock-pithy observations calculated for the enjoyment of the children that she herded about.

"Does anyone know why we call this painting *Impressionist?*" she asked, gesturing woodenly at a canvas to her left, completely ignorant of the fact that we were in the section on eighteenth-century painting and there was not an Impressionist painting in sight. Her hand eased out, a second too late, as if the gesture had been badly rehearsed—a film in which the sound doesn't marry with the action properly. One finger showed an enormous diamond engagement ring that glinted under the Metropolitan's lights. At least Daddy's trust fund wouldn't have to strain too much longer to make ends meet. "We call it Impressionist because it's *fuzzy*," she said, leaning over slightly on the last word for emphasis. A collective coo went up from the three-foot-high group.

"No reason. In particular," Robert said, addressing my last question about his profession. "Just thought it might be something to discuss." We passed several paintings that I knew and some that I had never seen before. "You really need to get out more and enjoy all that the city has to offer," he continued, as we glided in front of Brueghel's *The Harvesters*. He paused for a moment to look at the large canvas.

"I would get out more often if I didn't have to work all the time. And now, especially with the company putting me in therapy because of someone's complaints about my management style, I really don't have any extra time to put toward things such as art museums and the like."

"And that, my friend, is precisely why I wanted you to come out with me today to the Met. It helps clear the head. Hard to think about the office when you're surrounded by art from centuries past."

"I'd *like* to forget. Seems like I get rid of one problem, Reeda or Fartus or, well, pick someone, and then I get another to take their place. This therapist guy they're sending me to is the worst. And they're adamant that I go. Something about protecting themselves against a lawsuit."

We had managed to walk into the next section of the Met—the one containing nineteenth-century paintings. Manet's *Boating* sailed past with a throng of pastel-clad Midwestern tourists in front. "We have a copy of that in the dining room," one of the women said, adjusting her cat-eye glasses. Robert just shook his head. I continued. "I told them I refused to go but they claimed that my job was in jeopardy. And get this—this is the best part of the thing: While the company paid for the first visit, after I walked out and told them what they could do with their therapy, they now want *me* to pay for my own sessions. If you ask me, I'm paying for some CEO's summer cottage on Long Island. Seems I can't get away from people who want to take my money."

We strolled through most of the European section at the Met and then Robert came to a stop, standing before a painting of a man who appeared to be dancing. He was attired in red, almost the same exact color as the suit that the child in the Goya wore.

"Well," Robert said, as if coming out of a trance, looking at his watch, "I've got to get going. Can't keep the client waiting."

"Have you heard anything I said? We just got here and I had to pay the suggested price to get in, and now you want to leave?"

"I've got a very important lunch date with a young lady and I can't be late. Besides, you can stay and look around. I'm sure you'll learn something," and with that he sauntered off with his back to me, his hand held high in good-bye mode. It was typical Robertian behavior.

"And now if you children will gather around this way, we have a painting by Courbet," the guide was saying, her grating voice bouncing off the three-hundred-year-old canvases and gilt frames.

She and her group had caught up with me in the new section, right in front of the painting Robert and I had been looking at. I was suddenly surrounded by a gaggle of elementary school students. The whole scene was very Lemuel Gulliver amid the Lilliputians.

"This particular painting," she continued, oblivious to the fact that whatever was up inside the noses of the school children was imminently of more interest to them than nineteenth-century French painting, "shows the tenor Louis Gueymard in the title role of Meyerbeer's opera, *Robert the Devil.* " I turned now in her direction, not fully realizing why. "The painting is set," she continued, "inside a cavern of sorts and Robert has been gambling with two other individuals, probably servants. The evil Bertram, who is Robert's father, looks on in this scene." She paused to let the information sink in, and then, seeing that their interest was waning, decided to take it down a notch—more on the level of what they would understand.

"How many of you here believe in the devil?" she asked, and on the last word of her question she raised her right hand high and nodded her head—an indication that the small people in the party were to follow her example. But I was unaware that I had also followed suit. My hand was already a good three inches above my head when I saw the puzzled look on her face. Then the entire class turned in my direction and I felt like some Pompeian sculpture, trapped in those fatal minutes before Mount Vesuvius's eruption, awaiting the inevitable—wide-eyed and caught off-guard.

45

"I'm sorry I'm late, but Beau and I had to get married so that they wouldn't take him off to war and then I had to go for my cancer test."

It was Clarice, as usual, with one of her excuses for being late. I waited, patient in the knowledge that it was only a matter of time before the security camera revealed her mad pooper escapades and the report from the phone system illustrated the enormity of her conversations with Beau.

"That's okay," I said to her, grasping for something that would get her away from me and toward her own desk. "Just try not to let it happen again."

I was used to her stories by now; I just didn't feel like listening to them. One morning she had been late because she needed emergency surgery to remove a brain tumor, and another time she had been held at gunpoint by Canadian terrorists who insisted she strip naked for them and perform obscene gestures with a summer squash. Today was nothing new.

She waddled off and sat down. Within a few minutes she was on the phone, cursing and screaming at Beau about the fact that he had bought frozen string beans instead of the canned variety (they were living together). I tried not to listen yet couldn't help but make out pieces of the conversation—something about him accusing her of infidelity and his leaving beard trimmings in the sink. The list went on and on and on. This continued for a good twenty minutes until I couldn't take it anymore.

Since Clarice was preoccupied on the phone, I decided to call up the communications department to see where my report was—the one that would put her away. My only thoughts were of getting the upper hand in the situation. I imagined the report to be filled with hours of time she had logged, ranting to Beau about the price of tampons and his lack of sensitivity toward her sinus problems. When I reached the communications department they assured me the report was in the office mail and should be there any moment.

An hour later the report still hadn't arrived. I walked by Clarice's desk just as she was finishing a conversation, and of all things one *not* with Beau.

"Yes . . . yes . . . thank you doctor. Yes. Good-bye," and she clumsily hung up the phone.

"The doctor says I have cancer," she said, attempting to choke back her emotions.

"That's nice," I replied, not buying it, and put the latest document to be read on her desk. "Be sure to look at this manuscript about making tar. It's from some bigwig's brother-in-law or something—from upstairs. They want it done today." And with that I headed back to my desk. But as I was passing Perkel's cubicle, I heard him on the phone. His head was buried in a file folder, almost *inside* one of the cabinets in an attempt to procure a private moment. He had no idea I was anywhere nearby or I'm sure he wouldn't have braved the conversation he was having. It was truly an enlightening moment.

"Yeah, the guy's a real idiot. I've got him and everyone else thinking I've got nine kids. Nine *kids!* Can you imagine, me with nine kids? I can't stand the little bastards. And a wife? Sheez, what would he do if he found out I was gay? Yeah. Yeah, that's what I mean! He has no idea that I've got a second job I go to, and that I get paid for this *and* the other one at the same time! What a moron."

There was a pause. I tried to rationalize that Perkel was talking about anyone but me.

"Max. Yeah, the guy's name is Max," he continued, putting that theory away for good.

I tiptoed away as carefully as I could, back in the same direction as Clarice's cubicle. Then I walked around the side of the department toward Miss Pokey's office so that Perkel wouldn't notice me. I went out the back door leading to the restrooms and made my way to the front entrance of the office, just to be sure that Perkel didn't suspect anything. Then I created a loud commotion as I entered so that everyone would notice.

That weekend was the bringer of another revelation, for on my way to pick up a book from the library on voodoo practices and another called *The Art of Speakin' Jamaican, Mon!*, I saw Cloud hovering in a doorway at the side of some ratty buildings in the West Fifties. It was the same neighborhood she lived in. I ducked behind a van and watched. Within a minute or two, a shady character appeared and nestled close to her just inside the dirty, crumbling brownstone façade. While the conversation was quick, it lasted long enough for me to see him hand her a small package and she hand him an envelope. It wasn't hard to figure out that the package contained enough cocaine to light up the entire city of Edison, New Jersey, without the help of Thomas E. himself.

46

"The time before last we made a lot of progress with the hypnosis," Reeda began, sitting down across from me and crossing her legs (knee over knee) in a professional manner. "I'd like to start off with that this time and see how far we get."

She was a nervous wreck, waiting to find out the events of my life. It was also another chance for her to milk some more money from my impersonation fund. This having to be somebody else, complete with his or her problems and imagined income and life, was getting addicting. And now I had to contend with Reeda *and* Dr. Patchin *and* pay for them both. Why was it these people were so interested in what went on inside my head?

"What hypnosis?" I said, acting as though I remembered nothing from the last session.

"Exactly," she said. I could tell she was eager to get down to business. "Why don't we do the past-life regression part first, and then we can work on your book."

"Okay by me." I settled onto the filthy sofa after removing a Persian cat that was sleeping, gently setting it on the floor next to the chair where Reeda had positioned herself.

"I'm going to do something a little different today and I need you to work with me," she said as she set up the tape recorder. "I want to put you under even deeper and get to some issues that I think could help the book. That is, if you agree."

"Sure," I said. "Anything that would help my writing." Then I lied, eager to show her that I could be just as devious as she was. "I'm enjoying getting to the truth about who I am and what happened to me as a child," I said. "I have to say that you really know what you're doing. I'm very grateful."

She tilted her head a little, smiled, and said, "Well, thank you, Max. I appreciate that," and then she reached over and patted me on the knee. "Now I want to begin in the same manner as the last few times. Look up . . . deeeeeeep breath. Relax. Breathe again. And . . . exhale. I'm going to count backwards again from ten and I want you to feel yourself going deeper and deeper."

It was the same old routine, and while she played at having a job I managed to do some math calculations in my head, figuring out just how much money she had stolen from me over the past several months. She interpreted my furrowed brow and concentration as going under while the numbers in my head grew in size.

"I want you to think about how the horrible events of your childhood have affected you. Remember. Think back. You spoke about the Jamaican man. The accountant. Being raped in the bathtub. Remember?"

I nodded.

"Good. Now I want to take you to a dark place where you will remember all the bad things you did as—" but before she finished I jumped in for dramatic effect.

"No! Don't make me! No, stop! He's hurting . . . I can't . . . blood, blood, oh, this is awful." I managed to open my eyes the tiniest bit so that I could see her reaction. She was glued to the edge of her chair. I was aiming for the highest melodrama possible and evidently hitting the mark. It seemed that the more I played it up, the more she believed it—an unfortunate testament to her taste in entertainment.

"But I have to," I said suddenly in a high-pitched sweet voice, unlike the other one I had been using. And then in another voice—a Russian accent, very sinister and dark, "Ve vill have to keeeeel him . . ." I fluttered my eyelids slightly—another chance to see her reaction. She was mortified, thinking that she had stumbled upon a case of multiple personality. Even the featherless parrot was intrigued. From its perch came a faint, "Ohhhhhh."

Then Reeda spoke. I could tell from the sound of her voice that she was anxious. "Who are you? To whom am I speaking now?"

"Boy," I thought, "to *whom!* She chooses a time such as this to start using proper English?"

"Boris," I said authoritatively, using my best Russian intonation. "Ya Boris Olgavanovich Samaroff."

"And who *are* you, Boris? Who are you in relation to Max?" I could hear the scribbling of text as I spoke.

"I tell him vat to do. I make for him to kill de peoples. Hmmm, how to tell. Max, he is under my controoooool."

The only saving grace that Reeda possessed was the fact that she was actually as inept as she believed everyone else was. She really assumed she had stumbled onto something big and immediately entangled herself in the fantasy. Who was I to stop her?

"How many others are there? Are you the only one other than—"

"Maaaaaany odders. Ve all tell him vat to do. He kill many times because of us."

"Whom does he kill?" she asked (there's that *whom* again), at once nervous and fascinated. The word 'kill' had definitely snagged her. I was a bit impressed myself at this most recent turn of events.

"I tink you ask, um, how you say, maaaaany kuh-ves-tions. I go now. You speak vit my friend, Frasquina."

"Who is—"

But I cut her off, launching into my best Frasquina imitation. "Yuh too fass and facety. Galang bout yuh business," I said, doing my best to reproduce the coveted Jamaican accent. I had one hand on my hip and wagged my head back and forth with eyes closed even though I was on the sofa, leaning back. "Somebody tell mi say you dida talk bout me."

"I'm sorry, I can't understand you," Reeda pleaded. "May I please speak to Boris again?"

So I gave her Boris, but not before Frasquina let loose an "Uppity white bitch," and signed off.

"Dis Boris. Vat you vood like?" I said, hoping that I could come up with something, having no idea where this whole thing was headed.

"You mentioned something about killing earlier. What was that all about?"

"Must be careful. Max will kill for notting. He very sick man. He like to pretend he writer and then when have found way

238

into home of gentle woman who care for animals, he plan to cut her up in small pieces and make into stew for, um, how you say in your country . . . homeless peoples."

Once again I managed to squint and look at Reeda. She was a good two inches off the edge of the chair, just hovering. Her eyes and mouth looked like Clarice's. They could have been twins.

"I need to speak with Max," she said, hysteria rising in her voice.

"No. No Max. *Boris*. Ya *Boris*. You must no ask for this, um, Max person. He veddy bad. But not to fear him, for you veel know when he plans to kill your person. He veel send you tree-dozen red roses. Until dis time, you are safe."

"I need to speak with Max now. I'm going to count to ten and I want Max to—"

"Yes, what . . . what? Yes, I'm here. What's going on? Sleeeeepy," I said, slightly shaking my head. I furrowed my brow again and writhed slightly on the sofa, still not opening my eyes. In the distance I could hear smacking sounds coming from *Dog* as he licked his genitals.

"Who are you? Is this Max? To whom am I speaking?" Reeda asked, probably afraid that yet another personality had emerged.

"Dis ole oak tree almost as old as I is," I said, doing my best Miss Jane Pittman impression. "I likes me dat sports page and da vanilla ice cream," and then I smacked my lips. "Sho nuf. Sho nuf, sho nuf (smack, smack, smack)."

"Max, I need to speak to Max! When I count to ten—"

"Max," I replied, dreamily. "I'm . . . Maaaax." And then I added something completely outside the box but somewhat related to Miss Jane as I switched characters once again: "Do de name Ruby Begonia ring ah bell?" I said, trying my best to imitate a large black man.

"Max, I'm going to count to ten, and when you come out of this state you will remember nothing. Do you understand me? You will remember nothing."

And then she counted, and the numbers followed much faster than ever before. They piled up, one on top of the other like some bad freeway accident, until it was impossible to hear where one left off and the other began.

47

"I'm so glad we could have this little talk," I said after taking a sip of my cappuccino. "You know, Cloud, I really do like you and I don't want to see you get into any trouble, so I know you'll understand the expression, 'You scratch my back, and I'll scratch yours.' You have heard that one, haven't you?"

Cloud didn't say anything. She had agreed to meet me at the corner diner in her neighborhood—the very corner where I had seen her buying the cocaine. Le Cirque it was not. The fact that they even served cappuccino was a shock to me.

"I need to go to the bathroom," she finally said, pushing away her untouched food.

"I bet you do."

"What's that supposed to mean?"

"I think you know," I said. "I'd really hate for your little problem to become a big one for the company—sniff, sniff—you know, cause you to lose your job." She sat still; silent. I continued. "See, it's really a matter of you and everyone in the department making an effort to be nice. Not give me a hard time. See things my way. Basically . . . well, basically, doing whatever I like, when I like, and with no questions." I took another sip.

"You're a monster." She glared at me.

"That may be, but you and everyone else helped make me the creature of Frankenstein that I am today." I pulled at the sides of my neck, attempting to simulate bolts, and grimaced.

"I'll think about it," she said after a minute and fingered the edge of a tatter of wilted lettuce. She pinched off a small piece and it lodged under one of her bright red fingernails. "Okay. Fine. It's a deal. At least for the time being."

"Darlin'," I said, pausing for dramatic effect and smirking, "the time being is all I need."

Frasquina was easy. All I had to do was show her my homemade voodoo doll, complete with her own hair that I had procured from the ratty-looking brush she kept in one of her desk drawers. Then I managed a few phrases from the book I had acquired from the library, finishing off the conversation with a hearty, "Galang bout yuh business," and everything was set.

Perkel was much more fun. For him I had an entire scenario laid out. The next time he pretended sickness with one of his children, I told him that I had my car (of which I had none) outside and was going to New Jersey where he lived, on an errand for the company—that I'd be happy to drive him, especially since it was such an emergency. He blanched and protested, and after ten minutes I let him go. The next day I asked if I could see pictures of his children, which, miraculously for someone who loved his imaginary kids as much as he did, he didn't possess. I continued with questions about each of his brats and his wife with the caveat that I was trying to be a better manager—be interested in my employees. By the end of the third day of inquiries he was a nervous wreck. To top this off, I followed him after work one evening, carefully snaking behind him via subway and on foot until he reached his destination—a gay bar in the Village. I eased into the establishment so that he wouldn't see me, and managed to get behind him.

"Daaaahling," he was saying in a voice that Gloria Swanson could have sued over, his left hand dangling in the air somewhere between his head and Saturn, "this most incredibly delicious hunk of a rodeo hand from Montana was in town and *lost*, so I said to him, 'Precious, why not spend some time at my place?'"

It was odd, hearing a completely different voice come out of Perkel. At least his work voice wasn't affected. But then, he was playing another part at Bandomday. I couldn't really criticize— who wasn't?

He continued. "So after a few minutes of the most *exquisite* badinage, he mounted me, and just before I received penetration, he yelled out, 'Cowboy up!' and off we went!"

I crept back out of the bar and decided to wait on the sidewalk. To pass the time I made up names for drag queens, having been inspired by the seedy establishment and its inhabitants. "Sue Nami," I said to myself, thinking that if any female impersonator wanted to use it, she could appear soaking wet. Anne Thrax was next—an enormous four-hundred-pounder covered in white powder. Or how about Anna Bolic? She would have to be a bodybuilder. Miss Demeanor and Miss Creant could be a lovely perp duet with a handcuff motif. The minutes ticked by. This being a weeknight, Perkel wasn't in there long, and the look on his face as he exited the establishment was priceless.

"Uh, uh, uh, I was just looking for someplace to get a drink and I stumbled into this fag place," he sputtered at me, using his back-to-work-voice, while I stood up against the iron fence across the street. "Man, there sure are a lot of homos in there. I had no idea," he continued, shuffling from foot to foot, his hands in his pockets.

"It certainly took you long enough to find out," I said.

"What?"

"That there were a lot of 'fags' as you call them, in there."

"What? Me? I walked right in and then right out."

"I don't think so, Perk," I said, a huge grin coming across my face. "I followed you from work and I've been standing here for at least thirty minutes. Oh, and I managed to get inside for a while and overhear some of your conversation."

"Oh, man, shit. Shit, shit, shit, dammit to hell," he chanted as he danced around the sidewalk. "Man, you tell anyone about this, and I'll—"

"Correction, Sir Prance-a-Lot. I don't think you're in any position to tell *me* what to do. I, on the other hand . . ." and by the look on his face, I knew the message had been received.

But something else came to mind and I added it. "And another thing, I looked into your personnel file and then did some investigation via a special friend I have," I said, thinking about how Robert and his unlimited resources had once again come in handy. "Your last name is not Perez, it's *Weintraub*, and in case you haven't noticed, you're about a hundred pounds overweight. Double and triple whammy." He just stood there staring blankly for a moment and the silence was thick between us. Finally I broke it.

"I'll see you at work tomorrow," I said and began to walk down the street to the subway station. Just before Perkel was out of earshot, I turned and shouted to him to get his attention. He stood there waiting and I let him stew in agony, imagining what I could add.

"Cowboy up, dude," I said, and with that I headed for home.

Having no one left now but Clarice seemed, well, anti-climactic. I knew the report would come. I knew it would show her logging in hours of phone time to her loser fiancé. I knew that the security camera would catch her putting bags of excrement in front of the door, if not actually performing the polluted deed. But what happened was even superior, for as I tore into the report from the communications department, part of my mind said, "No, this is a mistake," while the other half said, "Just wait. It gets better."

This was Monday. Everyone was preoccupied with work, sitting at their desks, and as I wanted to check the validity of the phone report, I slid away to Miss Pokey's office since she was out for the day. I dialed and waited. When the person I had spoken with confirmed that I had been sent the correct report, I was livid.

"Then you need to check your equipment," I ranted, "because there's not a single phone call in or out on this list. Can you explain *that* to me? The girl is on the phone day and night and she's driving us nuts. There's got to be something wrong."

I was told that the equipment had been checked and re-checked and that there was no mistake—Clarice had hardly picked up the telephone in the last year. When I persisted, it was explained to me that while it took a while to get reports back, they could verify if she was on the phone at the present moment. That is to say, if she were to pick up the phone and start a lengthy conversation, right then, they could tell me how long she was on for. Technology—go figure.

"So what you're telling me is that if she's on the phone right now, it would show up?" I asked.

"That's correct." The person in the communications department was starting to get irritated with me. "Hold on one minute," I said, and put the receiver down. Then I carefully entered the readers' office from the back door—the one nearest Clarice's cubicle. Already I could hear her.

"Beau, you bastard! You hateful pig! How could you! And after all my parents did for you!" She went on and on with the usual sobbing and raised voice. I crept back to Miss Pokey's office.

"She's on the phone right now," I said. "Are you sure you have the right extension. Four, four, three, five?"

"She's not on the phone. No one is on that extension right—"

"Lady, you're crazy," I said, losing my temper. "I just walked up behind her."

By now the person in communications was getting fed up. "Sir," she began haughtily, "not only is that extension *not* in use, but *no one* is on *any* phone in that department with the exception of you, and I show you on a . . . Miss Pokey's extension?" she continued, obviously looking at some printout or screen before her, a question mark entering her voice as she read the name.

"I just saw her and—" but I stopped mid-sentence. Something clicked. Some bell went off. It was that previous warning that had said, "Wait, it gets better." I excused myself, apologized to the person on the other end of the line, and crept back into the readers' office via the back door again. As quietly as I could, I stole behind Clarice.

"You worthless piece of shit!" she seethed into the receiver. She was shaking from anger, her back to me. "How *dare* you speak to me that way! As far as I'm concerned, the wedding is *off*. OFF! DO YOU UNDERSTAND ME?!" and I watched for a good two minutes more as she ranted, the whole time with one fat finger firmly planted on the hang-up button.

The line wasn't active and never had been. Every conversation she'd had over the past year had been faked. There was no Beau, no doctor, no wedding. By my calculations, Clarice had been speaking into a dead receiver for well over a year.

48

"Look, you don't need any more work on your book. It's in very good shape and I don't think I could help you improve it." Reeda was still recuperating from our last session—the one in which Boris explained that Max would try to kill her when he . . . I, had sent her three-dozen red roses.

I had called to finish tormenting her (it was a slow day), as I figured she still had some payback coming. She possessed the most feckless existence I knew of and yet had somehow managed to bamboozle me. Plus, when it was decided a few weeks ago that I was officially finished with her, that I was only hanging on for entertainment purposes, I had decided to get my book in shape and submit it to Bandomday without consulting her. I knew all the necessary channels now and no longer needed Jungle Woman's help. I had the readers' department where I needed them; ready to receive *Mrs. Squigglemire et al.*

"But you've helped me so much," I said. "I feel as though a thousand pounds have been lifted off my shoulders. My writing has improved and I've gotten my self-confidence back. I really need to see you again and, as you said yourself, we can begin looking for an agent and pitching the idea to editors and publishers."

"No! I mean, that's not a good idea right now, what with, the, um, things I have to do. We need to take a break for a bit from this." I envisioned her with one hand on the doorknob, ready to escape, and the other poised to dial 911.

She continued: "We need to, um, er, let the writing sit for a while, like a fine wine. You know how wines have to sit for a while? Then we can go back and revisit it."

"But I feel like I'm just now getting to the real issue of what the book is about. I've been having these really disturbing dreams that seem to have surfaced from my childhood and I'd like to tell you about them. Because of your sessions I've started remembering all kinds of abuse that happened to me as a child. You were right—

the book really needs to be about pain, and I've got plenty of that. I had no idea I could hold so much pain. I'm in pain all the time now. Why, I'm in pain at this very moment."

"And the best way you can get through that pain is to just let things alone for a while. I promise, we'll get together again soon, but for now we need to take a break."

Reeda had one foot in hysteria and the other on a banana peel, but she had stolen hundreds of dollars and I was determined to make her squirm. She didn't know what to do with me now, but one thing was certain, I had made her sorry she'd ever probed into the dark recesses of Max Perkins's mind.

"Could we meet just one more time?" I asked. "I want to go over some ideas I have for the latest revision and I really need you since you've helped me so much." While I certainly didn't mean it, I wouldn't have minded torturing her in person with my Boris routine again. And I could use the money I was making from the occasional focus groups to pay for the sessions.

"Well . . . um . . . I'll have to call you when I get free. I'm really busy right now helping someone redo their screenplay and then I'll be able to get to you." The tone of her voice was machine-gun-riddled with anxiety—a regular Bonnie-and-Clyde scenario after an ambush of paranoia and fear.

"I think you're blowing me off," I said, attempting a slight hostility in my voice.

"No! No, that's not it! No, no, no, no, no, no, no," she said. Seven "Nos" in a row. I counted them. "I really am very busy," she added, just in case I hadn't gotten the message.

I couldn't resist and let my voice take on another quality—not an accent really, but something distant and far away. "Seven *Nos* in a row," I said, ethereally. "I've got to go now . . . Reeda . . . there's a . . . florist that I—" but it was too late—she had hung up.

Next, it was off to my weekly appointment with Dr. Patchin. I had endured his ravings and mock-Freudian assaults virtually in silence, having perfected my technique of lying in wait with Reeda. The two were so similar. At one point he had decided to take a vacation (thank God) and had told me of his plans: "Now you're going to resent the fact that I'm going away for a month and leaving you with no safety net. It's only natural. You'll probably exhibit some hostility and you may even hate me."

"Doctor," I had thought to myself, "I'm way ahead of you on this one." Instead, I said, "That's a little textbook, don't you think? I would hope that I'm mature and wise enough to rationalize your vacation. Plus, I could use the break from all the mind probing." I had finished with a little laugh just to show I wasn't angry.

"You're already exhibiting the hostility I spoke about. You're obviously incapable of caring for another human being and begrudge me my time alone." His response begged the question, "Which one of us is the person in need of therapy?" but I didn't say anything.

The vacation came and went. His rationale, or lack thereof, couldn't be overlooked, and I was forever trying to make sense of how his mind worked. Each week in his office I would point out some incident that had happened at work—at his request—and he would show me how I was the one with the problem.

"Frasquina has threatened to kill me again," I would offer up. "I don't think this is rational behavior. She should really get help," I would say.

"But can't you see it's *your* problem, not hers?" he had volleyed back. "Why *should* she behave the way you expect? Don't you see that by projecting your own warped idea of how others should act, that you're only hurting yourself?"

I would try and point out that, in a normal society, certain actions like killing someone weren't generally accepted. Dr. Patchin always had an answer.

"But again, there's that word *should*. You're expecting people to act a certain way and that's not right."

I tried other examples: Catching Perkel masturbating in the men's room; Clarice's lying; Cloud's post-nasal drip as a result of too much cocaine use. Nothing seemed to work. Every time I came up with an illustration of how people weren't acting properly or following what I considered normal protocol, Dr. Patchin would counter with, "Why *should* they act a certain way?" I tried to point out that society has certain standards, certain norms, and that if we violate them things will fall apart. I tried to point out that we all have responsibilities to one another with regard to common courtesy and manners. His response was always the same. I wanted to take the word *should* and shove it up into a vulnerable and dark part of his body located on his backside.

So at today's session—right after my last conversation with Reeda—I waited, knowing that he would step into my trap. After about four or five examples from Herr Doktor of "Here's what's wrong with you and why," he brought up the fact that I hadn't paid anything toward my forced therapy for the past several sessions.

"Why *should* I pay?" I asked, over-emphasizing the word *should* as he had done no fewer than five thousand times.

"Well, it's customary. Don't be absurd. You have to pay. It's the way things are done," he said, totally indignant at my shirking of financial responsibility.

"But you're expecting me to act in a certain way; to fit into a certain mold. You're projecting your, and society's ideas onto me," I said, spewing his pabulum right back in his face.

"But this is different," he countered. "This is what is expected."

"Who expects it?" I asked, turning my head to the side and squinting.

"We do. This office . . . society."

"You mean the way society and most people expect others not to masturbate in public places; the way people and society expect to be treated with courtesy and respect; the way it's not in the best interest to threaten to kill people?" I asked.

"It's not the same thing," he said.

"Oh? How? Tell me how it's not the same thing?" I asked. "Explain to me how not paying you is different from the examples in my life."

He couldn't and as a result I never returned to him. And I never paid him either. On this last visit, just before I exited his office, I asked, having remembered where I had heard the name Patchin, "Oh, and by the way, how is your devil-worshiping ex-wife,

Grace? You know, the one who lives in Brooklyn and speaks fluent Cockney?"

But he was silent; open-mouthed; at a loss for a witty comeback.

The student had become the teacher.

Part IV

Life is nothing but a competition to
be the criminal rather than the victim.

– Bertrand Russell

49

Scene: Tuesday. Spring. A meeting.

"I've called you all together today because we need to discuss your attitude lately and because I've decided to run the department in a slightly different manner," I began. I had asked my amalgam of *untermenschen* into Pokey's office since she was on her yearly vacation. She had just left a few hours ago. The psychological aspect of meeting in her office did wonders for morale. Even so, it amazed me that one of the staff—my money was still on Clarice—had left yet another baggie of excrement outside the door the day before. I saw it as a last-ditch attempt to get the upper hand but said nothing. A video was being made each night and I would be receiving a call any day now, telling me that Bandomday's home movies were ready for screening.

"First of all, Miss Pokey has put me in charge while she's away and I'd like all of you to be on your best behavior. I know you'll have no problem with this request." Looking around the room, judging by the complete silence and nodding of heads, things were right on track. It's amazing what having the goods on certain individuals will do for your career. I had Perkel in my pocket because of his closet case routine, Cloud because of too much nose candy, Clarice because of her imaginary fiancé, and all I had to do to get Frasquina in line was to hold up my Aunt Jemima doll, complete with miniature replication of her fuchsia-and-chartreuse outfit, and she would fall silent.

"Secondly, I've read a recent manuscript and found it to be one of the best I've ever come across. The office services department has made copies for each of you and I'd like you to read it. Put everything else on hold and give this one your undivided attention. Reports on it should be delivered to me no later than Friday." More silence followed. Then Cloud spoke up.

"I've got to be at a funeral tomorrow and then—" she started to say, but before she could finish I put my finger to the side of my nose and let out a loud *sniffffff.*

"Sorry about that," I apologized to everyone. "I must be coming down with a cold." Message received.

I continued: "The name of the manuscript is *Mrs. Squigglemire's Bustle"* and it's by a newcomer named Robert Hickenlooper."

Robert had agreed to let me use his name. If I had used mine, the book wouldn't have made it past the janitor. Besides, who makes up a name like Hickenlooper?

"We don't know much about the author, but the work came in through one of New York's most prestigious agents," I lied. "I understand that a top editor in New York, who wishes to remain anonymous, has worked on the book." Then I affected letting down my guard a little, for realistic purposes. I pretended to be on their side. "If you ask me, it's some kind of a test. You know, to see if we know what we're doing around here with regard to the quality of manuscripts we pass along. Someone upstairs marked it with a red flag, so if that's any indication to you as to how much energy you should put into the reading, then enough said." I handed out the copies, secretly glowing with admiration at my work and the fact that no one suspected I was not only the author, but the agent, editor, and upper management red flag person as well. It wasn't hard to do. When you've been as many people as I have, becoming someone else gets to be a walk in the park.

With everything set, I dismissed the group and we all returned to our cubicles. I was just starting to write up my review of *Mrs. Squigglemire*, having no need to read it since I had spent years writing it, when the phone rang.

"Perkins?" a voice asked.

"You got him," I said.

"Your tapes are ready. The ones you requested—the videos of the door to the readers' room this past week including last night."

"Did you look at them?" I asked, hoping that they would recognize whoever the culprit was and save me the trouble of having to watch the entire performance.

"We don't have time to watch every tape that comes through here. We save them for a few days and if no one has any complaints we tape over them. Jesus, do you know how cheap this company is?"

"Fine," I said. "I'll be up in a few minutes to get it," and made my way upstairs to retrieve the film.

Returning to Miss Pokey's office, I shut the door and placed the tape on her desk. "Time's up, Clarice," I said out loud and began to fumble with the video equipment in the corner. After plugging in some loose cables and scraping an inch of dust off the top of the machine, I put the tape in and waited for it to calibrate. Pretty soon a black-and-white picture appeared, complete with time stamp in the lower right-hand corner. I watched as my fellow employees came and went during the day. At one point Perkel and Cloud appeared in front of the doors to our office, conversing for what seemed like an hour. Miss Pokey was seen going out and returning a few minutes later. Frasquina walked dejectedly out the door and, judging by the time stamp, took three hours for lunch. There was a messenger, one of the cleaning people, and an electrician to put up some new lights.

After a while I grew tired of the plebian nature of the day and sped the tape up. "Three, four, and four thirty," the time stamp read, but in military hours. I translated in my head. Then I paused it. This was the end of the day and hopefully I would see Clarice leaving her obscene nightly offering. I started the tape again and watched carefully. One by one, each person in the office left. It was now five thirty and everyone had gone home. The camera stayed focused on the door—a tense few minutes passed and then the cleaning woman appeared. She entered the office and stayed for approximately twenty minutes, exiting with her cart, the now-full trash bags, and the radio that had sat on my desk since my third week of employment at Bandomday. While I was relieved to find out who had stolen the radio, its theft was secondary and I put it out of my mind. Besides, I was looking for someone who *left* things, not took them.

Again the time passed: Six thirty, seven, seven fifteen. I became bored, realizing that Clarice could have come back any time between now and early morning. Suddenly an image appeared at the front doors. It was seven-thirty, tape time.

At first it was just a blur, and the person wasn't wearing anything that I had seen my co-workers wear that day, so I squinted to try and make out who it could be. The culprit wore baggy jeans and a hooded sweat-suit top. The face was obscured. The mysterious visitor looked around nervously and then put a key into the office doors. The figure appeared to be female and was about Clarice's height.

What happened next was surreal. Since no one but myself in the department knew of the camera, what the hooded individual did was more than unnerving, for they proceeded to open both double doors to the office area and secure them with two chairs. Their choice of a place to create a makeshift stage couldn't have been better, for the camera now had a mezzanine view of the action. The gaping opening of the doorframe created a perfect proscenium arch to frame the action, and whether this was done to heighten the experience that was to come or to simply make a statement, it worked wonderfully.

The hooded figure proceeded with the evening's entertainment, taking a large plastic baggie from a pocket and opening it. When the pants dropped, the sex of the defecator was revealed. Or so I thought. It was a man, no, a woman, no a . . . I wasn't sure. I was convinced now that it must be Clarice even though the hood was obscuring the face and the graininess of the film footage marred the viewing experience.

The individual squatted over the baggie, and holding it with both hands behind—a gymnastic feat if ever there was one— produced the desired results. While I knew it was going to happen, the act of viewing someone actually letting the dachshund out the back door took my breath away. I know it's a bodily function, but seeing it take place falls under the category again of "a little more information than I needed to know." Sorry.

The perp finished and then began to put things back in order, giving new meaning to the phrase "anal retentive." Finally, the visitor locked the doors and placed the baggie in front, once again being careful to position it so that whoever came in to work first that morning would have to handle it before opening the doors.

But almost as if the miscreant knew what was needed, despite the hooded sweatshirt, despite the late hour, the individual turned just before leaving camera range and looked up, straight into the lens that was taping the action. It was then that I became truly stunned, for as the face hovered there, it seemed to be looking at the smoke detector—the new one that had been installed only a short while earlier; the one containing the hidden camera—and I could view every aspect of the person. And that's why it came as such a shock, for it wasn't Clarice after all who had been responsible for the unpleasantries, but someone else.

50

"The person leaving the goods is a hermaphrodite," I said to Robert over the phone. I was at home in Brooklyn and it was late.

"Which of the motley crew is it?" he asked.

I thought a minute. For some reason, something inside me went off—a bell, a trigger, something. I hesitated, not sure why. Instinct, I guess. I had watched the tape several times and by slowing it down been able to see two distinct sets of genitalia.

"I'd rather not say just yet," I said, sensing his disappointment. "I've got to confront the person first." Then I added, hoping that my reason would make my lack of immediate confession carry a more sincere tone, "It wouldn't be fair to tell someone else before I surprise the person."

Robert was silent for a moment, then he spoke. "Dude, *they* already know. It's the rest of us who are waiting for the news."

"Yeah, but this individual doesn't know they've been caught."

"True."

Just then I heard Spong's key in the door, in one of the tumblers. I knew I still had a good three minutes on the phone as we had no fewer than seven locks, each one an absolute potluck of chances on whether the position was actually locked or not. A person could easily spend half an hour on the wrong side of the door if one was accidentally locked while the others were open, never guessing which one was the culprit.

"Spong's coming in," I said. "He's been a real pain lately so I don't want to give him anything else to bitch about."

"Like what?"

"Like being on the phone in the bathtub, even though for what happens in this apartment, it's not that unusual."

"I can deal with Spong," Robert said.

"You don't have to live here with him, his three-in-the-morning talks—mostly to himself—his baby food. Something's been eating at him lately. I don't know what."

About that time Spong got lucky playing lock roulette. Bingo, he was in.

"Goddammit! Why did you lock every one but the third from the bottom? I went round and round trying to figure out what I'd done wrong. And you were in here, on the phone? You could have just gotten up and let me in."

"Told you," I said to Robert. He could hear Spong's tirade.

"Told you what?" Spong asked. "First the subway train stalls, then a passenger gets sick, then there's 'police activity,' " he continued, making little rabbit ears on the words *police activity*. "Then some asshole gets stuck in the doors. I've had it. Had it with the city, all the crap you have to put up with. There's got to be a better way than this. Who the hell are you talkin' to anyway?"

"Robert."

"*Robert,*" Spong mimicked. "Great big Texas asshole. That cowboy crap is strictly for fags."

"John Wayne? Are you gonna tell me he's a fag?" I said, my hand over the receiver. "I've got to go," I said, "and placate the beast within."

"Right. Give me a call later," Robert responded.

I hung up and turned my attention to Spong. He was flinging off his clothes. A tie landed on the edge of the tub, socks behind the Woodstock speakers. Eventually his shoes were thrown at the wall.

"Did it ever occur to you," I began, "that perhaps you'd be happier living in a nicer apartment, you know, spending some money on where you come home to?"

"I'm only here to change and occasionally eat. There's no need to waste what I make on fixing up this hole or finding another equally bad one."

"All I'm saying, is that you might spend some more time at home instead of being out on the town constantly doing God knows what."

I checked myself. I sounded like a nagging housewife. And what did I care where Spong spent his free moments as long as it wasn't with me? I thought about taking back what I had just said but chose instead to change the subject.

"I noticed you didn't get your copy of *Esquire* this month," I added, leaning back in the tub. "Did the subscription run out?"

Spong stuck his head out of his closet. "Why would you notice that?" he asked, running his fingers around the waistband of his Jockey shorts.

"I know how much you like that rag. Just didn't remember seeing it," I said, afraid I had set off a bell. Spong eyed me for a moment, then decided everything was okay.

"I'm switching to a new magazine," he said finally, "when the sub for *Esquire* runs out. Some new men's magazine about health, that sort of thing."

I thought for a minute. Health. Men's sports. Focus groups. This kneeling every day to pray to the drain god while dousing myself with a pitcher to rinse off was getting old. Also, there's something psychologically damaging about bathing in the same place you've just spent the last eight hours sleeping. I asked Spong: "You know of any good gyms around here?"

He just gave me a blank look. "The one I go to," he said, and waited.

"Never mind," I said. "I'll find one myself."

51

On her first day back from vacation, Miss Pokey seemed more irritable than usual. She was scowling at everyone and had been on the phone yelling at personnel about the lack of attention to detail that her staff was exhibiting. It just wasn't a good day for Pokey and I hated to be the bearer of bad news. Her day was about to go even further downhill.

I walked into her office, shut the door, and proceeded to sit down.

"I'm on the phone, Perkins," she barked after covering the receiver with one hand and waving me away with the other. She had not been happy with me since I had gotten out of company therapy, still trying to figure out how I had accomplished it.

"Then you need to get *off* the phone," I said, staring her down. "This is important. We have to talk about the employees, the department, and a few other things."

She put her hand over the receiver again and hissed in my direction, "Get out of my damn office . . . now! I'll deal with you later." Then she went back to her conversation, rolling her eyes for added effect.

There was nothing else to do really, so I walked over to the video equipment and put in the tape of the person who had been caught defecating into a baggie. I had cued it up to just a few moments before the culprit appeared and its grainy black-and-white footage began to roll. A slight hum accompanied the picture.

"Well, he'll just have to send it over now," Pokey was saying into the receiver, "he can't just up and—" but she stopped mid-sentence when she recognized the double doors to our offices.

"I have to call you back," she said absently to the person she had been speaking to, and sat transfixed. I didn't say anything but sat down again with my back to the video footage. I didn't need to see it again as it had unfortunately been etched into my brain for all eternity. But I did enjoy watching Miss Pokey's reaction. I could tell what part she was seeing by her expression: the doors being put back to prepare the mock stage; the stepping out of the sweat pants; the positioning of the baggie—all of it. She was in shock, unable to move. She was frozen to the spot.

As her face fell and her mouth dropped open I estimated that we were getting to the climax, and she confirmed this by her next choice of words.

"Turn it off! Turn it off now!" she screamed and somehow found her legs. She was moving toward the videotape, shaking violently. Her hand groped for the "off" button and she fumbled to remove the tape. Now she held it up between her thumb and forefinger as if it were the offending item that had been produced in the video.

"You're *disgusting* . . . how could you . . ." she attempted, but stopped when she saw the calm smirk forming on my lips. I said nothing for a moment but rather sat there with my arms crossed, leaning back in the chair—the way I'd seen Dr. Patchin do. I nonchalantly tapped at the edge of her desk with the toe of my shoe, calm and collected as though we had been discussing the merits of the latest Bandomday book on gardening. I waited, letting the full impact of the video sink in, allowing all the possible permutations the situation could hold make themselves known to her. Finally I spoke.

"I don't know," I began, not bothering to look at her, "I thought you photographed rather well, all things considered." I waited again. She was attempting to say something—I could sense her mouth moving even though I wasn't facing her. I finished, letting her know just where we stood on the issue: "You know, after all you've done to me while I've been here," I stated, "I'd like to tell you to go fuck yourself." I paused for dramatic effect; station identification; a sporty "time out," letting the full effect of having a boss who was not only a hermaphrodite but one who pooped into a baggie as well, sink in. Then I continued. "Problem is, I realize now that you'd be able to actually do it."

52

Weeks went by. I had everyone under my control at Bandomday. Perkel, Cloud, Frasquina, and Clarice had all given *Mrs. Squigglemire's Bustle* the thumbs up, and Miss Pokey was the easiest of all. She had been most helpful, promising to use all her pull in the company (she had worked there for over twenty years) to get the manuscript moved higher and higher. It was sad in a way, seeing her work so hard. She was there till almost ten o'clock every night, on the phone continuously; having lunch with anyone and everyone she could to push *Mrs. Squigglemire* high enough to get it published. And the whole time with Robert Hickenlooper's name attached. I still had not let on that it was my manuscript and wouldn't—that is, not until the time was right.

The scene in her office that day had been ugly—the one where I showed the tape where she gave birth to a lawyer and then laminated it. She had destroyed the evidence right then and there, furiously pulling out yards of squeaky plastic from the videocassette, as if trying to remove some giant tapeworm from the small rectangular anus that housed a physical representation of her innermost problems. But it had all been for naught, for when she had finished, I informed her that there were several copies, the most important of which was in a safe deposit box with a letter stating that "Should anything happen to me, please see that this tape goes to Channel Five News."

And so now she was hard at work, coddling my manuscript and a few others (I had to make it look legit) with glowing recommendations. The hard work paid off too, for in a matter of one month she was promoted to a higher floor, out of the basement, where she could do even more good for *Mrs. Squigglemire*. It felt good to have friends in high places.

I also got promoted, thanks to Miss Pokey, to her old position and began the task of redecorating her old office. Danish Modern wasn't my taste. My cronies couldn't figure out how I had done it (the promotion, not the decorating), but I'm sure they had some idea, knowing what I had managed to scrape up on them individually.

Pokey and I lunched often (she always insisted on paying) and she let me know the progress of the book, only occasionally questioning my rabid interest in it. She admitted that, while her hand was forced, the quality of the writing was original and the plot well thought out.

Then things began to get sticky about the second month into the process. One day at lunch she informed me that a top editor had requested an interview with the author. I hadn't thought about this part. I pretended to be dissatisfied with my croquettes of salmon—a foil for my real anxiety about how I would handle this problem—and then responded, thinking of Robert. "I'll get in touch with him for you."

Dropping her off at her floor, I made a mad dash to my office to call Robert.

"Just this one favor," I said, into the receiver. "I promise I won't ask for anything else."

"Max, I've gotten you jobs, found you story editors, roommates, places to live. Man, I can't keep going this way. At some point you've got to stand on your own two feet. You're in the publishing business; the book has gotten this far. You don't need me."

"But that's where you're wrong," I said. "I used your name as the author—just like we agreed—and now they want to meet him . . . you, me, whatever. I can't go in there. They'll find out I work for them, who I am, and the whole thing will be over. Besides, all you have to do is meet with someone in marketing and after you've signed the deal—"

"Signed the deal!"

"Well, you'll have to do it or else they'll know you're not the author. You just have to sign your own name and then give me the money."

"Oh, no. No, thank you. Nothing doing."

"Look, I promise I won't ask for anything ever again. Just this one last favor." But Robert held to his position. He didn't budge and hung up.

A few days later I saw Robert on the sidewalk, heading directly for a video store on Seventh Avenue in the Village. He was too far away for me to yell to him, so I ran to catch up. When I got to the store, to the bottom of the steps, he was already at the top going up to the second floor where the pornography was kept. Since I was out of breath I took a little longer getting up the steep flight and arrived just as he was asking the clerk at the desk for a copy of a video.

"It's called *Bonzo in the Jungle* and it was just released yesterday. Producer is named Fartus and the director is Rot, if that helps," Robert said to the clerk. I stopped cold. He hadn't seen me, so I stood very still, pretending to be just another customer waiting on line. I had heard two names that were familiar and my mind was reeling at what this bit of information could mean. Quickly I tried to rationalize. Perhaps Robert had said Roth, not Rot. Roth wasn't such an unusual name. Any number of people could have that. But Fartus? Perhaps I had misunderstood. The clerk searched his database for the title and my ears were given a second chance.

"You said Fartus was the producer?"

"Yeah, and Rot the director. Just came out yesterday. Maybe you guys don't have it yet."

Once again, I made excuses. Rot *could* be a common name, in New York—couldn't it? It was probably a man who was the director anyway. I was overreacting; jumping to conclusions. I was just being paranoid.

"No, here it is," said the clerk. "Reeda Rot. Aisle three, porn, next to the hard-core and kink."

Robert bid the clerk thanks and walked toward the aisle containing the tape.

"Can I help you?" the clerk asked now that I was the next in line, but my mind was a blur, trying to piece together what was going on.

For fear of speaking and giving myself away I just shook my head and waved a "No, thank you." Then I made a hasty retreat out of the store. I waited around the corner, and as soon as I saw Robert leave I made my way back up the stairs.

"Change your mind?" the clerk asked, and I responded sheepishly, "Yeah."

I looked around nervously. The guy at the desk probably figured it was my first time buying porn (it was), so he was patient. Finally I mustered up the confidence to speak: "I was just in here and overheard you and that other guy discussing a certain tape."

"Bonzo in the Jungle?"

"Yeah, that one. You wouldn't by any chance have two copies of it would you?

"Let ... me ... see," he said as he checked his database again. "You're in luck! Aisle three," and with that I made my way over to the exact place where Robert had gone—to follow in his footsteps.

It used to unnerve me as a youth, having our poodle watch while I pleasured myself—a mere twelve-year-old at the time on a date with Rosie Palm and her five sisters. I imagined the dog to be the reincarnation of my grandmother. A truly disturbing thought. It wasn't as if I sought the poodle out, but rather that the dog just seemed fascinated by the act and I was usually too far into it to stop by the time I noticed two beady black eyes staring at me through bangs of fur. That, plus I was lazy. Too lazy to get up and put the dog out of the room.

I imagined my grandmother doing her Aunt Pittypat imitation from *Gone With the Wind*—fan flapping the air; trying to recuperate after having witnessed her grandson choke the chicken—the small poodle paws reaching out for the glass of water being offered as the phantasmagoric thought played itself out. It was this mélange of salacious contemplation and reminiscence that rolled around inside my head as I auditioned my hand puppet early one morning, thinking that no one would notice.

I was wrong.

I had overslept and it wasn't the first time. Judging by the amount of knife scraping on toast above me and the slurping of coffee, it was past seven. Spong hadn't been kidding when he had said punctuality was everything to him, for at seven sharp that morning the board had been placed on top of the bathtub, sealing me in like some bad high school production of Poe's *Cask of Amontillado*. I knew better than to protest. The first time this had happened, I had pressed upward, thinking that I would simply climb out before Spong had time to put out the marmalade and coffee. But he had shrieked like a thirteen-year-old girl and I had relented, perusing (as he had suggested) one of the awful manuscripts that I had taken home from work.

So on this fine morning, having nothing to read, I decided to spank the monkey—you know, pull the handbrake? Wank-orama? Jackin' the beanstalk? I didn't think Spong, or anyone for that matter, could hear me. I mean, an eighty-year-old behemoth of a bathtub is pretty solid. What I didn't factor in was the reverberation qualities the thing had, even with the extra blankets and flashlight batteries.

"Wham, wham, wham, wham!" Spong's fist came down on the plywood.

"Guy, give it a rest. I'm trying to eat."

"Sorry. Didn't know you could hear me."

"And are you still using the blankets I let you borrow?"

"I promise to wash them," I said.

"Please."

I was finally released when the last breakfast crumb had been consumed, and proceeded to get ready for work. Spong said he was going to his gym first thing and shower there ("The sauna gets all the fuckin' poisons out of my system, man.")

I had no complaints.

Rationalizing that my watching of the porno tape the night before in my office (on the very video equipment that I had used to snag Miss Pokey) had set off some inner longing for companionship, I smoothed my ruffled feathers at not being able to finish. I decided to put my energy into getting ready for another fun-filled work experience at Bandomday.

All the while I did my morning ablutions I thought about the tape. Certainly nothing on it had excited me, but it was more the "idea" of pornography than the actual viewing that had piqued my interest. It was the idea of being paid for sex, in whatever form, be it movie or in person. The thought had always disgusted me, but now, after having experienced all life didn't have to offer, selling oneself didn't seem so bad.

The tape had been a revelation, but not in the way it was intended. *Bonzo of the Jungle* had indeed been a Fartus/Rot collaboration, but others were involved as well. Their names did not appear when the credits rolled at the end, but their faces and, well, other parts were recognized.

What had been most fascinating about the viewing was the capacity to reminisce about Reeda—that bastion of analytical abilities—for the entire production had been filmed in her filthy one-room apartment, complete with crippled menagerie and corn plant.

Horribly fake painted scenery had been crammed into the space to cover the bookcases and desk, and the photographic result wasn't much better than some cable program from the Midwest shown at three o'clock in the morning.

> Scene: Jamaican pen salesman with large pillow strapped to buttocks (and large blond wig atop head) assaults pencil-necked geek (Bonzo) who spouts lines from assorted Bette Davis movies. Bonzo seems uninterested and flips through various magazines during attack. Off to side, featherless parrot bounces up and down to cheesy drum music while sitting atop a cardboard palm tree--very Art Deco. Phobos (chariot god--a half-paralyzed dog with little fur, strapped into a contraption with wheels) squeaks up to the cleft palate geek (Bonzo, again) and begins licking peanut butter from some (thank God) unseen area. Geek spouts lines from old movie: "Fasten your seat belts . . . it's going to be a bumpy night."
>
> Jamaican pen salesman and Bonzo move to large claw-foot tub in center of room. "Hold baggie full of American doo-doo, fag-Jew-boy," the Jamaican exclaims. (Note: This is not a big budget film.)
>
> A large overweight man joins scene (holding jar of baby food) and attempts to speak Russian. He is balding with a flaking head and pompous manner. All pile into bathtub for orgy scene. Ferret scampers over the buttocks of the portly Russian, now exhausted and covered with sweat as he climaxes. Russian and Jamaican chime in together: "Hail, Satan!" Bonzo Cleft Palate is a few seconds late with lisp: "*Hair*, Satan!" he squeaks out. All three are panting. Finally Bonzo finishes the scene with a quote from *All About Eve*: "Cut!

Brilliant! What happens in the next reel? Do I get dragged off screaming to the snake pit?" In background, voice is heard, "That's a wrap, everybody!"

54

I waited outside of Robert's apartment, determined to confront him about what he had done. Three hours passed and still no Robert. Just as I was about to give up he came walking down the street. He hadn't been home from the night before.

"Out making more porn?" I said, holding up my copy of *Bonzo*. At first it didn't register for him. Then he saw the label on the tape's spine.

"Oh. You see it yet?"

"Yes, I saw it. You've got some nerve."

He brushed by me, heading for the door to his building. "Hey, you needed a job; places to stay. I was helping you out."

"Helping me out!"

"Did anyone else?" he asked as he opened the door to his building. I followed him up the stairs.

"It was bad enough that Fartus produced this piece of garbage, but then to send me to Reeda and have her suck me dry of all my cash, not to mention the fact that she pumped me for ideas for the porn industry."

"There are no guarantees in life, Max."

"Boy, you're not kidding." Robert was opening the locks on the door to his apartment.

"And then to find out that that Malcolm the cleft palate from Babley's was in the movie would have made things unbelievable enough, but that Mr. Babley was the Russian? I mean, why wasn't Anastasia in the production too, along with all my relatives and everyone I've ever come in contact with on the subway? Does the next one have a scat theme with Miss Pokey?"

"Hey, listen, some people enjoy making porn. Some just need the extra cash. In Malcolm's case he's got this fascination with Bette Davis movies. The guy knows every line from every one of her films. He thinks he *is* Bette Davis. This is probably the closest he's ever going to get to actually being her. And Babley, well, he just enjoys showing off. That and the fact that he and Malcolm are tight. He likes that little boy look. And Anastasia wanted too much money, though she did agree to do a stint in one of the seedier magazines."

"You owe me," I said, as we both entered Robert's apartment. "I'm surprised Marcel wasn't involved too," I added, seeing a brochure for his business on an end table.

"He's the clean-up crew for the films," Robert said, going into the kitchen area.

"Not him too! Is there anyone I know who's *not* involved?"

Robert waited a moment. Then he took a milk carton out of the refrigerator and drank directly from it. "Let me think," he said as he turned to me, a milk mustache on his upper lip. He took another drink and replaced the carton. "I'll have to get back to you on that one."

55

My phone rang at nine-thirty—at work. I answered expecting to hear someone from the company question me about one of the manuscripts that my group had sent upstairs. It was either that or news of *Mrs. Squigglemire*—perhaps a congratulatory call for finding the newest future bestseller.

"*Hola*," I said into the receiver, but the voice was unfamiliar.

"I'm trying to get in touch with a . . . Max Perkins," the female on the other end stated. Her voice was tinged with condescension and she was only into the first sentence of the conversation. I knew it wasn't going to be good.

"Speaking."

"Hi," she continued, somewhat more amiable now that she had confirmed her party, "I'll come straight to the point: I work for an employment agency here in the city and I have an opening to fill at one of the major publishing houses and was wondering if I could speak with you about it?"

"In what capacity?"

"Well, I understand you are the manager for your department—the readers' department—is that correct?"

"Hmmm."

"The position I have is at a most prestigious firm and pays well."

I let her go on, explaining the firm, the responsibilities, and perks offered. I wasn't terribly interested since I had my book to look after at Bandomday, but just as I was about to tell her to go somewhere else, she dropped the salary they were offering into my lap.

"How much?" I asked, thinking that I couldn't have heard correctly. It was triple what I was making—and I wasn't making that much as a manager. I still couldn't afford to move out of the hole that Spong and I shared on what I made. I hesitated a moment, wanting to see how serious she was. Even with better pay, a part of me still wasn't totally engrossed.

"Yeah . . . I don't know. I'm not really interested in moving right now," I said, and pretty much tuned out, waiting for her to talk herself to death or tire of the spiel. When I heard the new amount that they were willing to pay ("I've been authorized to go even higher!"), I sat up.

"Look, they want you. They asked for you personally but didn't want to call you themselves—bad form, that kind of thing. I'm not supposed to be telling you this, but they said they were going to do whatever it took to get you over to their company. Word is out about your reputation and they *want* you."

I sat silent. The voice on the other end of the phone jumped in, afraid of losing me.

"Don't you think you're underpaid?" she asked. Then she really dropped a bomb. "Let me ask you this—exactly how much is your bonus every year?"

The question sent a chill down my spine. It was common knowledge that the company didn't give bonuses. This had been a major bone of contention. I couldn't see how they expected to get the most out of their employees unless they offered some sort of additional compensation plan; something other than the meager four percent raises they gave each year; some incentive to work.

"We don't get bonuses," I said smugly into the receiver, careful to look at the doorway to my office, making sure no one was passing by.

Then she named a receptionist who had worked on one of the upper floors, asking if I knew her—a receptionist who had worked for the personnel department, for Ms. Philistine. I immediately called up from memory an incident that had happened to the poor creature.

In keeping with Bandomday's preoccupation with bodily functions, the girl's "relief" replacement had not come back from lunch on time one day, and having been told that she was under no circumstances to leave her post unattended, and in dire need of emptying her small bladder, she had relieved herself on the chair she sat in.

But the most intriguing aspect of the event had not been her lack of bladder control, rather the fact that she failed to mention it to anyone, including the replacement who *did* finally show up. It was only after the new girl sat down that the deed was discovered and by that time too late to be avoided.

"Yes, I know of her. You actually got her a job?" I asked, incredulous that anyone would have hired her after that fiasco.

"Not only did we place her, but we got her a twenty percent salary increase and an even larger bonus than she was getting at Bandomday."

"She got a bonus!" I screamed. "She gave *us* a bonus!"

"I would think that if the receptionist is getting a bonus, that you should be entitled—"

"Yes, I'm interested in the position," I said emphatically into the phone, and she proceeded to give me the necessary address so that I could meet with her, give her my application, and set up the interview.

I occupied myself the rest of the morning with odds and ends, that is, until the mail arrived. The usual fare was there, but one thing stood out. It was a small brown package: a videotape with no return address.

I was accustomed to receiving gifts from what I'll call "the stranger" but this one intrigued me the most. After all, it had a little more substance to it than the past items. The *Jokes for the John* book, the gardenia—they had only confused me. Then there had been the cryptic messages via telephone.

Tearing through the outer wrapping I pulled out a copy of the movie *Rosemary's Baby*—that 1967 Roman Polanski film set in New York. "Curious," I thought. "What could this have to do with anything?" and remembered that the movie had come to mind when I was apartment hunting; looking for something as grand as what Rosemary and her husband had lived in. That fantasy had been shot down quickly enough.

I decided to give the movie a look and walked over to the video equipment—that lifesaver of technology that had put Miss Pokey in her place—and popped the thing in. The opening credits began to come up and the haunting lullaby sung by Mia Farrow came floating out of the speakers. I closed my door so as not to bother anyone and stood looking at the opening shot. It panned over the New York skyline and then settled on that nineteenth-century apartment building, the Dakota.

"Scene," I said to myself, out loud. "Rooftops of New York. Camera moves slowly and we hear a simple lullaby sung by someone." Reeda had gotten into my head. I tried to shake her out.

Deciding after a few minutes that nothing substantial was going to be revealed (I had seen it years ago but couldn't remember much of it), I sat back down at my desk and began to peruse some of the manuscripts I was to hand out later that day. The film played in the background. At one point something caught my attention, you know, in an almost subconscious way. But I let it go. I continued to work.

I was on the phone when it happened.

"Yeah, you guys sent me this book proposal about herpes again," I said to a manager on one of the upper floors. "We've already read it and given you our—" but I stopped cold. Something in the film caught my ear. "Let me get back to you," I said vacantly to the person on the other end of the line. Then I grabbed the remote and hit rewind. I spooled the tape back a few minutes. There it was.

"Did you go to the bathroom?" one of the characters asks in the film.

"There? No," the husband replies.

"Guess what they've got in it?"

"A bidet."

"No, *Jokes for the John*."

That was it. *Jokes for the John*. But why? The mystery person had sent me a book titled that, and they were now sending me this movie. But what was the connection? And there was something else—some other bell that had gone off.

I hit the rewind button on the remote and started the film over again, hoping for other clues. I didn't see much resemblance to anything else I'd been sent and was just about to figure it as a coincidence when that previous "something" stood out. It was the thing my subconscious had heard earlier. It was as if my inner self caught it but some more rational and everyday part of me said, "Don't worry about it. It's not that unusual; not important."

I listened more closely this time to the dialogue:

"The previous tenant, Mrs. Gardenia, passed away only a few days ago and nothing has been moved out of the apartment yet," one of the actors intoned.

Now it was more than a coincidence. Gardenia. *Jokes for the John*. The tape obviously had something to do with the things sent to me. I abandoned all hope of doing work and started the movie over from the beginning, scanning each scene, listening to each word so as to be able to put the puzzle together. It was all there: Mrs. Gardenia; *Jokes for the John*; tannis root; Donald Baumgart; even the commercial Rosemary's husband was in—the one for Yamaha. Over the past several months I had also received a bottle of the perfume *Detchema*, the sheet music for Beethoven's "Für Elise," and a copy of the John Osborne play *Luther*. Those too were all there—all in the movie.

Then the word my anonymous caller had been repeating. It wasn't *castanets* but rather *Castevets*—the last name of the devil-worshiping neighbors in the movie.

I had written these things off as having nothing to do with one another—as if someone were cleaning out their garage and needed to get rid of various unconnected items. Now I realized they were all linked.

But why?

I knew now that the film was a culmination of all the objects and strange phone calls, but what was the person trying to tell me? And if they were trying to tell me anything, why didn't they just come out and do it? Why this drawn-out routine over the past nine months? And there was something else: At one point in the movie, the Castevets have Rosemary and Guy Woodhouse over for drinks, and they're serving vodka blushes.

"Vodka blushes," I said out loud to myself. "Where have I had one of those before?" and tried to remember. But before I could finish the thought, I saw it: a box on top of one of Miss Pokey's cabinets, near the ceiling. It was the Scrabble game someone had sent me on my first day of employment. Miss Pokey had confiscated it and hadn't disposed of it. She also hadn't returned it, and with all the work I was doing, and it being so high up, I hadn't given it much thought.

Climbing on top of a small table I reached up and took it down. I dumped all the contents on top of the desk, just as Rosemary was doing in the movie. With the film's soundtrack still going in the background, the timing couldn't have been more perfect. "The name is an anagram," a voice in the film announced and I remembered that first day at work. I remembered the note that had been attached. "The name is an anagram." But whose name? Was it a him or a her . . . or an object? Bandomday? Barely Broadway? What?

While the movie had shed light on the objects I had received over the past several months, I felt as if I were back at square one. And I spent most of that night trying to make the letters of the game fit into something rational. But nothing worked.

56

The face-to-face process didn't go well at my prospective new company. I felt a tension with everyone from personnel to the head of the acquisitions department. I had been instructed not to talk about salary, benefits, or anything but the most basic aspects of the job on this first interview, so I sat sullenly for the most part and let them explain. They were as vague as I was, and by the time I found myself once again on the street, I was questioning why the process had been allowed to get this far.

Calling the agency as soon as I was back at Bandomday, I let them know that I wasn't interested; that I was staying put for now. The girl on the other end of the line began immediately chewing my ear.

"This is the thanks I get for going to all this trouble? The least you could do is go on another interview with them. They love you! Are you so ungrateful that you won't see them at least one more time?"

"To tell you the truth," I said, "they didn't seem that interested in me."

"What! They loved you. The head guy over there said that if he had to, he was going to personally come over to Bandomday and drag you out kicking and screaming."

We argued over the next few days, back and forth, about whether or not I would go on a second interview. Finally, becoming disgusted with her tirades and attitude, and after having tried everything possible to get rid of her, I opted for something new. She wouldn't take "I'm not interested," so I chose a lie: "I've taken another position at another company and I've already signed the contract," I said. "They're paying me even more than what your company was offering and I'll be out of here in a week." It worked, for she stopped calling and left me alone. But the next day I was summoned to Bandomday's personnel office around noon.

I was told to shut the door by Ms. Stick-and-Bones—the original shrew who had placed me in the reading pit.

"We'd like to offer a proposal," she started out, smiling.

I waited. Tension hung in the air. I knew marriage wasn't in the works, so I thought perhaps she'd heard someone else wanted to hire me and the company was going to make a counter offer, so valuable were my services.

"We'd like for you to leave today." She delivered the words with the pleasure of an overzealous gardener scything through a patch of weeds.

"Beg pardon?" I said, leaning forward, not believing what I was hearing.

"We'd like for you to leave today. Someone is packing your belongings in your office as we speak. They will be sent to you at a later date."

I felt like Joan Crawford in *Mommie Dearest* when Mayer lets her go, only I didn't have her money, her career, or even Tina to go home and kick.

The creature continued: "Your card key is no longer valid in any of our security systems, so don't make any attempt to reenter our building after this exit interview." She was cold, calculating, rock-hard, and enjoying every minute. I tried to open my mouth but nothing came out. She continued.

"We were called by a . . ." and at this point she looked down at a piece of paper in front of her ". . . Camden Associates, who asked if they could fill the position of readers' manager—that would be you. When I told them that the position wasn't open, that we had someone already, they said, 'Oh, do you mean Max Perkins? He has a new job and will be leaving in a week—didn't he tell you?' Then the young woman explained how you had called her, asking her company to get you an interview at one of the firms that is our competition. I happen to know someone at that firm, and when I called them they confirmed her story."

She was on a roll—an even and hateful roll.

"It is our priority to protect ourselves with regard to filling positions and your underhanded way of dealing with other organizations is cause enough for us to legally terminate you. Is there anything you want to say in this exit interview?" she finally asked, lips smirking, arms crossed.

I had somewhat gained my composure during her long diatribe and while myriad ideas and questions circled my brain, only one thing came out of my mouth.

"Were you born without a personality and sense of humor," I asked, "or did you have them surgically removed when they sewed up your asshole?"

She had evidently pressed some unseen buzzer under her desk before the completion of my question, for no sooner had I finished than two burly guards opened her door and motioned for me to follow them. And I did—all the way to the lobby of the building with her a few feet behind, muttering under her breath.

Just as we neared the revolving doors they were to deposit me through, the guards spun me around to face the wicked witch. I had to wonder if the whole thing had been planned, so choreographed was the movement.

"I'll see to it you never work in publishing again as long as you live, Max Perkins," she seethed at me, her eyes two narrow slits, her less-than-amiable high heels tap-tap-tapping on the cold marble floor as she came to a stop only inches from my face. The guards were now holding me by each arm, slightly off the floor, so there was no way I could hit her, at least not physically.

"Honey," I replied loudly, suspended there while eyes on both sides of the glassed-in lobby focused their attention on me, "from your lips to God's ears."

57

Witness for the prosecution: "Yes, I met with Max Perkins. It was in reference to an opening that we had in the readers' department. He came to our attention through Camden Associates--they're a placement agency. Bandomday is a competitor of ours and we were told he worked there. I've been in the personnel department now for thirteen years. For some reason, Mr. Perkins was under the assumption that the job was managerial, paid more than he now made, and that he would receive a bonus. When I questioned the employment agency that sent him to us--again, Camden--they told us that the job had been described to him as what it was: lower level with no benefits. They claimed he had called them, asking for a position with us. Frankly, we couldn't understand why he was interested in the position. It paid less and there was no possibility at all for him to move up. We never really wanted to interview him but the agency kept shoving him down our throats so we saw him just to appease everyone. We rarely hire anyone from Bandomday.

"They fired me! The assholes fired me! That piece-of-shit employment agency—"

"The terms 'piece-of-shit' and 'employment agency' are so redundant that I can't even begin to address them," Robert said, as we made our way out of the subway station at Columbus Circle. Central Park was only a few feet away.

"I'm screwed. I live in a shit place, I have no real job, I have a psychotic roommate, and I've got bills to pay. I'm getting it from all sides."

"What you need is a totally new career change."

"No. No thanks. No favors. I'm through with whatever you're offering. You got me into that fiasco with Reeda, the porn film scriptwriter slash healer slash essayist slash anything you want person. I could have said, 'I want to learn to give head to elephants' and she would have said, 'That's what I do—I give head to elephants.' Jesus, isn't anybody a real person in this town? And I have to say, watching Miss Pokey take a poop in a baggie was one of the more enjoyable aspects of that snake pit—Bandomday—if that's any indication of the level of insanity and incompetence in publishing. No, you don't need to do anything else for me."

We headed into the park, down the winding concrete paths, across the asphalt street and onto the grass that led up to one of the smaller ball fields of Central Park.

"Speaking of giving head to elephants . . ."

"What?"

"Giving head—oral sex," Robert said, bringing us back to an earlier moment. We were now walking over one of the decorative bridges that graced Central Park. He hesitated for a moment, looking around. I sensed he was about to say something else but changed his mind. We stopped.

"You know, this is the bridge that was in *Sweet Charity*." Robert's mind seemed to be trying to find a way to the initial subject of the day—job changes—via an alternate route.

"What are you talking about?" I asked. Robert was leaning on the cast-iron railing that charmingly arched with the structure. Below us two bicyclists whirred past followed by a lone runner.

"*Sweet Charity*. You know. The movie with Shirley McLaine. This is the bridge in the movie where she meets that guy who almost marries her, depending on which ending of the movie you watch." He was gazing off into the distance now, not really looking at me.

"Been a long time," I said. "I haven't seen the movie in years. As a matter of fact, the last movie I saw was at work, a couple of days ago. Seems that—" but Robert cut me off, totally uninterested in what I had to say.

"Well, you know, it's an interesting story. Shirley McLaine is what you might term a call girl. Nothing too heavy, at least in the movie. She works as a dance hall hostess. Dances with these old

282

guys that come into the club. She fantasizes about getting out of the profession; changing the way people look at her, what they think about her. A career reassessment, if you will."

I stared at him. He was still looking out into the pre-green of the park. In the distance a horse whinnied and hoof beats could be heard.

It was then that something occurred to me; a light bulb of connection. I waited for a moment, uncertain whether or not to broach the subject. Then I did.

"It is you?" I asked.

"Huh?" He turned toward me.

"You. It is you that's been sending me the things; the tape?

"What tape? What things?"

"*Rosemary's Baby*. The gardenia. The joke book," I said. Robert said nothing.

At first I thought he was lying, but then I realized he wasn't—he was just uncomfortable. I tried to rationalize. "You like movies. Old movies. Lots of movies. You've even made a few yourself."

"Dude, what are you getting at?" He was genuinely confused. "Someone sent you a copy of that Roman Polanski movie? And a gardenia?"

"Yeah, and it wasn't you?"

"No way," he said, turning back now to lean on the bridge's railing. He seemed slightly shaken by something. The sound of the horse's hoofs came closer. It approached from the distance like the future—galloping nearer as we stood there high above the trail. I could tell Robert was annoyed by something, I just didn't know what. I still wasn't sure if he had sent me the tape or not, but something was definite: He was rankled by my admission of receiving it.

"Riding trail below," Robert said, changing the subject again, looking down for the first time since we had climbed to the top of the bridge. "You know there was that part in *Breakfast at Tiffany's*—the book, not the movie—where the main character talks about getting dragged by a horse through Central Park."

283

"Wasn't the male character in that movie a prostitute . . . and a writer as well?" I asked, still completely oblivious to where Robert was headed. But then the light began to shine at the end of that tunnel. The problem was, the beam was attached to an oncoming train. Robert straightened up and turned to me, leaning back slightly, a smug look on his face.

"Yes, he was. He most certainly was a male prostitute and a writer, my friend," he said, completely satisfied with himself.

Just at that moment, the horse that we had heard previously came charging underneath us, right under the bridge. It was galloping wildly and bouncing a young man who had fallen off but was still holding on with one foot in the stirrup and one hand on the saddle.

"And so," said Robert as he turned, watching the poor youth being dragged off down the path, "history repeats itself."

58

"There's no way in hell. Do you hear me? No way in hell that I'm going down that road. You've screwed my life up for the last time and this discussion is over. Got it?" I could see the Saturday late-afternoon traffic from Robert's apartment. The few trees that lined the sidewalk were beginning to bud. I should have known that something was up when he offered to fix me dinner. It had taken practically an act of God to get to see where he lived and now he was all too eager to entertain me.

"Max, Maaaaxxxxxx, just this once. After all, I'm doing you a big favor by pretending to be you at the contract signing, even if you did practically blackmail me after discovering that *Bonzo in the Jungle* tape. After it's all done and set in place, after the publicity is put in motion, they're not going to back out. And you think the people in management communicate with the promotion people? With that many books and most of them absolute crap? Think again. They won't even remember who I am . . . you are . . . we are. Whoever we're . . . you're supposed to be. I'm in and out in a flash. My signature is on the contract and then you're the one going to the book signings, the photo shoots, the interviews. No one anywhere within the organization is going to recognize you. Hell, they're all too busy with the next hundred books. And as long as they think the thing is going to sell, they won't say *boo*."

"You've gotten me into more disasters that I care to count. I'm done now. I don't care about the book. I don't care about becoming a writer. I just want out. Exactly how many people do I know who *you* know anyway? If I'd had any idea that New York was the small town it is I'd have stayed in Pennsylvania. And this is the reason you called me over?"

"No, I wanted to fix you dinner. Well, that and to discuss my latest proposition."

"No way in hell am I going to become a male hustler," I said, wrestling with a bottle of inexpensive merlot. The cork had broken off in the neck and I was attempting to pick out the pieces with a steak knife.

"And shouldn't you be doing this?" I said, giving him a nasty look. "Who's making *whom* dinner? Who's waiting on *whom?*"

Taking his cue, he got up to help, abandoning his comfortable perch on the sofa.

"You don't have to get all uppity. I need help since my client list has grown so. At least let me tell you about it."

"No. And where is Marcel?"

"All you have to do is show up, to this one place—I've known the guy for four years now. Four years, Max. He's harmless. All you have to do is show up and put the uniform on. And Marcel is out of town."

"I'm not showing up and I'm not wearing a Nazi uniform for anyone, anytime, anywhere."

"Put the uniform on," Robert continued, taking the wine bottle from me, "and just yell at him for a few minutes in German."

"I don't even *know* German!" I roared, retreating to the very place Robert had been sitting.

"There, like that. Just yell. He likes that. Two or three minutes and then after he's answered the bone phone you can go. You don't touch him—he doesn't touch you. No contact. And it's a painless two hundred bucks. How easy is that?" Robert had by this time extracted the mutilated stopper and was proceeding to strain the wine through a piece of cheesecloth to remove the bits of cork. His back was to me.

"Just go for me this once and then no more. I won't ask for another thing. I'm having the cabernet anyway—don't care much for merlots," he said, holding up the bottle to see if any cork was left inside. "Besides," he went on, carefully handing me the glass, the one in his left hand, "you need the money, I need the break, I'm doing you a favor, and this is the last time—I promise," and with that he raised his glass. "Cheers," he said and I raised mine as well, reluctant but not wanting to offend.

"This wine tastes funny," I said after taking a sip. "Like it has an aftertaste or something."

Robert swirled the wine around in the glass. The red liquid coated the sides. He held it up to the light, then he looked behind himself for a moment and then back at me.

"It shouldn't. Just a regular merlot. Mine tastes fine," he said, and took another sip. "Drink up, my man. We've got things to do," and with that I followed his lead.

After several more glasses of wine and dinner I began to warm to the idea that Robert was proposing. At least some part of me was. I didn't consider myself a big drinker so I was always careful about how much I consumed, but this wine was packing a wallop.

"What's the name of this?" I said, holding my glass up to the light. "It's got some kind of kick to it."

"It's just a regular merlot," Robert said, and casually lit a cigarette. The smoke rose around him theatrically. He smiled. "So what do you think of the proposal now, after you've been wined and dined?"

I smiled. I was feeling warm and fuzzy all over. "You know . . . I don't know what it is, but I really like you," I said, grinning from ear to ear at Robert. I felt like a potted plant—snug and lovable—a gift from the florist with card attached.

"Yeah, I like you too."

"I mean, I just feel that I can trust you, you know?"

It was as if someone else's mouth was speaking. I heard the words and it took me a moment to realize I had said them. Where was *this* coming from? The guy had set me up with every mental deficient within a fifty-mile radius and I was singing his praises. Talk about your out-of-body experiences.

"I'm glad. So how about that earlier proposition? The one involving, you know, you not having to do anything but stand around and yell?"

I leaned my head back on the sofa. My entire body was vibrating. Perhaps Robert was right—all I needed was a good meal, and this wine. "I'll think about it. I'm not sure. I mean, I do need the money, but some part of me still says no." What was I saying? I could hear the words again, but it was as if someone else had taken over my body. It wasn't an out-of-body experience; it was an *in-body* one—as if I someone else were *in* my body.

"Okay. No problem," Robert said, and looked at his watch. "What say we go for a little walk? I just have to make a phone call, so give me a sec," and with that he excused himself and went into the small kitchen area. I couldn't make out what he was saying and I didn't care. All I knew was that I was feeling stellar—the best I had felt in fact, since I had moved to New York. I tried to rationalize that it was because my book was well on its way to being published, that I no longer had to deal with Bandomday and every other worthless job in the city, and that this was possibly the best wine I had ever tasted in my life. Robert came back to the sofa and began to shuffle through some papers on the end table. The combination of wine and the feel-good of the evening caused a flashback to an earlier visit. Then I saw it. Again.

"Who is Ray-Bob?" I asked, remembering the envelope from the first visit and now seeing yet another.

"Huh?"

"Ray-Bob. When I first came over there was an envelope for him. Now I just saw another one. Ray-Bob something or other."

"Ramssey. You remember that?"

"Sure."

Robert waited, seemingly occupied with the mail he was going through. "Just someone I knew a long time ago."

"I thought you said he was the person who lived here before and that the mail had been mis—"

"That's right. He lived here before and I knew him. He moved. I'll have to have this sent back to the post office." He had reached the bottom of the stack. "Oh, look, and here's one addressed to 'current occupant.' Guess they'll deliver anything nowadays. How about that walk now?" and before I knew it we were out the door and heading toward the Upper West Side.

What irritates me most about people who insist on having sex with the dead is their pushiness. But then, I suppose that's what is attractive about the dearly departed in the first place—the lack of a "no" quotient; the imagined sycophancy; the selfishness the act reeks of; the total control over another individual, albeit a dead one. People attracted to this sort of thing obviously have some issues (more like the entire subscription), but when you think about it, they may be healthier than the rest of us who insist on the same qualities in the living. Who, I ask you, really has the sicker mind?

It had been three weeks since my initiation into Robert's world of late-night phone calls and summonses to suspect addresses—a world that ranged from badly decorated hotel rooms to Upper East Side society homes. The amount of strangeness I had encountered in these three weeks could have filled the pages of a novel the size of Manhattan's *Yellow Pages*.

There had been the eighty-year-old lady from New Jersey who wanted me to chase her around her bedroom with a vibrator, never actually touching her, while her Shih Tzu (dyed blue to match the bedspread and carpet) barked incessantly and ran in circles. Then the housewife in Manhattan who could not have been more accommodating; fixing me a full-course lunch and talking incessantly, never once mentioning sex. At the end of the visit she paid me in cash (I wanted to blow my brains out after six hours of non-stop chatter about a sale on throw rugs at Filene's Basement). And then the retired army captain in the Bronx who had insisted I take off all my clothes and stand on a chair with my back to him while reciting Allen Ginsberg's *Howl*. After delivering the entire poem I felt justified in being paid the two hundred dollars we had agreed on.

In short, there had been nothing too physically strenuous or sexually demanding throughout my experiences. Most of the individuals who asked for services wanted highly unusual things, but almost none of them wanted just sex. What seemed at the time to be a sheltering from the harshness of the job, was actually Robert's exasperation with those clients who were so odd.

And I never *really* had sex with any of them. *They* had sex—I was just in the room at the same time the event occurred. Even the high-level government official who flew me down to Washington on his private jet had been harmless enough. While no actual touching took place, I did have to soak in a bathtub of ice water for several minutes, lie perfectly still for half an hour, and try not to breathe or appear to be alive. The congressman, it seems, was into necrophilia and only wanted to do some whitewashing with Tom and Huck while I lay still, the whole time with Fox News playing in the background. He was an extreme right-wing Republican—what can you do? The fact that the hotel room he had rented was at the Watergate only made the act that much more morose.

In order to get to know me better (Why? I was supposed to be dead), he decided to have the limo driver chauffeur us around the Beltway and Washington environs between my performances as The Dead Whore. At one point our car passed the Mormon temple— that enormous glowing conglomeration of spires and marble on a hill overlooking Rock Creek Park. It rose, Oz-like, among the verdant trees and undulating hills surrounding it.

Approaching an overpass with the house of worship in full view, just in the background, we could see that some erudite Washingtonian had spray-painted the words, "Surrender Dorothy" on the concrete bridge structure. The Mormons, religion, and make-believe, it seems, were everywhere. I immediately had a flashback to my first days in New York, sans caffeine and blue jeans. Back at the hotel room, things weren't much better.

"Pope John Paul II visited Mexico this week. Crowds of adoring Catholics swamped the streets in order to get a better look at the pontiff," the television announced to the plush hotel suite while my back suctioned itself to the bathroom floor. It was May and the cherry trees around the tidal basin had finished blooming, but I couldn't enjoy them—there was a sheet pulled up over my head and I was inside.

About the only serious drawback from my capital experience had been the congressman's pushiness. He wanted my hands crossed just *so* and insisted on light blue lipstick to give me that realistic dead appearance. And he was never happy with the scenario he had planned out. He was always changing it.

"Okay, now I'm going to come into the *funeral* home and *find* you, but you haven't been *embalmed* yet, so try to look like you have *rigor mortis*," he yelled across the cavernous hotel suite. He had positioned himself in the living room area, its red-and-turquoise color scheme adding to the absurdity of the situation.

I tried to comply as best I could but his crankiness caused me to accidentally sigh heavily, and this seemed to ruin the effect for him.

"No! Now we have to start all over!" he screamed at me. "This time pretend you're still in the morgue," and at this point he covered me again with the sheet after instructing me to lie on the cold marble bathroom floor once more (the Watergate was nothing if not opulent). At least with the sheet in place I could mouth obscenities and cross my eyes without him knowing. The entire time, the congressman practiced the art of self-abuse a good six feet across the room. Just as he was about to achieve orgasm he cried out, "Who's your daddy?" to which I responded, having grown weary of the game, "How the hell should I know—I'm dead, remember?"

Later, the Washingtonian had complained bitterly to Robert about my performance as a corpse and as a result I was not asked back to the land of politics—a turn of events for which I will be forever grateful. Still, prostitution was better than working in publishing or being a writer, and as I had no other job at the time (other than the occasional magazine focus group) I persevered.

I was grateful that Robert had given me his non-sexual clients to start off with—those that didn't require any direct body contact. Because of Robert's and my similar looks (I had agreed to the flattop haircut finally and my arms were getting bigger thanks to my new gym membership, courtesy of a men's health magazine) the clients didn't seem to mind the slight difference. I was using Robert's *nom de porn* too. We had agreed that it was easier that way.

291

Besides, who wants to use their real name when they're a hustler? Who except Robert, and he had always figured that no one would believe it was his given moniker anyway.

"He's pissed because you ordered room service after he left—filet mignon, the best champagne . . . three salads!" Robert admonished a few days after our elected official's expedition to the other side.

"He left me in the room after making me pretend to be dead for an hour—something about Congress being in session," I said. "I felt I deserved something. I told the people at the front desk to just add room service to his bill. Besides, there was a VCR in the living room, the bedroom, the bathroom, and even the dressing room. The place was enormous. He can afford it."

"You were supposed to be dead," Robert threw back.

"I was only dead while he was there. After he left my health improved greatly," I said. "Besides, I need to know where my tax dollars are going," and with that I hung up.

Prostitution hadn't been the difficult transition I had imagined, but then there were reasons for this that I was unaware of at the time. I later learned that on the first evening of my foray into the flesh trade, Robert had slipped me a drug known in the more astute club circles as Ecstasy. And appropriately named it is, for all I can remember feeling at the time that I donned the Nazi uniform and yelled what little German I knew at the retired school teacher on Manhattan's Upper West Side, was that I wished him and everyone I came in contact with, love—in the deepest and most intense sense of the word.

"Wienerschnitzel!" I had yelled at him, thinking how much I wished him happiness, trying to coerce my voice into that which might have belonged to someone in the Gestapo. I held up a photo of a wiener-dog from a magazine and thrust it forward at him, forcing him to look at Fido's elongated figure and satisfied expression. My thumb was placed conveniently over the can of dog food the advertisement was hawking. "Dachshund! Verboten!" I rasped, and gave my best scowl, snapping the riding crop against my meaty leather-clad calf.

Then, seeing his dirty underpants lying on a nearby chair, I picked them up with the tip of my whip and demanded, "Vas is *dis?* Dumbkopf!" I couldn't think of the German for "dirty panties," not that I ever knew it, so I improvised as best I could. "Ve have vays of making you talk!" I seethed, trying to imitate some irate colonel I had seen on *Hogan's Heroes.* "Herr Commandant veel be ex-TREEM-ly upzet vit dis!" I vaulted in his general direction while he took matters in hand. Finally, just as I sensed he was approaching climax, I gave it everything I had: *"Deutschland über alles!"* I shouted at the top of my lungs—my best Schultz impression. Then I began to sing the German national anthem, and with that the former teacher of high school biology brought forth his part of the act of creation. Clarence Darrow would have been proud.

The bottom line on prostitution was this: It was less stressful, less humiliating, and paid more money than any full-time worker-bee situation I ever had. I could make more money in two hours beating someone's rear end than I could earn in one week kissing that same body part of a boss I didn't like. And for someone who had never had the experience of being a cynosure in high school, prostitution gave me an entirely new persona, complete with confidence, money, and the ability to take control of the situation. I liked the buzz of the pager against my hip—confirmation that I would soon be with yet another human being who desired my lusty companionship.

Granted, you have to be careful when going to a new client. I mean, you don't want to end up on the six o'clock news, found in an oil drum inside a barn on somebody's farm in Pennsylvania, all because you were careless and took on some nut case who likes to snuff out whores. But even with the danger element, it was better than corporate America.

For the time being I forgot all about the movie that had been sent to me—*Rosemary's Baby*—and all of the surrounding paraphernalia that had accompanied it. When you're having a sexual encounter of sorts, who needs a movie? Besides, I had probably overreacted to the film and its accompanying detritus.

And so, with my head firmly planted in nookie-land, I forged ahead in the sex trade. The high point of my hustling experience came when Robert instructed me to visit one of his long-standing clients. I had heard him discuss her once before, when visiting him and Marcel, and knew some of the kinky escapades she liked to partake in.

"She knows you're coming," Robert told me, "and it's really very simple. This one's a piece of cake—she lives in one of those high-rises on the East Side. She thinks *I'm* coming and since you're using my name to turn tricks, it doesn't really matter. For all she knows we're the same person." Then he laid out, step-by-step, what I was to do: "She'll leave the door open for you after the doorman buzzes her—we've done this a hundred times. She'll have already blindfolded herself and will be kneeling down, completely naked. You're to handcuff her, then tie her hands up to the whipping post. No talking."

"The woman actually owns a whipping post?" I asked, unable to believe anyone capable of living in a high-rise apartment building would stoop to such rustic decoration.

"Just listen. It's easy. She'll never know it's not me since she's blindfolded. Just tell the doorman to say, 'Your date is here.' Now, once you've tied her up, take out the cat-o-nine tails—I'll give you mine—and start lashing her as hard as you can."

"I don't know if I'm ready for this," I said, turning squeamish. "You know, there's a reason everyone had anonymous sex in the '70s. Have you taken a good look at some of the people out there?"

"Just wait. When you're through, untie her and whatever you do, don't take the blindfold off. Take the money—it'll be on the coffee table—and leave. Nothing to it. And remember, don't speak. She likes to only *imagine* who you are, so no reality. Oh, and I forgot. There'll be a camera there. You're to take a photo of her after you're done. She likes that. The tripod's set up and everything. Just pick up the remote and click away. She gets off a second time seeing the picture after I've flailed her. And absolutely no talking—I can't emphasize that enough. She'll freak out if you say even one word."

"I'm not sure about his one, Rob. Don't you have something a little more sedate?"

"Trust me, big guy, when you get there and see her, all your fears will fly out the window."

And he was right, for after I had made it past the doorman and into the apartment where the chunky woman was blindfolded and completely naked—waiting for the sting of my cat-o-nines, her concupiscence on display for all to see—I was delighted. The hard rubber ball-gag strapped in her mouth didn't hurt the scene either.

It was during the tying of her hands to the whipping post that it came to me—a rush of recognition after rattling my brain for the minute it took to secure the handcuffs to the pylon. There it was—the keloid scar looming out from her face. I wanted to say something but Robert's warning not to speak echoed in my ears, and as I brought the whips down on her, I thought to myself of my initial days in New York. I thought of Beaucoup books and the evil supervisor. I thought of how she hadn't wanted me to speak—her with her collection of Post-it notes and tally marks—and now, here in her apartment, I thought about how she still fancied she was getting the upper hand, insisting that Robert, or I, or whoever the person wielding the whip was supposed to be, wasn't allowed to communicate verbally—a sort of "who's really in charge game." I thought about it all, and as I brought the cat-o-nines down harder and harder each time, I said to myself, "Take that, Benny, or should I say . . . Bee-naaay!"

Before I left, I took the best picture I could—of myself—making certain that I got a clear shot of my face so she would be sure to recognize that scared and timid employee from the temp agency she had embarrassed so many months ago. Her words still echoed in my ears: "He thinks he's been sent here to write!"

Well, lady, I was, and I'm going to.

I had done what she had asked. I hadn't spoken the entire time I offered my services that day. I had played her game, with her rules, on her turf, and in my own way I had won. It's like the saying goes, "A picture is worth a thousand words."

60

My experience in publishing may not have been lengthy, but it was thorough. I'm sure the ramifications are the same for other areas of employment—banking, health care, McDonald's—but what made my experiences sting so acutely was the fact that I had perceived Bandomday as not only the "foot in the door," but a secure working environment as well; a veritable foundation where I could look down upon those poor hapless individuals who had chosen to try and carve a living from writing, music, or some other low-paying low self-esteem job. The sheer amount of knowledge I gleaned from subjecting myself to the likes of corporate America could fill a book and perhaps someday will. In the meantime, I'll include some ideas here, fragments really, for those individuals who have not figured things out yet and to commiserate with those who have. The rules of writing—or what every author should know. This, from what I've seen happen to other authors. It's my deference to Rudyard Kipling; my homage to the great "If" in the sky; that word that's usually followed by "only," or comes after "what." In this case it's used as . . .

> If nothing actually happens in your book, but there's at least one atmospheric phrase, then it will be called literary. In literary works there must be a total absence of plot.
>
> If there is actually some emotion shown by the characters, the work will be labeled "melodramatic."
>
> If there is a plot in your work it will be labeled a "mystery." Note: mystery works are not acceptable for most prizes, competitions, and awards.
>
> If the book can be made into a movie, rest assured that someone in Hollywood will steal what they can from it, hire someone else to write the screenplay, and leave out the fact that it is based on your novel.
>
> If you write in the first person ("I was born the son of a Quaker farm worker") everyone will insist that the book is autobiographical even though you grew up in the city and were raised as an orthodox Jew.

If you don't know what you're doing, and in the process write sentences that make no sense and are grammatically incorrect, the critics will call you a "new and exciting voice."

I pause here for a break—I know it's a long list, but trust me, if you're interested in the literary arts, you've got to know this stuff.

If you create well-rounded personalities, the critics will say your characters are inconsistent.

If you create characters whose personalities are consistent and make sense in their environments, the critics will say they are one-dimensional and flat.

If you write concise, to-the-point copy, your manuscript will be called "thin."

If you flesh out your characters with backgrounds, personalities, and histories, critics will say that you ramble on.

If you use humor of any kind, the work will be labeled "light."

If you don't use any humor, the work will be called "cynical."

If you use humor in a sarcastic or self-deprecating manner, you will be labeled "bitter."

Note: The work you are reading is a light, cynical, and bitter piece of fiction. But you knew that.

If you write a work and call it fiction, there are people who will insist it is the truth.

If you write a completely truthful non-fiction work—totally accurate and with backup for every statement—people will say it is made up.

If you actually have something to say, no one will publish it.

If all you have to offer is drivel that only a high school dropout could read and follow, all major publishing companies in the world will beat a path to your door. You will be rich and famous overnight and need special security to keep your illiterate fans away.

If you write about what you know, the critics will say you're limited in your experiences.

If you write about anything other than where you have lived for the last twenty years, critics will say you should stick to writing about your own life. What are those poor people who live in Idaho going to do?

If you win any type of award, the chance to publish an article, or land a job that enables you to write for a living, you've been sleeping with the right people and have at least a modicum of sexual talent, or you're a relative of someone in a high and important position, or this is a dream, or all three.

If you have never won an award, never had articles published, and are still asking, "Paper or plastic?" you need to seriously consider stalking someone who has some pull in the publishing world, or offer explicit sexual services in the *Yellow Pages* . . . or both.

If you do have connections in the publishing world, you've been spending too much time in bars, having sex, or compromising what little ethics you may have left after having gotten even this far with your talent.

61

"No, no, no," I heard myself saying. "No autographs. I've got to catch a plane," but the crowd wasn't moving. Hands reached out with pens, pieces of paper, even napkins and neckties to sign. Thousands of cameras clicked in my face. Greedy fingers stretched out to touch parts of my clothing. I was Max Perkins, that holiest of holy grails that everyone wanted to see, fondle, and be near. The police were trying to control the crowd but the mob's force was of epic proportions.

"I haven't seen this kind of crowd since the Pope was in town," I heard one of the policemen say, his arms outstretched to try and hold back the throngs of fans. "I've got to touch him, please!" one of my devotees screamed and lunged for a pant leg. I pulled away just in time.

"Just a few more feet to the limo, Mr. Perkins," another policeman declared. "We're sorry about this. The National Guard has been called out to try and ease the crowds along the route to the ceremony."

"That's fine," I said, giving the officer a firm nod. "You guys are doing the best you can. Who knew that they'd want to give me the key to the city, the Pulitzer Prize, the National Book Award, *and* the Humanitarian Award of the year all in one shot?" I said, and let out a little laugh.

But the policeman didn't hear me, for the chanting in the crowd was too great. "Squigglemire's *Bustle*, Squigglemire's *Bustle*, Sqigglemire's *Bustle*," they repeated, as if it were a sacred mantra, and with each beat their large signs bounced up and down.

"I've never seen anything like this!" another policeman shouted toward my left ear. "I knew authors could attain fame, but I had no idea it might be like this," and just as he finished, the crowd surged forward, pushing me into the opening on one side of the limo. I rode the wave as if it were some tubular phenomenon off the coast of Maui, and with luck and timing the long black car swallowed me up. Someone snapped the door shut and the din was cut in half. Against the windows fans mashed themselves, seemingly trying to squeeze through the molecules of glass. One overzealous female shouted "I love you, Max Perkins," her voice only a faint cry in the almost soundproof limo. Two middle-aged housewives flung themselves onto the hood and began taking off their bras and unbuttoning their pants. The crowd surged around the car, rocking it from side to side.

"Backup! Backup! We need some backup here in midtown," a police officer sitting in the front seat barked into his radio. "Get me some crowd control. We're not going to be able to get Sir Max"—I had been knighted only a week before—"to the award ceremony with this many fans around. Jesus! Two hundred thousand at the book signing this morning and now this! We simply don't have the force to handle this kind of thing. Get me the mayor for God's sake!" and then the car began to tip from side to—

"Perkins! Max . . . Max, where are you at, guy?" The rough voice shook me out of my reverie, along with an equally violent jostle. Some large man had his hand on my shoulder and was swaying me from side to side.

"I'm sorry I'm late," the voice continued. "Meeting with the promotion people. Your book," he said, and maneuvered over to his desk, "is what we need to discuss."

While waiting for the president of Bandomday I had been fantasizing about the success my book was going to have. Though I was somewhat worried about never being able to go out in public again without being recognized, I had managed to squelch my anxiety and make a mental note to set up an appointment with one of New York's renowned plastic surgeons. If things got really sticky I could always have them make me a new face. I imagined myself in the Paramus, New Jersey mall, sifting through racks of sweatpants just like any normal person, laughing to myself at the fact that no one recognized an author whose book had sold over two billion copies in the first month of its release.

"I'll get to the point," the man across the desk was saying. "Basically, well, your book has . . . bombed. No sales. The thing's a total waste. I knew we should have gone with the story of the serial parakeet killer in Iowa—that type of thing really sells."

I was confused. What did he mean, "bombed?" What about the hype, the interviews, my picture on the front of *The New York Times Book Review?* Every newspaper and magazine in town had said that I was the next big thing, that I was destined for greatness, that I was the up-and-coming *wunderkind* to watch. There were parties scheduled at the New York Public Library, Twenty-One, the Waldorf. There were speaking engagements, tours, private jets— the works.

"What about the parties, the tours, the—"

"Cancelled," he said, cutting his hand across his desk. "All gone. Finito. Caput. Down the tubes."

"But what about *The New York Times*, the book magazines, the private jet?"

"Do you understand? Listen to me, Max. It's . . . not . . . going . . . to . . . *happen*. The time has passed. The books aren't selling. We've done everything we could; *Mrs. Squigglemire's Bustle* is just not going to cut it. We shipped thousands of books to all the stores. We guaranteed that we'd have the publicity machine in place and we did. We even had the managers of all chains lie, as they normally do, about how many books were sold, just to get your book to the top of the bestseller list. And it got there. Number one for one week. But people caught on. Yes, they bought the book because they thought everyone else had, but then they returned it when they saw what junk it was. We've lost millions of dollars and all because someone in the company made a bad decision. You're through as an author and I'll be lucky if I keep my job."

Then, just as he was finishing pronouncing the death sentence of my book, the president of Bandomday stood up, dropped his pants, and began waving his penis at me, singing "I'm called Little Buttercup," from Gilbert and Sullivan's operetta, *H.M.S. Pinafore*. Out of nowhere ten or twelve old ladies in wheelchairs began frantically rowing toward me, intent on running me over. Cheesy salsa music could be heard getting louder and louder—something straight out of a '70s commercial. It was at that moment that I heard the fire engines coming closer.

"They're coming for you, Max—to take you away!" he sang, forgetting the words to the operetta. "We'll get a cell together. They're coming, Max! They're—"

I woke with a start, trying desperately to get my bearings, sitting up among the soaking-wet sheets that had wrapped themselves around my legs in the tub. Something loud and obnoxious was clanging away. The fire trucks? The police? I squinted and then looked at the object making the racket. Somehow, after all I'd just been through, I managed to remember that the instrument was called a telephone and answered it. I looked at the alarm clock. Five thirty in the morning. There's nothing more disturbing than a dream within a dream. You never know *where* you are.

"Hellooooo?" I said, irritation coloring every vowel and consonant.

"Max, it's Robert. Are you awake?"

"Well, I am now. Jesus, it's five thirty. What is it?"

"I need your help."

"You'd better, at this hour."

"Hey, you owe me big time since you photographed yourself when you serviced one of my best clients. She's still screaming at me."

"Fair enough. What do I have to do?"

"Now listen carefully . . ."

Scene: The West Village, early morning. Max meets Robert on Christopher Street, near the Hudson River. They talk for a moment, hidden in the shadow of a recessed doorway. Finally, we see Robert take a small package and slip it to Max. We hear the sound in the distance of a car moving over the rain-slicked streets. Toward the river, a shadowy figure lurches along the West Side Highway. Gulls are beginning to screech in the early morning light. As the camera moves closer, we begin to make out voices. Robert and Max are arguing, albeit in hushed tones.

Robert: "Just this one time--that's all. I won't ask anything again."

Max: "I agreed to cover your twisted set-ups with your clients and now this?"

Robert: "You know as well as I do that I couldn't fake being you as the author if I had to maintain all my other jobs. Besides, you're getting to keep most of the money. Just do this for me. Here's the address. All you have to do is deliver it at exactly nine o'clock this morning and everything else will take care of itself. Trust me on this one." We see Robert leave before Max has time to speak, ducking around a corner. Max follows quickly. The camera sees what Max sees. As soon as he rounds the corner Robert is gone, and with no real place for him to hide. It's as if he's disappeared into thin air.

Words flash across the screen: Nine o'clock that same day. We see Max ringing the bell of a seedy apartment building in Alphabet City, on New York's Lower East Side. As someone buzzes the door open he tries to move a wino over enough to enter the building.

We see Max mount a filthy set of stairs. The walls are covered with graffiti. He rings the buzzer to the apartment. The door opens only a few inches, and as Max begins to deliver the package, a rough hand comes out and seizes it, then slams the door.

Camera moves to front of building and we see Max exiting. He gently taps the dead wino with the toe of his shoe. Suddenly a window opens and a motley individual leans out. He's wearing a suit from the thirties-- double-breasted with a red carnation and a lapel that is wide enough to land a 747 on.

Gangster: "You motherfucker! This shit is no good! I'll kill you, motherfucker! You're one dead whore!"

Max hesitates for a moment, then we see that the gangster has a gun. He begins firing at Max. The bullets hit the pavement. Max begins to run.

62

"They need an essay for the paper; something written about *Mrs. Squigglemire*." Robert was asking since he was still pretending to be me for the moment.

"When do *they* need it?" I inquired, gritting my teeth. I was seething; so angry I could barely get the words out.

"Tomorrow. So, what's new?"

"What's new?" I said. "I'll get you the article tonight, but not until I get through tearing you a new one."

"What now?"

"What *now?*" I echoed. "You sent me to that burned-out neighborhood and the guy shot at me! Are you completely nuts? Are you trying to get me killed? I've been calling you all day."

"I think you're overreacting. Besides, you're wasting valuable energy chewing me out when you could be writing that article. Promotion, you know, got to keep those wheels turning."

"Have you heard anything I just said?" I asked, incredulous at Robert's insensitivity.

"Okay, okay. I apologize. I'm sorry, okay? It was my mistake and I've taken care of it. I spoke to the guy and it's all one big misunderstanding. Now will you get started on the article?"

"And when are we going to announce to the world that you're not really me?" I continued. "When did they say the book would be ready for production? When is the check forthcoming—the advance?"

I was worried. Robert had drugged me and then almost gotten me killed. Plus he had managed to coerce me into prostitution. Anything was possible and I didn't trust him. "I'm broke, even with the clients you gave me. I need the cash." I wasn't optimistic. I knew that it sometimes took up to a year before a book could get released. Still, I wanted to stay on top of things.

"Relax. You're getting yourself worked up over nothing. You can trust me. And just so you know where things are, I'll let you in on a little secret that should make you happy."

"I'm waiting."

"They started ragging me about my name, your name—the name of the author of the book. You know, Hickenlooper? This moron in marketing says to me, 'I don't think you're going to sell many books with a name like Hickenlooper,' and I said to her, 'What do you suggest?' So she tells me to come up with a pseudonym, a pen name. I came back yesterday with something and she seemed to like it."

"Such as?"

"How does the name Max Perkins strike you for my *nom de plume?*"

I was stunned. We had talked about how Robert would turn the book over to me once the ball was rolling; about how, before it was on its way to the printer we would announce whose book it really was in just enough time to straighten out the money, the photo shoots, the final details. But this? This was a stroke of genius on Robert's part.

"That's my name," I said.

"Nooooo."

"But won't they remember—"

"That you worked there? I don't think so. Companies like Bandomday are so big and such a mess internally that one department doesn't know what any of the others are doing, much less who works where. And you were only there a short time—in the readers' department in the basement. These guys making the decisions are fourteen floors up. And none of them wants to ever meet anyone from the basement. Besides, the marketing person laughed when I told her. She wondered how many people would remember that other Max Perkins who was Thomas Wolfe's editor. I was surprised she even knew who he was. You're safe, guy. Just sit back and wait."

It couldn't have been funnier. I had taken Robert's name when picking up his clients and now he had mine. I hung up

305

without any further argument and by that evening Robert had the article he needed. Here it is:

I love living in the past. It's so much easier and gives one the illusion of actually having some control over things. If properly worked, the mind can be convinced that events such as Vietnam, recessions, and President Reagan haven't yet happened. Yet if some new medical procedure or a convenience that makes life easier is called for—say, the car, fax, or phone—one can quickly step into the future, fix the problem, and then head with lightning speed back to, oh, I don't know . . . 1924. Ah, 1924—that magical time between wars when the great flu epidemic, mustard gas, and the sinking of the Titanic had passed, and we were yet to see the stock market crash, the Great Depression (the world's, not mine), and World War II. Perhaps I've just watched too many period soap operas, movies, and "Masterpiece Theatre" reruns. I long for a time when people said things to the servants with haughty condescension such as, "You're being *damned* impertinent," or "Good heavens, man, can't you see that the Bentley needs polishing!"

But why go back to just 1924? Why not all the way to 1889? People will frequently say to me, "You're living in the past." Damn right I am. What's so great about the present? If I can convince myself, as I sit reading the latest bestseller—Charles Dickens's *David Copperfield*—that World War I and global warming are decades away, then why shouldn't I?

Yes, if I could I'd decorate my home to look like something out of *Gone With the Wind* or the latest movie that takes place in turn-of-the-century New York—lots of crystal chandeliers and overstuffed sofas. If I choose to live without plumbing or electricity, then so be it. And who's to say that automobiles and the telephone are all they've been touted to be? Okay, so I do like having modern conveniences, but they detract from my fantasy and at this point in the grand scale of things, fantasy is all I've got left.

Enter the reason for *Mrs. Squigglemire*. I know bustles were uncomfortable and that there were no movie houses in 1889, but by setting my novel in a time well past I allow myself hindsight plus a much more civilized-appearing plateau on which to place my characters. I had often longed for a period novel—one in which I didn't have to worry about "the lights going out all over Europe" or my grandfather when he and his stocks plummeted to their deaths on Wall Street in 1929. But 1889? Sounded like a good year in which to set the action of *Mrs.*

Squigglemire and her cronies. And how many people do you know start their book off with a musical bustle?

So I chose to set my illustrious cast in England. The reason for this was simple: I couldn't find a company in the United States that produced musical bustles, much less ones that played something that caused people in the immediate vicinity to stand up. The only other option was Handel's "Hallelujah Chorus" and that would have forced me to set the entire action of the book at Christmastime or Easter.

But all this is explanation of a work that you'd be better off reading yourself; buying it when it comes out in the next few months. I hope you enjoy the journey—I know Mrs. Squigglemire certainly did. So, off I must be. My kentia palm needs watering and the under-house parlor maid just committed suicide in the attic.

A few days later, hearing nothing from Robert, I called his apartment. There was no answer and for some reason the machine didn't pick up. No Marcel either. Something was bothering me but I couldn't put my finger on it; something about Robert asking me to trust him. "Trust me" is one of those phrases I'm always suspicious of, like "You won't be sorry." If anyone ever tells you "You won't be sorry," run in the other direction as fast as your little legs will carry you. You will, without a doubt, be sorry.

So toward late afternoon I got restless and decided to do some investigative work. Besides, tomorrow was my birthday and I had no real plans. I needed something to take my mind off the fact that no one was throwing me a party and the snooping fit itself perfectly in with this. What I didn't know was just how much it would take my mind off of things.

I called the marketing department of Bandomday and pretended to be employed at one of New York's television stations. Again, not a hard thing to do for someone who has impersonated as many people as I have. But I hadn't thought the thing through well enough, for when I was finally able to speak with the person in charge of Max Perkins's book, I stumbled and said the wrong thing.

"Hi, I'm with Channel Five news—the entertainment division—and we received your press release about *Mrs. Squigglemire.*" I realized the second I said it that I was caught—that I had blown my chances—for to my knowledge there had been no press release yet for the book. For all I knew, the book wasn't anywhere near production and galleys weren't available. But what came out of the other end of the phone took me by surprise.

"Wow, that was quick," said the girl. "We only sent that out last week."

"Last week? But —"

"Yeah, and doesn't the release look nice with the picture of the author?" she went on, totally oblivious of the fact that I had no idea what she was talking about. Within a split second I checked myself. I knew that I had to play along to find out what was going on.

"So, you guys must be really excited about the book. It sounds extremely interesting; that's why I'm calling. We'd like to schedule the author for an interview and I was hoping you could tell me who is handling the publicity, if it's in-house or not?"

"Let me see," she said, and evidently began looking through some papers. I decided to press ahead and see what else I could find out. The fact that Robert hadn't told me about the release made me nervous.

"I know you might not be able to tell me this," I said, "but we were wondering if it's going to be made public how much of an advance the author is getting?"

"Oh, that's no problem. But . . . didn't you see it in the release?" she asked.

"What do you mean?"

"We actually gave out that information. Most times we don't and the author doesn't want us to, but since we paid so much we thought it would be a good marketing ploy—you know, 'Author receives half a million for first book'—that kind of thing?"

I had to keep my wits. It wasn't easy at this point. I swallowed hard. My head was swimming.

"But you haven't actually paid him yet. I mean, that's just the number he's getting. He hasn't received it yet," I said.

"Oh, yeah. We had a big photo shoot here last week— one of those things with the author holding a giant-sized copy of a check; shaking hands; that whole spiel," she said. And then, "Here it is, the name of the publicity person you wanted," but it was too late—I had hung up the phone and was well on my way to being sick. Within minutes my head was poised over the mouth of the porcelain god that everyone on our floor shared as I began driving the big white bus to Woof City. Next stop, folks? Revenge-land.

63

Scene: Robert and Max in a nightclub. New York. The Village. A smokey haze; the glue that holds the room together. Black walls. Lights focused away from the patrons. The proverbial clank of silverware and glasses that emanates from the kitchen when the swinging stainless-steel door is set free by a Latin waiter's svelte hips as he passes through with sandwiches and coffee. The raw squat honk and thrust of a sax over the predictable thump of double bass. The sizzle of high-hat cymbal. The cool noodling-doodling of a drugged trumpet hovering overhead, decorated underneath by punched-out piano chords--prosaic yet free, like some highly organized wanderer who's intent on going everywhere, yet always glad to come back home. All of it coming together, falling apart, coming back--pealing upwards and saying something, then returning to earth--an ordinary sex act that's over with just the cigarette left to smoke.

"They're good tonight," Robert said to me, leaning back slightly in his chair, one muscular forearm resting on the shiny black tabletop. Cigarette smoke fluted upward from his dangling hand; coolness personified. Robert—a veritable Buddha of sex without the weight problem.

"You know them?" I asked. I was guarded. Robert had requested I meet him at this location—a bizarre nightclub in the Village called the *Postnasal Elephant Mitten*—evidently some throwback from the sixties when odd names were the order of the day. And on my birthday of all days. Frankly, I didn't feel like celebrating. I was too angry to confront him after my phone call to the marketing department and I knew I needed to be calm if I was going to trap him and find out what he was up to. My first reaction to the news had been sickness. Then, moving onto seething anger I had made the trip into Manhattan only to stop myself before getting to Rob's door. I had returned to my bathtub in Brooklyn to try and formulate a plan—a way out of things . . . or into them.

"Nah. I come here about once a month and there's always a different group." He was unaware of what I knew about the book.

"So, these would be some of the few people in the world you haven't convinced to screw me over," I said in a good-natured manner. I wanted to play it close to home; try and show that nothing was different. It wasn't easy but I needed some information and the civilized jocular method seemed the best route. I was beyond anger; beyond betrayal. Besides, I had his number now. I no longer trusted him and was beginning to see him for what he really was. If he wanted to play the miscreant, then so be it. And I would do the same, meeting his coolness, his false façade, with one of my own. I absent-mindedly fingered a backgammon game that sat on the table—another part of the club's quirky atmosphere and attempt to keep the customers entertained. All around us patrons played Chinese checkers, chess, cribbage, or some other form of entertainment while they listened to jazz and drank.

Robert turned, extinguishing his cigarette into a black plastic ashtray. The receptacle wobbled slightly, giving off a counterfeit resonance when it settled back down—truth in a sea of deception turned inside out. "You don't understand," he said.

"At least we agree on that," I said. "No, I *don't* understand."

"We agree on a lot of things, you just don't give some of them enough time."

"You set me up," I said coolly, without malice. It was a statement—that was all. While I was referring to my book deal, I knew Robert thought the reference was toward the drug-running fiasco. I ran my finger nonchalantly around the edge of a backgammon game on the table as we talked.

"What are you worried about? You got away. I took care of it—that incident with the drug lord."

I paused, leaning back. "You know," I began, eyeing him, "I think maybe you knew that deal would go bad. I think you knew the guy had a gun." I marveled at my ability to stay calm. I was waiting to see a soft spot; move in for the kill.

But the moment was momentarily broken by one of the musicians announcing the last players and their contributions to the set: "Ladies and gentlemen, give a round of applause for that last number; Ray and Bob did a bang-up job. Ray on the sax and Bob on the double bass."

"Max. Dear sweet Max. You know I wouldn't do anything like that to you. I'm your best friend. You're getting paranoid," Robert continued, oblivious of the announcement.

I was heating up internally, and even with all the beforehand coaching I had given myself it was beginning to show. I wasn't sure how much longer I could hold out.

"Look, all I know is that I've had some pretty weird experiences because of you: the jobs; the roommate; and now this male plaything I've become."

Robert squinted. I wasn't sure if it was from the smoke or his reaction toward my latest name for his, and now my, profession.

"You worked, didn't you? You ate. You had a place to live."

"Well, gee, other than *that*, Mrs. Lincoln, how'd you like the play?" I closed the backgammon set and put it to the side, angrily snapping the latch shut.

There was an uncomfortable silence. "And stop saying that I had a job, food, a place to live. I don't know if you realize it or not, but those are basic requirements for staying alive. You always say that, like I'd be nothing without you. You also got me mixed up with some real lunatics. Don't forget Reeda," I said, crossing my arms.

"You and she have a falling out?"

"You and she have a falling out?" I mimicked in a sarcastic tone. "You know we did. She stole my ideas. She stole my money." I wanted to add, "Like you did," but didn't. "I've fixed her, though."

"You really shouldn't blow her off. After all, she knows some pretty serious people."

"Who? Like agents, publishers?" I asked, still sarcastic. He was beginning to get to me despite my vow to keep calm. Robert:

the great stud; the maniacal sociopath, sitting there pulchritudinous (look it up) and frank.

"It's just that she's going to remember your name when she sees it in print. You don't want any enemies," Robert answered.

I didn't think I could hold back any longer. It wasn't working, this game of cat-and-mouse. Robert had been the common and reliable thread running through the moth-eaten and tattered sweater from Goodwill that was my life, and now he was, for all practical purposes, gone. The tension was as thick as the smoke in the room. At that moment one of the other patrons came up to our table. "Mind if I use the set?" he asked.

"Huh?"

"The set," he continued. "The backgammon set. Trade you this Scrabble game for it."

"Sure. Whatever," I said, but the second I reached for what he was offering, all of the pieces fell on the table. I should have seen the omen; this Scrabble game that kept appearing, but I didn't. At least not yet.

"Story of my life," I said, and all three of us scrambled to move the letters to the center, herding them with our palms as if they were stoic alphabetic cattle. The pieces lay forlorn in front of me—the very meaning of life just waiting to be discovered in words.

"Sorry about that," the club-goer relayed and Robert and I nodded, indicating that no harm had been done.

"So, what's happening with the book?" I asked, changing my tone and the subject, moving a lonely *R* and *S* over with the rest of the group. I was sickly sweet. Anyone could have seen my fakery. My fingers now traveled absently about the Scrabble letters, not really trying to spell anything in particular.

"M-A-N," I spelled. It was easy. Not much effort.

Robert sat silent for a moment; hesitant; careful. "Oh, you know, it's coming along."

"Any word on the advance and when I'll be getting proofs?" I wanted to see just how badly he'd lie. Some part of me still hoped there was a logical explanation for everything; hoped that he was going to surprise me; put a check for half a million dollars in front of me. My right leg was imitating a sewing machine, up and down

313

underneath the table just thinking of the fantasy. I moved some other letters around, using the "M" in "Man" to start another word. "M-O-N-Y," I spelled, leaving out the "E," waiting for Robert's reply. "Maxwell "E" Perkins," I thought to myself. But what Robert surprised me with was something entirely different, for it took the wind from my sails and pushed all concerns about the book away. It was as if some great hand had come down and wiped the slate clean only to show something even more ominous underneath.

"Look, let's not argue," he said, smirking slightly. "After all, it's my birthday," and he looked around at the shady characters that filled the jazz space. Then added, raising his glass in the air, "I propose a toast. To Robert Hickenlooper, born June 28th."

But just as he said it, something resonated with me—some inner bell was set off as it had been that day I watched *Rosemary's Baby*. It was as if too many discarded clues had been piled into the attic of life, and the ceiling, now unable to take the weight anymore, was giving way; bowing out; getting ready to burst.

"I never knew your birthday was on this date," I said.

"Sure."

"But, *my* birthday is today."

"Cool. We should really celebrate. You know—go somewhere else," Robert offered.

"June 28, huh?" I said.

"June 28," Robert echoed, his glass hitting mine. I had raised my own automatically, just the way I had raised my hand that day in the museum when the trust-fund-tour guide had asked if anyone believed in the devil.

I sat in a daze. All hope of Robert coming clean with me was gone. His shameless self-promotion of his birthday was sickening, but there was something else; something worse than the comprehension that he was conceited, that he had stolen from me, that he was lying. Something about his birth date—my birth date— June 28—unsettled every fiber of my being. Why had I not seen this before? As Robert turned to the musicians I began rearranging the letters from the Scrabble game in front of me.

"And now we're going to do a set that I think you all will really enjoy," the piano player crooned into the mike. "Ray and Bob are with us again, so let's give them a warm round of applause, folks."

I had already begun lining up the letters, remembering back to the first Scrabble game sent to me and how it had tied in with the movie, and so now my fingers arranged the letters, spelling out the film's name. I allowed the small blocks to form the movie title *Rosemary's Baby*.

"What year were you born?" I asked, my voice taking on an ethereal quality as I moved the last letter into place. It was as if something had suspended me above the room and I was looking down—seeing things from a director's chair while making a movie.

"Nineteen sixty-six. Same as you," he quipped. Then he added the final brick through the window, "The year One," and with that, his last phrase, the ceiling gave way and all that had been stored up came crashing down around my head.

The music commenced and with it came a rush. A click. A whirr. "Ray on the sax and Bob on the bass. Ray-Bob. That day in Robert's apartment. Rosemary's Baby. Ray and Bob," I thought as my fingers began to rearrange the title from the movie.

Slowly I spelled, taking only what was there from the film's title. As the strains of sax, piano, and bass began their intertwining, it all came together. Robert had his back turned momentarily, engrossed in the performance.

It all made sense now—the things sent to me over the past year, the strange calls and cryptic messages, the videotape of *Rosemary's Baby*. Even Robert's birthday: June 28, 1966. The year One. The same as mine.

I had watched the movie when it arrived at Bandomday, before my firing. I had viewed it six, maybe seven times in an effort to try and understand what everything meant. And now, here, in this seedy dive of a nightclub in the Village, it was all coming together; the fragments piling on top of one another—the consequences resembling those caused by some ignorant tourist at the bottom of an overcrowded escalator who suddenly decides to stop and look around. It was as if some giant sped-up movie of a fern's growth was being shown to me—fiddleheads which should have gently unfolded now splayed themselves upward with the violence of a

New Year's Eve party favor, air-powered by a drunk who wobbled and lurched.

The realization came over me—petulant and warm—a feeling that I had emotionally urinated in my pants while standing in Grand Central at rush hour. I wanted to scream to someone for help, but held back. Robert knew more people than I could imagine and everyone in the city was suspect now. R-A-Y-B-O-B, I spelled with the letters from the movie's title.

I remembered the end of the movie—the scene where Rosemary discovers her baby in the next apartment. "The year One," Roman Castevet had said in the film. And the year One had been 1966.

Robert turned momentarily, causing me to freeze, then turned back to the musicians who were preparing for another set. He hadn't noticed my reaction; the horror on my face at the realizations. R-A-M-S, I continued, letting the letters move slowly over the tabletop.

"How many of you here believe in the devil?" The tour guide's pithy words rang in my ears as I remembered that day at the Met in front of the depiction of an opera character. It was all coming back—the movie; the painting; the New York Philharmonic concert with its fallen angel motifs.

S-E-Y, I finished. Before me was now a name—the name I had seen on the envelope that day in Robert's apartment: Ray-Bob Ramssey. But who was Ray-Bob and why did Robert want to keep him such a secret? Or was there really even such a person?

The flood of emotion was now constant. I wasn't sure what was real and what wasn't. Invisible angels and demons are the worst. Their cornucopia of black songs never seems to empty. Now they spilled out, eel-like over the stones of my life—a life set in mud. My mind was whirling from the realization of how the bits were careening into place. I scrambled the letters; a meager attempt to clear my head. The combination of alcohol, the music, the lateness of the evening—everything was coming together; falling apart; making sense and yet becoming more confusing. So engrossed was Robert in the next piece the group had launched into that he failed to notice as I slipped away from the table, intent on fleeing the club.

As I headed for the door, the band began to heat up. A sax swirled endlessly upward in the smoke-filled air, curling around the trumpet's lazy notes, and the sweet and steady swish of brush on cymbal underlined everything. It was an old standard—a song from long ago with countless connotations. The bass thumped out a steady but laconic and sexy beat. Then the female singer stepped up to the mike and I turned toward her before emptying myself onto the street.

"That Old Black Magic" was her musical choice. She sang in a sultry voice, caressing each word like a lover wanting to please, and with the first line of the song I found myself, confused and alone— in the middle of Greenwich Village.

64

I was only a few blocks from the club when I passed a pay
phone. It rang just as I got within inches of it. Normally I
would have kept going, but the combination of alcohol, the
evening, the revelation, everything, seemed to converge and cause
me to lose my equilibrium. I wondered if I were going insane. I was
trying to add it all up: the events, fortunate and unfortunate that had
happened; the connections; and now Robert's latest remark. Then
the final blows: Robert had stolen my book; he had taken the
advance that belonged to me; he had lied; used me. It must have
been this and the stress of the evening, for before I knew it I found
myself reaching for the receiver, intent on stopping the ringing that
had grown louder and louder. I had no real intention of speaking to
whoever it was on the phone, yet some part of me wanted to—
wanted to reach out to someone, anyone who had a better grip on
reality than I did.

If I expected anything it was someone to say, "Wrong
number," but that isn't what happened.

"I've got to speak to you."

The voice was urgent, almost hysterical; a simpatico
bedfellow in my present agony.

"Who were you trying to reach?" I asked. "Did you know
this was a pay phone? I think—" but before I could finish the voice
cut me off.

"Max?" the voice asked, and my mind began to try to
rationalize what was happening.

"Probably a coincidence," I told myself. "Max is not an
uncommon name. What are the chances that—"

"Max Perkins," the woman's voice said. Pause. I tried to
think, putting fear aside for the moment. Max Perkins was pretty
run of the mill. How many others had it?

"This is a pay phone," I said, hoping to keep whatever was
happening at bay, but then something took place that was

undeniable, something that couldn't be ignored, for it let me know that I was indeed the person the caller sought.

"Max, listen. I've got to talk to you. It's important. It's about Robert. Robert Hickenlooper," but before she could finish I hung up, completely shaken. As if Robert's strange birthday and connection to all the past calls and gifts hadn't been enough, now there was someone calling me at a phone booth. I looked around, scanning the sidewalk, the apartment buildings nearby. Was this just another continuation of his torture for me? Was this just one more sick joke he was playing?

"I'm imagining things," I said to myself, starting to walk quickly down the street, my hands in my pockets. "I've had too much to drink. I'm under a lot of stress. I'm not myself. I'm—" but I was stopped cold as I came in front of yet another pay phone.

It rang just as I passed.

"A coincidence," I told myself again, eager to get to the subway station and make it back to Brooklyn. I wanted the safe confines of my claw-foot tub, the angled walls, floor, and ceiling of the apartment I shared with Spong—anything to get back to reality or what I thought reality was. When the spirit is in pain, even unpleasant but familiar surroundings will comfort the soul.

Still, something stirred inside me. Some curiosity wouldn't let me walk by without answering. Besides, I reasoned, this one *had* to be a wrong number. I stopped and reached for the receiver, knowing full well that it wouldn't be for me.

"You hung up on me. Max, listen, I've—"

I didn't even give her time to finish. So unsettled was I that I slammed the receiver down and ran as quickly as I could, around the corner to the end of the block. This was too weird. First Robert and now this—this strange voice with two different pay phone numbers in the Village.

I was just about to regain control of myself, now a good two blocks away from the last pay phone, when I heard the dreaded sound: Ringing. I looked around. There was yet another phone about six feet from where I was standing. I didn't move. A few people passed by but no one attempted to answer it. It must have gone on for a good two or three minutes. I stood frozen to the spot.

319

Finally, rationalizing that it was some new fad—this calling pay phone numbers—I walked over to the jarring metal box. I didn't pick it up. I stuck my finger in the coin slot. Nothing. A couple passed and I motioned for them to answer the thing. It had been ringing now for at least two full minutes. Call me sick. Call me anything—just don't call me. I couldn't resist. This was the equivalent of a bad highway accident and I was rubbernecking.

As gently as I could I picked up the receiver but said nothing. I held it to my ear.

"Max? Please don't hang up. You've got to hear me out," the voice said. By now my defenses were gone. I was a lump of jelly. As casually as I could I tried to look around. Whoever it was could obviously see me. While this was disturbing, I tried to rationalize. My mind went into overdrive. I theorized that this woman had seen me coming out of the club. Perhaps she lived in one of the large old apartment buildings nearby. But this, this new development with me two blocks away threw me for a loop. Maybe she was some sick-o who'd taken down all the pay phone numbers in the city in order to stalk people.

I scanned the buildings around me. One empty office complex . . . mostly apartment buildings. One abandoned building. Someone could see me and I was getting scared. What if she were a sniper, a Son-of-Sam? The only way out was to see what the caller wanted.

"Yes, this is Max. Who is this?" I asked, literally shaking. I tried to keep my voice steady.

"This is Dory. You know, of Dory and Gray? Robert's, well . . . friend? From college?"

"Yes . . . but why are you calling me? . . . how—"

"I can't explain over the phone. I've got to see you."

"But how do you know where I am? What's going on?"

"Just do what I tell you. You're in danger and I can help."

I waited.

She waited.

I certainly felt in danger but I wasn't sure whether to trust her or not. She had just identified herself as Robert's friend and he, by now, had realized I was gone from the club, probably theorizing that I had figured out who or what he was. I played along. At that moment, all I wanted to do was be done with Mr. H and his companions, past or present.

"Okay. Where do I meet you?" I asked, completely void of any intention of carrying out her orders.

"The corner of Bleecker and Grove. Five minutes. I'll find you, just be there. It has to be far enough away from the club so he won't see us. Okay? Okay? I don't want to meet too close to where he is now. Just be there," and with that she hung up.

I didn't know who to believe or trust. The evening was not going well to say the least, and all I wanted to do was be free from telephones and the Village. I quickly darted across the street in the direction of Bleecker and Grove, but then turned a corner and pressed myself up against the side of a building. Wherever Dory was she could see me and I didn't feel comfortable. I crouched low and slunk next to an overgrown boxwood pushing its way out from an apartment building's front. Then I stayed close to the other buildings, finally turning another corner, heading in the opposite direction from where I was supposed to be going. Three blocks and five turns later, managing to zigzag my way back uptown toward Chelsea, I felt I had given Dory the slip. I was almost six blocks north from where the original pay phone call had happened and was feeling safe. As I continued to hide in the shadows, between parked cars and behind what trees there were, I was beginning to get my confidence back.

That is, until a pay phone rang.

So ardent had I been in my attempt to flee Dory and whatever it was she wanted to tell me, that I had failed to notice I was standing right next to one. I jumped a good three feet into the air. Then, taking a deep breath, figuring that I might as well see for myself—a sort of giving in to things, a realization that control over my life was not in this particular pack of cards—I picked up the receiver, believing momentarily in a God that would never do something so cruel to me as have this be the same person calling.

"What are you doing!" Dory screamed. "You're going the wrong way!" and with that, something clicked, reversing the giving up. The anger in her voice; the desperation, whatever it was, triggered in me panic. I let the receiver dangle and ran—wild and blind-eyed—right into the path of an oncoming limousine and into the delicious night of forgetting.

65

A black and starless sky slowly came into view. It was the inner roof of the very limousine that had almost done me in. Then a face appeared.

"You all right?" It was Dory peering down at me. We slouched in the back of the limo—my head in her lap—while the driver maneuvered through the crazy streets of Greenwich Village.

"What happened?" I asked, putting my hand to my head.

"You ran in front of the car—just got bumped. I think it was more fright than anything else."

I sat up and looked out the window. We were cruising toward downtown. The gray-blues, browns, and blacks of late-night New York slid by the tinted windows.

"What's going on? Why were you calling me every minute? How did you know—"

Dory held up the limo's phone. "We were driving around so we could find you. Saw you go into the club with Robert and spent the next hour getting every pay phone number for blocks around, just in case something like this happened. I saw you looking up, thinking we were in one of the apartment buildings. I had to get in touch with you."

"But why not just come up to me? Call me at home?" I whined, still in pain.

"Robert might have been with you. You might not have given me time to explain, and I didn't know what he'd told you about me—if he'd said anything to turn you against me. Besides, he's furious enough with me right now. He's trying to have me put away, he's so angry. Remember when you almost got shot? He's capable of getting people into worse scenarios."

"I'm all ears and obviously unable to escape. Let's hear what you've got to say," I said, still not sure I trusted her. My head was killing me.

"It's about Robert," she began. "He's not well."

"You're telling me."

"No, seriously, he's deranged. You got the things I sent—the gardenia, the movie?"

"That was you? But I thought Robert sent them. I mean, tonight . . . his birthday, the way he . . . Yeah, I got them, but why the cloak-and-dagger routine?"

"Robert again. I know it sounds far-fetched, but he's got some serious issues. For one, he thinks he's Rosemary's baby."

"Huh?"

"The movie, *Rosemary's Baby*. Robert *thinks* he's the kid—the devil."

"I don't follow," I said. "I mean, I figured out something along those lines tonight in the club. It was starting to come together, but I'm still not entirely sure what's going on. I thought he'd sent the movie, the gardenia, everything else. And then tonight in the club—the Scrabble game; the names. But when I unscrambled the title of the movie I came up with someone who used to live in the apartment Robert is in now. I thought Ray-Bob was supposed to be connected with *Rosemary's Baby*.

"What? What do you mean used to live? He still lives there."

"I don't—"

"You didn't think Hickenlooper was his real name, did you? Who has a name like that?" Dory asked.

"It sounded so awful I always thought it was real."

"His real name is Ray-Bob Ramssey. Max, the guy's from Texas. The only thing missing is a pair of cowboy boots and a toothpick dangling out of his mouth. I thought you knew that—knew that he'd taken that famous pianist's name a long time ago when he left home. That Olga somebody."

"Samaroff. Olga Samaroff." I waited. "So your Scrabble game was for naught. Your attempt to get me to realize who he was . . . is . . ."

"What I'm trying to tell you is that he *thinks* he's the spawn of the devil."

"This, because when you scramble the letters in the movie's title you come up with his real name?"

"Don't shoot the messenger."

"And again, why the mystery—why not just come out and tell me this months ago?"

"Long story."

"Short version?"

"He was playing me much the same way he's been doing you. I wasn't in any position to come right out and inform you for fear of what he might do."

"His parents actually named him Ray-Bob?" I said.

"I don't have to tell you that he knows everybody. I was working at an art gallery downtown and somehow got the notion to submit my mechanical installations to the owner under a different name."

"Ray-Bob?"

"Listen to me. I knew they would never take me seriously since I'd worked there. Robert was in on it—we decided to use his name."

"Been there, done that one," I said.

"Before I knew what was happening, Robert had become me, the artist, and had stolen a percentage of the money. We had a falling-out but I managed to bug his apartment with some listening devices before things got really bad. At one point I woke up in a mental hospital after Robert had drugged me. It took forever to get out but I managed it, and when he found out he was furious. Bottom line is, he's trying to get me committed to the mental institution again so he can gain control over my artwork. I'm living out of this frickin' limo right now and afraid to even be seen on the street. It's one from Gray's service—he's in New York, trying to make it like the rest of us."

"The monk thing not work out?"

"Robert's even done a number on him so I didn't want to stay in his apartment—that's how bad things are. And I wasn't sure until recently how you felt about Mr. Stud-Muffin. He's one sick puppy."

"You're not kidding," I said, still trying to make sense of everything. "And you got off easy—only a percentage."

Then what Dory had just said registered. "Bugging devices?" I asked.

325

"Remember when we were in college and I did the project with transmitters that would find lost skiers, alpine climbers—those things?"

"Oh, yeah."

"It came in handy. God, I'd like to have permanently eradicated that girl who got the prize for the potato cut-outs."

"Don't worry, she's probably on the board of the stock exchange now, and if things go the way they're supposed to she'll get jail time for insider trading."

" 'If things go the way they're supposed to' being the key phase here," Dory said.

"Right."

"Anyway, I got worried about halfway through this deal we had—the one where Robert would present my work to the gallery and when all was said and done, the truth would come out and I'd be established."

"Go on," I said, wanting to know, yet at the same time dreading the outcome of what she was going to tell me."

"As soon as I heard what he was up to I confronted him. I also overheard him talking about you and the book you'd written, and what his plans were for that. He told me that if I said anything he would pull the plug on my art deal and expose the whole thing."

"So let me get this straight," I said, coming to terms with what was going on, "this wasn't a totally selfless act on your part?"

"Well ... no. Sorry about that. I mean, he only got a percentage of my fee, and I did try to warn you—in my own way."

"Point well taken," I said. "There certainly were enough indications. But I just can't believe he would do something like this." Some part of me was still in denial, even with the recent revelations; Dory's elucidations; the ceiling falling in. She read my uncertainty.

"Think about it. Who got you the jobs you had? Who set you up with certain people? And how did it always turn out?" she asked.

"I know he screwed me over by recommending that story editor—she stole my material, just about everything else—but he couldn't have manipulated everything," I said, looking out the window as the limo turned down lower Broadway.

"You think it was a coincidence that you went to Grace Patchin's in Brooklyn that time?"

"You know about that?"

"I know about a lot of things. It all started right after college, this obsession that Robert had . . . has with thinking he's Rosemary's baby; that he's the son of the devil. Just because his birthday is the same as the kid in the movie and his real name is an anagram made from the title, he's convinced himself that he's Lucifer. Everyone he knows is into witchcraft or some tangent of it, and I don't mean the good kind."

"There's a good kind?"

"I was into it at one time, before I realized what he was doing to me. I was supposed to have a career in art. Robert was going to fix everything: spells; the people he knew; his connections—it was all supposed to come together for me, just the way you thought it was going to come together for you."

"But wait," I said, "Robert is from Texas. He didn't grow up in the Dakota apartment building—in New York. How could he think he's the baby of the devil just because he has the same birth date as the kid in the movie and his name is some anagram? I have the same birthday and I don't think I'm the devil. Hell, I'm not sure *who* I am right now."

"I said he *thought* he was Rosemary's Baby—and I didn't say he was sane," Dory replied. "He's not too grounded in reality in case you haven't noticed. And *Rosemary's Baby* is not a true story." Dory stopped; thinking for a moment. "At least I don't think it is."

Then it all hit home; all the detritus of the past year—lucent and sartorial one moment and jarring and saturnine the next. Robert was into stealing souls—he had already partaken of most people's bodies; it followed that he would want their very spiritual essence also.

"Oh, my God," I said, after the realization of what Robert had been doing set in. I had given him control over my novel; my work. I had put everything I had into that book; my very being. And now I had lost it all. Robert had his picture on the cover, was using

327

my name as his pen name, and had taken my money. In the process, he'd become me and I'd become him. I was now a hustler and he, a writer. I looked up at Dory's face, realizing that she was telling the truth about how Robert had set me up.

I thought for a moment. Then I spoke.

"I've sold my soul to the devil," I said, and then added, angry that even that had been a scam, "and not even the real one at that."

I awoke to sunlight streaming between the burglar gates on the window. Reaching up and grasping the cold edge of the tub, I pulled myself high enough to be able to see the alarm clock that sat, stoic and cynical. It was almost noon. If Spong had entombed me at seven o'clock I hadn't been aware of it. As I was stretching and yawning I noticed that the door to his closet was open. I glanced around. Spong was nowhere to be found and it was the weekend. At first I thought that he had possibly spent the night somewhere else, and for a moment I worried that something more serious had happened, but after stepping out of the tub I noticed that his blankets and few belongings were gone from the floor of the space he called a bedroom. It was then that I started to look around. The apartment had never held much, but the few traces of my roommate were obliterated. His cereal bowl, toothbrush, and roller-skates were gone, along with many of his magazines. It had all been there last night when I had come home after Dory's revelation and limo ride. But then, I *had* been drunk.

Witness for the prosecution, a Mr. Spong . . . Flagelatte: "I don't have anything to say. I plead the Fifth on most of this. My attorney has advised me that I might incriminate myself, so I'll just say . . . well, not much. Yeah, I left in the middle of the night. So what? It's not like that's a crime or anything. And I had paid the rent until the end of the month. Lucky bastard, Max. Yeah, I did accounting work for porn films, for a studio with that Fartus and Rot person--none of that crap I did for TV either--real accounting. And Max? At least he can sleep in the closet now instead of the tub. I'm gettin' outa here and going to Florida."

I wanted to find out what happened to Spong. I knew something was up and his disappearance was just one more event in a string of upsets. But as unsettled as I was, I tried to retain a semblance of normality. I pushed myself into believing that my schedule, my rut, would be my saving grace. I decided to head to the gym, hoping that once there I could completely entrench myself in denial and physical exertion. Plus, it was better than sitting around the apartment simmering in my own juices.

I would need to formulate a plan dealing with Robert on how to recoup my lost book and money, and the gym was the one place where I could concentrate on my biceps as well as on how to get revenge. One of my more normal clients-to-be (everything's relative) who Robert had set me up with wanted a meeting at three and I needed to be pumped. The exigencies of my life as a male prostitute required that I stay in shape, watch what I ate, and pretend to be generally someone I wasn't. The third point, again, was not hard to achieve given the enormous amount of practice each day was bringing. I was grasping for something—anything to retain normality. So it was settled—the gym it would be. I began to gather up my bag and workout clothes.

While it nauseated me to think of having anything to do with someone Robert had been a part of, I needed the money—especially since Boy Wonder had stolen half a million dollars. Besides, I was more than happy to take business away from the person who had so casually stuck his hands in my unsuspecting pockets.

Last night had been rough. The revelation that Robert was completely crazy—infatuated with a movie from the 1960s—was the final blow in an unsettling and miserable ten months in the city. Add to that the drug deal gone bad, the pay phones that had pursued me, the limo ride with Dory, and my lack of money, and it shouldn't be hard to see why I was on edge. But of all times not to fall apart, this was it. I could do it later, but not now. I had to hold on to what little sanity I had left. I slung my bag over my shoulder and negotiated the locks. As I was heading out the door, the phone rang.

"Mr. Flagelatte?" the voice said over the line when I answered.

I thought quickly. Spong was gone and I had no idea where. Obviously the person calling didn't know either, but perhaps if I found out who it was, some light would be shed on the situation.

"This is Spong Flagelatte," I said.

"Oh, good! I'm glad I caught you. We're doing another focus group and need a last-minute replacement. This one is very—"

"I'm sorry," I said, "but I'm not interested." I was about to hang up.

"We're offering five hundred dollars as we've only asked a limited number of individuals—only those people with more than fourteen magazine subscriptions. I *am* speaking to Mr. Spong Flagelatte, am I not?"

I caught the receiver before it hit the cut-off button, right after I heard the words "five hundred."

"Five hundred?" I asked.

"Yes, you see, we're taking only people who—"

"Five hundred?" I was still smarting from Robert's scam. The thought of making money and dealing with at least semi-sane people for one hour sounded nice.

"When exactly would this group meet?" I asked, hoping it wasn't at three o'clock, the same time as my client.

"Three o'clock today," the woman on the other end said.

"Great," I thought, "now I'm going to have to call the patron and reschedule." I did need the money but hated to do this as it was only the second time I had met the guy, the first having been in passing one day when Rob and I were doing lunch. "Rob," I thought to myself as I let the caller wait on the line for a moment. Why hadn't I seen that before? Rob. And that's what he had done— robbed me. The focus group was paying more for the one hour than the would-be client, so I decided I would call Mr. Had-To-Pay-For-It and cancel.

"I'll be there. Three o'clock," I heard myself say to the moderator who was still holding the line, "conference . . . room . . .

331

number … five," I continued, writing down the location. "Okay. Great."

I headed over to the gym, deciding to phone the client from that location as the time got closer to the appointment. I hadn't eaten all day and I was cranky, not really caring whether he'd be upset or not, especially since I now had the five hundred coming from the focus group. After three sets of sit-ups and twenty minutes of treadmill I located a phone.

"Hey," I said to the guy, "it's Robert. Robert Hickenlooper." I tried not to gag on the name and remembered that Robert's real one was some hokey Texas label. "Sorry, but something's come up," I said.

I figured he wouldn't know the difference between Robert and myself, and I was only too eager to let him think I was Mr. Scumbag. I listened. The guy sounded disappointed. After a few minutes he offered me twice what he had originally agreed to pay.

"You don't understand," I continued. "I can't. It's nothing personal." He persisted. What was up with this money thing? People just kept throwing it at me. Before, everyone had their hands in my pockets. I figured my time had come and my luck was changing, you know, something about a horse as a gift; something to do with looking in his mouth? I can't remember.

"Guy, lighten up. Are you terminally ill or something?" I said. "Can't you wait until tomorrow or even later tonight? What's the rush?"

But he wouldn't take no for an answer, so I agreed to meet him outside the hotel where the focus group was to be held.

"Meet me there at four," I said, "I've got a meeting in a conference room at three o'clock and I can get to you right after that. We'll see what we can do—find a place to go. Meet in the lobby."

I was in the middle of my workout. Thinking that lifting weights would get all my frustrations out had been a misconception. Now I was angrier than ever. I needed to set things straight, get my money back from Robert; put an end to him. It was all rolling around inside my head but as yet I had no plan formulated.

332

Before I moved to squats (today was arm-and-leg day), I decided to call the answering machine at the apartment and see if Dory had left any messages. While I still didn't trust her totally, she was a better bet than Robert. I'd given her my number at home so we could further discuss Mr. Beelzebub. After last night I wanted to know more about the direction Robert was heading since it had taken me down roads I'd rather not have traveled. So it was a shock when I put in my code and retrieved the first message. It wasn't from Dory.

"Max, it's Robert." The very sound of his voice irritated me—that combination of verisimilitude ($4.75) and speciousness ($3.50) that swirled together in a vertiginous state. "Look, about last night. I know something's upsetting you and I want to make it up." He had no idea about my conversation with Dory; what I knew.

Robert went on: "Let's get together today. Oh, and by the way, you know how I told you to mend your relationship with Reeda? She does have connections, even if some of them are rather seedy. Max, I know how you are; that you wouldn't do anything—so I did: I had three-dozen red roses sent to her—with your name, of course. And don't worry about the cost. My treat. Give me a call later, big guy."

67

What had I done? I had bullied Robert into making an appearance as the author of *Mrs. Squigglemire* and he had taken me for everything. But the truth was, he had planned the entire escapade. I had only *thought* I bullied him. His act of not wanting to help was just that—an act. That was Robert's talent: getting you to do what he wanted and yet making you feel as though you had asked him for a favor.

It was the ultimate smoke-and-mirrors game; a virtual setup after setup in which things went from bad to worse so that I was forced to rely on him to fix the latest problem. He had long ago learned that people will tolerate bad behavior if you're good-looking enough, and he had used every moment to his advantage along with the bad experiences he offered, knowing that I'd come running back to try and extricate myself from the latest situation. That's when he really got me, for he made sure I went from bad to worse until my defenses were broken down and I had nothing left.

The most heinous part of it wasn't the money but the fact that he had stolen my life's work, my very soul by means of absconding with years of creative effort. But what else could I have done with my limited resources? If anyone at Bandomday had found out before my book came out that I had lied and tricked the company into publishing a novel, they'd have pulled every string they could to exact revenge.

As I waited for the subway to carry me into Manhattan to my focus group, I wondered what Reeda had made of receiving three-dozen red roses from me. Surely she remembered the words of Boris—that made-up Russian—when he . . . I, had pretended to be hypnotized. My only hope was that she wouldn't act on impulse and call the police. I remembered that she had taped the sessions and prayed she had not saved any of the cassettes. But I couldn't think of that now. The advance I had been counting on had been stolen and I needed the money from the focus group and the new client. Every bit I could get was important so that I could try and pry the half million from Robert's greedy hands. All of this rolled around in my head as I traveled underground.

I found myself in midtown, having survived the jostling subway trip, and climbed up the steps at Fiftieth Street. The walk would hopefully clear my head of all that had happened.

Today's focus group was being held in a fancy hotel banquet room at one of Manhattan's posh establishments. As I jaunted across midtown I tried to shake off the pain I was feeling. Stopping at a street corner I noticed two men who had been on the subway with me. Nothing unusual in that, but with all the goings-on of late—the pay phone calls last night, the revelation about Robert, Dory, the flowers sent to Reeda—I began to get worried. When you think the entire world is out to get you, you begin to perform some serious analysis of your environment. I began to walk faster, eager to get off the street and into the hotel.

I turned up Fifth and crossed Fifty-Sixth, then I turned again, circling an entire city block. They were still behind me—the two men. Strange, definitely, but then, this was a big city with all kinds of people. I wondered if they were interested in my services or just lost, or worse yet, after me. I tried to put them out of my head. After all, I was surrounded by people. If these two were dangerous, they'd have to come after me in full view.

But the city was beginning to take its toll and I felt anger rising in my throat. I remembered the drug deal gone bad and wondered if Robert had really taken care of things as he said he had. Were the two men out to exact revenge, thinking that the bad dope was my fault? I didn't know, but I began to see them and everyone else not as people, but rather as one more thread of the tapestry that was the city. It was as if they had merely become a tendril of New York, bent on my destruction, carrying out orders from the top.

Abhorrence seethed up inside me for a city that was in itself a living, breathing thing. Abhorrence for all the people in it—for all the businesses, for the corruption and vice, the decay and dementia. I was taking my frustration out on a metropolis that had cheated me, comparing my life to the movie *Midnight Cowboy*—that enormously proportioned film about a male prostitute trying to make it in

335

Manhattan. How ironic it seemed that the main character in the movie had come from Texas, just as Robert had. And I was both the star and the supporting actor, for while I was physically the hustler, I was emotionally a Ratso Rizzo, the scruffy sidekick. I looked around, seeing things from a pair of eyes that now belonged to someone else, and caught myself just as a taxicab almost slammed into my legs.

"I'm walkin' here! I'm walkin' here!" I shouted, and limped off through the center of midtown.

My experiences had come back on me; an over-taut and rusty mile of barbed wire less than one year in scope. It snapped back to its original form, circling and cutting me as it traveled—a three-dimensional preparation for the crucifixion to come.

I headed angrily east, toward the hotel. At one point I stopped in front of one of the city's enormous glass skyscrapers, pretending to look at my reflection. My first day came back to me—the one with the Mormons on Broadway. I peered deeper; Heckle and Jeckle were still there, tailing me. They seemed a representation of everything bad in the world.

My mind-set was sinking into a morass of desperation and depression, and it seemed that things would only get worse, but I pressed on. I was only a few steps from my destination. It was as if a hand were at my back.

I padded my way up the carpeted outer steps of the hotel and was ushered into the cool interior, glancing around for the pair who had followed me. They were gone, and with them my depression and angst seemed to depart. Echoes greeted me, along with a throng of Kentia palms, chandeliers the size of small solar systems, and an aura of history and wealth. You could smell the money. It's amazing what that particular scent will do to the emotions. I felt buoyed now; momentarily free; upbeat again.

Finding the registration table in front of the banquet room after a few moments—it was on the third floor—I approached the lone woman who sat nervously in back of the hunter-green cloth-covered table. A few brochures and media kits were pitched loosely around. Other than that, you wouldn't have known a meeting was going to happen. The place seemed deserted.

"Is this where the focus group meets?" I asked, sensing something wasn't right. She nodded. An uneasy silence followed. She cut a look to the side. So did I. Something was up. Then she adjusted herself in her seat.

"Name, please?" she asked, pen in hand, poised to write my identification *du jour* down on the clipboard she had in front of her.

"Spong Flagelatte," I said, as if I'd been born with it. Then I added, "Can you tell me where the men's room is?" I heard myself say the words, but just as they escaped my mouth I saw a sign pointing the way. I figured I would kill a few moments relieving myself and the others would be milling around when I came out.

Standing at the urinal, lap taffy in hand, I proceeded to let go. I was about halfway into the deed when the door opened and in popped my four o'clock client.

"Hey, guy, what's going on?" he said, and saddled up next to me.

"I told you four o'clock," I said, irritated that he had found me early, and in the exact location where the focus group was to take place. I realized then my mistake of giving him the address of the hotel and telling him that I had a meeting right before his. But I didn't want the money thwarted and I didn't want to scare him off. He wasn't exactly skimping on what he'd be giving me.

"Yeah, yeah, I know," he bantered, removing his trouser snake as well and giving it a few shakes.

Two regular guys, us.

"We are going to have sex, though, right? I mean, you are a hustler, right?"

"Escort," I corrected. "I'm an escort, and yes, I promise, sex."

"What about now? We could do it right here?" he persisted.

"Look, I've got some business to attend to right now—"

"I can see," he said sleazily, looking down at my crotch, my baloney pony in full view.

"I'll get to you later. Four o'clock," I said. But before I knew what was happening, he reached over and took hold of my most coveted possession with such ferocity that I feared its removal. He had one hell of a handful of meat and potatoes and wasn't letting go.

"Hey! Hey there! What are you doing!" he yelled at the top of his lungs, and then pulled me to him. We were chest and chest.

"What am *I* doing?" I thought. "Boy, *you've* got things backwards," but before I could move, the door to the men's room burst open and three enormous New York city police officers fell in, the most irritating of whom had a camera. He snapped a picture of Mr. Vice-Grips, and before I knew what was happening the other two were behind me.

"This is him," the would-be client said, his tone changed now to something harsh and demeaning. "Robert Hickenlooper—the guy's a hustler. You heard him—what he said. You guys get everything with the wire?"

But before the policemen could begin to read me my rights and cuff me, another set of cops burst in, fast on the heels of the first three.

"Everybody freeze!" one of them shouted and all three of the most recent group pulled their guns, thoroughly confused by the presence of the additional backup.

"Max Perkins, you're wanted on suspicion of murder," one of the new group offered—a *Pithecanthropus erectus* if ever there was one (I have a client who would love him). "You have the right to remain silent," he continued, but was cut short by the arrival of the two men who had been following me ever since I got off the train at Fiftieth Street. They surprised the gun-thrusting cops from the back. The police, stunned by the new consortium, wheeled around, ready to defend themselves, not sure who the newcomers were.

"We're FBI," said one of the agents, shocked by the large number of police and drawn guns pointed in their direction. The two men hurriedly held up their badges. "We're here to arrest Spong Flagelatte—fraud and embezzlement. That's him. The one you guys have got there," one said, pointing to me. "He stole tens of thousands from a major television network."

The first two sets of police looked at one another, guns still drawn. The whole event was beginning to take on an atavistic Keystone Cops air; a non-sepia and surreal episode. I prayed for a quick list of credits—anything to end this bad mock-celluloid experience. Where is Charlie Chaplin when you need him?

"That's Robert Hickenlooper. He's a male prostitute," the setup man said, still holding my reproductive organ in his tight grip, somehow afraid that I'd escape from a ten-square-foot room with no windows, six cops, and two FBI agents.

"Sorry, guys," one of the second set of cops said, "but we're taking him in for murder. Max Perkins. He's *our* perp."

I wanted to ogle at the canned dialogue fructifying before me, but held back. These guys had seen too many "Dragnet" reruns.

By now the small men's room resembled a bad law enforcement convention. The only thing missing was the doughnuts. I looked toward the doorway to see the mousy meet-and-greet woman who had been at the registration table—a now obvious part in the whole setup—attempting to peer between the burly criminal specialists.

"Don't you guys ever coordinate your efforts?" I asked, hoping to break the tension. "Does the right hand ever know what the left is doing?"

Then, all of the men, somehow sensing that one of the other groups might get credit for the latest catch, pitched forward and I found myself crushed to the floor. It was a freak accident, full of sound and fury, signifying everything. The only saving grace was that the pouting nerd who had been wired decided to free Willy. I thanked him. My meat puppet thanked him. And we all fell down.

The police piled on—eager young recruits at this year's training camp for the NFL. By the time they finished I had three sets of handcuffs on. Each team was determined to get credit for capturing Robert, Max, Spong, and anyone else they could find. I lay there—an old piece of clothing tossed onto a highway, continually run over by semi trucks until all shape and form is completely gone. Most people are nameless and faceless, but my problem was just the opposite. I had too many identities, and when all is said and done, the end result is the same. It's one big canceling-out of ideas—you're a nobody.

Jail was not pretty. Fuliginous and prosaic, it incorporated every bad cliché known on film. An open toilet whined in one corner and an equally bad-smelling wino snored in another. Pasted on one wall, on a small piece of paper, was a quote from *The Rubaiyat of Omar Khayyam:*

> I sent my Soul through the Invisible,
> Some letter of that After-life to spell:
> And by and by my Soul return'd to me
> And answer'd, "Behold Myself am Heav'n and Hell."

I was staring at the passage on the third day, after meeting with an appointed attorney, when it was announced that I had a visitor.

I jockeyed up to the bars, hoping for the Messiah. Instead I got a swarthy Italian of about forty-five. He looked strangely familiar and it wasn't until I was up close that I realized who it was—the very man that Robert had sent me to with the bad drug shipment. I gasped, and before I could step back, he reached through the bars and manhandled my collar, almost pulling me through.

"Now you listens to me, punk," he started out, still in character from the last time we saw each other, his monologue sautéed in a nasty Brooklynese, "yous pissed off one of New York's premier crime families, what with that phony package yous delivered. De picture of you, 'cause of duh arrest—it's all over. In de *Times*, de *News*. Ya'a known entity now and we *knows* where to find yous."

I had somehow been under the mistaken impression that I would be safe in jail; that Robert had taken care of the bad drug deal; that things would straighten out for me; that a place like this would keep away undesirables—anyone in the Mafia or publishing.

The Italian continued: "We'd like to rub yous out, jail or no jail. We gots friends in places like dis. Haf de police department." Then he relaxed a bit and his grip eased up. A confused look came over his face. He looked around, from side to side. Finally he finished, his tone almost affable, familiar: "De trouble is . . . we can't figures out who de hell you is."

I waited. His hand was still holding my collar though not as rancorously as before. I swallowed hard and looked around sheepishly. "I'm having a little trouble with that myself right now," I said, and attempted a smile.

68

The trial was short. No need to spend New York's tax dollars on me. It was a media frenzy thanks to the publicity department at Bandomday, eager to up the sales of any book for any reason. There was time to reprint the dust jackets even though it didn't matter—Robert and I were practically indistinguishable. And they refused to try and straighten out the many problems with my check, claiming that it had been cashed and their hands were tied. Like mine weren't?

> Witness for the prosecution, a Miss Penelope Crewel. (You can't even make up a name like this.) Here she is: "I'm head of the marketing and promotion department at Bandomday. Twenty-five years in the business. I consider myself an expert. By the time we knew what was happening the book was already at press. The publicity had been done, the money paid. It was a done deal. Low-hanging fruit. The fact that the author was arrested was a stroke of luck. You can't buy that kind of publicity. What did we care that he had worked as a reader at one time for Bandomday? So, yes, we are paying his legal expenses. The amount of sales this trial has generated so far for the book is astronomical. And we'll recoup most of the rewards from his stroke of bad luck. Do you have any idea how little we actually *pay* most authors?"

So many things went wrong. I briefed my lawyer on what had happened, all the right questions to ask, and what role Robert had played in the whole thing. I thought it would be easy, but I still didn't know all the angles to this sick scenario. Robert truly did know everyone.

But you want details—everyone does. Back to the trial.

"Now Mr. Perkins, if that is your real name," the sleazy (redundancy alert) prosecuting attorney slimed at me during the kangaroo convention. He leaned onto the wood-paneled partition in front of the witness stand, leering at me for dramatic effect. "Why don't you just admit that you're responsible for this whole thing, hmm?" Then he turned back to the rest of the courtroom, his arms outstretched as he swaggered in their direction. "We've looked up *every* address you gave us, called *every* phone number, spoken to *everyone* we could find . . . and still . . . there . . . is . . . no . . . Robert . . . Hickenlooper." He turned again toward me, a drama queen of immense proportions. "THERE IS NO ROBERT HICKENLOOPER, THERE NEVER WAS A ROBERT HICKENLOOPER, AND THERE NEVER WILL BE A ROBERT HICKENLOOPER!" he shouted, bringing his fist down on another partition for added effect.

It worked.

I jumped.

Then he was back to his slimy condescending manner, settling in for the kill: head nestled on neck, eyes slightly shut, smirk on lips. "Now why don't you just admit that he doesn't exist; that you and he are one and the same? I'm sure we'd all *love* to know just how many people you really are! Then we can all go home!" he finished and topped the thing off with a condescending little snort.

I could hold back no longer and jumped to my feet. "Aren't you going to object?" I shouted at my attorney, real fear rising in my voice. "I gave you the names, the addresses. Didn't you check them? What about Dory? What about all the others?" I said. "Spong and Marcel testified. Why don't you ask them about Robert? What's going on? Why did you let them testify and not ask about the things I wrote down?"

The courtroom began to titter, then explode with laughter; snickering, muttering. They were as one now—a perpetual God sticking his finger down my throat, assuring me emotional bulimia is best; that I had better refrain from any more outbursts.

The judge's gavel came down TV-style. It could have been any courtroom anywhere with anyone. Same drama, same time. Only it was me.

"Does counsel wish to cross examine?" the judge asked. I held my breath.

"No need, your honor. We plead guilty. My client is clearly insane," he said, standing and buttoning his jacket, preparing to vacate the premises.

"But I didn't agree to any plea! What's going on? Who *are* you people?" I screamed. "My attorney is a con artist. He's the one who got the letter from Fartus—the one about the donkey suit! I've seen him in the bathroom, changing into the thing! They're in this together!"

I was lost; all at sea. The walls were closing in; old walls; the courtroom walls; walls that remember things; windows in those walls that allow the masses to peer into the soul of a man and then tear him to shreds. Media. Cameras. General Mayhem reporting for duty, Sir!

And me.

> Scene: Courtroom madness. We see the churning heaps of cheap huddled-together flesh that have come for the trial. The bailiff is wrestling with Max now. Max's hands are cuffed behind his back. As he's pulled from the courtroom, kicking and screaming, the din increases. Camera moves up to high point. Then, a close-up of Max's face just before he is pulled out of sight:
> "I'm innocent, I tell you! I know it sounds like a cliché, but it's true. I'm not insane . . . everyone else issssssss. Ahhhhh!" and then the camera moves into Max's gaping mouth and we fade to black.

The charges brought against me during the trial were so numerous that I can hardly begin a tally. I'll try: Fraud; solicitation; drug running; obstruction of justice; dealings with organized crime (is there such as thing as unorganized crime?); possible connection to several tri-state murders—the list is endless, and all because I was trying to be myself in a world that wanted someone else. The wonderful city of New York even managed to throw in a parking ticket—a veritable cherry on top of the criminal sundae—even though I don't own a car and can't drive. Logic—what can you do?

Robert had disappeared, and later, after testifying, Marcel and Spong went that route also, as did a host of others. I was looking at a prolonged stay in a mental institution, my health was shot, I had a permanent criminal record, and everyone I had counted as a friend had deserted me. All in all it was just another typical day.

69

Getting even—a general follow-up for those of you who adore minutiae:

I've always believed in karma—reincarnation. What goes around comes around—that sort of thing. It's my contention that if you hate children and can't stand being touched, your chances of coming back in the next life as a cute fuzzy bunny in Miss Thompson's third-grade class are pretty much guaranteed.

Imagine the anxiety each day as recess approaches and every child contracts for five minutes to coddle Thumper. So I've tried to live my life the best way I know how. Problem is, other people won't let you. Compound this by living in a large city where events get sped up—one year in New York is the equivalent of ten anyplace else—and you can see why attributes like morals, scruples, and conscience become derelict. Now the thing is this: when I look around, this karma, this universal idea of sow and reap, seems only to apply to me. It's as though the rest of the world got inoculated and I was left out. ("Sorry, no more serum. Guess you'll just have to make do with karma. Nurse! Make sure this one comes back an artist during a bad economy!") Well, okay, some people get theirs, but some don't. You decide.

I eventually got the safe deposit box person to send the tape of Miss Pokey and her cable-laying talents to several people at Bandomday. They, in turn, did the only thing they could—they promoted her. By the end of the month she was a senior vice president. People say the cream rises to the top. What they don't tell you is that other things do as well.

With regards to that pithy note from the agent—the one on fuchsia paper telling me to go get a story editor—I understand through the grapevine that she's practically killing herself trying to get in touch with the author of *Mrs. Squigglemire* in the hope of representing him, me . . . whatever. Lady, I wish you luck because you're gonna need it. And get some manners while you're at it.

And remember Anastasia—that cornucopia of football-field-sized jewelry? She was eventually hit by a tour bus and died, unfortunately quite instantly. I heard that Malcolm and Mr. Babley attended the funeral and made quite the lovely couple.

The headhunter-slash-agency-person-slash-rude bitch that got me fired from Bandomday is now making sausage clips in New Jersey for minimum wage. Seems that she got lead poisoning from chewing on the end of her pencil while trying to think up ways to screw people over; the metal greatly affecting the few brain cells she had. Perhaps there is a God.

Last but not least . . . Reeda. She ripped off yet another budding young writer, who, thinking that his book was now in tip-top shape, sent his manuscript to Bandomday. The offending piece of literature landed on Miss Pokey's desk and was promptly sent back with not only a scathing note, but a box of her excrement as well. The dejected would-be writer—because of the realization that Reeda had pulled a fast one—fashioned Miss Pokey's intestinal efforts into small candies, dipped them in real chocolate, put them in an empty Valentine's box, had the thing shrink-wrapped, and sent it to his former teacher with a note saying, "Thanks for all your help." Reeda, having no sense of smell (think farting dog), ate every last bit and, well . . . died. Her family, learning of the bizarre circumstances of her death chose wisely not to prosecute for fear of having everyone know that Reeda Rot died from eating shit. The world is now a safer place.

As for the good employees at Bandomday, they still work there and that in itself is punishment enough.

Conceivably I had been too harsh on New York, for deep down it really is no different from any other place—there's just more of it. And a large majority of the more disturbed components come from far-off lands—places such as Illinois, Utah, Florida, and Texas—ordinary people with that worn-out look (the result of attempting to make an honest living in today's world) who haven't yet figured out how to play the game.

347

But for those suffering from low self-esteem, insecurity, or an uneven personality, New York is a veritable neurosis hothouse. I hear the only place worse is Hollywood. Moving to New York from someplace else can exacerbate symptoms too. What was a nervous tick in an Iowa cornfield can become a full-out *grand mal* seizure in the city. Cautiousness in Utah develops into a bad case of paranoia, and a healthy ego and ambition from down Texas way turns into overzealous and rampant toe stepping and people squashing.

But another contingent helps make the rules. They're the ones who cause everyone else to suffer. They set into motion the greed, the mistrust, the anxiety. They are the over-pious who commit the worst sins. The sharks who feed on any and everything, just because it's in their way. New York is all this and more: the super rich and the super poor, and not a lot in between; a heaven and a hell on earth simultaneously mingled for seemingly no rhyme or reason; a painted whore who gives the appearance of lust, only to reveal prudishness underneath, and the pedantic hypocrite who specializes in sleaze and debasement. It's all there for the asking, the taking, the pushing, the shoving, and finally . . . the letting go.

Epilogue

The definition of insanity is doing the same thing over and over and expecting different results.

— Albert Einstein

The definition of insanity is doing the same thing over and over and expecting different results.

— Albert Einstein

The definition of insanity is doing the same thing over and over and expecting different results.

— Albert Einstein

I have to wrap things up now. Everyone, and I mean *everyone* is becoming suspicious. I'm just biding my time until I can formulate a plan to escape. I've managed to give most of the nurses the slip with regard to my meds, at least for a few months— the length of time it's taken me to complete this manuscript. And I have to say that I couldn't have done it without the help of my fellow inmates in this mental institution. For those of you who've never been in an insane asylum, let me tell you, it's not the walk in the park that you'd imagine.

Where to start.

I should tell you first about the psychiatrist they've assigned to my case. While he's not overly bright, he's easily manipulated. Been my doctor since the beginning of my forced stay. He's ubiquitous—a real Dr. Eckelberg who sees everything, always trying to patch things up.

Then there's the head nurse. She's a piece of work, always telling you one thing, then changing her mind; regaling you with stories of the animals she nurses back to health. That's what she *does*. Reminds me of someone I once had a *very* bad relationship with. Claims she's writing a novel—who isn't? Add to this her preoccupation with nose goblins and you've got one messed up individual. Bodily functions and the mentally ill—they just seem to go together.

There are others too, though most are not known to me by name. There's the American Indian woman who's in here for cocaine addiction; the overweight Jewish homosexual who hates everyone and labors under the delusion that he's straight; the girl who never closes her mouth, preferring instead to leave it in perpetual O-gape mode. She's a walking ellipsis; a nonexistent parenthetical insertion. Some say she's in with us because an old boyfriend raped her. Some say she has a fetish for writing implements. And others think that the boyfriend doesn't really exist. Who knows? Personally, I think her obsession with her own excrement is the ticket that landed her in this Whitman's Sampler of loonies. But think about it: Would you want to be obsessed with someone else's? Perhaps she's onto something.

Oh, and she's got company, this fecal-zealous mental midget I just told you about. There's actually another nut-job (as if anyone *needs* more than one), but no one has been able to determine exactly what "they" are. And he/she has this little orange bendable horse they carry around; something to do with a cartoon from the '60s. A Gumby and somebody. I don't know. I can't keep up.

Then we have the following: one resident cleft palate; one overweight older gentleman; a middle-eastern female janitor with a funny name, and even an anal-retentive dwarf. Literally, there are too many to mention. They all congregate here, in the recreation room for the most part, the exception being myself. I like to check out old movies from the nurses' station and watch them in the tiny alcove off to the side—the one with the chained-up video equipment. This, to get away from my fellow fellows. I think I've gone through just about every movie ever made—some two and three times. *Midnight Cowboy, Sybil, Gandhi, The Exorcist, Rosemary's Baby, Valley of the Dolls, The Snake Pit, Mommie Dearest, The Picture of Dorian Gray*, every Bette Davis movie known to exist; even the cartoon *The Jetsons*. You name it; I've seen it. Strange, but the only one they don't have is *One Flew Over the Cuckoo's Nest*. Pity. Then again, when you've got what we have (and here I insert my best Jewish accent complete with shrugged shoulders and upward inflective hump in the middle of the last word), "who needs a movie?"

Oh, and lest I forget, there's my very special acquaintance: The lady I made friends with the first day they locked me up—Our Lady of Perpetual Insanity as I like to call her. She does have her moments of lucidity when she's not playing with Mr. Potato Head and all his parts or stuffing a regulation nut-house pillow down her panties. So we made a pact during one of them (her periods of lucidity, not the Mr. Potato Head parts or her panties): If ever we thought we were slipping—going into that land of never-ending madness—we would come up with a word or phrase that one could say to let the other know they weren't crazy. Something like *Squigglemire, Bunghole, Precious, Mother of God*, or even *The Book of Mormon*. Something off the beaten path. Shibboleths—go figure. Only trouble was, poor thing, she suffered horribly from Tourette's Syndrome, so half the words we invented, along with every obscenity known to man, came flying from her lips.

"Piss! Shit! Fuck!" she would rant in between the words we had conjured, along with entire sections of the works of Hemingway, Wolfe, and Fitzgerald. The projectiles would land on whoever was nearest. "Incoming!" the cleft palate would yell, and we'd all find ourselves covered in obscenities.

And that's the way I remember her the day they carried me off—all taped up in the chair—to my hydrotherapy session. I had seen her, standing there behind the glass and chicken wire, with bandages streaming down from her wrists like Chinese flags on New Year's. I tried to make out what she was saying. What was it? One of our secret words? She was mouthing it slowly so that I could understand.

It had come to me, this revelation, when the orderlies were strapping me into the tub and stretching the canvas over me. Cold water, constant motion: It's supposed to be a shock and it is. It was while I was in the tub that it had become clear: *Katzenjammer.* A secret code of ours along with *Beelzebub* or *Recalcitrant.* Something no one else would recognize. She was telling me that I was sane; that it wasn't my fault; that the world around us had gone mad.

"Haven't you guys ever seen *Valley of the Dolls?*" I had tried to scream though the thick duct tape they had plastered over my mouth that day. I looked for a hole in the canvas covering the tub, à la Patty Duke with big toe sticking through, but the thing was tight. I was sealed in—one more diminutive gherkin ready for sale by a God with not enough stock on his grocery shelves.

Then, when therapy was through, they put me back into my room—nothing more than a closet really, it's so small. I lay there, flipping through the countless magazine subscriptions they've doled out to us, thinking about what some philosopher said: "Did God invent man, or did man invent God?" For that matter, did I invent the devil, this Robert, this Ray-Bob, or did he invent me? It's the same conundrum for me now, and things are so convoluted that I can't remember. Was it that the city, my life, the absurdity of the situations, made me this way—unstable, loopy, without a mental foundation? Or was it that karma took over and my idea of hell is now being cooked up especially for me; funneled through that giant karmic feeding tube in the sky? ("Now Mr. Perkins, we're going to have to go through the nose if you don't open up!")

```
        Witness: A Dr. Ralph (we pronounce it
     "Rafe") Patchin--head psychiatrist for Penn
     State Mental Hospital. His comments here:

        The patient who calls himself Maxwell
     E. Perkins is delusional.
```

Don't tell him that! How did *you* get in here anyway? *You're* delusional, you A-hole.

> As I was saying, the patient suffers from multiple personality, over-projection of ideas, and schizophrenia. He actually believes his name is Maxwell E. Perkins, though we've found out that his real name is Mike Praxenwells.

Oh, Jesus, this and all my other dirty laundry from this (space dot space dot space dot space) lunatic. What's next, something about anagrams?

> This, because of the fact that when you rearrange the letters in the name Mike Praxenwells, you come up with Maxwell E. Perkins--the name of that famous editor to Wolfe, Hemingway, and Fitzgerald. It has taken months to uncover his true identity. Patient has a tendency to take elements around him and weave them into fantasies. In addition, he spends hours each day watching old movies: *The Three Faces of Eve*, *Sybil*, *Portrait of Jennie*, even that old 1947 Crawford film *Possessed*. We had to literally pry his fingers off a copy of *The Exorcist*.

Your mother sucks cocks in hell!

> Also, he's completely worn out a video collection of old Tarzan movies, and, after viewing the movie *Midnight Cowboy* seventeen times, he became adamant that he had been a male prostitute in New York. Mr. Perkins/Praxenwells has been with us at Penn State for years and has never actually seen New York. *The Picture of Dorian Gray* is another favorite of his.

I'm screwed—big-time.

> Lately his obsession has been with the 1960s film *Rosemary's Baby*. So rampant is Mr. P's paranoia that he believes all of us to be in league with the devil. He's currently being given a regimen of medication to abate these fantasies, but the staff has been unsuccessful in getting Mr. Perkins to take his meds orally. Hydrotherapy has also been tried, usually in the morning hours, between seven and eight. This involves sealing the patient in a bathtub and filling it with cold water. As with his medication, this has proven ineffective. His only real friends at our facility seem to be a patient with Tourette's Syndrome, and a rather muscular orderly.

I give up.

> Other than that he is distant and withdrawn, choosing instead to live in a fantasy world and in the past. His only additional form of entertainment seems to be the game Scrabble which he plays with the aforementioned orderly and patient. It should be noted that Mr. "Perkins" always wins.

Who to believe? My shrink claims I'm delusional and I claim he is. All I know is that this place is an improvement over the world of publishing and corporate America. Let them think what they want—I'm safe here. Safe from editors, publishers, the public, the devil, and most of all, the critics, be they professional or amateur.

Of course, nowadays it's exceptionally bad—a real free-for-all where anyone and everyone gets to voice their opinion. Some people (for lack of a better word) write in on various websites, reviewing books: "The best book i efer red," one might see—some evaluation from a high school student whose glue-sniffing experiences have gotten out of control and who has entirely too much time on his sticky little hands. (Just try and shake that *Playboy* centerfold loose *now*, you perverted little circus of hormones.) Of course it's the best book you ever read, you dimwit—it's probably the *only* book you've ever read. Kids today. What can you do? What can anyone do, really, with the realities we're given?

Then there are those jealous ones who slam the books: "Bad book. Bad plot. Bad everything! Ugh! How did this get published? This is the first book I've ever thrown in the trash!" all the time criticizing your grammar and typos while they misspell every other word and dangle participles like meat before a crocodile's snout.

Item: "The metafors or so *clunky* I couldn't even finesh it! Whoz editng this thing anywhay? The righting is at best meatyoaker."

And if I read one more reviewer's description that contains the phrase "deftly done" I will honestly blow my gooey little brains out.

Who is really writing this stuff, these reviews on the Internet? Are they real people, or would-be writers bent on bringing down someone who has had the will power and know-how to actually get something done? You have to have a license to own a gun, but not to write a review and point your .22 caliber criticism at an author's head.

So, with that we're back to the chronicles of the powerless (uh ... that would be ... me). In these last few months I've been able to smuggle out this manuscript, scribbled down on napkins, the backs of patient charts, and anything else I could find in this Godforsaken place. "How did I get it out of here, this story, this papyrus representation of what happened to me, this thing that records my insanity?" I hear you ask.

Robert again.

He's promised to give me the money this time. As if I actually believe him. Besides, the state pays my way and the people in here are much nicer *and* saner than those on the outside. A regular *King of Hearts*, this institution. And I know something's up because Robert slash Ray-Bob tells me that he's thinking of changing his name—again. Says Hickenlooper just won't cut it, especially if he has to go back to turning tricks someday. Spank Wexmiller is what he's come up with. Certainly *sounds* more like a male escort, doesn't it? Spank . . . Spank Wexmiller.

Trouble is, I don't want to burst his bubble, this Robert; Ray-Bob; Spank, but Spank Wexmiller is really nothing more than an anagram for Maxwell Perkins. But then, I think he already knows that. I'll play along for now.

"Robert," I said to him one day as he was lifting me out of my wheelchair, "just give me a *sign* that I'm not really nuts; something, some key word—anything, dude. Maybe the title of my next book?"

"We'll see, big guy," was all he said, and sauntered off. Our conversations are mostly hit-and-miss these days.

And *Mrs. Squigglemire's Bustle*? Well, it did finally make it to the bestseller list, but only for a short while. No wonder it sank like a stone after what the editors did to it. When they finished "editing" (I do like a loose term) it became the tale of a Romanian peasant girl who sails for America in 1863 so that she can enlist as a spy for the Confederate forces during the Civil War. The editors gave her a hoopskirt instead of a bustle, a wooden leg instead of Tourette's Syndrome, and a CD player that she had brought back with her from her time travels into the future—1989 to be exact.

In this new and unimproved version she mistakenly gets on the wrong boat and ends up sailing to a remote island in the Caribbean where she is eaten by natives after failing to appease them with her modern auditory invention and a recording of "She Drives Me Crazy" by the group "Fine Young Cannibals."

Irony isn't what it used to be.

Don't look at me—I had nothing to do with it.

The brilliant people at Bandomday also neglected to change the title, and as there was now not a bustle in sight, I fear a large segment of the public became confused and passed on *Mrs. S*, thinking that she was simply a busy woman with a complicated name. Then there was the cover. It was a modern-day picture of a muffler that had fallen off a car—close-up. What that had to do with anything *none* of us could figure out.

But enough about *Mrs. Squigglemire*. This story is supposed to be about Robert and his machinations; his draconian measures in the key of turmoil.

I see him now, Mr. Hickenlooper, coming toward me as he pushes the wheelchair that will take me back to my room. The medications they've put me on—the ones they force me to take since they've discovered I duped them for months (how else could I have gotten this story out?) have rendered my legs almost useless. I'm a rag doll; a limp pile of people parts; an emotional and psychological Frankenstein's monster of everyone's making.

He's getting closer, Mr. Hickenlooper. And how nice of him to take this job—one of the many he's had—in this state hospital for the insane, just so he could be near me. Penn State Mental Hospital. Penn State. Sounds somewhat like a university, don't you think? "Do you offer a course in film history?" I'm about to ask, to no one in particular, but things are getting a bit foggy now, what with that new tranquilizer they've put me on. Wait. Is that Robert coming this way, or someone else? They all look the same after a while anyway. And I suppose it doesn't really matter—the majority of them are relatively harmless . . .

       Witness: Name's Jackson Tippett McCrae. Been an orderly now for over six months in this God-forsaken loony bin. Came here to look for new material; you know, fodder for the next book. Boy, what a gold mine I stumbled on. This co-worker (big beefy guy with red hair, muscles, small tattoo) would give me these packages to mail to a very famous publishing house. Like I wasn't going to open them, me being a writer and all. So I guess you could say that I didn't exactly come by this story honestly. But then, consider what everyone else is doing in publishing. And the writing style isn't really mine either. What the heck. By the time the guy with the tattoo and his over-drugged sidekick figure out what I've done, it'll be too late. Like they were going to get an award for honesty anyway,

357

either of them. Confusing, you say? Hell, I'm
still trying to figure out who's telling the
truth. And I'm going to ask the publisher to
do something really sleazy to try and sell the
book--you know, put some comment on the front
such as "Soon to be a major motion picture."
Anything to get people to buy it. Plus, I
figure it's not that far from the truth . . .
at least in the mind of Max Perkins, Mike
Praxenwells, and a host of others. You factor
in that their fascination with the movies has
to get them somewhere, sometime. It's the
least I can do.

I told Robert what I was writing, and he read the manuscript
before he sent it off to Bandomday, in dribs and drabs. Mailed it out
in small packages. "A Foucauldian tale with twists and turns just like
my own life," I said. I ask him again today if he is worried about me
telling the story.

"Dude," he says, as he swings my wheelchair around,
"nobody is ever going to believe it," and he may have a point. I
know he'll probably keep the money from this one too. Says he'll
insert his own comments into the book, just to make sure no one
thinks I might actually be sane. Like there's any chance of that. I ask
him if he's mailed the last few pages of my work yet; the latest
installment of my life.

"Don't worry," he says. "Gave it to the new person to drop
in the box—that McCrae guy. It's a done deal."

> Scene: Robert wheels Max around and
they make their way down a long corridor in
the mental hospital. As they slowly recede
into the distance, the area where they've
previously been comes to life with the other
patients. We see the credits begin to roll.
Background scene becomes only a small picture,
and moves to upper left-hand corner of screen
with action continuing. Rest of screen is
black with white credits. Real sounds of the
mental hospital fade to background and we hear
the following dialogue, spoken by Max:

358

"As he wheels me down the hallway, I look at those big Popeye forearms of his; this Robert, this caretaker of *me*. I see the small tattoo he has, just peeking around from underneath the soft underbelly: It's the tiniest little devil—blue ink this one—and he's holding a pitchfork. It's nothing too serious, just this mischievous little fellow with a smirk on his handsome face and a miniature pair of bulging biceps. He seems to be waiting to delve into the archaeology of my life. But that doesn't bother me. I've got everything I need, right here. And it's funny when you think about it. I mean, this place is not so bad. See, the really crazy ones, the ones who are dangerous, the ones who ruin everything, ruin the world . . . well, they're out there with you . . . still walking around."

        Credits continue to roll . . .

        Screenplay by Jackson Tippett McCrae,
    based on his best-selling novel, *Katzenjammer*.
    Credits continue and we hear the theme music
    begin as sounds of hospital fade out. The
    music is a Patsy Cline standard . . .

                "Crazy"

Jackson Tippett McCrae has worked for various magazines and publishing companies in New York. His other books include *The Bark of the Dogwood—A Tour of Southern Homes and Gardens*, and the short story collection *The Children's Corner*.

Also available
by Jackson Tippett McCrae

The Bark of the Dogwood—
A Tour of Southern Homes and Gardens

"Downright hysterical. An entertainment potpourri. I couldn't
stop reading."
The Sanford Herald

"Rich in complexity . . . not for the faint-hearted."
Southern Scribe

"Can make you laugh out loud. Scenes with the power to disturb
and to haunt."
Echo Magazine

"Thoroughly engaging novel . . . a highly recommended and
compelling tale."
Midwest Book Review

The Children's Corner

"McCrae laces his stories with allusions to art, music, and
literature . . . (he) has created characters with complicated lives
and conflicted hearts. A generous and thoughtful look at the
human condition."
Southern Scribe

"A stunning literary achievement. This Pulitzer Prize-worthy
collection of short stories ranks as highly as some of Pynchon's
works or those of Gabriel Marquez or Flannery O'Connor . . . a
bittersweet compilation of loss, life, love, and insight into the
human heart. A truly great collection from a great writer."
BookReads

Reader's Guide for *Katzenjammer*

- How many references to the past can you find in the book? How do many of the references tie in with movies mentioned in the novel?

- The original Max Perkins was fond of saying "The book belongs to the author." Why is this ironic given the experience of Max Perkins in *Katzenjammer* and his experience with publishing?

- The original Max Perkins was of a New England temperament and possessed many dichotomies. How is he similar to the Max Perkins in *Katzenjammer*?

- The original Max Perkins once said, "When a man does you a favor, he owns a little piece of you." How does this compare to the favors that Robert does for *Katzenjammer's* Max Perkins?

- How do music, art, dance, and film figure into this novel?

- Compare how *Katzenjammer* gets published and whose name gets attached to it, with the story of Robert and his attempted entry into a piano competition (chapter one).

- What part do the epigrams play at the beginning of the different sections in the novel?

- Discuss the "What you hate, you become" theme.

- For all the discussion and themes of sex, there is no actual traditional sex act in the novel. Why do you think this is?

- What do you notice about the number of chapters in this novel (excluding the prologue and epilogue)? How is the number significant? What sexual connotation does it have?

- What do you notice about the climactic chapter in the novel? Why is its chapter number significant?

- Discuss the different writing styles used in the novel. Contrast the "Scene" sections with the rest of the writing. Also, discuss the author's style when describing music (New York Philharmonic concert and the jazz in the night club). How are the styles related to the music the characters are listening to?

- Discuss the style of writing whenever movies are mentioned.

- Even though Max is aware that people are using him at times, he nevertheless continues associating with them (Reeda Rot, Robert, certain bosses). How does this figure in with the epigram(s) at the beginning of the epilogue?

- Discuss how the author ties together the idea of movies with fantasy, the story editor, and the general theme of the book.

- What is the significance of the quote from the *The Rubaiyat of Omar Khayyam?* How does it fit in with the novel and the movie *The Picture of Dorian Gray?*

- What is the significance of mentioning the "pothos vine" in the book? What is the common name for this vine?

- How many references to movies can you find in the novel?

- Discuss the idea of "What you say about other people is usually a reflection of yourself" and how it figures into the text.

- How many references to the devil can you find in the text?

- Compare this story to that of *Faust.* What are the similarities—the differences?

- At one point in the relationship between Thomas Wolfe and the original Max Perkins, Wolfe—who was known for using his life and those around him in his writings—decided to write about Scribners, Max, and things that Mr. Perkins had said to him in confidence. Contrast this with *Katzenjammer's* "Max" and how he writes about the publishing world. In this particular article that Wolfe wrote—"No More Rivers"—he eventually changes the main character's profession to be a concert pianist. How is this similar to what happens to Max in *Katzenjammer?*

- Discuss the idea of paranoia. How does this relate to the book and movie *Rosemary's Baby?*

- Discuss the similarities between the magazine focus groups that Max attends and a group therapy session.

- At the beginning of the novel, and then later on, the movie *Midnight Cowboy* is mentioned. Compare what happens in that movie to what happens in *Katzenjammer.* How many similarities can you find?

- Where does the title of the book come from?

- Discuss the connections between the prologue/epilogue and the main portion of the book. How many connections can you find? Example: Max is forced to sleep in a bathtub each night and in the mental institution he's constantly being put in a large tub and sealed in for the purpose of hydrotherapy. There is also a connection regarding drugs, neurotic behavior, etc. Discuss these as well.

- What purpose does the New York Philharmonic's musical program serve? What are the pieces and how are they connected to the story?

- Discuss the use of the anagrams and how they relate to the book and movie *Rosemary's Baby*.

- Do you think the story really happened, or is the narrator really insane even before the book begins?

- How does the Oscar Wilde quote that Robert speaks during a modern dance performance fit in with novel? Where does the quote come from? Why is this significant?

- How is Robert Hickenlooper similar to Dorian in the book *The Picture of Dorian Gray?*

- How is the German language used in the book? What is the tie-in between German, Dory, *Mrs. Squigglemire*, and Our Lady of Perpetual Insanity?

- How is the writing style and period setting of the brief section of *Mrs. Squigglemire's Bustle* similar to that of the Oscar Wilde story *The Picture of Dorian Gray?*

- In the movie *Midnight Cowboy*, the male prostitute and his sidekick live in an abandoned building. How is this similar to where Max and Spong live? How is Spong like the character Ratso Rizzo in *Midnight Cowboy?* How is Robert similar to the character of the male prostitute in that movie?

- Why do you suppose the author had the "Scene" sections of the book set in a different type? What do you know about screenwriting and why he may have done this?

- The writing in *Katzenjammer* has a more commercial tone than the author's first novel. Why do you suppose this is? How does this tie into the idea of being successful and getting published?

- Do you think the writing style and subject material fit together in this book? Do you believe the author achieves what he set out to do as far as style and tone?

- How does the subtitle of the book, "Soon to be a major motion picture" fit in with the theme of advertising and promotion in the book? How does it fit in with the theme of movies that appears in the book?

- What characteristic do all of the names of Max's places of employment have in common?

- How does the author tie in the original Max Perkins's "Piss, shit, and fuck" reference to the content of the book? How are these bodily functions used as themes? How do they tie in with publishing and prostitution?

- Discuss the symbolism of the closet that Spong sleeps in. Despite his bragging about the opposite sex, do you think he is homosexual or heterosexual?

- How is the idea of changing names used in the book? Discuss Olga Samaroff, why she changed her name, and how it connects with the idea of self-transformation.

- How does the author tie in the book *Jokes for the John* to one of the themes in the book?

- Discuss the names Dory and Gray and how they are linked to the movie *The Picture of Dorian Gray* and the Oscar Wilde work that the movie is based on. What themes in the movie do you see in the book?

- How does the fact that Dory is an artist tie in with the movie *The Picture of Dorian Gray*? How does the theme of corruption in *Katzenjammer* tie in with the movie?

- Discuss the similarities of theme and journey in the movie *Midnight Cowboy*, with those in *Katzenjammer*.

- What do you know about the original Max Perkins? Do you know what his favorite type of punctuation was? How does the author use this type or types of punctuation in *Katzenjammer*?